THE
SPOILERS

THE
SPOILERS

A Novel by

DAVID HOOKS

ARBOR HOUSE/New York

Designed by Richard Oriolo

Manufactured in the United States of America

10 9 8 7 6 5 4 3 2 1

This book is printed on acid free paper. The paper in this book meets the guidelines for permanence and durability of the Committee on Production Guidelines for Book Longevity of the Council on Library Resources.

Library of Congress Cataloging in Publication Data

Hooks, David.
  The spoilers.

  I. Title.
PS3558.056S6   1985   813'.54   84-24255
ISBN 0-87795-628-6 (alk. paper)

For Mother

ACKNOWLEDGMENTS

The author wishes to thank:
Presidents Ronald Reagan, Gerald Ford, and Jimmy Carter, and
  their campaign staffs;
The United States Secret Service;
The librarians at the University of Texas Library System;
Marcelle and Mike;
Emma Lee and George;
Vele, Betty, Malinda, and Marilyn;
Ricky, Allen, Geray, John, and Frances;
and the rest of my family and friends.

"We're behind you all the way."

—SUPPORTER TO A PRESIDENTIAL
CANDIDATE

"Just don't get too far behind."

—CANDIDATE

CONTENTS

PROLOGUE

IN FLIGHT

He noticed it immediately.

It lay on one of the plane's vacant seats waiting to be picked up. Cliff Hawkins had been making his way down the aisle when the magazine's cover caught his eye. He hadn't seen this latest issue of *Newsweek,* but it was obvious that someone had. Hawkins picked up the bent and wrinkled magazine to examine it more closely.

Otis Meade was on the cover, looking straight at him. Steely eyes, pursed lips. His face was stern and unyielding. "Gruff" always came to Hawkins's mind. The caption beneath the photograph read "Coming Up from the Depths." "Oh, is he?" He thumbed through the pages and quickly found the cover story: A STRUGGLING PRESI-DENT.

Bending the magazine back, reversing the middle crease, Hawkins moved past several of his entourage to the front of the cabin. Taking his seat, be brushed aside the reports Randy Perrin had given him and began to read the article.

The correspondents were discussing the president's struggles to handle his increasing domestic troubles and their effects on him during the upcoming election year. After all, there had been the gas-oline shortages . . . the farmers . . . the economy . . .

Hawkins read several paragraphs and couldn't go on.

Why was he reading this?

Nobody had to remind him about Meade's domestic troubles or this coming election year. Hawkins had been obsessed by both for the past two years. The nation had nearly gone bankrupt morally and economically because of Meade's policies. Every time Hawkins thought about them he felt a surge of anger.

While his eyes drifted back to the article, his mind went back to the past. No, nobody had to tell him—he knew. He'd been through it too.

Cliff Hawkins was one of the most successful, influential religious leaders in the world. He'd been bringing his message of Christianity to millions since the 1950s, evangelizing from the cold war through Ronald Reagan and beyond. It had taken four decades, but his fol-lowers, and America, had made him a religious superstar.

During those decades, his books were best-sellers; every season his television and radio shows increased their Nielsens ratings, and there was money, lots of money. Dollars outnumbered supporters fifty to one. Even impoverished people would mail in five dollars or ten dollars a week, while others sent in hundreds, even thousands, a month. At his Dallas headquarters Cliff Hawkins's investors bought up surrounding land as fast as it was listed. Construction tripled. His staff numbered well over a thousand.

But even with all his success Hawkins had never really been tested before. By the end of the 1980s his test had finally come. Nationwide production was down and morale was down; suicides, divorces, and bankruptcies were up. Pornography was commonplace. Having al-most died out during the Reagan years, the feminist movement expe-rienced a violent rebirth. Homosexuals were screaming for equal rights. Meanwhile, the Russians announced a series of break-throughs in defense technology that sent shudders throughout the Western world.

Everyone was bitching. Even America's allies had begun to worry.

The American people needed guidance. Someone who could help turn the country around, someone who understood, someone like them! They needed a man who could offer them the spiritual guid-ance they lacked and the common reasoning they deserved.

A lot of people thought the country needed Cliff Hawkins. Hawkins thought the country needed a miracle—a miracle he called "moral rebirth." A return to basic values, to biblical morality, sensibility, patriotism, and the concern for America that he felt had been placed aside for too long because of personal pursuits. If anyone was going to do it, it was Hawkins. His advisers agreed.

So Moral Americans, Inc., was formed. A nonprofit conservative political branch of his own Christ Church Worldwide (CCW) organization, it gave him the vehicle he needed to speak out on what he called "America's Five Greatest Sins": abortion, pornography, humanism, the broken family, and homosexuality. He spoke out more fervently than ever. People noticed. His supporters doubled in number, as did his critics. Quickly Christ Church Worldwide and Moral Americans, Inc., became the most powerful evangelistic enterprise in the world. By the end of 1989 Hawkins's empire had over eight million followers and five hundred million dollars in the bank.

But was it enough? Hawkins asked himself, as he gazed at his reflection in the plane's window. He knew the answer: No. No, because, although they had made great strides in the effort to turn America back to God, he and his organization had been too limited within the confines of Moral Americans, Inc., to make any further impact on either legislation or the public's attitudes. He had seen that months ago, even a year ago, as had his advisers. So Moral Americans, Inc., was dissolved, and Hawkins stepped aside, letting another group pursue the ultimate goal for him—the presidency.

WASHINGTON/The White House

Otis Meade stood on the balcony Harry Truman had added to the South Portico and watched as snow blanketed the South Lawn. Beyond the grounds and past the Ellipse the president could see the Washington Monument in the distance, its huge limestone contour shrouded by the gray wintry skies of Washington. He took a drag from his pipe as snowflakes drifted lazily past him. He never wanted to leave this place. He relished the presidency.

Meade, cultivating the political field for years, had finally reaped the presidency, but hanging on was going to be even harder. Over the past three years new problems had occurred with uncanny regularity. Had he wanted a scapegoat, Meade could have thrown the blame on his predecessor. But everyone else was doing that. The worst part was that, save for an unfortunate downturn in the economy during the old man's last year in office, his predecessor hadn't done so badly. For Meade almost nothing had gone right. Programs and policies that were designed to operate one way often went the other. Meade invoked the Taft-Hartley Act to end last winter's coal strike and the miners ignored him just as they had Jimmy Carter years before. He asked corporations to follow prescribed price constraints and they snubbed him. He introduced tax incentives for Americans to ride mass transit buses, but they refused to ride them. He tried to strengthen ties with the post-Castro regime and almost severed them.

In spite of himself he sometimes wondered if it was all worth it.

The snow was falling more rapidly now and chilly winds began to whip through the portico's columns. He turned to go inside, then suddenly pivoted around for another look. He wondered who would be standing here next year. The election was ten months away. Barely enough time. He remembered seeing several of the other candidates on television in New Hampshire looking for support. But let 'em. They were Republican has-beens, not a strong one among them. Yet the more he thought about his record—ah, well, he was an incumbent Democrat. By 1988 the nation had had it with the Republicans and his party affiliates had helped sway the election. This time, despite the growing threats to his own presidency, he hoped it would again.

If so, Meade thought, next year might not be that bad.

He was wrong.

BOOK
ONE

LOOKING
BACK

1

The Mexicans could not believe it.

Juan Ortega sat perplexed. He glanced at General Eduardo de la Cruz to his right. General de la Cruz raised his eyebrows. Both men turned toward Luis Pérez, who also seemed puzzled. Together they looked across the table. The Americans were waiting for a response.

Finally Ortega broke the silence. He removed the cigar from his mouth, flipped a few ashes into the White House ashtray, and said, "My friends, I don't understand what you are asking us. Perhaps it is my English . . ."

Tony LaCross, chief negotiator for the United States, repeated it again. "It's the seventeenth clause, gentlemen, it has to come out."

Ortega turned to Luis Pérez, who took the cue. "Señor LaCross, I do not believe you are aware of what you are asking us to do. If we remove the seventeenth clause, we will be breaking Mexican law."

He continued, "You see, gentlemen, our law says that any enterprises undertaken in Mexico, such as a construction job of this type, must employ one of our own firms and hire Mexican workers. It is an old law, but still in effect." He shrugged. "We simply cannot break the law."

There was an awkward pause.

Tony LaCross privately cursed the Mexicans for stalling the talks so late in the afternoon. For three hours things had been running smoothly and now this. He sighed. He should have known he couldn't pull the clause out so easily, but he still had to try. The whole thing had been a mistake and now the clause was going to become an issue all its own. And with good reason—money and oil.

A pipeline was to be built running from Tampico, Mexico, to Houston, where an estimated 350 million barrels of crude oil would be refined yearly for America's use. When the White House announced the pipeline, it would be hailed as another North Slope, and Meade's administration would be sitting pretty. Job opportunities would open up, money would come in, and the United States would have its oil.

That is, if the negotiations were ever finished.

Relations between the southern border country and the United States had been strained since the American farmers became an issue in 1989. That was when farm lobbyists stepped up their pressure on the government to decrease the flow of Mexican agricultural products coming into the country. Goods ranging from alfalfa, cotton, and refined sugar to lettuce and tomatoes were costing the American farmers billions of dollars in business a year. By 1989 the farmers were hurting so badly that they would fold unless something drastic was done.

A decision had to be made. On August 17, 1990, Otis Meade had stepped into the Rose Garden and announced his decision to the press. He would cut all incoming Mexican farm products by 35 percent effective immediately.

The farmers were jubilant. Labor unions, farm associations, the Vegetable Growers of America, and everyone else connected with agriculture praised the president for a courageous decision.

Mexico was furious. The Mexican government lashed out at Meade from the United Nations, the Mexican embassy, and the Palacio Nacional. President José Portillo closed the borders for ten weeks in protest and warned that Mexico was considering a closed-door policy against the United States, and other Latin American countries joined in the protest. Meade had momentary regrets about the ramifications of his actions, but as the days and weeks passed, the protests eased and he forgot them. There were many, however, who felt that the president *had* overextended himself and was losing the United States any chance of regaining the diplomatic relations with Mexico that it had once enjoyed.

Late in 1990 Secretary of Interior Morris Finner, aware of a growing fuel shortage, conceived of an oil pipeline, similar to that in Alaska, running from Mexico to the United States. Finner explained the idea to the president in a confidential memo, and Meade bought it. Within days Meade had various Department of the Interior personnel, along with his staff, ironing out rough proposals to send to Portillo. It was to be given top priority and done in complete secrecy.

In December of that year the United States sent the secret proposal to the Mexican president.

Portillo balked.

Meade wasn't surprised; he had been warned beforehand. Knowing just how strained their relations were, and also aware that he couldn't very well rescind his agricultural decision so soon, he decided to shelve the proposal until he had a stronger hand to play.

The next year governor Slim Wallbanks of Texas, unaware of the dusty proposal in Washington, took actions that greatly worsened the relationship between the United States and its neighbor. In October Wallbanks announced that Texas would no longer allow Mexican migrant workers into the state because they were taking too many jobs away from American farm workers. Specifically Texas farm workers.

With his own political future to worry about, Wallbanks wasn't going to take any chances. Border patrols were stepped up and Mexican workers in the Rio Grande Valley were denied seasonal permits as fast as they applied.

The Mexicans were incensed. Meade saw it as a blessing. If Mexico would agree just to *talk* about the pipeline, Meade would cajole Wallbanks into rescinding his decision. Then they could discuss the agricultural import quota once the negotiations were under way.

Portillo, realizing how seriously his country was being hurt by the decreased exports, agreed. Meade succeeded in getting Wallbanks to back down. Two weeks later Mexican representatives arrived in Washington to negotiate.

Now, as the Mexicans continued to stare at him and his colleagues, LaCross realized these people were very shrewd. On paper the seventeenth clause appeared to be a legal necessity. Off paper there was no reason why Portillo couldn't disregard the construction law. After all, the man had taken power by having his own cousin assassinated. How sacred was the law to him?

It wasn't, but money was.

Everyone in the room knew that whoever received the contract for building the eight billion dollar project would stand to make an astronomical profit. For Portillo the money would go directly into the government's hands, meaning his. For the construction firm doing the work there would be a fortune.

"We simply cannot break the law . . ."

Bryon Knowles, who had been sitting next to LaCross rummaging through some papers, broke the impasse.

"Gentlemen, I think I've found a loophole to pull the seventeenth out legally."

Heads turned.

"Now, if I'm correct, under Mexican law 90 percent of the employees of a firm doing work like this must be Mexican citizens. However, if qualified personnel are not available, then only 51 percent of Mexican worker participation is required by law, which any foreign company could achieve simply by hiring local workers."

He was smiling. The others were not. He caught their bewilderment. "Don't you see? We wouldn't have any trouble at all in securing Mexican workers for the pipeline. Any American firm would be more than willing to hire them. And an American company could still get the contract, which is, I think, what the president really wants. It solves the problem."

General de la Cruz looked very disturbed. Beads of perspiration formed above his lip. "I'm afraid it doesn't, señor. You are overlooking the first part of the law—*if qualified personnel are not available.* Let me assure you, we have many workers looking for jobs, many firms that meet the 90 percent requirement. A Mexican company must *still* do the work."

LaCross spoke up. "But your president could override the law if he wanted to."

General de la Cruz raised his eyebrows. "You don't seem to understand me, señor. El Presidente Portillo does not wish for any other firm other than one from my own country to do the construction . . ."

The words hung in the air like the smell of foul fish. *El Presidente Portillo does not wish . . .*

* * *

Meade's head was between her legs. He could feel the sweat from her skin moisten his cheeks, smell the scents of her sexuality. She was nude, buried in a sea of sheets. She tried to control her writhing but Meade's tongue teased her. It became impossible. Unable to harness her movements, her hips rocked back and forth, faster and faster, rubbing her slippery flesh over his entire face. The heat grew more intense. She clung to his head and her body soared in uncontrollable flight. She cried out and her body was flooded with spasms. Mercilessly his tongue probed deeper. She cried again. Her back arched, then snapped in one sharp movement as her insides exploded.

The president lifted his head and glanced at the panting movements of her chest. Her breasts were flat and glistened with perspiration. Her nipples hard and red. Meade moved up a little. His eyes met hers. No words were spoken, nor were any needed. He knew, as she did, that he had satisfied her once again.

Now he felt her exploring his body. She discovered his pectorals, his small masculine cleavage, the belly he worked so hard to keep firm, then his navel. As her long, rich black hair swept carelessly across his chest, her tongue moved farther and farther down. Meade felt her circling his penis, then bathing his testicles, teasing and arousing them. A stirring grew in his groin. He shifted his body. He was growing. She lifted her head up. His pulse quickened as her tongue made love to him. He became hard. Moaning, he pushed her head down over him. Her movements began with natural timing, moving from the tip of his penis to his testicles, then up again. Over and over until she worked him so thoroughly that his legs were covered in sweat, his penis stabbing at her. Within seconds she mounted him, thrusting him within her, gasping in delight.

Their movements were hurried. With each thrust they became faster and faster. Perspiration lubricated their bodies and she rode him like the crest of a wave, until finally she cried out something in Spanish, shuddered, then toppled over him.

Later her head rested comfortably on Meade's chest. Quietly she listened to the gentle beating of his heart as the afternoon passed into an early winter evening. They stayed like that for almost a half hour, and when the bedroom began to grow dark, Maria Vásquez lifted up her head and said, "What time is it?"

Meade glanced over his left shoulder to the clock on his nightstand. "Four thirty."

He shut his eyes and took a deep breath. Maria lay there looking at him, gently tracing the outline of his chest with her finger, thinking about the afternoon and about him. Not too long ago, on another afternoon much like this one, he had told her there had never been anyone better than her. She wanted to believe him then, just as she did now, but she knew he had been lying. He probably lied to all of them. One could guess she wasn't the first twenty-two-year-old tour guide he'd wanted badly enough to take to bed. Still, there were moments, moments like this, when it was nice to dream . . .

She was about to shut her eyes when someone knocked.

It startled them both.

Meade raised up, moving Maria off him, and grabbed the phone. "Security? Where's Mrs. Meade?" He hung up. "It's got to be Howard. He's the only one who'd have nerve enough to do this."

Howard Hickman, chief of staff, stood waiting outside the president's door. He was a legend of sorts and the most despised man in the White House. Not only despised, but feared. He acted on his whims, and his lack of consideration, callousness, and hard drive for perfection had generated a list of firings longer than that of any recent administration. He was like a hurricane, protecting Meade at the eye and blowing the others away. He was capable of destroying a person's reputation as easily as breathing; his attitude was Meade first and screw the rest. It prevailed over everything, from refusing a king or prime minister's request to see the president to informing the First Lady that Meade was entirely too busy to see her.

Hickman watched as Otis Meade fumbled with his robe, half-covering his burly athletic body. He knew he should have telephoned, but he found himself enjoying the element of surprise. He decided not to apologize for the intrusion.

"Howard? How many times have I told you not to disturb me during my nap!"

Hickman strained over the president's shoulder and eyed the naked Maria curled up on his bed. "Mr. President, somthing's come up. The pipeline talks have stalled."

Meade raised his chin. "And?"

"And it's your seventeenth clause. They're bitching from here to Tampico. LaCross says when he brought it up they got all pissy. He pushed them, and now they're refusing to talk about anything until LaCross concedes on the seventeenth."

"Sonofabitch. It's Portillo, isn't it?"

"LaCross thinks so."

"I knew it. He's holding out on us because he wants that construction contract too. They're not budging?"

"That's what LaCross said."

Meade didn't reply.

"Look, I know how much this contract means to you. I know how important it is for you to see we get the job, but it's standing in the way of more important things. These are only the preliminaries. If this thing stalls, we won't be able to lock it up until summer. I really think you should concede on that clause."

"And let them build that pipeline? Howard, you ought to know better than that. It's not just the United States' interest in the pipeline, it's ours as well. We've got a debt in Texas that's been due for three years now, and unless we pay it back, we might as well kiss those contributions good-bye."

"And besides," he added when Hickman stood silent, "if a bunch of half-assed Mexicans screw up the pipeline, I'm going to be taking the blame, not Portillo."

"So your answer is no?"

"My answer's *never!*"

Hickman bit his lip, then pivoted to leave. "Don't forget—you've got a campaign-strategy meeting in ten minutes."

Strategy meeting? Meade had forgotten all about it. As he closed the door, he glanced at the bronze body lying in his bed. She got up and walked to his bathroom.

"Can you come in for a shower?"

"No, I can't," he snapped, "and I don't really like the idea of going into a meeting smelling like the aftermath of a Roman orgy!"

Maria leaned her nude body against the frame of the bathroom door. "Well, you don't have to yell at me! And don't refer to my people as half-assed Mexicans . . ."

The president had gathered his clothes and was hurriedly putting them on.

"I'm sorry."

"No shower?"

"No."

The next thing she knew, he was out the door.

2

In the Oval Office, seated in front of the blazing fireplace with only a coffee table between them, were the president's men: Paul Rampling, Reed McClellan, Joseph Krantz, Jerry Ecklecamp, and Tony LaCross. Rampling, young and ambitious, was Meade's top political strategist, one of the few in Washington politics who had never lost touch with reality. He was capable of reading the pulse of the nation with extraordinary insight. And he was fair.

Fair.

That's what's wrong with me, Rampling thought. In the Meade White House, politics wasn't fair. It wasn't how you played, but how you won. To lose clean was still to lose and Meade's world had no place for losers. To win, by any means, was victory. That's what campaigns were all about, he told himself.

Next to Rampling, studying a list of computer printouts, sat Reed McClellan, the president's pollster. The president liked McClellan. He was one of the few who had enough guts to tell him the truth—whether he wanted to hear it or not. While McClellan was poring over his printouts, Joseph Krantz sat next to him on the end of one of the Oval Office's matching couches. Krantz's mind was on the media, which he loved to manipulate. He delighted in using the

White House reporters, network correspondents, publishers, columnists, and editors from all over the country for his own ends, and in the past he had manipulated Walters, Bradlee, Rather, Mudd, Graham—everyone.

Opposite Krantz was Jerry Ecklecamp, Howard Hickman's senior aide. The moment Hickman and the president walked in, Ecklecamp knew he would have trouble. As always, his palms turned clammy, perspiration beaded his forehead; it would be a miracle if he didn't wet his pants. Ecklecamp was afraid of the president. With his barking manner, raw humor, lust for women, vengeful attitudes, the president could be frightening, and Ecklecamp lived in constant fear that his time was up.

It was one of the reasons that he was a nervous wreck. He smoked too much, drank too much, kept the wrong company, and hung out in all the wrong places. But there were other reasons too. Jerry Ecklecamp had a few secrets. One, he was the source of a great many leaks to the press. It wasn't that Ecklecamp wanted to be a leak, but he needed friends in the press because if anyone could do him harm, they could. Why? Well, that was his second secret . . . a secret that no one must ever know or even suspect. *Ever.*

Sitting next to Ecklecamp was Tony LaCross, who had two things on his mind: the pipeline negotiations—particularly that damn seventeenth clause, which Hickman now said he had to get in—and a rumor he heard from a friend in Texas, a rumor he couldn't believe, at first, but then began to worry about. LaCross wanted to mention it to someone all day—the president, Hickman, Rampling—but there hadn't been time. So he'd just wait and tell them after the meeting. It was crazy as hell . . .

Meade came in, followed by Hickman, and took a seat before the fireplace. "Gentlemen, it's been a long day, so let's cut the informalities and get down to business. Hughes Martin over at the President Meade Reelection Committee phoned me. We're going to have to hit New Hampshire after all. Three months of telling me we don't need to, and now we do. Hughes has gotten wind that we may not be alone in the primaries after all."

Ears perked up.

"It seems," the president said with a certain amount of disgust, "that sonofabitch Jackson Chambers, our fine senator from New York, may be announcing within the next month or so. I've already talked to Cuomo and some of the others, and told them exactly what I think. If they don't get the message to him, I don't know who will, but if he runs against me for the nomination, there's going to be *a lot* of shit."

He paused and lit his pipe.

"But Chambers isn't the issue. It's New Hampshire. If he runs, we'll need the state. If he doesn't, it won't matter. Hughes wants us to file right now. I told him I'd talk to you people. That's why you're here. Do we go to New Hampshire or not?"

"It's all dependent on your strength there, Mr. President," Rampling said.

"Right, and right now," McClellan said, "if I may be so blunt, it's not promising."

"You have the figures?" asked Meade.

"I've brought along some charts. New Hampshire's on it."

Meade shifted in his seat. "You haven't run any polls on Chambers, have you?"

"No sir, but we can. Right now, they're all yours."

Meade took a drag from his pipe. "What've you got?"

McClellan got up, went behind the sofa and pulled out several charts and a collapsible easel. He propped the easel up in front of the President's desk and placed the first chart on it. They studied it.

President's Dec.–Jan. Figures
Compiled by PollWatch, Inc.

	GOOD	SATISFACTORY	POOR	UNDECIDED
December	47%	21%	23%	9%
January	36%	19%	37%	8%

"You've lost eleven points from the *Good* column and gained fourteen in the *Poor* column."

Mead shook his head. "Christ, I knew this would happen."

McClellan said, "A lot of the criticism that has been fired at this administration lately seems to be having an effect."

"Cliff Hawkins," said Meade.

"Yes. Cliff Hawkins, among others," agreed McClellan. He held up another chart and moved away from the easel. He pointed to a line running from the upper-left corner down to the lower-right side. Along the line there were sporadic jags upward, indicating a rise in Meade's polls, and then dramatic shifts downward. The chart ended with the beginning of January 1992.

"This shows not just a gradual decline in the president's popularity among the electorate, but a marked dissatisfaction with the government in general. And . . ."

Hickman waved his pen again. "What about New Hampshire, what do the figures say?"

"Worse." McClellan pulled out another chart. The president's performance was thought poor by 48 percent of New Hampshire's voters."

"Ah, Christ," Meade huffed in disgust. "These people make me sick. Look, do we have enough to take the New Hampshire slate or not?"

"Right now, among the Democratic voters canvassed, 54 percent would be for you."

"Well," said Meade, a little more relaxed, "it's a majority."

"But," McClellan went on, "that's against an *uncommitted* slate."

"Oh, shit." someone moaned.

Meade swallowed hard. He looked extremely uncomfortable. Perhaps it was the fireplace against his back, perhaps not. He removed the pipe from his mouth and gave Hickman a worried look.

"Are you sure about those figures, McClellan?" Hickman asked. "That 54 percent figure is just a little bit . . . well, against an uncommitted slate, it's a little . . ."

"Pathetic," said Meade.

"I didn't say that, Mr. President."

"Nobody had to," he snapped. "Fucking pathetic. I can't even pull a decent majority against an uncommitted slate? God!"

McClellan was now eager to interrupt. "Mr. President, believe me, a majority is a majority and right now . . ."

"Right now that's a damn shaky majority to put any money on. Don't you agree?"

He looked at the others. They all nodded and twenty minutes later they had nearly decided.

"All right, let's blow off New Hampshire," Meade said. "Screw it. The last thing we need is to get grilled while I'm still unopposed. We're not going to throw ourselves to that bloodthirsty electorate. Anyway, if that bastard Chambers does announce, we're going to have to give everything we've got to the really big ones: New York, Ohio, New Jersey, Texas. No doubt about it."

The others agreed.

As if on cue, Meade stood up and Hickman indicated the meeting was over.

"Gentlemen," the president said, "thanks for coming."

He shook their hands as they left. First Rampling, then McClellan, Krantz, LaCross, and Ecklecamp. LaCross paused with the president and said, if possible, he'd like a quick word. Meade glanced at his watch, then saw the earnestness on LaCross's face and acquiesced.

"Only a second, though," the president said. "What can I do for you?"

"Well, Mr. President, this isn't going to come as a total shock to you, but Cliff Hawkins is going to run for president."

It took Meade a second to decide whether he'd heard him correctly or not. Meade turned to Hickman, then quickly back to LaCross.

"He's *what?*"

LaCross repeated it.

"You mean he's going to endorse this . . . this idiotic draft movement that's been trying to get him on the ballots? That . . . he's going to take them up on it?"

LaCross nodded again.

Hickman sneered. "That's absurd. He's seen what it's doing to the country. Those people, that whole draft movement, they're nothing but a bunch of right-wing lunatics."

"It'll never work," said Meade, clearly disturbed. "It'll never work. It'd be like Jerry Falwell or Billy Graham running for president. They're television evangelists, not presidential candidates."

"But," LaCross said, "Hawkins—or at least his people—think it *can* work."

"But the gays, the women," protested Meade, "they all hate him, despise all that rhetoric. It just can't be done," Meade kept repeating to them. "It just can't. Can it?"

LaCross shrugged uneasily. "I don't know. Look at the support he's got behind him."

"Look at the opposition," countered Meade. "Even if he were to enter the race, he . . . he certainly couldn't get far. Hell, we don't even know if he's a Democrat or not."

"Republican," Hickman said flatly.

Meade's face tightened. Then, after LaCross and Hickman were out of the Oval Office, he poured himself a drink.

Fifteen minutes later, after downing a double scotch on the rocks, Meade finally assimilated what LaCross had told him. Confused, angered, but more than anything else uncertain, he finally tried to erase the image of Hawkins entering the presidential race, and started for the private quarters. He turned back and picked up his phone. A White House operator put him through to her apartment. On the third ring she answered. When he heard her voice, he hoped that for a moment at least he could forget everything on his mind. When he heard the tone of her voice, though, he knew he'd made a mistake.

"And whom do I owe this gracious call to?"

"Just me. What are you doing?"

"Pulling out a TV dinner. Sound appetizing?"

"Not really."

"I didn't think so. How can Swanson's Chicken Dinner and I compete with the White House chef?" she asked facetiously.

"Listen, I didn't call to argue, just to . . . I don't know."

"Well, did you make your meeting on time?"

"No, we were late and I looked like shit. Any other questions?"

Now Maria's temper flared. "So what if you looked like shit? You were making love to someone. So what? You're the president, who do you have to answer to?"

"My wife."

3

Katherine Meade stood at the foot of her husband's antique bed, gazing at the crumpled sheets and damp towel. She couldn't fool herself any longer. It was too obvious to ignore. She had never caught him, had never seen a nubile young body fleeing into one of the private quarters' elevators, but every instinct within her told her she was right. There were others, *had* been others. And to think, she told herself, as tears welled up in her eyes, it had all started off so well.

Hadn't it?

Katherine had known Otis Meade since their high school days in Evansville, Indiana. He had been the young man filled with dreams of success. The tall, handsome outstanding student, who seemed to excel in everything. She had been the young girl four years his junior—the eldest of the three children of furniture baron Eustes Myrer. Her father reaped millions from the southern Indiana timber, and Katherine was his only daughter. He had always called her a tomboy and, though she never appreciated the reference, she knew it was true.

Her mother and governess tried their best to keep her in ruffles, but it never worked. Trees, rooftops, woods, and the banks of the

Ohio River were as familiar to the carefree thirteen-year-old as they were to her two brothers. She loved the wonderful Indiana outdoors and, though she was older with friends of her own, Katherine would constantly pester her brothers to take her along. When fights broke out, neighbors would watch in horror as the furniture tycoon's daughter tumbled through the grass with her brothers. They were the only boys she had ever paid any attention to until she turned fifteen.

Then she met Otis Meade.

She had seen and heard about him ever since he had moved to Evansville two years earlier. In drugstores or ice cream shops after a baseball game, in the school hallways, on the way home with friends—his name always seemed to come up. Their first encounter was purely by chance and, even though reporters had asked her a hundred times since for the details, Katherine could only remember the evening in general. It had happened on a Friday night. She had been at one of Eustes Jr.'s baseball games, sitting behind the backstop. Toward the end of the game, between innings, Eustes Jr. came up to her and told her that they were going to give Otis Meade a lift home.

After the game she found herself sitting next to him in the back seat.

Unlike most of her friends, who were still inhibited by the presence of boys they didn't know, Katherine immediately began talking to him. She asked him about the game, school, anything she could think of. He, in turn, talked to her as if he had been around her all his life, something that most of her brothers' other friends didn't do. They talked until they pulled up in front of Otis's modest home. As he thanked them and got out, Katherine felt a warm rush within her, a tingling sensation she had never known before.

The next day she was still thinking about Otis when Eustes Jr. came in and said he'd run into him downtown. "He asked me about you. Wanted to know how old you are, if you can date, all kinds of junk. And," he said teasingly, "he told me he thought you were pretty. Can you believe it? I told him he was crazy."

Katherine's eyes grew very big. She grabbed her brother by the collar.

"Hey, I was only joking, sis."

Pretty? she asked herself the rest of that day. Yes, pretty. It was the first time anyone had really noticed her, and although they never got together in high school and went their separate ways in college, Katherine never forgot the feeling she'd had thinking about him or about the word he'd used.

By the time she fell in love with him, so many things had changed. Her father died shortly after her graduation from Wellesley. Her mother, devastated, was incapable of handling the family's business, which now spanned thirty-two states. Her younger brothers were still in college, but Katherine was determined not to allow any outside interests to become involved. So she quickly found herself at the helm of an empire.

For nine years she was so consumed by the business that she barely had time to breathe. When she did, she discovered that she did not like being the head of a major corporation. In the meantime Otis Meade had been elected to Congress four times. She remembered his first campaign vividly and had even sent him a contribution, but the remaining campaigns, like much of the past, was nothing more than a blur.

Katherine felt she was missing so much, even though she had energy, money, and youth to enjoy things the most. There were moments when she longed for a social life, for relationships that went beyond wrapping up a business deal, then going out to dinner. In fact, the idea of falling in love and marrying appealed to her very much. She assumed all of this would eventually happen, but didn't know when because there never seemed to be time. In the mornings she would sift through various social invitations, take one look at her business appointments calendar, and reject almost all. Still they continued to come in, and after a while Katherine became one of the most socially sought after women in the state. Her name was synonymous with Indiana's booming furniture industry and, still unmarried at twenty-nine, she made an excellent dinner partner for rich young bachelors.

After her thirtieth birthday Katherine's longing for a life beyond marketing meetings and boardrooms finally grew so intense that her brothers began to take notice. Having more than adequately learned how to oversee the family fortune themselves, they gently urged her to resign and enjoy herself.

Katherine took less than three days to decide, and when she did, she left without regret and without looking back, moving easily from one life-style to another.

Whatever memories the people of Evansville had of Katherine as a tomboy quickly faded. She stepped into society as easily as she ate beluga caviar and drank Dom Pérignon champagne. The family estate came alive with dinner parties, teas, and receptions attended by people from all over the country. Newspaper photos of her captured a smiling face framed by long willowy hair; the pictures also emphasized elegant attire and a diamond necklace, typifying wealth and a sense of style matched by few. Within a matter of months her parties became a standard for other hostesses to emulate, her invitations among the most prized in the state.

As time went by, it seemed as though Katherine could turn any function into an elegant, charming success. No one was more aware of this than the finance chairman for Otis Meade's fifth congressional campaign. He desperately needed help. As his latest reelection campaign neared, the polls indicated that he might be in trouble. For eight years rumors had circulated in Washington about Meade's passion for women, his affairs with various members of his staff and with the wives of other congressmen, but only recently had the gossip begun to filter back to his district. Katherine had heard them just as many of her friends had, but she simply brushed them aside. Others hadn't or wouldn't, and slowly Meade's image began to tarnish. Not only were his polls slipping, but his financial support was waning. To survive, he would have to clean up his image and bring in some money. What better way than through Katherine Myrer?

"Will you help?" the man asked.

"What do you need?"

"Money. And support. You see, Congressman Meade is getting some, but not enough. Especially from the more established, conservative constituents."

"But so many of those people are his friends."

"And yours."

Cautiously Katherine asked, "What do you propose?"

"Well, your endorsement would help a great deal. And if you could give it in a very visible manner, all the better."

"Money?"

"Of course."

"How about a fund-raiser?"

For the first time in her life Katherine found herself involved in politics. She had agreed to host a fund-raiser not because she was interested in seeing Otis reelected but because of the opportunities such an event would present. While it was true that the majority of people attending would be friends and acquaintances, Otis was still bound to be surrounded by many people she didn't know. People her own age. Maybe . . . just maybe . . .

The evening of the fund-raiser the estate looked magnificent. Muted lighting guided the guests up the drive to the mansion's entrance. Stepping inside, guests were taken aback by the stunning beauty of the interior. Marble flooring extended all the way up to, and beyond, the two curved staircases on opposite sides of the foyer, and an enormous chandelier glittered in the middle of the room. Orchestra music drifted in from the ballroom. In the gardens in the back gardenias and lilies were floating in the pool and fountains, and violinists strolled through the pavilions.

Meade had arrived late, a little perturbed at having to walk from the road because too many limousines were blocking the drive. They met in the great foyer, Meade standing there with his hat in hand and Katherine finding herself shy for the first time in years. Both forgot whatever they had been thinking about. After what seemed like an eternity, Katherine remembered that she'd wanted Otis to introduce her to some of his friends, but when she talked to him, when she felt his hand touch hers, she didn't want to meet another soul.

Katherine had one of the servants bring him a glass of champagne, and then she showed him around the place, her arm within his. Then she had the servants summon everyone into the ballroom. Meade was formally introduced, and after giving his campaign remarks, he thanked them all for their support, especially Katherine. There was the expected applause and then the orchestra resumed. As it played "When You and I Were Seventeen," Meade guided her into the sea of bodies on the ballroom floor.

"Do you know how much I appreciate this?" he asked her.

"I'm glad I could help out."

"You've done more than that," he whispered.

The orchestra drifted into "What'll I Do?" They moved in perfect rhythm to the music. When the music slowed its tempo, Meade, with his hand on the small of her back, pressed her to him, "I don't think I've ever told you how beautiful you are."

They stopped dancing. "I don't think you've ever had the chance."

"My loss," he said smiling, holding her close.

By the end of the next year they had been dating for fifteen months. Otis had been reelected to the House, and they saw each other on weekends by shuttling back and forth between Evansville and Washington.

On the surface they were an ideal political couple. They went to parties and receptions in Washington and throughout Indiana as much as possible. When not guests, they played host with lavish, glittering parties of their own. Meade's public image soared. He was no longer a womanizing, irresponsible congressman from Indiana, but a respected man of integrity—and a man definitely moving up.

But beneath the surface the political life had already begun to sour for Katherine. She tried to like it because Otis did and she loved him. In fact, she wanted to spend the rest of her life with him. Talk of their marrying was a constant in the gossip columns, but she had no more idea of when he would propose than anyone else. Every time she tried to bring it up, he changed the subject. Confused, distressed, it gnawed at her so painfully that she finally decided to act. One night she phoned him from Evansville and gave him an ultimatum.

"I've waited and waited, but I can't wait anymore. I need something more complete, more permanent. This shuttling back and forth is more than I can handle."

He remained silent.

Trembling, crying, she said, "Do you hear me, Otis? Don't you understand? It's come down to this: tie the knot or cut the strings. One or the other."

He laid his head back in his bed and let out a deep sigh. "Look, Kat, I think you're just tired. Have you been back at the office?"

"No!" she cried. "You know I haven't. It doesn't have a damned thing to do with the business, and I'm not tired. You've got to decide what you're—"

Meade didn't let her finish. "Kat, I know there are problems, things we have to talk about. ... I understand. But you're out of sorts and so am I. I was asleep and I'm still kind of groggy. Let me call you in the morning. I'll be able to think more clearly then."

"All right. I'm ... I'm sorry I woke you. I do love you, Otis."

"I know," he said and hung up.

Chondra Reeves, one of his legislative aides, felt him shudder, then come. She pulled her head up. "Having troubles with the ladies, Congressman?"

"Shut the fuck up."

* * *

Katherine was still standing at the foot of the bed—the president's bed—clutching the damp towel. She was thinking about that phone call twenty-five years ago. They had been married one month after that. She never knew about Chondra Reeves, but it wouldn't have surprised her. Not now, in the presence of crumpled sheets and the scent of . . .

. . . of what? Of something you haven't smelled in a long time?

of . . . perfume. No, it wouldn't have surprised her. It hurt. Hurt like hell. But what was she going to do about it? She didn't know. What *could* she do? If . . .

If only I knew for sure. Had some concrete evidence.

If . . . only she hadn't decided to stop by his room on the way to her own.

But the door was open.

That was the worst part, that she still loved him. Not as much as she once had, but things hadn't started out well, even in the very beginning . . . And yet she'd lived with other things in the past. She would live with this too.

But for how long?

4

TEXAS/Austin

When Cliff Hawkins bounded up on the stage, immaculately dressed as always, the enthusiastic roar of the audience could be heard on television sets from Newport to Palm Springs. Eighteen thousand people were in the audience and over fifty-five million more were watching on television. Even Hawkins's contemporaries, such as Billy Graham, Oral Roberts, and Jerry Falwell, didn't command the television audiences that Hawkins normally did. No one in modern times had cultivated such a successful following by means of the Bible as he had. Sociologists and religious leaders had a stockpile of explanations for his popularity, but the most obvious reason was that Hawkins wasn't a stereotypical evangelist: his suits weren't polyester, his shoes weren't patent leather, and he ordinarily didn't have a Bible in hand. When he did, he didn't wave it from the pulpit, didn't blast the Devil at every turn, go into graphic descriptions of a burning hell, or rant and rave like a zealot. When he spoke, Hawkins gave the impression of being a lawyer rather than an evangelist. He had a series of logical arguments, all backed up by the Bible, as to why you should be born-again, and why the nation was going morally and spiritually bankrupt. Tonight it would be politics, the nation, the family, and other patriotic subjects. For what Cliff Hawkins, like other evangelists, had was a strong and influential conservative voice. In a nation whose populace included over thirty-five million evangelicals and fundamentalists of voting age, the tune Hawkins had been singing about the moral and spiritual collapse of the nation went straight to their patriotic hearts and their sense of godly duty.

Thus a presidential draft movement began.

From its inception the movement ran into severe opposition. It brought out not only all of Hawkins's old foes, but new ones as well, who were at once horrified and stunned that a group of people—a group representing thirty-five million, six million of whom were actual followers of Hawkins himself—could even consider placing him in the White House. It wasn't just the fact that he was a liberal's nemesis, but the fact that he was an evangelist, a *television evangelist!*

The movement not only survived its first few months of controversy, but grew at what political scientists agreed was an alarming rate. The backlash that Hawkins had previously encountered through his association with Moral Americans, Inc., renewed itself with even greater force. But the voice of Hawkins's supporters grew even stronger. Hawkins himself had remained mute for months, neither endorsing the group's efforts nor opposing them. Simply letting the tide flow. Until now.

"Live from the Frank C. Erwin Center in Austin, CBS presents a full two hours of ministry—music and words of inspiration from America's best-loved evangelist. . . . Ladies and gentlemen, founder of Christ Church Worldwide and minister of the Lord, Cliff Hawkins!"

The cheers went up and Hawkins greeted them with gracious acceptance. The routine of those crusades was so pat that Hawkins could go through the entire show without glancing at his teleprompter or script even once. During the first hour Hawkins brought out his good friends Johnny and June Carter Cash, who offered their testimonies; introduced Debby Boone and B. J. Thomas, who sang a duet about "giving up my ways of sin/loving you and being born-again"; and spoke to the audience about the importance of accepting Christ. During the second hour of the program the "target hour" as Hawkins called it, he zeroed in on the theme of his crusade, his trademark: America's Five Greatest Sins.

"One of our greatest presidents, Abraham Lincoln, once said that 'if destruction be our lot, we ourselves will be its author and its finisher,' and never before have I believed that so strongly as I do now."

He paused and then turned his blue eyes directly toward the camera, right into the homes of 55 million Americans.

"We are on a road to destruction, America! Destruction by our own hand! You've heard me talk about our five greatest sins tonight. You've heard me read the prophets' words about what's in store for us, and yet I must ask you. Are you listening? Do you hear what I'm saying? Are you thinking about it? And if so, what do you plan to do about it?"

He gazed into the audience, stretched forth one hand and passed it in front of him.

"You hold the key," he said softly. "You are the ones who must decide. Are you going to go home tonight, think about what I've said, and hope our nation's self-destruction won't come about? Or will you turn off the television, pick up a book, and forget about my words?"

He shook his head sadly.

"I hope not. By the faith I have in Jesus Christ, I hope that you are not so blind or naive as to believe that you can ignore what I've said—and hope things get better."

He paused and then said in almost a whisper, "Look around you. Are *you* better off than your parents were? Is our nation as strong as it was when you were young? Do we as a nation have the respect, the power, prestige, we had when you were growing up?"

"Look at our dollar," he said slowly. "Our military. Our welfare. Look at the products we're turning out. Are things, as our government and this present administration would have us believe, really as good as they used to be? I don't have to answer that for you. You know."

His face tightened, his body tensed, and his voice rose sharply. "You know what the truth is. You know things aren't better, and the reason—the reason, my fellow Christians—is that we have lived with second-rate products, policies, and platforms for so long that we've forgotten what it's like to be first-rate! We've sold ourselves out. Not only to the world, but to God. We've been passive while our homes have broken up, our divorce rate has soared, and pornography and abortion have boomed. And unless we do something, unless we decide to commit ourselves to turning this country around, to turning this country back to God and the moral standards by which *he* meant this nation to live, then our destruction is going to come about. And it will come about, as Abraham Lincoln prophetically claimed, by our own hand."

He paused again to let this sink in. The camera moved in for a close-up.

"I am calling on you, each and every one of you, to unite together as Christians and Americans, to enlist our Jewish friends and the nonbelievers in our cause and to raise your voices—loud and clear—and let the entire world know that America is not finished, that we *are* going to bring back righteousness, solidarity, and a moral and spiritual rebirth to this nation, to our peoples. If our fellow Americans won't save themselves, then we, right now, are going to work to save them. That should be our commitment, that should be our goal, so help me, Lord Jesus Christ! Amen and amen!"

The cameras moved in and applause exploded throughout the center. People rose up, cheering, screaming their approval. Then, just as quickly as he had bounded up on stage, Hawkins was ushered off, without so much as a glance, a handshake, a blessing or prayer, to any of them.

"Well, how's that for histrionics?" he asked Randy Perrin, his campaign manager, as they moved through a cordoned-off security area with Gordon Wade, president of Christ Church Worldwide.

"You're going to be a natural on the campaign trail."

Hawkins, on his usual high after delivering a fiery message, said, "By God's holy grace, I hope so. It's going to be the best thing that's ever happened to this country! The Lord has blessed us with a great mission!"

They approached the limousine in the underground garage. The chauffeur, who had been leaning on the fender, quickly brought himself to attention and scurried to open the doors. Before getting in, Hawkins paused and looked at his two closest advisers on the opposite side of the limo. With sudden seriousness he said, "You know, I just thought about it. Tonight was my final crusade, wasn't it?"

Wade said, "No, Cliff. This election is going to be your final crusade."

Hawkins reflected on that for a few seconds, then gave a slight smile. "Or the one for my reelection four years from now."

The three of them laughed and got in; the garage door raised, and the car sped off into the dark cold January night.

The plane touched down in Dallas at 9:47 P.M. Within minutes they were in another limousine speeding to the Christ Church Worldwide compound, where Hawkins lived.

Much of Dallas was just coming alive for the evening. Discos and bars were receiving their first serious spenders, and the city's elite were entering the luxury restaurants and clubs. The tables in the French Room at the Adolphous Hotel would be filling up, as would those at the Mansion on Turtle Creek, and the Venetian Room at the Fairmont Hotel. But the three men rushing through downtown were oblivious to the nightlife around them. They had more important things to consider.

"How are things going?" said Hawkins. "With the election, I mean."

"Your supporters' draft movements are already exceeding their goals, getting more people faster than were expected," Perrin answered.

"But the opposition—" Wade said.

"—is really beginning to hurt," said Perrin.

"How bad?" Hawkins wanted to know.

"Not as bad as it will be later. Those opposing the movement are doing so because they think the people behind it are just a bunch of religious fanatics. They don't realize you're actually going to step in."

"And when they do—" said Wade.

"I know, I know," said Hawkins. "But we've faced tougher battles before. Our supporters are solid. Just look at our reception tonight."

"But once this thing gets into motion it's going to be a very different situation. What with the press, the gays, the feminists, and . . ."

". . . and we're going to counter them—and Meade—with people of our own. They're one of the main reasons I'm getting in this thing anyway."

Gordon Wade rubbed his brow and looked out into the night. He said reflectively, "Who would ever have thought ten years ago, even twenty, that we'd need a man like you? That we'd have to call upon a religious leader to put the country back on the tracks of decency and moral righteousness?"

"Who would have thought it'd be *me?*" asked Hawkins. "I wouldn't have believed anyone if they had told me this is what I'd be doing. But then . . . twenty or thirty years ago I wouldn't have believed I'd be an evangelist."

"You were a lawyer, weren't you?" asked Randy Perrin.

Hawkins nodded, his thoughts already slipping back to the past.

"Indeed I was. A young, ambitious lawyer who never wanted to be an evangelist."

It was true. Cliff Hawkins had *never* wanted to be an evangelist. From his earliest memories religion and evangelism had been synonymous with poverty, degradation, embarrassment, pain. His parents had been evangelists since they were newlyweds. Their lives had been frugal but dedicated. At times they were like bedouin nomads wandering from town to town, searching for whatever food, warmth, and shelter they could find, but always preaching and always holding to their beliefs that God would provide. When Cliff was born, their beliefs were reaffirmed.

"The Lord has given us a son," his father said, "and he will be the heir to his word."

By the time Cliff was two years old his family had quit roaming and settled in a dilapidated two-story frame house that Cliff's father inherited from an aunt in Texarkana, Texas. Though poor, his parents were determined to carry on their ministry, and eventually the Christian Home for the Wayward was born. Over the front door hung a shabby sign: PEACE BE TO ALL WHO ENTER HERE.

Hawkins still shuddered every time he thought about the place: peeling wallpaper, cold floors, outdoor plumbing. Originally it had been a comfortable house, but when his parents moved in, fifty years had passed since the place was built and Cliff's great-aunt had long since left. The neighboring town was now at their doorstep, bringing with it all the poverty and ravages of the Depression. There were as many sleeping vagrants infesting the house as there were termites and roaches. Food was bought through donations from local businesses and churches, and even then there was usually just enough to buy ham hocks and beans. Food was served off an old oblong maple table, where whores, winos, and bums would line up single file for their rations and then move on. Cliff and his parents were always the last to eat and, when there wasn't enough to go around, which was often, his mother would sigh and say, "Just remember, in doing the Lord's work we must all sacrifice." So he would be put on his mattress in an upstairs bedroom, cold and hun-

gry. Why couldn't he eat when everyone else was being fed? he
wondered. He would cry himself to sleep, but even sleep was elusive
because the evening was Richard Hawkins's favorite time to preach.
When his father went into one of his religious tirades, ranting to
those transients who would listen, few could calm him.

Even now, whenever Hawkins thought about it, he could still hear
those ravings as clearly as when he was a child.

"Oh, my friends, my friends!" his father would shout. "You have
sinned against the Lord! Taken his words and commandments and
thrown them away for the pleasures of this godforsaken world! Lust!
Wine! Sodomy! Oh, by the mercy of God, I can see the anguish on
your faces! The confusion! You need to be saved! Saved!

"Jesus said: 'Submit yourselves to God, resist the devil, and he
will flee from you! Come near to God and he will come near to you!
Wash your hands, you sinners, and purify your hearts. . . .' Repent!
Repent and know that you shall have salvation!"

Cliff was terrified whenever his father yelled like that, and since
he did it so often, the son grew to dislike him intensely. It was not
until ten years after they'd moved into the Christian Home for the
Wayward that Cliff realized it was not his father whom he disliked,
but what his father did.

The Wayward Home reached its peak at the height of the Depression and, once that had passed, the decline began. To offset the
decreasing donations, Cliff's parents held street corner services for
contributions.

Richard Hawkins, now in his thirties, would wave his tattered
red-leather King James Bible before the crowds and espouse all the
apocalyptic revelations that his own son would use years later. But
back then Cliff had no intention of following his father. He had not
forgotten the humiliation or the cheapness he felt during those im-
pressionable years, when the street corner services were nothing
more than God-excused begging. He remembered the faces of all
those who walked by his father. Looks of disdain and contempt
written on their faces, the corners of their mouths curled in snickers.

He could see them still.

They had stopped. Taken notice. Some stared. An eyebrow would
lift, a giggle would be stifled. On occasion someone would laugh
openly. Many stormed away in disgust, while others huffed in des-
peration, tossing the nodding, praising-the-Lord man a dime or
two—anything to be left alone.

Cliff had noticed that those looks went beyond a fleeting sense of curiosity or bemusement to a feeling of underlying pity. Pity so strong that he felt waves of shame pass through him. His family was not like other families. His father was not like other men on the street, his mother not like the women. They were different, but he didn't know how. They were poorer for sure, but it went deeper than that.

When he was fifteen, he realized why. Those people who passed him weren't relying on God to meet all their needs. Religion wasn't a crutch for them. It was something personal and private, not an escape as his parents had made it, but a relationship of understanding between themselves and the Being that guided them.

Had this hurt them?

They didn't seem to suffer too much if it did. God's wrath wasn't an excuse they invoked at every setback nor was his good proclaimed at every stroke of fortune. These people didn't believe they were going to perish in a burning hell or be devoured by the serpents of Revelations, as his father had predicted. They didn't need to; they had everything in the world. Cliff had seen their automobiles whizzing by. They were heirs to all the world could offer—money, furs, jewels, comfortable homes. What more did they need? They had never eaten at the same table with winos or prostitutes. Their feet hadn't almost frozen from lack of heat. They weren't clothed in hand-me-downs. Their homes had running water, and mice were nonexistent. Their children never scrounged for pennies just to see an arcade, nor was their Christmas tree a pathetic potted plant.

They were different! And Cliff longed to be like them.

"They're instruments of the devil," Cliff's mother said. "Not God's chosen people like us."

"Then why do they have everything we don't? Why doesn't God punish them if they're so bad?"

His mother would raise her hand in the air, shaking her head. "Don't be so doubting, Cliff. God will provide . . ."

God will provide!

He had heard it so many times it sickened him. God had *never* provided. They lived a life of bare subsistence. By the time he was sixteen they were forced to sell the Wayward Home and move into an apartment that in the summer reeked of stale urine and the putrid odors of dirty diapers from the neighbors across the hall and in the winter had no heat.

God will show us the way!

But he never had. Their street missions were their only means of support. Every day after school Cliff reluctantly went with his parents to the corners downtown.

Forget not all his gifts!

What were they? The shoes on his feet were old and worn, the clothes on his body were used and faded. He was tired of his life, tired of the humiliation he felt at the street services. Tired of being called white trash. He prayed for a chance to flee from all the poverty he had known.

When he was sixteen, he still didn't know how he was going to leave his surroundings, but his yearning for a better life had made him more independent. He tried to release himself from the religious and emotional grip his parents had on him, and he no longer went with them on their street corner missions. The town's high school was now taking all his attention. He was studying to get an education, working harder than his parents had ever expected.

The determination of their boy!

They were losing him and knew it. They didn't understand the dreams their son was always talking about, and in their own innocent way they were resentful. Cliff was the heir to God's word. They had known that from the beginning, the sanction had been made at birth, but now what had become of it?

"Just try to accept the Lord's will, son!" his father pleaded.

"I have, and his will is for me to make something out of myself, be my own person!"

"You're running away from your inheritance, boy! Jesus said to witness . . ."

"Just go with us after school," his mother pleaded. "That's all we ask. We'll have the services done before dark, then you can do what you need to . . ."

Cliff refused. He wasn't going anywhere with them after school, and he enrolled in his high school's debate program, one of the few in the state. He loved the program, not only because it required him to stay after school every afternoon, which was a welcome alternative to the street services, but because he was actually a good orator. As the semesters passed and his debating challenges increased, so too did his mental resources, his vocal abilities, and his confidence. Cliff's mind was quick. When debating, he reasoned his arguments with electrifying speed. Refusing a flow sheet, he would take a presentation, note the points for each argument, then repeat his own responses in fast, precise chronological order to a stunned opponent. His vocabulary increased by leaps. Soon he became known as the sharpest, most articulate high school debater in the state. In researching his topics he came to love reading and devoured book after book from the public library. His grades soared and Richard and Gloria Hawkins sat in awe as their son excelled beyond anything they imagined possible. His debate coach, a man named Bud Dyon, also watched in proud amazement.

It was during the second half of his senior year that everything changed.

As his graduation approached, Cliff grew depressed. There was no money for him to go to college and thus no escape from the world he loathed. He felt he was destined to live out his life in an in-between state, never completely leaving his past and never fulfilling his future. What would he do? Where would he go?

One night he actually found himself praying for help.

Nothing happened. He didn't expect anything to.

His graduation was approaching.

Reluctantly, almost shamefully since he felt so hypocritical about it, he prayed again.

Nothing.

Three weeks passed. He was in such a state of anxiety and melancholy that it began to affect his studies. When his teachers took notice, he was summoned to the principal's office, but not for the reason he'd suspected.

"Congratulations! It looks as though you're going to be our valedictorian."

"Which means—"

"Which means you're not only at the head of your class, but the recipient of a full four-year scholarship."

When he heard the words, he fell back in shock.

"A godsend for you," his father said quietly, but he and his wife feared they had lost their son forever.

One afternoon, right before graduation, one of Cliff's debate partners pulled him aside.

"I hear you're going to UT."

"It's the only university where I can apply the scholarship."

"Prelaw?"

"I don't know yet. Lawyers make a lot of money, don't they?"

"If they're good, they do."

That was it. Cliff's freedom, his hope. Just as college would become his new life, law would become his goal. His studying would only be interrupted by a girl named Charlotte Astor.

5

Charlotte Astor Hawkins stood beneath the vanity light in the powder room just off the library. Leaning over the marble countertop, she breathed onto the mirror. It fogged up, but she couldn't tell anything. She tried again. Still nothing. Cupping her hands in front of her mouth, she breathed once again. Okay. As far as she could tell, he wouldn't be able to detect a thing. She glanced at her Piaget watch and let out a sigh of relief. She examined her eyes too, just to make sure, then turned around and walked out.

In the library Charlotte took a quick glance around and decided everything was okay. Instinctively she glanced at one of the bookshelves and decided that even though the book looked right you never could be sure. So, for what must have been the third time in the last ten minutes, she went back to the shelf, pulled the hollow book out, opened it, tightened the flask's top, then put the book back.

Now she was sure everything was okay. She had had a couple of hours to get sloshed and then a couple more to sober up. She'd done it before and covered it up. She was going to do it again. She went upstairs thinking, everything's okay. She pulled off her robe and crawled into bed and wondered, is it really? Or do I just keep telling myself that? Why the questioning? Why all this damned battling with myself . . . Why?

She knew why. As she heard Cliff's limousine pull up, she knew Cliff was everything she wasn't. She was everything opposite to what he must have wanted. If only *he* could see that. She saw it. Had seen it for years. He had done so much with himself.

She supposed she could have done more with her own life than she had. In fact, she was sure of it. But she had made the decision to stay with him after he'd gotten into religion a long time ago and this was the price. His career had taken off with meteoric speed and everyone from her father on down made it clear that *his* life, not her own, that should be her top priority. It hadn't been a bad price, she told herself. After all, Cliff was one of the most famous men in the country. Had he been a lawyer, she doubted he would have gone this far. Despite the fact she had never been as religious as Cliff, he had helped her overcome a lot of personal anxieties about life. He had given her much to think about and she had found some peace in that. She'd been able to calm down the fiery spirit of her youth, had even learned to play the role of loving, supporting housewife well enough to fool everyone. For that I should get an Oscar, she thought. She even found herself enjoying this life of theirs, now and then. At one time she hadn't believed this possible.

When they first met, he was midway through his last year in law school and Charlotte was struggling through her sophomore year as an undergraduate. She was strikingly beautiful, vivacious, a flirt, and very rich. Coming from a large family whose men had shrewdly retained their oil money during the Depression, she had neither the interest nor diligence to suffer through four years of college simply in the hope of becoming richer or gaining a better life than the one she had known. So, from the moment she arrived, Charlotte knew that studying and classes weren't for her. She was on scholastic probation more than she was off, but her father kept sending her checks and she kept having fun. When she wasn't lounging about her apartment, tooling around in her roadster, or socializing at her sorority house, she was at countless fraternity mixers and eventually in the bed of any one of a dozen fraternity men. Weekend partying was even more dizzying. When nothing official was slated and Charlotte wasn't in the mood to throw a soiree of her own, she would fly home to Houston to reassure Daddy that everything was fine. Then, quick as a tornado, she would be off, back to college, back to fun, but never back to books.

It was through her avoidance of books that Charlotte discovered Cliff. Forced to go to the counseling center after her grades had dropped to the point of almost no-return, she needed a tutor desperately. Her tutor was young and good-looking and had the most charming smile she'd ever seen. He was a law student trying to earn some extra money. His name was Cliff Hawkins. He promised to help her and he did. They spent numerous weekends working on her assignments, trying to pull up her grades. Cliff gave her tips on how to stay awake during the most boring lectures, how to take better notes, and how to retain more of what she studied. Occasionally she skipped class and he would scold her, but her determination finally took hold and her grades began to improve.

They dated throughout the fall. When they weren't going out, they were eating at Charlotte's apartment or talking on the phone. At times they'd spend two or three hours discussing everything from world events to their own frustrations and hopes. Cliff wanted to work in a small law firm, then go into politics. Charlotte wanted to get out of school, go back to the horsey set, or get married.

She never did go back to the horsey set, though three years later she almost wished she had. It would have spared her the pain of seeing Cliff knocked down by something neither of them could control, something that came so quickly it gave no warning, yet changed their lives forever.

Cliff was on his way to junior partner status in a growing law firm he had joined in Austin. Charlotte was pregnant with the child who would be their only son, Blair. One evening Cliff awoke coughing uncontrollably—a wheezing, hacking cough. Charlotte sprang up and asked, "Cliff, are you all right?"

The coughing continued. "Yeah, I just . . ." he coughed again, "I just caught a cold or something. I'll be all right." Charlotte laid back down, listened to him cough a few minutes more, and then all became quiet. Cliff drifted back to sleep. Neither of them gave the incident another thought.

Several weeks later Cliff awoke again with the cough, only this time he had a temperature and was feeling dizzy. Charlotte had heard him throughout the night and tried to get him to take something. He refused. It would be over by the next morning. But it wasn't. When he got out of bed to get some cough syrup, he nearly fainted. Dazed, he stumbled back to bed, his body rattling with each hacking cough. The spell lasted two days.

A week later the same thing happened, but this time the coughing didn't stop. On the third morning Charlotte woke up and screamed.

"What's happened to you? Cliff! Are you all right? Wake up!"

In a daze Cliff raised up his head. "What's wrong, honey?"

"There's blood all over you! On your pajamas, the sheets . . ."

Cliff looked around in confusion, coughed some more and felt warm fluid fill his mouth. Seeing it, he felt even sicker. Then a pain seared through his chest. His breathing grew faster and the dizziness returned.

"Charlotte . . . I feel weak . . . I can barely breathe. What's . . . wrong with me?"

"I don't know but I'm calling the doctor." As she reached out for the phone, she felt his body fall back.

He had fainted.

After several tests and what seemed like countless examinations, the two doctors who examined Cliff had enough evidence to support what they had already surmised. When they told Charlotte, she broke down. Telling Cliff was worse. She had gone into his bedroom, agonizing over the best way to word it but determined to remain composed. She failed. When she saw him lying there, pale and exhausted, she broke down again. Laying her head on his heaving chest, she sobbed for several minutes.

"Honey, come on. It can't be that bad. What's . . . what's the matter?"

She struggled to get the words out, but something within stopped her. Finally she realized that if she didn't say it, she probably never would, and so she heaved out in one breath: "It's in your lungs . . . they said it was in your lungs . . . everywhere!"

Cliff did not move. "What?"

"Tuberculosis."

Sitting up in her bed in Dallas, waiting for Cliff to finish with Randy Perrin and Gordon Wade downstairs. Charlotte remembered how his reaction was so unlike the man she knew now. But they had both been so young, and tuberculosis was still a deadly disease then. . . .

The first three days after he had been told the diagnosis he denied it. Could not accept it. Then he did accept it—and went into a state of depression so severe it delayed the beginning of his treatment and worsened his condition considerably. He was killing himself and knew it. But he didn't want to fight. Fourteen days after the onset of treatment he began refusing his medicine. Charlotte, less than a month away from delivery, grew desperate. She pleaded, begged, even threatened him to cooperate, but he wouldn't. Instead he began to talk openly about dying. It took Charlotte to the brink of collapse.

As the days turned into another week and then another, Cliff grew even more depressed. Charlotte, trying to bring him back into the world, brought him books and every magazine she could find, even brought him the Bible. It irritated him, but he said nothing. Finally he asked her not to bring him anything else. Almost in tears, she asked why. He told her he wanted to be alone. And so he was . . . with his thoughts and his fears.

When his parents showed up, things began to change. Cliff had begged Charlotte not to write or call them about his condition, but she insisted. She had no other choice. When she told Cliff, it aggravated his depression. He had been staving off a meeting between his two families for three years. His memories of the Wayward Home and the filthy apartment were still too close to him. He never wanted to expose Charlotte to his past, and now she would know everything. Everything that had been ugly and unpleasant: the humiliation, the degradation, all of it.

"They're not like you," he told her.

"I don't care."

"They're not like your parents. They're poor. Poor and simple."

"My parents don't care. We only care about you, getting you well."

When he first saw them, standing at the foot of his bed, Cliff said nothing. Instead he wept. Seeing their son, his father and mother wept too. Charlotte and her parents left the room. Within the closed room the reunited family talked for hours, trying awkwardly to reach out to one another. When Charlotte checked on him later in the evening, his condition had grown worse, accelerated, Charlotte was sure, by the trauma of seeing his parents again. Yet, even though their presence had had an adverse affect on him at first, she felt that in the long run he would be better off with them there.

For three days they remained at his bedside. What they discussed or prayed about with her husband, Charlotte wasn't sure, but the effect it was having on Cliff worried her. His coughing grew worse and the blood in his lungs, gone for the past week and a half, reappeared. His temperature climbed, as did his temper. At times Charlotte could hear arguing behind the bedroom door, then pleas, even crying. Once she noticed Cliff had been weeping. She asked him why and he simply turned his head away from her and asked her to get the Bible. She did, then went and called his doctors.

His doctors wanted to move Cliff to Brackenridge Hospital because their treatment seemed to be losing its effectiveness. But Cliff, surprising everyone, refused. What was wrong with him? Why was he doing this? Charlotte asked if he enjoyed seeing how they suffered because of him. Cliff was losing the battle. They knew it. He knew it.

"But I've got to think about things," he told her.

"What things?"

"My life."

"Keep this up and you won't have a life," she snapped.

"That's just what I mean!"

Not understanding, Charlotte turned and walked out in tears.

Cliff's father stopped her in the hallway. "Honey, I know this is driving you crazy, but *he's* got to decide whether he's going to live or die."

Charlotte became enraged. "What are you talking about? He's already made the choice, no thanks to you! What have you been talking about in there all this week?"

"The Lord," replied Richard Hawkins softly.

Several hours later Cliff called Charlotte into his bedroom. He looked like a man on the edge of death. Instead of turning back and running, she steadied herself and knelt beside him, wiping the perspiration off his brow and telling him how much she loved him.

"If you love me," he said in a whisper, "then please don't be angry at me for what I have . . . to tell you."

"What . . . what is it?" she asked softly.

"I'm not . . . going to be . . . a lawyer anymore. Not . . . not after this."

Charlotte, more concerned about his health than what he was saying, replied, "That's fine. Do anything you want, but please, we've got to get you to Brackenridge."

"No," he said, "the worst is over now. I can feel it in my lungs . . . I'm going to be all right."

"Not if you don't . . ."

"Yes! Yes, because the Lord's going to heal me."

"Wha—?"

"That's why I'm leaving law. I . . . I'm going to be . . . an evangelist."

"What? But why?"

"I'm giving my life to God. Right now . . . just . . . just as my father did."

"Your father? Cliff, what does he have to do with . . ."

"He had it."

"What?"

"*TB!* Just like me." He shut his eyes, then opened them, and, amazingly, began to speak with more strength than he had before. "This happened to him over thirty years ago. They knew for years it would happen to me too. A vision told them. And now . . . now it has."

"But—"

"The only way for me to survive, Charlotte, is to give my life to God."

He was crying now. He cried so hard he ached. Charlotte held him. "I never thought I would," he said. "I hated it. But I've seen the truth."

Within hours he was improving. He never turned back. He had never wanted to be an evangelist, but in the years to come that's what he became.

Yes, she mused, he went on to be something I never thought he would. From lawyer to evangelist without the courtesy of even asking me. Just deciding. Maybe that's why I was so bitter at first. Or maybe . . . maybe it was because I was afraid that he would . . .

Would what?

. . . would end up being like his parents. That's such a cruel thing to say, but they were different from us—all of us. So fervent in their beliefs it was almost frightening. I could have left him, almost did. But Daddy, thank-you-ever-so-much, Daddy put an end to that. Waved a $7 million trust fund in my face and showed me how fast he could dissolve it if I ever left Cliff.

So she stayed. For the money at first, and then for Cliff. It was true that, for the most part, she enjoyed their life together more than she ever thought possible.

Yet there were times, times like tonight, when all the doubts would crop up again, when she thought about all she could have done and still wanted to do. Not live the life she was currently leading. What it was she wanted, Charlotte wasn't sure. That was when she drank. Tonight, though, she had drunk for a different reason. Things were changing. It was at once exciting and frightening. Cliff was actually going to run for . . .

Her thoughts left her when she saw Cliff walk through their bedroom door. As was usual after a crusade, he was smiling. He wanted her. She, too, put on a smile and the act began once more.

BOOK TWO

THE PRIMARIES

6

NEW HAMPSHIRE

It was a miserable day in New Hampshire and Senator Sheldon Roberts concluded that whatever reason he'd had before for braving the extremely low temperature—minus six degrees—was now totally unjustified. He didn't care what the other candidates were doing, this was absurd. He made his way to one of the last houses he would visit that afternoon and knocked.

An elderly woman with dingy gray hair appeared at the door. She was bundled up in a sweater with a light scarf around her neck, and behind her Roberts could see a crackling fire ablaze in the living room. She did not recognize him and moved to shut the door.

He talked fast.

"Please, Senator Sheldon Roberts. I'm running for president . . ."

"Roberts? Good, you just do your running somewhere else."

The door was shut.

"Things are going to be a lot better this time," he'd promised his staff. But Roberts had promised many things and promises were as short-lived as the voting.

Discouraged, but not giving up, he trekked back to the sidewalk, met his aide, and moved on to the final house. He jabbed the doorbell.

Screams greeted him at first. A mother in her twenties with two bawling children hanging from her neck opened the door. She swatted the youngest child. "Yes, what is it?"

"Good afternoon, I'm—"

"Damn it, quit pulling my hair!"

"—Senator Sheldon Roberts."

"Mary Louise! Do that one more time an' I'll blister you!"

"I'm running for—"

The door slammed so quickly Roberts didn't have a chance to step back. He touched his nose. A trickle of blood appeared on his finger. Disgusted, he pulled out a handkerchief and walked back to the sidewalk.

It had been a disaster for the Republican senator.

Larry Broder, the former governor of Colorado, had stumped quickly through the town of Claremont, north of Manchester, where Sheldon Roberts had spent the day. He then headed east to Concord, where he was scheduled to address the Oil for All lobby, an organization—much like Larry Broder himself—dedicated to demonopolizing the oil industry. At every stop his theme was the same. Dismember the multibillion-dollar corporations. Expose them for the loopholing, conniving, lying conglomerates that they were and punish their sins by transferring their control to the United States government. End the gasoline lines, dig through the industry's records, audit their accounts, and funnel their profits into exploration. Sever our reliance on imports, increase our production, seek alternative energy sources, all for America's future. This was such an unusual Republican message that some swore Larry Broder was a closet Democrat.

Broder had been sure he would take the state by storm. But, as the past few months of campaigning taught him, only the northern blizzards were capable of that. Still on this day in Concord things were more harried than usual. Broder had been to so many places within the past eight hours that by now he didn't even know where he was or to whom he was speaking. He assumed that he was somewhere in Concord speaking to the Oil for All group, but hell, he couldn't keep track. Besides, that's what his staff was for. He spoke for about fifteen minutes and started winding up what he thought were some pretty damn good remarks. Harried, true, but the day had gone well.

"... It's been happening for years. We've been selling out to

Exxon, Texaco, and the rest because we don't have the leadership to stand up to them. We've evidenced this in the limp legislation the president's introduced, the wrist-slapping rulings handed down by our courts, in every sector!"

His aide was waving in the back of the auditorium. His face was disturbed. Must be running late, Broder thought.

"We've given in to the sanctimonious oil interests, who claim they're working for the nation. But they're merely working for their own profits."

His aide was motioning to him frantically now.

"People ask me all the time if a lot of this didn't begin with the OPEC situation about two decades ago. It escalated then, but its beginnings go back much further. In fact, when I was still young, my father took me along with him on a goodwill mission to Vietnam to tour the battlefields . . ."

He paused again. His aide was almost hysterical in the back of the room. What in God's name was wrong with him?

". . . and as we toured the battlefields, we flew over some oil refineries. American refineries. All bright and beautiful and quite oblivious to the war raging about them. When my father asked our Vietnamese guide why those most obvious targets weren't bombed . . ."

Shaking his head, his aide begged him not to continue.

". . . he replied, 'Oh, don't you know? The American oil companies pay the Viet Cong off.' "

Broder glanced around. The men and women sat in silence. In shock. Several squirmed. One man dotted his forehead with a Kleenex, several others looked noticeably disturbed. Confused, Broder hurriedly finished his remarks. He thought he'd done rather well, yet they were acting so queer . . .

Larry Broder had made one mistake.

This was not the Oil for All lobby he was supposed to have addressed. That was at the Sierra Club. It wasn't even close. He had just spoken to the All for Oil group—another lobbying interest whose main purpose was to counteract Oil for All. All for Oil hated the other group and loathed Larry Broder. The sea of faces before him were the group's main financiers: influential and astute businessmen from around the country.

Men of big business, connected with big oil.

* * *

If Concord wasn't good, Rochester was worse. Booker T. Smathers was a conservative Republican congressman from Washington, D.C., and the only black presidential contender the modern GOP had ever had. Smathers stepped out of his government-authorized Winnebago, took a position in front of the restaurant, and offered his hand to the first person he saw.

"Booker T. Smathers, congressman from Washington and running for president. I'd—"

The patron disappeared inside the restaurant.

"—appreciate your . . ."

Another person came up.

"Booker T. Smathers, congressman running for president. I'd—"

Smathers was frustrated, but not unused to it. He had been working New Hampshire and the eastern seaboard for the past six months and the reactions had generally been the same. Damn, if life wasn't a bitch. With somebody new, someone like himself, the Republicans finally had the chance to recapture the White House, dump that racist Meade, and counteract the stereotype against their own party for being so Waspish. Smathers couldn't even get a handshake out of them. Sometimes he wondered if he was in the right party. Nobody seemed to give a fuck. There was about as much interest in his running for the presidency and these primaries, he thought, as a nun's funeral. What they needed, he decided, was a nun's gang-bang. A spark! *He* was supposed to be the spark.

America's first black president!

Here he was, the lonely nun, lifeless and being carried to an early grave without even getting screwed. His eighty-year-old father had said it best the day he learned Booker was going to run: "These people don't give a shit about you. You ain't got nobody's sympathy or nobody's interest. Fuck that shit."

Smathers told his father that he was wrong. Times had changed. The barriers once standing between the nation's highest office and his skin color were falling fast. But now Booker wondered if his father hadn't been right. Just look at the reception he'd gotten today.

He was about to call it quits when his aide popped out of the restaurant pursued by a large swarthy man wearing a chef's hat and an apron with smears all over it. Smathers thought he was either a distressed cook or a harried owner. He was both.

"Mama mia!" he said, throwing his hands up in the air. "You causin' all the trouble? Huh? Huh? You gonna havta leave right now! Fellini don't wanna anybody disturbin' his customers."

Fellini kept raving. Smathers said, "Okay, okay. We got the message. We'll leave in a minute, all right?"

"No," he cried. "Right now. Right now."

Smather's aide quickly escorted him back to the Winnebago.

Once inside, Smathers walked to the rear of his office-on-wheels. He could see the bulky figure of Fellini still standing at the restaurant's entrance. A little girl was staring at

BOOKER T. SMATHERS FOR PRESIDENT

painted on the side of the van. Sliding back one of the windows, Smathers poked his head out. "I'm Booker T. Smathers. I'm running for president. I want you to do me a favor. Tell your parents to vote for me in the primary. Booker T. Smathers, just like the sign says. Understand?

The girl gave him a quizzical look, then stuck her tongue out.

7

TEXAS/Dallas

Cliff Hawkins opened one eye and zeroed in on the digital clock. He was running about ten minutes late, but that was all right. The world could wait another ten—he'd had the jitters all night and wanted to stay in bed as long as possible. He'd already said his prayers; now he wanted to think.

This was it.

All the emotions, anxieties, and hopes he'd been accumulating for the past eighteen months were making his stomach flutter. He was nervous, but he had to control it. They all had to. Wade, Perrin, the board of directors, even his son, Blair. They had all laughed casually, jokingly, the first time he mentioned the idea to them. When people began to take his political opinions more seriously and contributions shot up, he mentioned it again. They only chuckled.

But when the draft movement began right after his first—and most brilliant—speech on America's Five Greatest Sins, none of them laughed. Instead, realizing what they were on to, his advisers called in media consultants and hired a public relations firm, as well as an additional direct mail firm, and began a series of lengthy secret discussions with some of the nation's top political strategists. They did a careful audit of Moral Americans, Inc., funds and discovered that both the money and the manpower were there. All they needed was a candidate.

Hawkins was the man.

"It's gotten to a point where I don't have a choice," he had told them. "The people are calling me—and the Lord. The draft movement's proof. People are out there, Christians like myself, who see this nation falling under the weight of its own sins. I can only stand behind God's pulpit for so long before people quit listening. It's going to take more to save this country. I've got to be able to make them realize this. I thought I could do it through lobbying, through Moral Americans, Inc.—and we did do more than I ever thought possible, thanks to you, Father—but the nation is sicker than I thought. Its sins have spread like a cancer. They're eating away at it, and the very foundation of our freedom and democracy as well. It's ... it's like that woman, that crippled woman I tried to heal years ago at that crusade in ... where was it? I knew ... I knew that I was only a contact between her and the Lord, but I'll never forget how she looked when I failed. God didn't fail, I failed. There was such a pain of disappointment in her face. And yet it's the same face I see now, all over the country, wherever I go. Faces of disappointment, reflecting the promises of Meade's administration—and how he's failed."

He now got up out of bed and started toward the dressing room.

"Cliff?"

He paused and turned. "I didn't mean to wake you, I'm sorry."

Charlotte sat up stretching. "You didn't. I've got to shower ..."

"I'll be right out."

"Cliff ... aren't you nervous?"

Hawkins walked over to her and sat down on the bed. "Of course, I am. But I also believe this is what the Lord wants me to do."

"But ... what if you misread his message, or ..."

Hawkins laughed, "Charlotte, are you scared?"

"Terrified."

"Don't be. The worst that can happen is that I'll lose. The best that can happen is ... well, you know that."

Charlotte said nothing.

8

Howard Hickman rushed past two White House tour guides and collided with a group of visitors as he raced past the Diplomatic Reception Room and the Map Room. He slammed through some glass doors, miraculously not breaking them, and flew the short distance between the main mansion and the West Wing offices. He stopped only to flash his badge at the Secret Service agents before entering the Oval Office. Suddenly he was before the president.

"Howard! What in God's name—"

Hickman pointed to Meade's desk. "Your TV. Flip it on!"

"Huh?"

"Never mind," he replied, already behind the president's desk, pulling out a long drawer with controls in it.

Meade looked up, perturbed. "What in hell are you doing?"

"Look," he answered, pointing to the television set opposite the president's desk. "I saw it on a set in the East Wing."

Meade's eyes riveted to the screen where he saw Cliff Hawkins standing before an army of microphones.

"The sound, Howard! Where's the sound?"

Hickman turned the knob.

"... Once again, to repeat, evangelist Clifford Hawkins has just announced here in Dallas that he is a candidate for the presidency of the United States . . ."

Clutching Hickman's arm, Meade said, "Jesus, he's crazier than I thought."

9

TEXAS/Dallas

Cliff Hawkins was on the ballot in Massachusetts. The reaction was swift. Newspapers and magazines begged for interviews. The "Today" show and "Good Morning America" phoned. So did Dan Rather and all the major political columnists. Letters, telegrams, and phone calls flooded the offices of Christ Church Worldwide for two days. An army of journalists from around the world set up camp at the religious empire's headquarters.

Hawkins stood at the window of his office suite, on the top floor of the main building of the CCW complex. Eight stories below him was an encampment of newsmen waiting for his departure to Massachusetts. Behind him his suite was a flurry of activity. Secretaries dashed in and out, telephones rang endlessly, and news service reports poured in over the wire. Everyone was talking at once, computer printouts were flying, and the road to the presidency, once only talk, had now burst into living color.

Gordon Wade, propped against Hawkins's expansive desk, was conferring over the telephone with their regional and state offices. The foreign offices in Belgium, Holland, England, and Germany had phoned as well. Randy Perrin was behind the desk on another phone gauging the influx of letters and telegrams.

"Calls are still hitting every office we have," announced Wade.

"In Ann Arbor more demonstrators are showing up. And San Francisco's gays are throwing fits."

Randy Perrin cupped his phone and said, "Fifty thousand telegrams in the past forty-eight hours, sixty thousand letters from within the state alone."

"What are they saying?" asked Hawkins, smiling.

"They're split right down the middle."

The smile faded for a second, but then quickly returned. "We knew it would happen this way."

Wade said, "Our New York office is on the line. *People* just phoned. You're on the cover next week with Charlotte, if you want it."

Hawkins's eyes glowed. "Of course I want it."

Just then Malinda Mayer, the evangelist's girl Friday for the past eight years, came in. "Secret Service says time to go. Your luggage is in the limo."

Hawkins waved to Perrin, and pulled on Wade. "Let's go. We'll talk in the car."

Accompanied by his newly assigned Secret Service protection, the presidential candidate emerged from the building amid a wave of flashing lights and whining motorized Nikons. Flanked by his agents and aides, he tried to push through the sea of journalists to his waiting limousine.

"Reverend, do you think your position as an evangelist will help or hinder you in Massachusetts?"

"It'll certainly help me with my fellow Christians. I hope that the voters who aren't Christians at least share my views enough to vote for me."

The Houston Post asked, "There's already been a lot of criticism about your involvement in politics. Don't you think this is going to increase even among other Christians?"

"Not as much as we expect the support to increase."

Dallas Times Herald: "Reverend, have you considered the implications of such a candidacy in respect to the constitutional provisions regarding church and state?"

"Yes, I have."

"And you don't see yourself as a threat to those provisions?"

"Of course not."

"Reverend," NBC News called out, "where do you draw the lines between church and state?"

Hawkins, now begining to feel a little self-conscious at the barrage of questions, replied, "I draw the lines exactly where the Supreme Court draws them."

ABC News asked, "Does that mean you're in favor of their ruling against prayer in public schools?"

"No."

There was an excited flurry of follow-up questions and Wade pushed in between the thrusting microphones and Hawkins, saying, "Gentlemen, please! So many questions!"

Hawkins stopped walking and the clamoring group immediately surrounded him.

"It's all right, Gordon. To answer your question, I oppose the ruling because, as I've said many times before, I believe it infringes upon the rights of Christian children everywhere and attacks the spirit of the First Amendment. I believe the public is with me. A recent Gallup poll said that as of January of this year 74 percent of those with children in school—people who are and are not Christian, by the way—want their youngsters to have not only some sort of prayer but also some religious instruction."

"But if the Court ruled—"

"I said I draw the line on separation of church and state with the Court. That doesn't mean I agree with every Court ruling relating to either the church or the state."

Hawkins noticed that several reporters were scribbling furiously, and decided to continue. "Nevertheless, ladies and gentlemen, I do believe that by banning prayer in schools you're stepping on the rights of millions of American children who want to acknowledge the Lord together before doing their schoolwork. This is exactly what our Founding Fathers wanted to avoid: the denial of an individual's rights to free religious expression."

Associated Press: "If elected, whose laws are you going to go by? The Lord's or the court's?"

With characteristic aplomb, Hawkins said, "I'll do both and, believe me, I won't buck the system doing it. If you glance at Romans, chapter 13, you'll find that this is exactly what the Lord wants."

"What does it say?" someone asked.

" 'Everyone must submit himself to the governing authorities. . . . If you owe taxes, pay taxes; if revenue, then revenue; if respect, then respect; if honor, then honor.' And that means respect and honor for the courts and the Congress."

"Reverend, are you aware of the protesters at your headquarters in Ann Arbor and Saint Louis?" asked the *Los Angeles Times.*

"I'm aware. It doesn't matter. If they want to protest, that's within their rights."

"Reverend, have you heard any reactions from the White House?"

"No, I haven't," he said with a smile, "but I don't imagine I'll be asked to give a blessing at a state dinner anytime soon."

Everyone laughed and, before they could ask anything else, Hawkins was pushed into his limousine and whisked away. Going out of the complex, they passed his television studio, radio station, auditorium, and mail building—past thirty years of his life and into his new one.

On the plane Hawkins took his seat behind the small desk they'd equipped his aft-cabin office with. He glanced up and saw Randy Perrin sitting against the opposite wall, scribbling something on a yellow legal pad.

Perrin was by far the most important member of Hawkins's team, at least as far as the public was concerned. Serving as both press secretary and campaign manager until the race heated up, he was the one person besides Hawkins whose face was going to be continually before the public. Perrin was much younger than Hawkins, and his age and wholesome appearance would help pull in the more skeptical young voters. Politicians and political columnists everywhere acknowledged him as one of the shrewdest of the young poli-sci grads with pragmatic views on American politics. Hawkins had the money to hire him and got him. Also in the cabin office were Gordon Wade, CCW president and former Wall Street financial genius; Coco Province, Hawkins's media specialist; and Winny Foster, his pollster.

"As we expected," Wade began, "the reactions have been volcanic. Telephone calls, letters, telegrams. Cliff, as I told you at the office—and Coco, you should oversee this—*People*'s putting you and Charlotte on the cover. I'm sure *Time* and *Newsweek* will too. This is probably the biggest publicity coup of the year for them. As far as our opposition goes, no one has issued statements and that includes the White House."

"We have demonstrators," added Perrin.

"Which we knew we'd have," sighed Wade to Hawkins. "Right now it's your small-time civil rights groups, leftists, liberals, and general antireligion or anti-Hawkins people. But we'll be hearing from the gays, the feminists, the blacks, and all of our other friends too."

"How bad is Ann Arbor?" asked Coco.

"Last reports indicate it's getting worse. The police have set up barricades around our office up there to keep the people back. But they're throwing eggs and all."

Hawkins shrugged it off. "We anticipated all this; don't worry about it. The Christians out there who are with us, they'll see those people for what they are—the very ones bringing this country down."

"Or else *make* them see that," said Coco facetiously, "through our friends in the press."

During the next twenty minutes Perrin and Coco filled the group in on the various members of the press who'd been assigned to cover the Hawkins campaign. They told them who was friendly, who wasn't, who was neutral, and who could give them plugs when they needed it. Going through a file the Secret Service had given him, Perrin went over each name and asked them all to make an effort to connect the names with their faces. He pulled out photographs to help.

"They're going to be the ones who ultimately make us or break us," Perrin said. "We've got to keep them as happy as possible, even if it kills us."

"Oh, also, we're scratching the patriotism ads for now," Coco informed them.

"But why?" asked Hawkins. "Those were terrific! And they cost us a fortune."

"Because of the reactions since the announcement. Hamilton and Zinn, our firm, thought it'd be better to go into Massachusetts with something more identifiable to the voters than your red-white-and-blue song and dance . . ."

"I think it deserves a little more credit than that," said Hawkins.

"You know what I mean."

"So, what are you going to do?"

"Plug in those other commercials. The ones of all those people from Massachusetts talking about why they're glad you're running for president. How courageous you are for stepping into the race, how they think the country needs a man of God, how much they agree with you about America's Five Greatest Sins, all that. We can run a sixty-second commercial and the sound track can be used for radio ads without having to change a thing. I'll play it for you."

She pulled out a cassette from her briefcase and popped it into a tape deck. An anonymous but soothing voice issued forth.

In a time when the greatest nation on earth is suffering from moral decline, suicides, bankruptcies, inflation, crime, and pornography, there is one man—one caring, understanding, concerned American—who stands above the rest. He is a man like you and me, but so much more. A man whose inspiration and leadership has brought him into the homes of millions of people; a man who talks to us, who listens to us, and who helps. His name is Cliff Hawkins and for almost four decades he's heard the cries of a needy America. He still does. . . . That's why he's here now, in Massachusetts. Ready to help our nation in a new and exciting way, ready to help turn back the clock to a time when we not only knew our life in America was good, but felt it. He wants to help us and we have the chance to let him. Cliff Hawkins—yesterday, today, tomorrow. He's standing up for America, let's stand up for him! Vote Cliff Hawkins in the Massachusetts Republican primary.

Coco reached over and stabbed the eject button and the cassette popped into her hand.

A phone buzzed. Perrin picked it up. He listened, not believing what he was hearing. He looked up at Hawkins, then to Wade, Coco, and Foster.

"Well, we're going to have problems in Boston. That was the state coordinator on the phone."

"What did he say?" asked Hawkins.

"The mayor isn't meeting you at the airport as planned."

Foster and Coco shifted in their seats.

"Why not?"

"He said, when you were scheduled to come it was as Cliff Hawkins, evangelist, not Cliff Hawkins, presidential candidate—"

There was considerable grumbling.

"He said it just wouldn't look appropriate."

"Well, it's plausible," offered Wade. "We scheduled this a month ago without mentioning the race . . ."

"It gets worse," said Perrin. "Not only is he refusing to meet us at the airport, he's also revoked the Key to Boston ceremonies as well."

Hawkins looked momentarily stricken. "What?"

"Somebody must be pressuring him," said Coco. "They must be."

"It sounds like it," said Wade.

"I thought the same thing," Perrin said. "But if they're putting the heat on him, they're doing it to everyone else connected with us as well."

"What do you mean?" Wade asked.

"Not one other Republican leader in Boston is willing to meet us there either. Nobody will touch us. What's more, our Boston office received a bomb threat a little while ago."

"Good Lord," said Hawkins.

"It's all over the news."

"I'll bet it is."

Wade put a cigarette to his mouth, fumbling to light it. "Anything else?"

"Isn't that enough?"

10

EN ROUTE TO BOSTON

Twenty thousand feet over Greenville, South Carolina, making their way toward Boston, they were relayed the newest poll on Hawkins, the first one taken since the announcement.

"Our crudest figures," said his pollster, Winny Foster, "but the ones we can surmise as being indicative of the electorate are as follows: 38 percent are enthusiastic about your running, 23 percent are not, and 39 percent are undecided."

"That's not bad," said Hawkins. "There are 38 percent for us. That's only 13 percent away from a majority!"

"Cliff," Foster said, "it's awfully hard to count on making up 13 percent when so many people are undecided about you."

"And," he sighed, as if bringing more unpleasant news, "that's not all. Between Larry Broder, Booker Smathers, and Sheldon Roberts, your biggest worry is Larry Broder. Next to him your chances are split right down the middle. You have an edge over the others, but it's going to be Broder that gives you trouble."

"Roberts was supposed to be the one giving me trouble, not Broder," protested Hawkins. "That's what you said all along."

"Roberts is already running out of money and support faster than anyone expected."

"But Broder," said Hawkins, leaning forward in his chair and looking directly at Foster across his desk, "and I are on completely opposite ends of the political spectrum. Everyone knows that. He's a closet Democrat! Why would he be taking support away from us?"

"Because you are both so distinct on your stands. We haven't been in this race two days and people seem to be cutting this right down the middle. Either you want a staunchly conservative—and controversial—candidate, or you want Larry Broder, crusader for the left."

"It's too black and white," said Wade.

"It is," agreed Perrin. "Broder should have given up on Massachusetts. It was supposed to be Roberts's state. That's who we should be fighting in this primary."

"But it's not going that way," Foster explained. "This country's split is a lot more definite than I calculated."

"If the figures are right."

"They are."

"Well," asked Hawkins reflectively, "what's the verdict on the state? Can we still win Massachusetts or not?"

"I don't know. It's too early to tell how this publicity in Boston is going to affect us, but I don't think it'll be good."

"We don't really expect to win Massachusetts anyway, you know," Perrin said. "I mean, just make a strong enough showing to establish credibility, and let it sink into the voters' heads that we really mean business."

"That's true," said Foster. "But we also didn't expect this to turn into an embarrassment so early."

"It's not an embarrassment," snapped Wade. "We haven't lost yet, and we certainly aren't going to let these figures dictate our campaign for us."

"We knew what we were facing when we got into this thing," Hawkins said, "knew it would be tough. What we didn't know is that we'd be slapped in the face so early, that there'd be bombs in our offices. But that's okay. Just remember our long-range goals. Remember that there are Christians out there who want us to win! And 38 percent is good, but it's going to get even better. Count on it. God's with us. And with him on our side, we can win!"

"Amen."

They landed in Boston. Witnessing the throngs of waiting supporters and press outside the runway's fence, Hawkins felt confident about their chances in the Massachusetts primary. The Secret Service had estimated at least twenty-five hundred people were there, in the freezing cold. All of them pinning their hopes on him to take over the helm of this nation and turn it back to God. He said a prayer of thanks and went down the jet's ramp. Before he could reach the edge of the runway, members of the national press corps were already upon him, joined in turn by a throng of local media representatives. The press had found out just minutes before about the mayor's deliberate absence as well as the cancellation of the Key to Boston ceremonies, and everyone wanted a statement.

"Reverend!" they called above the cheering of his supporters.

"What's your reaction—"

"Sir, how do you feel about Mayor Boisvert's refusal to meet you?" one shouted.

"The cancellation of the key ceremonies?" another yelled.

"Smile please!"

Hawkins smiled directly into flashing cameras and television Minicams.

"To answer your many questions, I'm after the presidency, not a key to a city. I know Mayor Boisvert has many duties and I'm glad he didn't drop them simply to come out here and meet me. If he did that everytime someone flew in, he'd never get anything done. Anyway I don't feel its a reflection on me or my campaign. Now, if I were president, it might be different. "But," he said wryly, "I'm not president yet, am I?"

Before they could ask anything else, he quickly started shaking hands up and down the fence and greeting his supporters.

11

In his suite at the Ritz-Carleton Senator Sheldon Roberts had gathered his family and staff for a small party. The New Hampshire primary returns were coming in, and Roberts was pulling a bit more votes in than they'd expected. Larry Broder was still running far ahead, but since Cliff Hawkins had announced, nobody knew how the voters would react. Even though Hawkins wasn't on the ballot in New Hampshire, all the political scientists were predicting mass confusion at the voting booths.

Yet that hadn't happened. Roberts's party wore on. They patted each other on the back at his gaining percentages, then suddenly watched in horror as Governor Larry Broder's gains accelerated. . . .

Five hours later, in Manchester, New Hampshire, Booker T. Smathers was glad he wasn't the Catholic nun he'd thought about last week. New Hampshire had screwed him bad enough and, had he been the nun, he'd have been dead by now. With all major precincts reporting in on the first primary of the election year, Smathers now officially knew what the exit polls had already told him: that they were going to pull only 11 percent of the Republican primary vote.

Not only was this personally embarrassing, but it was one of the most politically pathetic failures he'd ever encountered. Too pitiful to call a press conference. But, being the politician he was, Smathers had one anyway. Citing poor organization—which he had—and mismanagement—which he had also had—he conceded his poor showing before a handful of reporters, mostly from *Ebony* and *Jet*. The rest of the media hadn't bothered to show up. Typical, he thought.

We shall overcome? Bullshit.

WASHINGTON/The White House

Otis Meade, sitting in front of the three-screen television console in the West Sitting Hall, felt unsettled by the primary results. Larry Broder had come out ahead in the contest, pulling 34 percent of the vote, Sheldon Roberts brought in an unimpressive 24 percent, and Smathers, a ridiculous 11 percent. At first Meade was encouraged by Broder's lead, feeling if Broder kept it up, he could go into the Massachusetts primary with enough momentum to cream Hawkins right off . . . and that would be the end of that. But it hadn't worked out exactly that way. Broder had stayed ahead, but 31 percent of the votes were cast under the uncommitted slate.

Why? Who were they waiting to commit those delegates to?

That's what bothered Otis Meade the most. Hawkins, a force to be reckoned with in a presidential race? Did anyone actually take this seriously? Were the people really so desperate? Meade stared at the television screen. He scoffed at the very idea. No, the voters had chosen the uncommitted slate for other reasons. Obviously they just didn't like anyone the Republicans were offering this year. That had to be it.

And yet . . .

Meade had the uneasy feeling that there was possibly more to it than that. That there were other reasons he just didn't want to think about.

He shook his head and turned off the sets.

No, Broder's going to get the nomination. Things were a little off this time around, but Massachusetts will set everything straight. He's still going to be my opponent in November. And I'm going to blow that little sonofabitch out like a match.

12

MASSACHUSETTS/Boston

Randy Perrin's itinerary for Hawkins couldn't have been worse. His first serious mistake of the campaign had been neglecting the most obvious factor—the weather. From the moment they landed it began snowing and didn't let up for two days. Power lines were down, roads were blocked, Brookline had lost its power, Somerville had a snowbound traffic jam, the airport was shut down, and every stop Perrin had planned for Hawkins, save one, depended on good weather. Their tour of the Hancock-Clarke House in Lexington was canceled. In Boston the Quincy Market was deserted, Harvard called off classes, and even the downtown Rotary Club failed to show up for their weekly meeting.

By their third day Perrin and many of the staff were growing depressed and desperate. The local and national press had already enjoyed the embarrassment of Mayor Boisvert's refusal to greet Hawkins and had wrung everything they could out of it. They were even more delighted when the weather—and the cancellations it brought about—practically wrote the rest of the week's dispatches for them.

Perrin wanted his candidate to leave Boston as soon as possible, to start regaining what they had lost. But Hawkins, the eternal optimist, the man whose faith in the Lord had made him famous, wasn't about to leave. Instead he did a series of radio and television interviews, taped commercials for Coco to use later, and begged Perrin to take him some place where he could meet voters.

"Are you kidding?" Perrin had asked. "The only place that hasn't shut down in this weather are the malls, and I'll bet you we won't find ten people shopping in them."

Hawkins disagreed. "No, they should be packed. Where else can you go in weather like this? There's one five minutes from here, with three residential neighborhoods surrounding it. Let's go."

Perrin insisted it was time to leave the city but Hawkins insisted on going to the mall. They went.

The mall was indeed packed. When ten Boston police officers and several bulky men in overcoats and sunglasses started combing through the crowds, a wave of murmuring spread through the various shops. Within minutes the main entrance was roped off and walkie-talkies were crackling from strategic points throughout the shopping area. A crowd began to form near the entrance. Protected by the central heating, they stood and talked among themselves, watching the huge glass doors leading into the parking lot, not really knowing what to expect.

"What's going on?" someone asked.

"Dunno. Cops everywhere, though."

"Jeez."

Within ten minutes the crowd had tripled, and beyond the parking lot with its sea of snow-covered cars they could make out a motorcade of flashing red lights moving slowly toward the mall.

Half-murmuring questions quickly rose to open speculation. Arguments broke out. It was the president. It was not. The crowd grew even larger. Shoppers were leaving the stores, and even store managers made excuses to step out for a moment. The row of flashing cars drew closer. Someone yelled that it *was* the president. Screams erupted. People began shoving. Suddenly the press was there. Television cameras and lights were turned on the crowd, microphones appeared. News photographers darted here and there looking for shots. Then the motorcade turned in.

"He's coming!"

Several neatly groomed young men and women, campaign volunteers bundled up in coats and scarves, rushed through the doors and moved through the crowd, passing out leaflets.

Then it happened.

The advance cars and limousine came to an abrupt halt in front of the entrance. The Secret Service quickly surrounded the automobile and the cameras and newsmen, turning away from the crowd, moved toward it. The door opened and there he was, in living color, evangelist-turned-candidate getting out and meeting the voters. The mall's doors opened for Hawkins as if he were a king. People swarmed around him. Immediately there was a mixture of cheers and booing, combined with a forward thrust from the back of the crowd by people who obviously wanted a better glimpse of the candidate. Hawkins assumed his role and played it as true as any seasoned politician. The crowds pushed in closer. Camera flashes popping, Nikons and Minoltas clicked away. The crowd was electrified. The candidate and his Secret Service agents were caught in the middle of the pandemonium, the cameras recording it all. Those agents closest to Hawkins pleaded with him to leave. Instead he plunged deeper into the crowd.

"Are you crazy?" an agent asked him.

"This is the best thing that's happened since we got here," said Hawkins.

That evening all three networks gave the event lead coverage on their news broadcasts. They reminded their viewers of Hawkins's clumsy start in Boston, but then pointed out that his reception at the shopping mall was unusually enthusiastic. Perrin was pleased with the reports. So was the candidate, who prayed that the coverage would help win over most of the 39 percent of undecided voters. If it didn't, Larry Broder would not only defeat them in Massachusetts, but in Vermont's simultaneous primary as well.

VERMONT/Mount Snow

The snows had fallen for three days in the Northeast, and continued to fall the day Larry Broder dropped in on one of Vermont's most popular ski resorts. It was an unplanned trip, forced on the former Colorado governor because of closed roads in other parts of the state, but Broder found himself more appreciative of the weather every hour he stayed.

The drive had been beautiful. With three inches of new snow on the roads, the journey had been slow, but Broder didn't care. He'd heard about the ski resort for years and, as they wove up the mountain, he was sorry he'd missed it before. Flakes drifted lazily past his car window, and in the distance he could see pines and spruce, their branches bending under the weight of snow. Traffic was backed up for a mile and, dotting the white mountainsides far off in the distance, one could see chalets similar to those at Saint Moritz. Puffs of smoke were billowing from their fireplaces. It was known as Little Switzerland and Broder could see why. Flags representing the various nations of the world flapped in the wind and, as they neared the top, Broder could see dozens of skiers whizzing down the slopes, a gondola struggling upward toward the mountain's peak, and several of the chair lifts rocking back and forth as they brought skiers to and fro.

The thing Larry Broder did not appreciate about this trip, or anything else having to do with the campaign, was the sudden appearance of Cliff Hawkins in the presidential race. True, he was aware of the Hawkins draft movement and he knew that behind Hawkins's smiling thanks-be-to-God persona was a deeply ambitious man, but never would Broder have dreamed Hawkins would actually run for the presidency. But he was running. Campaigning now in Massachusetts, on his way to Vermont. Planning to come right here in Larry Broder's own territory. His campaign manager, Randy Somebody, had said on the news the other night that Cliff Hawkins planned on entering every primary from here on out, which meant every primary Larry Broder would be in.

Broder didn't like it. Didn't like it one damn bit. This was supposed to have been *his* year and his year alone. Hawkins was on one week now, and the press was gloating over his candidacy like Elvis Presley risen from the grave. Broder had wanted to say something all week, but hadn't. Don't attack him even before he does anything, his campaign manager had said. It'll make us look worried. We don't need that.

Well, after seeing the coverage Hawkins was getting, they did need it. Broder was now ready to knock Hawkins's face right off the screen. He was tired of keeping his mouth shut. At the ski resort he hadn't answered more than three questions when it came up. He was holding a press conference in a room hastily provided by the resort's management.

"Governor, have you decided to break the silence on Cliff Hawkins's candidacy?" the reporter said. "If you have, how do you feel about his running? Do you think he will represent any serious threat to your campaign?"

Broder laughed. It was a mocking laugh. Almost wicked. Then he grew serious. His eyes were wary.

"To answer your question, Jim, no. I don't think he represents a threat to my candidacy or any candidacy. What I do think his candidacy represents," he paused for effect, ". . . is a threat to the very basic principles upon which our nation was founded. Particularly the provisions regarding separation of church and state. Men and women left their homelands more than three hundred years ago to escape the very influence that Reverend Hawkins is obviously trying to restore through his candidacy. Reverend Hawkins obviously wants to ignore that. He wants to take his morals, his beliefs, and his religion, and shove it down the throats of the American people. And I, for one, don't think they're going to buy that."

"Are you saying he doesn't have a broad base of support?"

"I'm saying that his followers are not the only people in this nation. So who are they to shove their religion and morality down the rest of our people's throats? Who are they to come in and take control over the government and dictate policies that will affect people they blatantly dislike?"

"Meaning?" another reporter asked.

"Meaning the Jews, the Catholics, the homosexuals, the lesbians, you name it. Even the liberals. God, yes, every liberal's a Communist, didn't you know that?"

"Governor!"

"I'm not finished yet," Broder snapped. "I'm appalled that Reverend Hawkins has even considered running. I'm totally disgusted that he's in a race where he obviously does not belong. Hawkins's present pursuits are secular when, if he were being true to his profession, they should be directed at teaching the Bible. Instead he's opted to try and influence the laws and policies of our country from the White House instead of from the pulpit, and that, ladies and gentlemen, would be the biggest disaster to ever hit Washington. Does he honestly think there's a place for him in Washington? Our country is too diverse for a man like him. What sort of policies would he consider? Would he want to impose his morals on every piece of legislation before him? I don't know. That bothers me. It should bother all of us. Every American who's interested in maintaining the sort of system our forefathers fought and died for. Cliff Hawkins is a fine man, but his race and election would, without a doubt, be the biggest calamity to ever hit this nation."

"Governor! Governor!" a dozen voices called out.

"Yes, Frank," he answered pointing to one of the journalists.

"Governor, you've made some pretty blunt charges today. Do you feel the other Republican candidates would agree with you?"

"I hope, for the sake of this nation, they do."

He was right. It was as if Sheldon Roberts and Booker T. Smathers had been looking for something to latch onto to give their campaigns the needed coverage Broder and Hawkins had been taking from them. Within a matter of hours they each had press conferences of their own, questioning Hawkins's true motives for running, his seriousness as a candidate, his chances, and the issue of separation of church and state.

Smathers, while not openly calling Hawkins a demagogue, did say—without any pun intended—that it would be a "dark day in America for blacks if Cliff Hawkins even wins the nomination, and an even darker day if he were to ever become president."

Roberts, normally a reserved man, charged Hawkins with "trying to blackmail the voters into thinking their votes for the presidency are either anti-God or pro-God with nothing in between. For a man of religion to even attempt this is morally appalling."

And in Washington? The White House informed the press that "President Meade will reserve comment on the matter until the seriousness of Cliff Hawkins's candidacy has been established."

13

URGENT   URGENT   URGENT   URGENT
FOR IMMEDIATE RELEASE
BOSTON (AP)
Cliff Hawkins, evangelist-turned-politician candidate, categorically denied a host of allegations leveled at his campaign yesterday by his opponents in the Republican primary sweepstakes.

Hawkins, at an often heated news conference here this afternoon, blasted the former Colorado governor Larry Broder, Senator Sheldon Roberts (R-Va.), and Congressman Booker T. Smathers (R-NJ) for "erroneous statements made in an entirely callous, malicious, and calculated manner."

This is perhaps the strongest wording Hawkins has used concerning any of his opponents so far.

Hawkins said that while he agreed with Governor Broder's charge that his pursuits were secular in nature, he said that "it is secular issues that are ruining this nation, so I've got to address them."

Responding to Broder's words that his campaign threatened

the separation of church and state, Hawkins said, "I firmly believe in separation of church and state and have never been for anything close to resembling a national religion. If we didn't have this [separation] and the national religion was, say, Catholicism, then I would never have been able to run openly on my beliefs, so how can I not be for it?"

"But this is not to say," Hawkins continued, "that I believe in government turning away from God. This is precisely where our nation's downfall began in the first place and it goes against everything our forefathers wanted. Just look at our coinage: 'In God We Trust.' But we haven't been trusting in him, have we? From the office of the president down to the constable in the smallest county in the nation we've got to return to basic trust in God, and who would be better to set such an example than the president himself?"

Responding to Representative Booker T. Smathers's allegation that Hawkins's campaign and possible election would be detrimental to blacks, Hawkins said, "I'm not running for any group of people, but for all the people. Christians, Jews, blacks, and anyone else who is worried about the direction our nation is heading."

Hawkins, referring to Senator Sheldon Roberts's assertion that the evangelist was "trying to blackmail" voters into believing the race for the presidency was going to be "either anti-God or pro-God with nothing in between," said Roberts was "totally off base."

Elaborating, Hawkins said that "the issue isn't anti-God or pro-God at all . . . instead it comes down to whether you want to turn this country away from the road to ruin, working to turn the tide and saving this great nation of ours, or whether you want to see this country bankrupt itself morally far more than Rome ever did.

"If a man is non-Christian, even atheist, but believes in the unity of family, is against homosexuality, abortion, all the issues I've addressed before, I'd rather have that man serving in my Cabinet than a Christian who is diametrically opposed to me on every issue. You can bet on it."

People here, and in the sister state of Vermont, may or may not bet on it. Polls released today by both Harris and Gallup show Hawkins trailing noticeably behind Broder in both states and not much ahead of Smathers or Roberts. When asked about the polls, the evangelist replied, "I think we'll surprise a lot of people. Especially the pollsters. Our organization's strong and there's a good silent majority out there listening to us."

14

If Cliff Hawkins had wanted to surprise the skeptics, he surprised none of them. He did, however, surprise himself by losing the first two primaries he entered.

Although it wasn't official yet, almost all the major precincts in Vermont and Massachusetts were in and the next day newspapers and television and radio broadcasts would make the election results their lead stories. The world would know that Cliff Hawkins had lost. There was disappointment throughout the ranks of his campaign staff, but Hawkins stepped before the cameras and microphones to tell them and the rest of the world that he wasn't giving up. Looking as clean and crisp as ever, with a charming smile, Hawkins told his supporters not to let his losses bring even a shred of doubt that the presidency couldn't be his. They could still save the nation from its impending moral collapse. It was only a matter of time.

At the end of his press conference his supporters broke out in cheers. Hawkins beamed.

Two thousand miles away Charlotte Hawkins was on the first campaign trip she'd ever taken in her life, in Florida, trying to drum up support for her husband with the aid of a half dozen staff members and sixteen media representatives. Florida was the next primary battleground, one of the biggest they would hit. Although it was still weeks away, as soon as the results were in from the last two primaries, attention had zeroed in on the Sunshine State—and on Charlotte.

All things considered, Cliff thought, she was adapting to the life of a campaign trouper rather well. Nevertheless, there was some strain, he could feel it, hear it even though the distance that separated them was great. It was a strain whose vibration carried across all those thousands of miles of telephone lines and hit him in his gut. For her matters weren't the worst they could be, but they weren't the best either.

"You said the worst thing that could happen would be losing," she said. "Well, you're right."

"Don't let it get to you. The Lord is with us."

"I'm not talking about the Lord. I'm talking about losing, how it affects us. All the attention that's focused on us is maddening, Cliff. Microphones always in your face. Cameras. They practically follow me to the bathroom."

Hawkins, used to professional scrutiny for years, had forgotten how unsettling such attention could be at first. "Charlotte, it's something everyone has to deal with. Political wives, especially the wives of presidential candidates, have always had it rough. It's part of the pressure, you know that."

She knew about pressure all right, and about a hundred other things. She knew but, thanks to her handy bottle, didn't dwell on it.

"Look at Katherine Meade. Look at all the pressure she's under. It's probably a thousand times worse for her, but she handles it. She's had to learn to."

"I wonder . . ." Charlotte said.

WASHINGTON/The White House

That evening in her bedroom on the second floor of the mansion Katherine Meade sat in a chaise longue flipping through a *New Yorker* too quickly to read the copy. She was passing time in a world that for years had offered her no time of her own. From the day they had moved into the White House there had always been a reception or opening, a luncheon, an interview, a state dinner or speech, but never a moment to call her own.

Outside her bedroom door she could hear the muffled voices of her husband, the vice president, Howard Hickman, and several others. They were discussing the latest poll concerning the upcoming Florida primary. She didn't know what they were saying, nor did she care. They had been talking about the election and about the Republican opposition since dinner. She was tired of it. Tired of politics, tired of Washington, everything. She felt the polls, all the other stuff didn't really matter. She would still be trapped in this mansion next year . . . and the year after that . . . and the . . .

Katherine flipped through more pages, took a long sip of the Tom Collins she'd been drinking, and, plagued by boredom, dropped the limp copy on the carpet and got up. She supposed she should catch up on some of her correspondence, sign a few cards, or do something else that fell within her unofficial duties as First Lady. But the hell with that. She walked over to the window and parted the curtains. Gazing out at the South Lawn fountain, with its splashing almost hypnotically, and beyond that past the majestic lawns, Katherine noticed automobiles speeding in the night past Avenue E.

She stood there for a moment captivated by their movement, their lights, their racing bodies . . . racing into oblivion. She imagined she was in one, fleeing, like them, away from this place, this prison of hers.

Katherine let the curtain fall back and returned to the chaise longue. She picked up her drink, drained it, then settled back down. The fire crackled in the fireplace. Voices from the other room continued to filter into her room. She thought about getting another magazine, doing the correspondence, but the thoughts disappeared. Her eyes concentrated on her bedroom door, and her mind centered on her husband on the other side of it.

Katherine wondered if the president could sense her need for him now, her craving for him to be the husband he hadn't been for so long. To caress her, fondle her, envelop her in his arms, and say, "I really do love you." She fantasized how she would react if he suddenly burst into her room, swooped her up in his arms, threw her on the bed, and made flaming, soaring love to her. She gazed longingly at the bed. She envisioned their movements, their bodies meshing in eros and passion, his deep thrusting, her body moving in rhythm with his.

The first time they had made love was after the fund-raiser Katherine had given at her estate when Otis was seeking reelection to Congress. When the guests had departed and her own family had retired for the evening, they sat in a small study and talked for hours. As if they both knew there was nothing left to say, they kissed. Then Otis suggested they go for a walk.

They moved silently through the estate's darkened grounds. The night air was chilly and the moon was shrouded in a light mist. Walking through the gardens with Otis's arm around her waist, Katherine mentioned the guesthouse nearby.

"There's a fireplace and some things for hot buttered rum in there," she said.

They entered through the small building's french doors. Katherine made drinks. Otis built a fire in the fireplace. She told him a joke and they both laughed. Side by side, standing at a small counter just off the kitchen, they sipped the hot rum and gazed at the fire. It now offered the only light in the house. The fire snapped, Otis put his cup down on the counter, took Katherine's and put it down too, then reached for her and kissed her. She responded with passion. He kissed her again and then again.

"Fifteen years ago," she said, "I wouldn't have thought I'd be doing this."

"Neither would I."

"I want to make love to you."

"I want you to."

He took her hand and guided her away from the counter. They walked over by the fireplace and he paused.

"Here?" she asked.

Otis looked at her, amused. "On the rug? Kat, everybody's done that . . ."

She giggled and followed him into the bedroom.

The covers were thrown back, the pillows fluffed. They left the bedroom door open and light from the fireplace seeped in, casting shadows about the room as they removed each other's clothes. In between kisses they regarded each other's naked body and quickly fell into bed.

Katherine laid back and shut her eyes, feeling the weight of his body move over hers. She took a deep breath and reached for his penis. Finding it, clutching it, she guided him in and his movements began.

After a few seconds Otis noticed a tear roll down from the corner of her eye.

"Kat?"

She sighed, wrapped her legs around his back, and held him very tightly.

Another tear fell.

"Kat? Is everything okay?"

She nodded and wiped the tear away. "If you . . . if you only knew how long I've waited for this."

There were many more nights, passionate nights filled with such strenuous lovemaking that sex took on a new meaning for Katherine. Otis was a more powerful lover than any man she had known. He pleased her, aroused her, and brought her to heights of ecstasy she never imagined possible.

Before the last congressional election was over, she was seeing him daily. Over breakfast, lunch, dinner, and any other time she could steer him away from the campaign. She was in love with him as she had never known love. She was hungry for love and he fed her hunger. Throughout the campaign and the weeks that followed it, she was completely his, wishing the days with him would never end.

Katherine would look back on those years as the best in her life. Carefree, exciting, luxurious. Otis Meade finished out his fifth term in Congress and wanted to run for the Senate. She persuaded him not to after a long series of debates. She wanted him to forget about politics for a while and enjoy himself without the responsibility of answering to a public. They hadn't actually taken a honeymoon and it seemed a perfect time. They had money, energy, and the rest of their lives. At first Meade said no, but finally he gave in.

With her hand in his they began a three-year honeymoon that took them from the crowds of Cairo's Khan el Khalili bazaar to lunch at the Savoy in London, dinner at Maxim's in Paris, shopping on Beverly Hill's Rodeo Drive, and a suite at the Hassler in Rome. They passed through the customs gates of sixty-two countries, sailed eight seas, swam and played in the Mediterranean, watched porpoises stream past their yacht in the Caribbean, skied the slopes of Saint Moritz and Pontresina, sunned in Eleuthera, and downed margaritas in Puerto Vallarta.

But while Katherine dove into their travels with all the enthusiasm of a child, Meade's disposition varied as much as the countries themselves. For weeks he would enjoy himself, relishing the freedom he had never had in Congress, and think about nothing more pressing than where they would go next. Evansville and Washington never entered his mind. Then there were nights when he and Katherine would be lying in bed, and all of his deepest thoughts would pour forth. He talked about the ravages of Vietnam, of Watergate, and the effects both had had on the nation. He felt guilty that he was not politically involved in the healing process the president said the nation was going through, and wondered if they weren't simply escaping from the uglier world. Katherine said no, they weren't. Every couple deserved a honeymoon, regardless of the world's political situation. She kissed him, asked him to make love to her, and tried to make him forget. During their last months she thought she'd succeeded.

She had not.

She wouldn't know until years later that during all those nights of reflection, those mornings when he would scavenge about for an American newspaper or listen to American news on the radio, that an idea had been forming. A determination to run for office again. To move on to more ambitious heights, and most of all, to win.

When their private jet touched down in Evansville, his mind was already made up, although he hadn't told Katherine. He was going to run for the U.S. Senate. Even better, while he and Katherine were abroad, one of her brothers, Edmund, had been elected state Democratic party chairman. Now the Myrer family wasn't only financially prestigious, but politically influential as well.

Over the next two years Katherine pleaded with him to stay home. But Otis Meade traveled throughout Indiana speaking out on various political issues, lending his name to Democratic causes, and with the help of Edmund he met the state's top Democratic leaders. His feet were firmly planted in the political soil. When he sent up trial balloons for the Senate, however, he was shot down.

"You'd be facing Harroll, you know," his brother-in-law said. "And your chances against him are zilch. Even with your reputation—which is damn good, I might add—it'll take a helluva race to beat him."

"But his record—"

"Doesn't matter. He's been sitting pretty ever since those organized crime hearings made him a star."

"Well, what am I going to do?" snapped Meade. "Your sister

thinks I'm gonna play tennis for the rest of my life, which is bull-shit."

"Does she know you want to run?"

"No, but I'll tell her."

"I'd love to see that."

Meade shifted uncomfortably in his chair. "Let me handle her, just answer my question. What am I going to do? I've wanted that seat for so long I don't know what to do."

Edmund thought for a moment, then leaned forward. "Well, what do you think about being governor?"

His race took off like a bullet, and Meade was filled with so much determination that the biblical forty-day flood couldn't have stopped him. Thanks to Edmund and his cronies, Meade mobilized far more support than he'd ever had as a congressman.

As Edmund and Meade had suspected, Katherine resisted his decision to run, then realized there wasn't a choice. By the time Meade told her he had already mapped out his strategy from his announcement to his inauguration. While Katherine wasn't overwhelmed with the idea of campaigning from town to town with him, she reasoned that if he had given her three years of his life abroad, she could give her ambitious husband a few in the governor's mansion.

Katherine sold her interest in Myrer Furniture for almost twenty-eight million dollars and used part of the settlement to help finance Otis Meade's campaign. Once again she opened up the estate for fund-raisers and dinners, and notables and celebrities flew in from around the world.

Meade's name was soon plastered across billboards and television screens all over Indiana. Newspapers carried daily stories about the campaign, accompanied by photos of the candidate shaking hands with a supporter or greeting a Hollywood star at the estate. Radio commercials blared out his position on the issues hourly. His face was seen at every turn. The press went into spasms over Katherine, hailing her as Indiana's Jackie O. As for Indiana itself, the state just sat back and enjoyed it all. The people had never seen such a campaign by the Democrats and, when they were polled, the majority couldn't remember his opponent's name.

It could have been a theatrical production written in Hollywood. When the voters went to the polls, there wasn't a doubt about the election's outcome.

Meade became governor.

Then he got the laws changed and ran again and won again.

It was an obvious move by a man driven with obvious intentions. He was seeking more power, more prestige, and eventually higher office, and he knew this before he was well into his second term.

The years had changed them, she thought now as she gazed over at the bed: their marriage, their love, and much of their lives. She looked at those gubernatorial years as the beginning of the end. Even before Otis Meade had been inaugurated as governor the first time she regretted the moment she agreed to his running, resented the fact that she had given so much of herself all these years, only to be driven to the limit before it was over. The months of the first governor's race had left her feeling as though she'd been on a satellite doomed to circle the earth forever. The fund-raisers had left her exhausted; the banquets and dinners, ribbon cuttings, and interviews seemed endless. His tour of the state had taken her to the brink. When the voting began, she collapsed on a couch in the family mansion, praying for a vacation. But when the votes were in, she found the state and party coordinators loudly knocking on her door.

She had to select a staff.

Coordinate the inauguration.

There were formal balls.

Dinners.

Invitations.

She had to pack.

Move.

Redecorate.

Entertain.

Smile.

Laugh.

Wave.

It never stopped.

The satellite never returned to earth, but she managed. She managed because she loved Otis too much not to. The governorship had totally consumed him. Hardened him. Sucked him into a pit she couldn't pull him out of.

He went deeper into the pit. He became distant. There was always a squabble going on with the legislature. He formed enemies, grew distrustful, vengeful. His staff was no help. Her needs were secondary to his work. They told her so. They held him by chains to his office. He was theirs. And the state's. And he wanted to be. A captor, and Katherine hadn't wanted to guess what the ransom might be.

o

Finally, he took a separate bedroom, claiming his late hours would disturb her. She protested, but he insisted. It was for her own good. She knew what was good for her, she cried, but it was useless. The chains were too strong. Weekends away from Indianapolis were nonexistent. Vacations were unheard of. The doors slowly closed on her, his love drifting further away, locking her out. One night, she recalled, the separation became complete.

She had been reading when he entered her bedroom. She glanced up, smiled, and moved over as he got beneath the covers. It was so seldom that he came to her. She set her book on the nightstand beside her and Otis kissed her.

"I'm so glad you came," she said, "I need you."

"How are you?"

"Fine," she replied too quickly. Then, "No, I'm not. It's been so long ... I was kind of giving up hope."

"I've had a lot of work to do," he explained. "But tonight ... I needed to see you."

His lips met hers and her mouth automatically parted. Her tongue reached out for his and touched it. She shifted beneath him and pulled him to her, resting her hands behind his neck.

"Thank God, the years won't always be like this," she said. "After all, you can only be governor twice."

"Aren't you happy?" he asked her.

"It's ... just that I'm so tired of all this."

"Please don't say that, Kat.... You've got to stay with it, be strong, to keep me strong."

Katherine smiled and his weight rested on her. She parted her legs and his frame shifted between them. He opened her gown and his tongue moved over her breasts. He could smell the desire burning within her, the yearning for his familiar touch. His tongue roamed.

When it was over, Katherine stroked his hair and said, "I love you."

His eyes met hers. They weren't, she recalled now, the eyes of years before, when they were both young.

"Do you love me?" he asked. "With all your heart?"

Anxiously she nodded yes.

"Good, because I'm going to run for president."

That was when my naïveté died, Katherine told herself, still gazing at the bed. I realized then that Otis's ultimate concern was going to be Otis, nothing else. And I suppose it's always been that way, hasn't it? Right from the beginning. He didn't marry me because he loved me, but because I had the right name and the right connections. I was someone to show off. But someone to love? No, no I suckered myself into believing that, didn't I? I really thought he wanted to marry me, but he never loved me, did he? He's never loved anyone. There isn't any room for love there, or for a wife. He's married to himself, to his ambition, to the presidency, to power, and politics. But me? Me? Never me.

"No . . ." she whispered quietly to herself. "It's really not true—is it?"

But she knew it was. And knowing it, all the anger, the hostility, the self-pity, the hatred for her life, for Washington and politics, resurged. They were emotions that had been building for years, building during those lonely nights in an empty bed, those moments of lost passion when Otis was away. Things could have been different. She knew that. She asked herself a hundred times why she'd stayed with him, and a hundred times she'd answered, because I love him. I really do love him. It was bizarre that she still did love him, knowing Otis the way she did. But she did.

There had been other factors too. One very important one was their only child, Alexandra. Barely nineteen, Alexandra was as much of a reason for Katherine's staying with Otis as anything else. Now a freshman at Radcliffe, bright and absolutely beautiful, she was one of the few people who actually made Otis proud, brought what little love Katherine had known inside him to the surface. It was a very special close relationship between the two of them, much closer than Katherine had with Alexandra herself. Although she had been away at school for almost seven months now, Katherine could feel the strength of her daughter's bond with Otis as strongly as the day Alexandra had left—the day she saw Otis for the first time in his life actually cry. It had so startled Katherine that she too began to cry. But she cried for a different reason: not out of sadness that their daughter was leaving, but at seeing a glimpse into the soul of a man she thought she knew, and didn't. This told her as much about their marriage as anything else. She should have known that Otis was capable of shedding a few tears, but in twenty years of marriage she had never seen him do it before. It was this simple act of his that told her how horribly shallow their marriage was, and yet at the same time told her how much she still loved him. But she had to decide: was she going to continue her role as First Lady, or was she going to get out of this marriage? She had thought about it then, standing on the South Lawn with Otis as a military helicopter lifted up into the summer sky, taking their daughter off to college, and she knew almost immediately she would stick it out—for as long as she could.

A buzz shook her from her solitude. Katherine picked up the phone next to her.

"Yes?"

"Higgins—Secret Service. Routine check."

"Thank you, I'm fine." She hung up the phone. How long? I don't know. But I do love him . . . want him . . .

She parted her nightgown and moved her hand down to where her yearning burned . . .

Oh God, I need him . . .

Her gaze again went to the bed and her fantasy returned. She thought of their making love.

Her hand went deeper within her, her breath quickened.

Then she heard voices beyond the door. She pulled her nightgown together and the door opened. Otis was giving Howard Hickman an order while bidding the rest of his group goodnight. Finally their voices trailed off and Otis Meade came into her room.

Katherine prayed her fantasy would come true.

"Well, things are looking up," he said, coming over to her. "It looks like Broder's going to take Florida too. If this keeps up, he'll get the nomination—Cliff Hawkins or not. I can't wait to get hold of him in November."

Katherine shifted back in the chaise longue. He sat down. "That's what you want, isn't it? Broder to get the nomination, then you finish him off in November. A landslide, right?"

"Nothing's a landslide. My polls suck, really suck. But with Broder running against me . . . well, we've got a chance. Especially if we dig up those idiotic remarks he made in 1988 and some other crap. Then we'll destroy him."

"Four more years," she interrupted, glancing down at her gown. "I guess I can live with the idea."

Meade's smile waned. "What do you mean live with it? I didn't know you had any problems living with it. You've wanted this as much as me. Worked your ass off, financed us. You wanted to get us here."

"No, you wanted to get us here."

"And you didn't?"

"Look, if you'll be happy for four more years, I'll stick with it. How long, I don't know, but if that's what you want . . ."

Tears were welling up in Katherine's eyes, and he asked, "Kat, what *do* you want?"

She sighed. "I don't know. To go back to Evansville, home, away from all this. That's what I'd really like. But most of all, to get you back with me." She looked at him. "I love you, isn't that clear to you?" She leaned forward and kissed him, bringing his hand up to her breast. "Make love to me," she whispered as tears rolled down her cheeks. "Please make love to me."

"I'm tired."

"Don't you love me?"

What little sympathy he'd had for her turned to anger. Katherine stroked her smooth hand under his chin, waiting for his answer, but he didn't have to say anything. It was all visible in the flames reflecting in his eyes from the fireplace.

"Otis—?"

Meade pushed her hand away, got up, and walked to the door. He paused and looked at her. Tears streamed down her face. The president turned and said, "I told you, I'm tired," and left.

Katherine watched the door shut behind him. Her fantasy had died.

15

FLORIDA

From the moment Cliff Hawkins flew into Florida the columnists and pollsters were spelling his defeat. The latest Gallup and Harris polls showed Broder several leaps ahead, but gave neither candidate a clear-cut majority. If Hawkins's campaign was doing anything, it was driving the voters back into their homes and away from the polls. Projections showed that record numbers of Republicans were going to abstain from voting in the primary. They didn't like the choices. Newspaper editorials around the state were already asking Hawkins to withdraw from the race because, as many said, "It's doing more harm to the system than good." Television commentators continually asked, "Is Hawkins serious about this?"

Hawkins told everyone, "Yes!" Many believed him. Even as doomsayers were calling Florida a flop, the number of volunteers coming into his offices around the state tripled. Contributions were coming in more frequently and larger than ever before.

But his detractors were more audible at every stop. Demonstrations by gays, feminists, proabortion groups, antimilitary and antinuke groups, and university students had increased by a third. They were growing more and more vocal in their opposition to him, and more violent too. There had been further bomb scares, and Hawkins could barely go anywhere without seeing opposing rallies.

If any of this had an effect on him, it didn't show. He continued, as always, to be the epitome of optimism and determination. His opponents, he said, drove home the point he had been making all along—that anti-God, antilife, antifamily and antidefense groups were going to bring down American society. Apparently more people were beginning to believe him. Every time Hawkins defended his candidacy on television a flood of contributions and letters of support would follow. It boosted the morale of almost everyone connected with the campaign.

One person, though, on whom the demonstrations and attention had had an adverse affect and whose morale wasn't boosted by each new influx of letters and contributions that came in, was Charlotte Hawkins.

Charlotte made sure the bedroom door leading into their enormous hotel suite was shut. She crossed to her dresser, yawning. It was past two in the morning. She was starting on her third week in Florida. She'd been up since early yesterday morning, campaigning in Lake City and Jacksonville, and was damned tired. Although she and Cliff had finally met up today and would be traveling together for the rest of the week, even that had not lifted her spirits.

She opened the dresser drawer, felt underneath her lingerie, and pulled out a small silver flask. She turned her head back and swallowed.

Good—God, that feels good.

She took a couple of quick breaths. She put the flask to her mouth and drank again. Quickly she thrust the flask back in the drawer.

She had decided sometime a week or so ago that the vodka was the only thing keeping her going, the only thing that made this horrible business bearable. She didn't like campaigning, she knew that now. Didn't like meeting the people, smiling when she didn't feel like it, being friendly to people she cared nothing about, none of it. Nor did she like the fact that Cliff was still in the race, that this whole escapade of his had now been strung out over a period of four—or was it five—weeks. There was no end in sight. The tougher the going, the more determined Cliff got. What could she do? She hadn't wanted him to get involved in this race in the first place. It had been his idea, his dream. How wrong we've been, Charlotte thought. It's not working the way it was supposed to. This is a state where Cliff's always been very popular—but look around us. Who are all these people hounding us? Throwing eggs and tossing bottles, breaking out the office windows? It's maddening. And they haven't stopped. Haven't let up for one minute . . . newsmen always swarming around me, around Cliff . . . on our tail for anything—and everything—they can get.

Cliff had told her, "People eventually come around to support the underdog, believe me. It's happened time and again. And even though they're hurting us right now, we'd hurt ourselves a lot more if we answered every charge they level against us. I don't want to be seen as a subversive narrow-minded evangelist who's trying to undermine the Constitution and start a civil war between liberals and conservatives."

"Then what can we do?"

"Just what we're doing now. Use the media, not let them use us. Take our case to the American people and keep our faith."

That isn't enough, Charlotte told herself. He's wrong. Neither what they were doing nor what they were believing would deliver them from the political disaster that awaited them. That made her mad. Mad at Cliff, at the press, the people, everyone. But more than anything, it hurt her. Hurt badly. This state was only the beginning, only the first of four big primaries they were to hit within four weeks' time. Next Illinois, North Carolina, and New York. Four of the biggest prizes any candidate could get in the sweepstakes. If they didn't pull through those . . . if they at least didn't win one . . . knock Broder and the others out just once . . . she didn't know what they would do. She glanced back at the door, undressed, then went to bed. Within minutes she was asleep.

Hours later, as Charlotte lay sleeping soundly next to him, Cliff was awakened by Gordon Wade. It was his usual campaign wake-up call at 6:30 A.M. He got up, careful not to disturb Charlotte. He spoke in the phone.

"Running on time?" Hawkins asked groggily.

"Yes."

"What's . . ." he yawned, ". . . on the agenda today?"

"Orlando, Miami, and Tampa, believe it or not."

Hawkins shook his head. He breathed into the phone. "Busy aren't we?" Then, going back to one of the problems they had hit upon in their discussions the previous night, he asked, "Anything on Fort Lauderdale? Daytona? The Tallahassee thing?"

"I put in a call just a few minutes ago. Government won't approve that much in gasoline allocations."

"Is it legit?"

"It's hard to tell. Nobody can keep track of the actual fuel the candidates are using because none of them want to admit they're going over the limits through the black market. So the only way we can check it is on the actual mileage they cover."

"And?"

"And it seems legit, but you never know. Not in this race. Lord, sometimes I think we shouldn't even be on the Republican ticket."

"Well, it'd never work on an Independent slate. Besides, we've got a lot of friends in Congress, remember that."

"True," Wade said. "At least we're hitting Miami, and they've got all the Jews. We need them a lot more than those WASPs in Fort Lauderdale."

"Anything else?"

"No, I'll let you wake up before the briefing." He paused to hang up. "I did hear something on the morning news that might interest you. A shame, really. Happened in Dallas."

"What?"

"Mayor Freeport's been indicted."

Tom Freeport was an old golfing buddy of his. "Indicted? Why?"

"Apparently for accepting bribes from . . . oh, whatshisname?— Gianni? Francesco Gianni."

"The racketeer?"

"Yeah."

Hawkins sighed. "That's too bad. Tom's all right, or seemed to be."

Cliff showered, washed his hair and towel-dried it. Then he got dressed and went over to wake Charlotte. He was about to nudge her when something within him made him pause . . .

He stared at her in the room's semidarkness and suddenly all the thoughts that had made falling asleep difficult last night came back. What was it? He couldn't be sure. And yet . . . something told him last night, when he bent over to kiss her goodnight, when his lips were about to touch her and he smelled her breath, that . . . could it have been what it seemed?

Was it possible that it was happening again?

Here? Now?

Last night seemed so far away now. So far that he told himself emphatically that it was impossible. He knew her too well. She was older now, so much more mature, so much more capable of handling things now than she had been then. Yes, he had to believe that, had to give her more credit.

But was it?

Cliff reached down and awakened her.

16

It hadn't been Howard Hickman's favorite morning.

First off, their press secretary had been hounded once again by the White House press corps during the regular morning briefing for a statement on Cliff Hawkins's candidacy. This morning, as he had done every other morning since Hawkins announced, the press secretary said the president had no statement to make. So the press turned to Hickman instead. His phone hadn't stopped ringing until an hour ago.

Then Hughes Martin at the President Meade Reelection Committee phoned and said he'd received a hot tip about Jackson Chambers, Democratic senator from New York and possible opponent to the president for the Democratic nomination. He'd phone back as soon as the rumor was confirmed.

Next Reed McClellan called and said he had some polling to bring over. The results were bad. Why not go directly to Meade? Hickman asked. You take everything else to him. Well, McClellan had explained, this wasn't the type of news Meade would welcome. Besides, the polls were far too speculative to be of any real use to him until later in the game.

Finally there had been the news out of Dallas, which Hickman had just seen stuck on page four of *The Washington Post*. It might as well have been on every billboard in Washington. Francesco Gianni had once again been publicly linked with an influential politician. It was a great coup for the reporter whose investigation had led to the indictments of Dallas's mayor, Hickman fumed, but a fucking nightmare to anyone else linked with that underworld slime, including us. The pipeline contract would take care of that, but how in the fuck does he expect us to get him the pipeline contract if he keeps stepping in shit? Well, the damage is done. Right here—

Hickman stared at the story. Because of one stupid, greedy little mistake, Gianni could very well cost them the entire pipeline. But it wasn't just that, it was all the other things that had happened. Martin's call about Chambers, McClellan and his polling results. . . . From now until November it would probably get worse. Meeting later with Reed McClellan only confirmed this.

"All right, what's the big secret?" Hickman asked. "You're being so damned melodramatic."

"Well, you could offer me a seat," replied McClellan, taking one anyway.

"Please—do you want me to breast-feed you too? Don't be a pain in the ass. You phoned saying you've got something hush-hush, Hughes Martin's got some tip on Chambers, the press is hounding us about Hawkins, and—ah, forget it."

McClellan unbuttoned his coat and relaxed. "Howard, look, I didn't want to go to the president with this. There isn't, as I said on the phone, any need yet. But I want you to be aware of this."

"What?"

McClellan handed him a folder. "In there you will find two private polls I ran this week completely at my own discretion and seen by no one but me. However, they're accurate and frightening. Shocking really."

"What kind of polls?" Hickman said suspiciously, ignoring the folder.

"The first is ideological, the second a projected voter preference."

Hickman looked puzzled. "Ideological? Meaning what?"

"Meaning I took an extensive poll, or rather our staff did, on the current political mood of the country. But more than that, the poll asked a cross section of voters certain questions about what they believe is wrong with the country, what they believe is right with it, and what should be done about it."

"And the other one—the one that had to do with voter preference?"

"Right."

"Between whom?"

"Well, I'll get to that in a minute. The second poll was taken only after we'd gotten back the results of the first. It's purely hypothetical, based primarily on a lot of ifs. If such and such happened, if so and so doesn't win the primaries, et cetera."

"So what'd you find out?"

"That the people are getting much more emphatic in their beliefs as to what is wrong and isn't wrong with our nation. That slowly, very slowly, they're getting angrier at this administration and at the Democratic party."

"Meaning . . ."

"Meaning they *are* going back to the conservatism of the Reagan days."

"Are you sure?"

"Well," he said slowly, "it's either that or they're simply so fed up with Meade that they're gravitating toward these beliefs because they're the only visible alternative. Ideologically, that is.'

"And?"

"And you know who that's going to help, don't you?"

"No . . ."

"Incredible as it seems, he's the right man for them. Almost perfect."

"Who?"

"Cliff Hawkins."

Hickman was nonplussed. "Come on, Reed, he's an evangelist. They wouldn't gravitate toward him. They're not even voting for him. Shit, he's barely keeping his campaign alive now."

"Wrong. You and I both know he's been getting more attention now than he ever has and . . . and, this is the clincher, he's got a lot of detractors but his supporters are increasing and will continue to increase right along with their growing discontent with Meade."

"Bullshit."

"I'll stake my reputation on it. I've seen the figures."

"What's—what's the second poll say?"

McClellan looked down, then gave Hickman a grave, serious stare. "That the rank-and-file voters are beginning to accept him as a presidential candidate."

Hickman's eyes locked on his. "What did you say?"

"You heard me. Given the way the ideological tide is turning and the continued media attention Hawkins is getting, he's slowly becoming fixed in their minds as a serious candidate. One who could very well be the president of the United States."

Hickman shut the folder. "Are you sure? He can't even beat that pansy Larry Broder and you're saying they think he's a serious candidate? Why, he probably won't make it into New York's primary."

McClellan shook his head, "I don't agree . . . everyone's underestimating the possible impact he could have on this election, save Hawkins himself, and nowhere is the evidence for this stronger than in these two polls."

Hickman opened the folder again, this time much more seriously. He flipped through the pages of the report while McClellan continued. "You'll see it, Howard. Everything's ripe for something like this to happen. We thought firebrand conservatism had died after Reagan, but it hasn't. Instead it crawled back into the woodwork for a few years and is slowly coming out again, even stronger and more determined than ever before. Believe me, it's scary. The conservative faction doesn't have anyone as visible or as moneyed as Hawkins. He's their torchbearer. Or will be."

Hickman sighed. "As if I don't have enough worries without this."

His intercom buzzed.

"Wait," he said picking it up. "Yeah? Oh, put him on." Hickman glanced toward McClellan, "It's Hughes. Yeah, Hughes, what's the scoop?"

Hickman listened for a few seconds and then his face flushed with anger.

"That asshole. Of course, we all knew it, Hughes, but . . . uh huh . . . okay. Thanks—for nothing." He slammed down the phone.

"Trouble?" asked McClellan.

"That's not the word for it. This was supposed to be a wrapped-up reelection year, right? Then why the hell is everything going wrong?"

"What is it?"

"Hughes Martin just confirmed that Chambers is going to run against us for the nomination."

"Great day, huh?"

"Reed, about those polls ... don't mention them to anyone, okay?"

"It's why I'm here. They're confidential."

"Good, good." He paused, then asked gravely, "Do you really think he's going to last? I mean, beyond New York?"

"All of my colleagues in the business are saying no, but my gut instinct is saying yes—and it hasn't been wrong yet."

17

One week later Reed McClellan's colleagues in the polling business were still saying Hawkins wouldn't last, and his defeat in Illinois's blockbuster primary the next night—his fourth defeat in a row, including Florida three days earlier—seemed to reaffirm this. Nevertheless, McClellan was holding fast in his belief—and fear—that Hawkins was going to pull through. Eventually there would be a turnaround. Looking at all four primary results, he easily detected a pattern: the percentage by which Hawkins was losing had been *decreasing* with each primary. If Hawkins and his money held out—and both looked as if they would—there would definitely be trouble for the other candidates.

Coming back from a lunch break at her hotel, Charlotte Hawkins stepped out of her limousine and was immediately engulfed by reporters and supporters. The crowd had grown so large lately, the thrust of their bodies so powerful, she felt as if she were going to be swallowed up or trampled to death by them. As her Secret Service agents pushed her through the mob toward the stage, she wanted everyone to back off, leave her alone. By joining this campaign, she lost the one thing in her life that had meant so much to her—privacy. She had built it up for years, protected it, and now it was being

destroyed . . . destroyed by people like these newsmen, the overpro-
tective agents, her campaign aides, even Cliff.

She had never been a public person. About a year after Cliff had
decided to evangelize and Daddy bound her financially to their
marriage, Charlotte realized Cliff's dedication to the ministry was
real and lifelong. Slowly she began to adjust and quickly learned to
avoid further animosities concerning his career by avoiding it alto-
gether. Using their baby, Blair, as an excuse, she stayed away from
her husband's crusades, relinquishing any involvement with his
ministry and leaving Cliff's affairs to Cliff alone.

Over time Charlotte built a cocoon around herself to guarantee
peace, tranquillity, but most of all, privacy. She made sure nobody
bothered her, no charities asked for commitments, no organizations
called upon her, no society clubs sought her time. She wanted to live
her life with their growing son and the husband she still loved, and
forget about the rest.

But it was impossible.

With Cliff on the road on crusades and expanding his ministry
into the empire it would eventually become—and her determination
not to become involved in "his affairs"—Charlotte soon found herself sitting at home, sheltered by her cocoon but also smothered by
loneliness. With the loneliness also came a hunger. It was a hunger
that needed nourishment, a hunger that comes when your husband's
away and the attention and loving have left with him. A hunger that
charities, country clubs, even friends can never satisfy. She needed a
release . . . and found it in alcohol. In the beginning it was only a
drink or two. Then it became worse, until finally it was so bad that
Cliff came home one night and found her passed out on the living
room floor. She sought counseling and for almost a quarter century
she had suppressed the urge. It worked—until Cliff got serious
about running for President.

Charlotte noticed they were now approaching the steps to the
stage. The agents tightened their grips on her. She cringed and
turned to one of them. "I can walk just fine, thank you. Just keep
those people away." The agents stepped aside, constantly watching
the crowd, and Charlotte began the ascent up the steps, holding onto
a railing decorated with red-white-and-blue streamers with one
hand and waving to the applauding crowd with the other. She
smiled automatically, first to the crowds, then to the officials on
stage awaiting her.

Suddenly she tripped. As she began to fall, amid audible gasps, one of the officials closest to her caught her.

"Oh!" she gasped, as he helped her regain her balance.

"Are you all right?"

"Yes," she slurred, "thank you very mush."

For an instant an alarm went off in the official's head. Looking into Charlotte's glassy eyes, catching that ever-so-faint smell on her breath, he understood the problem. He wasn't the only one who noticed. Among the dozen or so photographers and journalists who'd been traveling with Charlotte since she began campaigning was Herman Morris of *The New York Times*. After she'd stepped out of the limousine, Morris had been close enough to catch—only for a second—that foggy, slightly out-of-focus look.

Walking steadily now, almost in full control of her faculties, she couldn't help but think of how humiliating this whole business of greeting people was. They were losing. Cliff's dreams weren't working out. Something was wrong. The people were listening but weren't going to the polls.

Four primaries in a row! she said to herself, while greeting some plastic-faced imbecile in front of her. Four primaries and it's not looking any better. The projections are already looking bad for North Carolina and New York . . . and still over two dozen more to go!

Why? Why is he doing this to me? To himself? Doesn't he get the picture? Isn't it clear enough to him that they want him in the pulpit and not in front of the presidential seal?

He knows, she told herself smugly, still feeling the effects of the drinks she'd had in her suite after lunch. He knows, but he doesn't care. All of us be damned. Myself, Blair, the whole organization. To hell with us, he's not going to give up, no sir. Even with all the strain it's putting on us—on me—he's going to stick it out.

"The Lord's testing our faith," he'd said. "We've got to believe in him, believe he's not going to let us lose in the long run—that he wants to continue what we've begun. It's his will."

Is it!?! she asked as she sat down, waiting for her introduction, gazing out at the crowds. Is it his will, Cliff, or *yours?* Lord, Lord God, you've got to help me.

Hawkins sat at the head of a long boardroom table scattered with computer printouts, polling reports, newspaper clippings, ashtrays, and coffee cups. Seated around the table were his four closest advisers, Perrin, Wade, Coco, and Winny. There were also seven other top-ranking campaign members. For more than an hour Hawkins had been listening to individual reports from each member on the current status of the campaign as it related to a specific area and the particular problems each one was facing. Together they told him in general terms some of the reasons they were continuing to lose, the most overriding of which was his image.

"My image?" he asked matter-of-factly.

They nodded.

"You're still coming across like Cliff Hawkins, the religious leader, not Cliff Hawkins, presidential candidate," said Coco.

Randy Perrin added, "Coco thinks we can change your image subtly, but enough to make a difference."

"Cliff, what we're talking about now isn't just a few changes in your attire and speech content. I think, and I'm sure the others will agree with me, that part of the basic problem—in fact, the overriding problem—is that you've had to defend yourself so much that it's drawn attention away from your main—and ultimate—opponent: Otis Meade."

"Meade is your nemesis," she continued. "We'd all be better off if our efforts were aimed at him, not wasted on Broder or the others. Those people can only bring you down. To some extent they've already done that. And that ends up hurting everyone's image, particularly yours, because you're being seen as a troublemaking newcomer to American politics."

"In essence I'm a spoiler," he said.

"You are all spoilers," she said. "So you might as well take on the president himself. After all, you're after his office. You're going to have to show the American people why. He's done everything he can these past four years to bring us closer to ruin than any other president in history. You can hit him on everything: leadership, defense, his urban policies, his economic policies, his disastrous relations with Cuba, Mexico, the Middle East. These are things presidents or would-be presidents need to hash out."

Finally she sat back and looked at him. Hawkins let out a deep breath. "So we campaign offensively now. Attacking Meade to draw attention away from our own controversies, is that it?"

"That's it," said Randy Perrin.

"Gordon, what do you think?"

"I think we're all in agreement on this, Cliff."

They could see that Hawkins was reluctant to change his tactics so quickly, and, sensing this, Coco said reassuringly, "Cliff, don't worry about it. You're not going to be the only one attacking him, believe me. Meade's going to have enough trouble on his hands with Jackson Chambers. This will make the going even tougher on him"

"Chambers is announcing today, isn't he?" Hawkins said.

"They're expecting him to within the hour."

NEW YORK/Great Neck

Whenever Jackson Chambers spoke, the left side of his mouth moved slightly upward, the result of a harelip he'd had since birth. It had been corrected by surgery and was not a particularly noticeable feature, but still it was one of those things you never miss on a person. Something that makes that person real.

Jackson Chambers had never known himself to fail. In the past he had succeeded at everything he'd set his heart on. It had been that way from the beginning of his career when he was county commissioner and later when he was in the New York legislature and also when he campaigned for the U.S. Senate; now he hoped his streak would continue with the presidency. Some said it was his astrological sign, Taurus. Others said it was his political crassness and nerve, his ability to draw blood from his oponents and unravel their support. Others said it was simply political shrewdness. But whatever it was, Chambers, now a senior senator from New York, was banking on it to carry him through the almost two dozen primaries remaining and on to the Democratic convention, where he would finally get the best of that sonofabitch Otis Meade.

Chambers had wanted the presidency for a long time and had plotted for years to get it. He had sprinkled every political favor with hints that he planned eventually to call in his markers for support, had written speeches specifically to rouse the ire of the White House, and had steered his career wherever the spotlight was conveniently focused. The announcement was his first declared move in an undeclared candidacy that went back more than a year.

Chambers was behind the podium in the reception area of his newly opened campaign headquarters, standing before a sea of reporters and press. His wife and two homely but well-dressed daughters flanked him. In the back of the reception area many of his workers held up freshly painted signs. The television lights broiling the candidate made the air-conditioning useless. Chambers waved at the cheering group, coughed as the harelip rose, and then he began.

True to his profession, Chambers immediately thanked those who buttered his bread: his supporters. After thanking his staff for their efforts and the press for coming, he apologized for the cramped quarters.

"But I guess that's a good sign, isn't it?" he joked.

Several laughed purposely.

He then said there wasn't any question as to why they had all been asked there: the signs, placards, bumper stickers, and ribbons were answer enough. The reason he was there *was* important. Within a minute, never at a loss for words, Chambers launched into a tirade against the president and his record.

It lasted ten minutes and would be the lead story on every major network and in every newspaper.

Within an hour after Chambers's announcement the press was already begging the other candidates for their reactions. The White House had "no comment" on the matter, but the others did. For the most part, their responses were predictable. Since they were Republicans and Meade and Chambers were Democrats, they wished both men a good fight but were careful to emphasize how their own candidates and subsequent election would serve the country far better than either their fellow opponents or the Democratic contenders.

Only Cliff Hawkins took everyone by surprise.

The journalists, expecting a predictable may-the-best-man-win statement, were agog when Hawkins not only concurred with Chambers's assessment of Meade, but was far more scathing.

It was Hawkins's first direct fire at the president as a candidate, and it almost upstaged Chambers's announcement during the national news broadcasts ... which was just what Hawkins and his staff wanted.

Hawkins was leaving his hotel en route to a convention, to participate in a forum that included his three opponents, when Perrin announcd that the candidate would hold a short question-and-answer session in a room off the lobby. At first Hawkins seemed a little uneasy in his new tough role, but after two questions his responses were rapid-fire and cutting.

Answering one of the questions, he said, "Otis Meade has been in the White House for four years doing a lot for this country—a lot of harm. And, let me tell you, the people have had it. I know because they've been sending us letters by the truckloads. They're furious with the way the president's running this country—or not running it—and I think Senator Chambers's thoughts on this matter are an understatement at best."

"Reverend," the *Los Angeles Times* called out, "can you elaborate for us?"

"If you'd like. The senator said, and quite eloquently I might add, that much of our nation's demise is due to a lack of leadership from the administration. I say it's due to a lack of leadership from many administrations, though President Meade's is surely at the top of the list. He's vacillated on almost every major issue that's arisen during these past four years, made a complete mess of our foreign policy, particularly with regard to the Saudi Arabian situation and Egypt and Israel, and nearly got us into a war with Cuba. Under his so-called leadership his administration has given the nation the greatest federal deficit we've ever seen, the most exhorbitant interest rates we've even known, and tried to make a mockery of the free enterprise system with federal regulations that are almost criminal.

"To make matters worse, the president has slapped the American people with a long list of requests to 'conserve,' to 'sacrifice,' and to 'bite the bullet,' while at the same time he's increased his White House staff by almost 25 percent, asked for a larger expense budget and even had the gall to request a 17 percent pay increase. Let me tell you, the people are mad and they're not going to listen to this anymore. They're tired of seeing America having dirt tossed on it by an administration that's ready to send this country to an early grave."

A dozen voices began calling out questions at once, but Hawkins continued.

"Almost every letter I've received, ladies and gentlemen, asks the same question: where is the leadership in this country? Where are men like Theodore Roosevelt? Presidents with the legislative abilities of Ronald Reagan? Men with dreams like Woodrow Wilson and John Kennedy? Administrations with the honesty and integrity that Abraham Lincoln brought to government? Are they in Washington now? In the White House? Not by any means, nor are they within the ranks of my fellow candidates. And I want to ask you and the American people this: are you willing to have men like this run our country for another four years? Are you ready to put God's most glorious gift to the world in the hands of men like Otis Meade for another four years? Can we afford to?"

Hawkins's eyes looked sad and sincere.

"I don't think we can. This nation took a big gamble during the 1988 election and it's obvious that we lost. Otis Meade isn't a bad man, he simply isn't good. The American people don't have to review his records, look over his statements, compare his positions with mine, they know where he stands because they're suffering from his stands. And neither they nor I want to see this happen again."

Again the journalists all began to speak at once and Hawkins held up his hand for silence, like a schoolmaster calming his students.

"It comes down to leadership. We don't need just any leader. After all, that sort of man could lead us anywhere. Instead we need a man who knows what America wants and what Americans are feeling, a man with the common sense and dedication to put this nation back on the road to greatness. A man who can restore confidence among our allies and answer the economic challenges we're facing. I sincerely hope I am that man."

After a moment Hawkins walked out of the room and the most one-sided press conference any of the journalists had seen in a long time came to an end.

18

WASHINGTON/The President Meade Reelection
Committee

"But, Mr. President . . . I know, sir . . . We've been getting calls too. I realize that. But, Mr. President, I . . . what? Of course, sir. None at all. No, sir, we won't issue any statements until you tell us to. What? You're telling us to now? . . . Mr. President, we couldn't say that. Right, right. Yes, sir, good-bye, sir."

Hughes Martin placed the phone back on the receiver and wiped his brow. It had been a long morning at the President Meade Reelection Committee offices. That phone call hadn't helped. Larry Peterson, his top administrative assistant, regarded him with sympathy.

"He's mad, isn't he?"

Martin nodded, "He's fuming. Absolutely fit to be tied."

"Well, everyone wondered when it would hit him . . . "

"Guess it finally has," said Martin. "Never have I heard such language."

"What'd he say?"

"He wants us to issue a statement concerning Hawkins and Chambers and tell them to, and these are his words, get fucked."

"He said *that*?"

"That was one of his milder statements," answered Martin. "He isn't thinking straight. He's livid."

"But he knew Chambers was going to announce. He's known it for months."

"Not Chambers, Hawkins. Nobody cares about Chambers. Hawkins is the one that really set him off. Christ, you should have heard him!"

"I'm glad I didn't."

For two days Otis Meade controlled his rage about the recent series of events. Controlled it so well, in fact, that every time he read or heard Hawkins's remarks or watched Chambers's announcement he merely winced. He had to do this if he was going to control himself. So his eyes never glared at the television, his lips never tightened. His hands hadn't balled up into fists, nor had he cussed or breathed fire. In fact, the only noticeable change during that time was his posture. When standing, Meade was rigid as a West Point plebe: tall, firm, erect. This kept him intact and allowed him some sense of composure in what was turning into a very unsettling state of affairs.

It was true that Meade and his staff had anticipated Chambers's jump into the race for almost two months and were more than ready for a battle. Meade was on the ballot in all the imminent primaries, McClellan was running new polls weekly, Krantz had pumped more than two million dollars of the reelection committee's money into commercials; new offices were opening around the nation daily, telephone banks were operating full-time, and a campaign itinerary had been drawn up for a series of rallies if the president needed more media coverage. War had been declared between the two Democrats, but the president hadn't said, "Charge!" Instead he said nothing.

Until the news was three days old.

He was shaving when it finally hit him. He was being *opposed*. His nomination was not locked up, nor was he the sole Democratic candidate. Meade was being challenged. Attacked. Targeted. Singled out.

The razor snagged his chin. Blood appeared.

In an election year, when his nomination should be the least of his worries, it was going to be one of his biggest. If Chambers built up any momentum at all against him, that would be more trouble than Meade needed. But Chambers himself was not what bothered Meade the most. It was Hawkins, a man who was trying to humiliate him, slander him, kick him in the balls.

Meade stood there, staring at his own reflection, his face half-covered with shaving cream. Why am I even concerning myself with him? He's not a serious candidate. He hasn't won a damned primary yet. Probably won't before he's forced to concede.

Quickly he finished shaving, put his razor under the running water and rinsed it, and then tried to stop the bleeding.

The image of Hawkins came back. Is it possible that people would actually take him seriously?

He dried his face and combed his hair, and paused. How far can a man like that go? How much will the public buy? Would they consider electing an evangelist for president?

He tried again to think of other things as he went out of the bathroom and while his valet helped him into his clothes. But Hawkins plagued him. It wouldn't work, would it? Of course not. He doesn't have any experience, no governmental service. No political record. He's a novice. He doesn't know the first thing about . . .

. . . but what do they care? What do the American people care about all that? This is a nation that elects its leaders over the television. The voters are video idiots. They don't care about things like a man's record, his accomplishments, his stands on various issues. I should know better than anyone. . . . It's whoever comes across best on television, isn't it? We've known that all along. The man who looks the most presidential, who has the charisma. The electronic presence. Kennedy, Reagan. It's all in the image.

Meade felt himself getting angrier as he dressed. The image . . . that's what those fuckers out there are buying. Screw the fact that he's unqualified, that he doesn't know a damned thing about running a government. Fuck it, if they like what you say, they'll vote for you. I know because I was elected the same way. It actually *could* happen. He *could* get the nomination. He *could* be facing me in November.

For the first time in months the reality of Hawkins's candidacy hit him. Meade sat down on his bed, ignoring the stares of his valet. They're listening to him . . . I know they are. I read . . . shit, where was it?—in *Time*. The percentages by which he's been losing are dropping. Not much, but dropping. Or was it McClellan who told me? No, he hasn't mentioned Hawkins much. Whatever, the fact remains . . . he could conceivably pull out ahead of Broder. After all, Broder's message is old. People don't like him, he's too weird. And Smathers? A nigger for president? Roberts? God, he's already in debt up to his ears.

Hawkins has the money. The organization. The support. What

was it? Six, eight million people contribute regularly to his church? Eight million people?

And now he's coming after me. He really *is* serious about all this shit.

Meade stood and straightened his tie. He had been humiliated, slandered, and challenged. He couldn't put off acting any longer. As the president was leaving the bedroom, his valet saw in him a rage he had not seen in quite a while.

"I want to know exactly where we stand," Meade snapped. He sat behind his desk in the Oval Office with Krantz, Rampling, McClellan, Hickman, and Ecklecamp in a semicircle. "I want to know what in hell you people are planning to do about this shit. This whole fucking thing was supposed to be locked up a year ago. I spoke with every Democratic leader in the country and they said we'd be unified. Unified like hell. Now we've got Chambers. A no-good, lying, conniving sonofabitch who wants to throw the whole race out of kilter. And worse, we've got that egomaniacal evangelist out there who looks like he's getting serious. I want to know what are we going to do about it?"

They all began talking at once.

"One at a time," growled Meade. "Paul, say something."

Paul Rampling leaned forward. He pushed his glasses up on his nose and spoke calmly. "Mr. President, our standing's okay. I don't think you should be overly concerned with Cliff Hawkins at this point. He simply hasn't proven himself as a viable presidential candidate. Granted, his press conference certainly didn't help us, and it drew a helluva lot of attention to him, but I think he came across like a demagogue, not—"

"Wrong, wrong, wrong," snapped Meade. "He came across like a fucking sincere father giving advice to his children. That's what pisses me off. And he did it at my expense."

"Mr. President," Reed McClellan said. "We've had worse things thrown at us before. It's not the first time; it certainly won't be the last. Paul's right, don't let it bother you. Chambers is the one who's our most immediate problem. Our standing—as far as readiness, as far as not being caught off guard, and all that goes—is very good. We've known that he was going to do this for months. Sure, we thought some of the party leaders would talk him out of it, but obviously they didn't. Nevertheless, we've got our own troops in order and are more than ready to fight."

Meade pushed back his chair and stood up, staring at McClellan. He turned and looked out the window directly behind his desk, then pushed his chair in and began pacing. "Fight, huh? Well, we'd damn well better be ready to fight because it's becoming evident to me our problems don't end with Jackson Chambers. One, we've got Hawkins. Two, we've got Hughes Martin over at the President Meade Reelection Committee with a staff that sits around with their fingers up their asses. Hughes isn't bad, but he doesn't have the initiative we're going to need from someone in that position. But what can I do? He's there because of a political debt I owed and now we're stuck with him. So the race is going to be completely up to us. Hughes'll give us staff, funds, all that crap, but the planning, the decisions, that's going to have to be our ballgame. Your ballgame. Understand?"

They all nodded.

"Good," Meade said and sat back down. He pulled a pipe from his drawer and packed a blend. He lit it as he spoke. "Now, Howard ... since Chambers has the pissy-assed pleasure of announcing in time for the North Carolina and New York primaries, you'd better have me scheduled for some things, especially in New York."

Hickman nodded, "It's already been done."

Meade was surprised. "And what about North Carolina? Wisconsin? Pennsylvania? Texas and Indiana?" He was getting angry again. The whole week had put him on edge.

"Mr. President," Joseph Krantz said calmly, "we're working on them. Your itinerary's not complete in all those states, but it's coming."

Meade blew smoke in his direction. "It better be. And what about around here? Can we beef things up around this place? Get the press in more? I want my face to be on the six o'clock news from now on without fail—and I want positive coverage. I want to block them every chance I get, understand?"

Krantz nodded. "Mr. President, you've had a 22 percent increase in air coverage for the past two weeks to help cover this thing. You're also scheduled for a full round of media events throughout the rest of this week until you leave for New York."

"Good! Howard, you get that?"

Hickman nodded.

"Good, we'll get both of those bastards yet."

The meeting ended seven minutes later when Jerry Ecklecamp asked to be excused: the bathroom. Hickman bit his lip.

After they had all left the Oval Office except for Hickman, whom Meade had asked to stay, the president reached over and stabbed his intercom.

"Yes, Mr. President?"

"Cancel my eleven to twelve appointments, okay?"

"Yes, Mr. President."

Hickman, who was sitting in front of Meade's desk, gave him a puzzled look. "What'd you do that for? I thought Jong was bringing over that proposal on the World Economic Conference in Delhi."

"So what?" Meade shrugged. "He can have a courier send it over. I'm going to the residence and take a nap. It's not even eleven and I'm tired as hell."

"Well, I'll leave if there's nothing . . . "

"No, I wanted you to stay because I wanted to ask you about the pipeline. How's it going?"

"You noticed Tony LaCross wasn't here?"

"That's what made me think of it."

"He's still negotiating."

"What about the seventeenth clause?"

Hickman sighed. He knew the president wasn't going to like what he had to say. "They've shelved it for the time being. It was dragging down their morale by the constant haggling, and some technicalities came up in other spots . . . "

Meade's face tightened. "Howard, how many times do I have to say it: that clause has got to get through—and soon. We've got to get Gianni off our backs and give him the construction contract or we can kiss this whole campaign good-bye."

Hickman knew exactly what the president meant. Since a court ruling in the late 1970s had allowed private groups to supplement a campaign's expenditures, several groups, which were not regulated by the campaign-finance law, had been established to help support Meade's efforts. Most of them were legitimate, but some were not— most notably one called Americans for Democracy, which was spearheaded by front men acting for Francesco Gianni. So far Gianni had "contributed" more than three and a half million dollars to Meade's current effort, yet it was clear to everyone involved that it was a loan to be repaid. During Meade's first election Gianni had "loaned" them two million dollars, but none of it had been repaid. Meade thought, what would be the best way to repay him for this year as well as his contribution of four years ago? A fat construction contract that would have his business interests building the Mexico-U.S. pipeline. The seventeenth clause would allow this.

"So," Meade was continuing, "you tell LaCross to pull that clause back off the shelf and *make* them accept it."

Hickman sighed, "Yes, sir."

Sitting in his favorite chair next to a window, Meade glanced occasionally at his untouched bed. He hadn't really wanted to nap, but he needed to get away from the office. It was rare that he did this, but he felt good about it. He had taken along a stack of intelligence briefings just in case and, seeing them now in his lap, he didn't want to study them. He'd had a week of bad news and these just compounded it.

He picked one up—a confidential briefing, filed by the Company's Mexico City bureau, warning him about growing anti-American sentiment in the ranks of the extreme wing of Mexico's Partido de Fuerza Popular (National Action Party), and cautioning that the party's national leader could be extremely dangerous.

> He is described by Intelligence contacts to be both neurotic and violent. Possibility that he may be victim to acute paranoia as well. Understood by all analyses to be dangerous and unpredictable by nature. Currently considered a possible threat to the United States. Though surveillance has been somewhat successful, his movements are so well shielded that consistent monitoring has been hard to maintain. . . .

Great, Meade thought. That's all I need is some crazed revolutionary running around in Mexico unwatched who could take action against us at any time. . . . Christ! He tossed the folder in a stack with some others and stared out the window.

He thought about Katherine. It was hard not to, since her bedroom was in the same wing. She wasn't there, but he felt her presence.

Finally thoughts of her left him as well. He forced them away. He was feeling sleepy after all. In his sleep he dreamed about Maria Vásquez.

Meade knew he would be late getting back to the office, but didn't care. As the elevator descended from the residence, his military aide kept saying, "But, Mr. President, I don't understand why we're using this one. It's going to bring us right down in the middle of a horde of tourists. The other one would have been much better for security ... "

"Screw security, Benson. I want to see these people."

Suddenly the elevator doors opened and there they were. At first nobody noticed the doors opening, but then the gaping tourists being guided through the mansion realized this wasn't a dream, that they were seeing none other than the president of the United States. As soon as Meade stepped out of the elevators, the commotion began. Several alert Executive Protection Service guards came rushing down the center hall to surround him, as did several Secret Service agents, all of whom were wondering what in the hell had made him take this elevator. He'd have to be drunk to come this way. They tried to guide him away from the excited crowd, but Meade refused and moved into the group.

Hands reached out, children giggled in delight, and two old ladies reached out to kiss him. Meade took a peck on each cheek and with his famous political ease moved through the group saying, "Hi," pressing every hand he could and even stopping to sign someone's brochure.

It was when his persistent agents moved him toward the front of the group that Meade noticed her. Standing several feet off to the side with another tour guide, Maria Vásquez blushed from cheek to cheek when she saw him. Meade noticed her body twitch and knew it was a sign. A spontaneous smile broke across her face and her eyes spoke to him.

That's what I wanted to see, Meade thought.

His eyes met hers, their line of vision merged. Her message was soft, loving. She was trying to tell him something amid the confusion, the excitement. So was he, but his message was very different.

Is it guilt or pity?

Meade's eyes locked with hers and the fury burning beneath his pupils reached across the hall. The emotion surged between them. He continued staring at her. Her face contracted. Her lips folded. She backed off and trembled. Her eyes filled. Meade noticed a tear.

Cry, he thought. That's what I wanted to see.

Then, as quickly as he had come, the president was gone.

INTERLUDE

WASHINGTON/The White House

Maria Vásquez nibbled uncomfortably on her cold beef sandwich in the basement lunchroom of the mansion. She thought she would vomit if her friend mentioned it one more time. She did, but Maria restrained herself.

"Did you see the way he looked at us? So serious, but oh, so dreamy. His looks could melt you in a minute. God, I'd give up anything just to spend one night . . . "

Maria put down her sandwich and stopped her cold. "Will you please shut up?"

Her friend was aflutter. "Why, Maria Vásquez! You act like you couldn't care less. The day the president steps off the elevator. I suppose you, Miss Vásquez, in all your worldly travels have seen more exciting things?"

Maria tensed, her voice raised. "Lay off, okay?"

"What's wrong with you? Ever since we broke for lunch you've been acting so weird!" She leaned forward and whispered, "Look, if you're on the rag, say so. Nothing I don't know about myself."

"It's not that!"

"Well, don't get so testy about it. I happen to be discussing the president . . . " She paused and indulged in fantasy. "He's irresistible, isn't he? And you," she said, coming back to earth, "don't even want to talk about him. Honestly I don't know what's gotten . . . "

It happened so quickly. The girl glimpsed Maria's arm at the same time she heard the crash. Her head spun and she saw an ashtray shatter against the wall. Others jumped at the crash. Heads turned. Maria was breathing over her now, her face burning.

"I asked you to lay off, you stupid bitch!" she shouted.

Inside the women's restroom her hands were shaking so badly Maria could barely open the bottle. Damn safety caps! She struggled with it a moment longer, wanting to smash the fucking thing against the sink. Open the fuck up! she screamed silently. Finally the cap popped off and, trembling, she doled out four tablets and put them on her tongue.

She swallowed, thinking, I've got to stop this. I've got to get off these. They're destroying me . . . no, he's destroying me! I can't take it! . . . Not both of them at once . . .

19

Three weeks after Reed McClellan had shown Howard Hickman his private polls indicating a growing conservative shift in the country reminiscent of the Reagan years, Winfred Foster pulled out some polls of his own showing that not only was Hawkins's negative rating dropping, but his popularity was rising at the same time.

"In other words," Foster said, "we're gaining on them. People are starting to listen to you, not to your critics."

If this was good news to Hawkins, it was bad news for his fellow Republican opponents. Larry Broder had been hitting him on every conceivable issue, especially his religion. But his attacks were having much less impact now than six or seven weeks ago. People were growing weary of his mudslinging, and of Broder too. Broder's polls slipped even more. As far as Sheldon Roberts's campaign was concerned, what little money he'd been able to keep coming in had all but stopped. Roberts did not have the spunk, political acumen, or spirit that he needed to keep his supporters and his bankers happy. The fact that his platform was just about as exciting as oatmeal didn't help. But Roberts was determined to stick it out as long as possible. Booker T. Smathers, on the other hand, considered dropping out of the race a week ago, but for vanity's sake decided to remain in at least until the New York primary.

Thus on North Carolina's primary day in 1992 Cliff Hawkins was out there fighting for every last vote. Demonstrators were still plaguing him at each stop, but the crowds who turned up in his support were growing larger and larger, which kept Hawkins undeterred in his quest.

By early evening, while voters were still filing into polling stations across the state as they'd done since morning, Hawkins concluded his primary day tour with a long hot bath in his suite at the Raleigh Hilton.

He was exhausted both mentally and physically, having stumped the state for the past seven days nonstop.

At times the pace seemed worse than anything he'd ever experienced during the early years of his crusades. He was pushing himself more than most men half his age do. The world around him became nothing more than a blur . . . a hurried, relentless blur painted with lost faces, dates, names, and words. But he kept going, confident in his faith and encouraged by what Foster had told him.

With every stop, every speech, and every question-and-answer session he felt he was getting closer to the hearts of the people, penetrating their psyche, establishing a trust with them that he hadn't had before.

The only thing to blight this was the constant presence of the press. As if they could sense the growing bond Hawkins felt, the media, determined to make sure it didn't materialize, tried to trip him up, ensnare him in either a controversy or a statement that would tear down the fragile foundations he'd built over these past six or seven weeks. They hounded him on his various positions, asked for clarification after it had already been given, sought comments on the latest criticisms lodged against him by one group or another: feminists or gays, entertainers or publishers.

But, instead of defending himself, Hawkins began shrugging and saying everyone was entitled to his own opinions, himself included. He would then turn the question around and use it against Meade or his record. The press, though no champion of the president, obviously didn't like his change in tactics. Newspaper articles began calling his responses toward his critics "evasive" and "aloof." His charges against Meade and his administration were labeled "desperate" and "publicity ploys." Editorials both in print and over the airwaves became more acidic, barely mentioning the fact that Hawkins was gaining in the popularity polls. How much effect this would ultimately have on the North Carolina primary as voting continued was still unknown, but it definitely bothered Hawkins.

Gordon Wade told him over dinner in their suite, "There's only so much you can do. You've done it. No matter what happens, we're going to keep on all the way to Wisconsin and New York."

Instinctively Hawkins said, "Right," but for the first time he wondered how long it would be—how many more primaries it would take if they lost this one—before he wouldn't mean it. If they lost this one, it would be number five. Although he'd been prepared all along for a string of initial defeats, he was vulnerable enough to let it nag at him. He remembered the words: "Consider it pure joy, my brothers, whenever you face trials of many kinds, because you know that testing of your faith develops perseverance ... " The words rang as true as any he'd come across in the Bible, but, like any man, questions of a more pragmatic nature continually surfaced and it was in these moments, right when he should be filled with a sense of spiritual peace, that he was most unsettled. He had persevered, and his faith had never seriously faltered. He took pride in that. Never cracked, not once. But could it? If ...

He got an indication of how the evening would be running almost as soon as he'd stepped out of his bath. Winny Foster came into his bedroom in the Raleigh Hilton suite with the results of the exit polls, ones taken as soon as the voters left the voting booths.

"We're trailing Broder again."

"By how much?"

"Not nearly as bad as before, and quite a bit better than Illinois."

Hawkins's face brightened. "You mean there's a chance that ... "

Foster slowly shook his head, "I don't know. I'm not going to say. These were taken at key precincts. There are a lot of rural counties out there that could turn everything upside down."

"But still, we could ... "

"We could, but I'm not going to say. It's just too early."

So that's the way it was going to be, cat-and-mouse.

By midnight Hawkins's suite was filled with people surrounded by clouds of cigarette smoke. Everyone, it seemed, was smoking, each one of them either talking on one of the many telephones or watching the returns on television. The "Good Luck" fruit basket provided by the hotel's management had been devoured long ago, as had several buckets of chicken and two cases of Cokes. Although the race had narrowed considerably since early evening and even the most reserved television anchormen were expressing surprise at Hawkins's strength, the tension that should have filled such a hotel room on election night wasn't there. His people were hoping for a victory, praying for one, but even now with the latest projections they knew that victory wouldn't come. Another loss.

At 12:30 A.M. Hawkins was on the phone with Gordon Wade, who'd flown up to New York just hours earlier.

"Things aren't looking any better."

"No," Wade said, "but they look a lot better than they have before."

Then it happened, so suddenly and with so little warning it gave everyone an ecstatic surprise. A flood of returns started pouring in from the rural precincts, returns held up by a computer breakdown, and to the dismay of all his critics gave Hawkins the first lead he'd had over Broder in any primary.

The suite erupted in cheers. Hawkins seemed stunned by the figures. They flashed on the television screens. He was winning. Was actually winning. He somehow knew, just knew that this was going to be it—their first victory! The Lord had not let him down! Not at all.

Thirty minutes later Hawkins was still surging. He was now in front of Broder by a good five points. The press was going absolutely wild. Phones were ringing, people were coming and going, camera crews came in, photographers from *Time* and *Newsweek* arrived, and, sure enough, it was finally, after four defeats, going to happen. Magical number five!

"Hawkins has a definite lead now," an anchorman for CBS told the world from his desk in New York.

"A most startling show tonight, folks," said NBC's political analyst.

Word came that AP and UPI were already declaring Hawkins the winner. Someone else in the suite got a call from Washington saying the *Post* was ready to go to press . . .

Fifteen minutes later everything changed. Two precinct boxes that had previously been having computer trouble came in with a plethora of votes for Broder and Roberts, throwing everything off. An election official announced that regrettably an alert technician had found a programming error in one of the main computers, completely reversing Hawkins's lead.

The suite listened as the news reports and corrections flashed on the television screens. They were losing. Not by much at first, but, as the minutes passed, the gap grew wider, the news worse.

The photographers and camera crews, already in the suite for Hawkins's victory, now turned their lenses on him in yet another defeat. For the first time since the race began, the agony of defeat showed clearly on his face. People hovered around him. The press wanted a statement, the phones continued to ring, and the camera shutters fired away.

It was over. All of it. North Carolina was number five. Not the magical number five he'd hoped for, prayed for, but defeat number five.

He looked around him, at the sea of faces, at the cameras, lights, microphones, and backed away. It was as if he were observing them from the inside of a fishbowl, the water around him distorting whatever words were flowing from their mouths. He turned and went into his bedroom and shut the door behind him.

Twenty minutes later, with the bedroom door firmly locked, he was sitting on the edge of his bed asking himself the same question he'd asked when he first sat down: why?

"Is this another trial for me?" he asked God softly, almost inaudibly. "Is it? I need . . . I need to know."

But God did not answer.

20

NEW YORK CITY

Howard Hickman gazed scornfully at the fabulous sprawling Sherry-Netherland apartment that was part of an entire floor the president was using. "How much is this place costing us, Rampling?"

Paul Rampling, rather frayed from the president's whirlwind schedule, glanced up from a comfortable but priceless chair and said, "Not a cent. Lord Rathby's more than glad to do it. You know him, anything to be rubbing shoulders with the president so long as there's a half-assed chance Meade will get reelected."

Hickman surveyed the apartment, taking inventory of its Waterford chandeliers, Edward Fields rug, Chippendale chairs, mirror from Lloyd-Paxton, lacquered chinoiserie, paintings by Miró, Chagall, Picasso. "Shipping industry must be doing very well. Bet you ten to one Rathby wants some maritime legislation signed."

"That's a realistic assessment. If that's what he wants, the president will probably give it to him."

Hickman didn't respond and the conversation ended in awkward silence. Crossing over to one of the apartment's windows, Hickman gazed out on Central Park. Earlier that day the president had given what was supposed to have been a rousing speech at City Hall Plaza. All the right ingredients were there: appearances by New York's popular mayor, a handful of other well-known figures, several thousand New Yorkers, dozens of news media representatives, two bands, an eighteen thousand dollar stage dressed to the hilt in red, white, and blue, and most important the "right" speech. It was a direct, hard-hitting speech that their speech writers had labored on for almost two days, covering issues they knew were dear to New Yorkers. Meade's delivery was by far the best he'd given in a long time, but Hickman wasn't sure whether Meade had accomplished anything. The reception was lukewarm at best.

The same thing happened later that day at a rally for Meade in front of the New York Public Library at Forty-second Street and Fifth Avenue. With police helicopters circling overhead and a crack team of sharpshooters keeping their sights on several thousand New Yorkers who'd left their offices to hear the president, Meade's arrival was dramatic and perfectly staged. When his motorcade pulled up, the people cheered. And when the doors to his limousine were opened and the band struck up "Ruffles and Flourishes," they went wild. Meade stepped out of the bulletproof Lincoln into a wave of flashing cameras and harried journalists and, like an Egyptian pharaoh venturing into the streets of ancient Cairo or Alexandria or the pope moving through Saint Peter's Square or a king descending into a mass of his country's peasants, he moved confidently through the crowds. But things went downhill from there.

Standing at the window, Hickman thought perhaps the problem had been in the speech itself, but it had been one of the president's best. The people had listened, Hickman recalled, but how well? Where were the cheers? The tiny American flags waving furiously in the air? The signs with Meade's name on them bouncing up and down as the band played? The "Reelect Meade" hats flying into the air? Oh, there'd been a few flags, a few hats tossed up into the sky, a few placards waved about, but it wasn't a Broadway show. The enthusiasm was reserved at best. Krantz and his advance people had done their best, but what happened?

Hickman stood at the window for several minutes thinking about it. He glanced away, looking over at the French doors that shut off Meade's bedroom where at that very moment the president was undoubtedly screwing that Mexican cunt, and then gazed back out at Central Park.

Hawkins . . . Chambers . . . the sonofabitches. They're the ones that have thrown everything off. It was bad enough when Hawkins decided to run. Of all the fucking things to happen this year, Mr. New Right Evangelist has to throw the entire electoral college off. Hickman thought about the polls McClellan had shown him, about the coverage Hawkins was commanding now. It was almost as if he were a celebrity instead of a politician. The film clips he'd seen of Hawkins and his wife up in Wisconsin, smiling and walking among the wheat and dairy farmers, were disgusting.

What are we doing here anyway? The president doesn't stand a chance. It's Chambers's home state. But if we lose here, that's going to affect us in Wisconsin, Pennsylvania, Texas, all the rest.

Worst of all, Hawkins was going to be in New York tomorrow, speaking to the same group Meade's speaking to. Chambers was going to be in the city as well.

Hickman drummed his fingers on the windowsill. The timing is the worst thing of all, he thought. It's going to turn this whole trip into a circus.

Hickman tensed and stood erect.

A circus . . . a fucking three-ring circus with Hawkins and Chambers on both sides of us. Chambers was their most immediate problem, their real target. But what weighed most heavily on his mind wasn't Chambers—

—it was Hawkins.

If Hickman was worried about Cliff Hawkins, Meade wasn't . . . at least not at the moment. The day had been a success for him, so everyone told him, and because he wanted to believe them, he did. The crowds hadn't been quite as energetic as he'd wanted, but the president blamed the heat on that, knowing in his own mind that he'd given the best round of speeches he possibly could.

He had been celebrating for the past hour.

Maria Vásquez lay on her stomach in the middle of the bed. She was completely covered in oil. Meade was behind her, propped on his knees.

"Now what?" she asked him with a hint of resignation in her voice.

"Just raise up your rear," he replied, grasping her slippery hips with his hands while trying to lift her up.

Maria's buttocks raised in the air to a graceful height, her breasts, shoulders, and head resting on a pillow. Meade's hands parted her. She felt his stiff penis move between her cheeks. His hands slid around front and she felt both penetrations at once.

"No ... " she moaned, " ... you're not going to. You'll hurt me."

"Just relax."

He gave her a forward thrust.

She whimpered.

"Otis, please. Oh, God. I can't take it, I can't."

He thrust forward again, this time more violently. She screamed out in pain. Her body flushed when his movements began.

Over and over she protested as tears ran down her cheeks.

"Otis, please ... it hurts ... it's killing ... "

He thrust even harder. She gasped for air. His movements quickened and in front his fingers began working on that ever-so-sensitive spot within her.

"Oh, God," she cried, "I love it!"

After they had come, their slick, hot bodies lay back on the sheets. Meade's arm was around Maria, her head rested in the hollow of his shoulder. She was almost asleep when Meade felt it—

—a quick, nervous tremor that ran from her toes to the tip of her nose. It was a vibration, odd and unmistakable, different from just the unwinding of tight muscles or nerves.

It struck him as strange.

"Maria," he whispered, rousing some half-conscious state within her to perk up.

"Huh?"

"You okay?"

She took a deep, lazy breath. "My ass ... is so sore ... "

"No, I meant ... well, I felt something."

She raised up her head and their eyes met. "Like what?"

"Well, like ... like a nerve twitching or something."

Maria gave him a guarded look and didn't answer. It was then that Meade noticed her pupils were constricted.

21

If Meade's first day in New York wasn't an overwhelming success, his second was a disaster. After spending a restful night in his Sherry-Netherland apartment, Meade flew to Albany the next morning to try and get support from New York's state legislators. He failed miserably. Not only was the legislature Jackson Chambers's political alma mater, but many of the state's politicians remembered all too well a long list of unfulfilled promises made by Meade during the 1988 campaign. They chastised him in private meetings and later—though much more diplomatically—at a news conference.

In Syracuse the reception was downright hostile, climaxing when his limousine was pelted with eggs and tomatoes during a downtown motorcade—all of which was duly recorded and filed in wire reports by Meade's traveling press corps.

In Poughkeepsie that afternoon the press informed Meade of the latest Gallup and Harris polls showing him running far behind Jackson Chambers in both New York and Wisconsin. Meade was pissed the rest of the afternoon, but didn't show it until he was back in New York City that evening.

That was when he and Cliff Hawkins finally met face to face.

The president was walking through the lobby of the Waldorf-Astoria with an entourage of Secret Service agents and press people, heading toward the Grand Ballroom, where he was to address the Civil Service Employees Association. Across the lobby and down the steps came another entourage of agents and press. The moment he looked in front of him he knew who it was. Although Hawkins was surrounded by bodies and couldn't be seen clearly, Meade's agents and advance people had warned him earlier that Hawkins would be at the Waldorf. But they had promised him—*promised*—that Hawkins would be gone before he arrived.

Then the commotion began. Both groups of media representatives recognized what was happening and began making the most of it. Photographers clamored for the best shots, television Minicam lights came on, microphones appeared. The Secret Service agents spoke hurriedly into their hidden twoway radios, frantically trying to establish some sort of cohesive security. Meade tried to sort out his options on what to do. Hickman, who was walking directly behind the president, leaned forward and whispered, "We can't ignore this. Repeat, *can't* ignore this. You've got to meet him."

"Damn it, Howard," said Meade under his breath, trying to maintain composure, "you promised . . . "

It was too late. The two groups merged. As cameras whirred and microphones were thrust in their faces, both men found themselves facing each other.

From those first seconds everything seemed a blur to Meade. There was Hawkins, standing in front of him surrounded by at least a dozen reporters and agents . . . and the sound of what seemed like a thousand voices calling out questions. The cameras. The flashbulbs. The cackling of twoway radios. There was pandemonium. It ran through Meade's head like floodwaters.

He tried to decide what to do. Instinct and protocol told him to put forth his hand and smile. But when he looked directly into Hawkins's eyes, something held him back. He couldn't do it. His anger overwhelmed him.

Hawkins's hand went out to Meade. "Mr. President, we finally meet." Meade did nothing. Absolutely nothing. Hawkins's hand came forward a little more—perhaps Meade hadn't seen it. Again Meade made no attempt to shake it. Meade could hear the gasps of shock and dismay from the journalists and saw the surprise and bewilderment on Hawkins's face.

And then the president moved on to the Grand Ballroom, his entourage following, completely stunned by what he had just done.

It was later in the evening, with Meade safely back in his apartment at the Sherry-Netherland, that the reports began to make their way across a surprised nation. The incident, carried on all the networks' newsbreaks, quickly became the lead on the local and national late-news broadcasts. Meade had already decided he wasn't going to apologize. After watching a television playback of the incident, he realized how serious the whole thing could be, but he would stick to it. So all that was left were the repercussions.

"They could kill us," Howard Hickman told him and the rest of the staff.

"He isn't a serious candidate," snapped Meade. "I send money to preachers, not shake their hands."

"Do you realize what this could do to us?"

"Of course I do, but I'll be damned if I'm going to apologize to that sonofabitch!"

"You've got to!" insisted Hickman.

"He's right, Mr. President," said Joseph Krantz. "This isn't going to sit well with anyone. Especially the voters."

"It's without precedent," Paul Rampling told him.

"I don't care. Somebody's got to have the balls to do a few things."

"The people want a civil campaign," said Hickman.

"Bullshit. If they don't like it, I'll tell 'em what I just told you. In fact, since the fucking press keeps hounding us for an official statement on his campaign, we'll let that be it."

"Mr. President," Rampling said, "with all due respect, that is absolutely ridiculous."

"Ridiculous? You're telling the president of the United States what he's saying is ridiculous when he's got a fucking evangelist opposing him? I think you'd better reassess the situation!"

"But, Mr. President, Paul's right. We can't just leave the things the way they stand," said Hickman.

"Howard," barked Meade, "don't tell me what we can and can't do! Get that straight, right now. All of you!"

Meade went into his bedroom and slammed the door behind him.

An hour later, as Hickman and Meade's press secretary were fending calls from what seemed like half of the United States Congress as well as from the First Lady, the press, and several Democratic party leaders, the stillness in the president's apartment was shattered by breaking glass. Two of Meade's Secret Service agents looked up from their card game and glanced nervously at each other. Hickman raised his eyes from the telephone and looked at the press secretary. There was another crash, followed by another. Hickman and the others turned and stared at the beautifully carved Louis XV doors leading into Meade's bedroom. The president's chief of staff could feel a migraine coming. Beyond the doors they could hear Maria Vásquez's angry voice.

"You sonofabitch! If I want to go outside I'm going to. Nobody's going to stop me!"

"You're not leaving this fucking apartment!" roared Meade. "I've got enough problems."

"Tough. I'm sick of this place, you hear me? Sick of it. First time in my life in New York and all you do is keep me in this damned bedroom!"

"It's where you're staying too. I didn't haul your little ass up here so the whole world can see the whore I'm screwing!"

"Whore? Whore!" she screamed.

"Put that vase down, Maria!"

There was a crash. Hickman and the others shifted uneasily. One of the agents cautiously drew out his revolver.

"Since when am I a whore?"

There was another crash, followed by a loud scream.

"Leave me alone," Maria cried. "Keep your hands off me!"

"Shut the fuck up."

"Don't pull that presidential power trip on me." Maria laughed wickedly. "It isn't going to work."

There was some scuffling and Maria's laugh grew mocking. "I should have listened to my mother! She warned me about you. She didn't even vote for you. She knew the kind of asshole you are!"

"You cunt!"

"You're hurting me! Leave me alone! Who in the hell do you think you are?"

There was a loud tear, then an exploding crash.

"Cunt! Quit biting me!"

On the next crash the Secret Service agents rushed to the door. Hickman hurriedly intervened.

"You'll only make him madder."

"Out of our way."

Hickman stood firm. "Look, it's happened before. You know him. Nothing to worry about. Don't upset him."

"Upset him? We've got to save him."

There was a scream, another crash, and then a thud. Just as the agents shoved Hickman aside and moved to storm the doors, the president swung both back and met them face to face. He was sweating, heaving like a raging bull, clad only in his underwear and a badly torn shirt.

"Well? What in godsakes is it?"

Embarrassed, the agents drew back, explaining hurriedly. "Well, we heard some . . . we . . . ah . . . thought maybe . . . "

The president stepped back into the bedroom and slammed the doors so hard that one of the hand-painted china knobs flew onto the carpet.

Rampling, who'd been standing nearby, shook his head at Hickman sadly. "Poor Lord Rathby. You know, you were talking about him getting some maritime legislation signed? Well, now the president's going to have to. I mean this whole apartment's going to be demolished before we leave."

"Oh, get screwed," fumed Hickman.

A short time later the shouting subsided and the familiar rocking and squeaking of the mattress subdued the atmosphere into temporary tranquillity. The agents struck up a game of gin. Rampling and Krantz went over some work. And Hickman stood at the antique bar drinking, thinking about the people who'd demanded to see Meade later that night about the Waldorf-Astoria incident. It was twelve midnight. The night had just begun.

Until almost three in the morning, after he had cleaned up and dressed, Meade met with a stream of national and state leaders who'd been scheduled to come earlier but, because of the incident at the Waldorf, had been rescheduled. Only during a campaign would one find the president of the United States so oblivious to time. He didn't care that some of the people who had gone to bed had to get up again to keep their appointments with him. Although nobody wanted to discuss it, the Waldorf incident came up, but it was overridden by everyone's concern over the growing strength of Hawkins's campaign. Meade reiterated that Chambers was his real concern, not Hawkins. But nobody was fooled, least of all Meade. Hawkins's name was the one people kept discussing. They all expressed grave fears that, given just one victory, Hawkins could take his campaign, now akin to a tropical storm, and turn it into a political hurricane.

"It won't happen," Meade told the last of his visitors, the former New York governor Mario Cuomo, during their conversation.

"I hope not, Mr. President. I really hope not."

It was two thirty-five in the morning.

At the same time in Meade's apartment the bedroom was breathing. The walls were inhaling and exhaling, blowing their stale breath upon Maria Vásquez. She could hear Otis somewhere nearby. She heard his voice, he kept calling people by their first names. People had been floating in and out of the apartment for over two and a half hours but, had anyone asked her, she wouldn't have been able to tell you where she was.

It was finally happening . . .

Trembling, feeling another cold sweat sweep over her, she rolled over and knew she shouldn't have given them up.

But I was popping too many.

She had fought it as long as she could, arguing with Otis merely to retain some grip, but for the past twenty-four hours it had been next to impossible.

The room coughed. Maria cringed. It *was* happening.

The president had noticed the change yesterday, and this evening too. The last coherent thought she had was of Meade withdrawing in the middle of their lovemaking, saying, "What's wrong with you? You're as pale as a ghost. And your eyes! They're . . . different. Have been for a couple of days. What's happening to you?"

She couldn't tell him because she didn't know. She had never just stopped before—ever! Her connection said she was crazy to try. Yet four days earlier Maria had been staring at four of them in her hand, about to pop them, when she heard herself say, God, how long can you do this? You've got to stop! It's killing you! The next thing she remembered was a stream of colorful little capsules being poured into her toilet. It was the most self-destructive thing she could have done. Cold turkey.

Her body had started to crumble from that moment on . . .

At first she tried to cover it up: disappear into a bathroom until the shaking stopped, set a glass of tea down when it began to shake, laugh off her profuse sweating. But now she couldn't hide it and she was fighting it alone. With each passing hour her control had gone a little more.

Her body . . . her mind . . . couldn't take it. Things were happening to her that she didn't understand. Why didn't they tell her this would happen? Maria gazed up from the bed to the chandelier hanging from the center of the room, its dim yellow lights struggling to brighten a world of darkness. She had gazed at it some time ago, and then followed the ceiling to its edge, where it was met by the wall. From there Maria trailed the gilded molding around the room until it formed a box.

She had wanted to scream when the box began to spin.

Like Dorothy's house in *The Wizard of Oz,* the room spun around and around. All her hidden fears began to surface and swirl as well.

Faster and faster.

She shuddered. *No . . . stop it! It can't be happening again!*

But it was, the process sped up like clockwork gone wild.

Faster and faster it spun.

The windows blew out! A cold rushing wind burst in, blowing the sheets and her clothes into the air like tissues. The walls were breathing again. Contracting and expanding. Exhaling, inhaling, sucking at her, then spitting her out. The few pictures still hanging on the walls leaped from their hooks and danced a jig. There was laughter. Someone was laughing at her.

Her body . . . her mind . . .

Got to relax . . . got to go through this like everything else . . . got to . . . but why didn't he warn me? Why?

Breathing, spinning, dancing. It was too much! Maria trembled and felt an electric shock jolt her into an upright position. As the sheets blew around her, wrapping themselves in her wet sticky body, she commanded her feet to find the floor. Her legs swung over the side of the bed, and she tumbled forward. Maria thought her head would burst.

The laughing grew louder, hysterical.

Ripping away the sticky sheets, Maria stumbled into the bathroom and shut herself off in the shower. A cascade of water poured over her, but it didn't help. She shook. Her eyes hurt so badly she could barely see. Once, she could have sworn a bat flew over.

It did fly over you, yes it did! HAHAHAHAHAHAHA!

Stop laughing at me! Stop laughing at me! Got to relax . . . got to re . . .

Swinging open the shower door, Maria tumbled back into the bedroom and suddenly everything stopped. The windows were shut.

The walls were still. Everything was the same, as if nothing had happened.

A glimmer of reality swept over her, and for the first time Maria saw the enormity of the damage she and the president had done. There was a pair of love seats facing each other with a demolished crystal ashtray scattered across the table between them. Behind one of the love seats hung a smashed eighteenth-century gold leaf mirror, and propped against a wall was a Cézanne original which Meade had removed for safety but which had been sheared when Maria threw the phone through it.

The wall to her right, opposite the double doors, ran the length of the room, and much of its space was taken up by the bed. On each side of the bed was a Louis XIV end table and four inches from the closest one were the crumbled remains of a Jean Michel Frank lamp executed by Diego Giacometti. A shiver ran down her spine. She gazed past the bed to the draped windows, highlighted by oils on both sides; seeing one of the paintings splattered with Coca-Cola and the remains of a Ming dynasty vase in the corner, she suddenly gasped for air.

It was coming back.

Maria stood just outside the bathroom a moment longer, then somehow found her way to the nearest corner. Slowly, effortlessly, she sank to the carpet. Fear overwhelmed her.

The room coughed. The windows blew open. Hanging from the chandelier was a tiny black man, his teeth bright as the sun, singing. The room began to shrink. The walls were contracting. She felt their force squeezing her frail naked body, pushing her toward the center of the room. But where was the center? In the oriental rug in front of the bed? No, there was only a black hole there now. A large black hole. A pit, really. And it had a suction so strong Maria felt herself being pulled into it by a giant vacuum. The wind was blowing the drapes like flags, and the tiny black man kept swinging from the chandelier.

The room spun faster than before. Pictures leaped from their hooks and whirled around the singing black man like a miniature tornado. The grandfather clock near the doors tipped his hat and bowed, and then started dancing, his chimes ringing a deadly "Ding . . . ding . . . ding . . ."

The telephone receiver jumped back through the Cézanne, and in the distance Maria could hear: "Operator number nine. Yes, I have the time. Operator number eight. Would you like a date? Operator number seven. You and I were made in heaven ... " The walls were coughing and spitting, the wallpaper falling about her and wrapping around her. Maria felt herself choking and wanted to scream. Instead she began to cry.

"It's ... not supposed to be like this. ... It's not!"

"Operator number five. Baby, what's the latest jive? Operator number four. Honey, you ain't talkin' to no whore."

She thought she would go crazy.

Howard Hickman stirred in his chair when he heard the noises. They were faint, almost inaudible, like a puppy crying for its mother. The president and Mario Cuomo were seated a few feet away on the couch, but he doubted they'd heard them. Meade was carrying on about the absurdity of Cliff Hawkins's race and Cuomo was politely nodding his head.

Cocking his head back, Hickman strained his ears for a second, but the sounds disappeared. He breathed more easily; then they suddenly resurfaced, this time louder. What in the hell was it? He glanced at the president, who was still talking, and then around to the others. No one seemed to notice. God, was he going looney?

No. They were there all right, and it was crying he heard. Hickman tensed and noticed Rampling heard them too. Their eyes met and they exchanged alarmed looks, but neither stirred. Hickman calmly eyed Meade and Cuomo; Meade was still carrying on. Rampling caught Hickman's attention with a nod. The sounds were coming from behind Hickman.

Shit! The president's bedroom.

Maria managed to stand up, her back facing the pit, thinking somewhere between the cracks would be an escape, but it wasn't any use. She dropped to her knees and tried to grasp anything she could to keep from being sucked into that ... that grave. Her body slumped forward, her head wedged in the corner. Then her knees were pulled out from beneath her. She fell on the carpet, being pulled by something while the man overhead kept singing.

She felt her feet being tugged toward the center, and knew it was a losing battle, but wouldn't ... couldn't give up. Clutching the doorframe to the bathroom, she tried to fight back, to stay in the corner. She held tight to the frame. But there was another tug and her hands slid off the frame as if it were greased.

Got to hold on! Got to stop them! Grave ... dirt ...

Struggling, she pulled herself back to the doorframe against the suction from the pit trying to pull her away.

But I can't hold on! Oh, God! It's sucking me in! . . . It's eating me alive!

She went down, her legs pulled toward the center of the room. Her hand lost hold of the doorframe. Frantically she clutched the edge of the carpet at the bottom of the frame and, using all her strength, tore the carpet up from its tacks.

But the suction grew stronger!

And you can't escape! No, you can't! We've got you little girl! HA HAHAHAHAHAHAHA!

Pulling away from the wall . . . she was being pulled away from the wall, toward the center.

She now noticed the exposed carpet linings nailed to the floor and tried to clutch them in a furious, insane determination not to be pulled any farther toward the center. The carpet tacks sunk deep into her hands, drawing blood.

Something yanked her . . .

You can't escape! We're going to get you, oh yes we are! HAHA HAHAHAHAHAHAHAHAHAHA!

. . . and yanked her again. She jerked back toward the wall so quickly that three fingernails snapped off her fingers like bottle caps.

Maria cried out in pain, watching blood stream from the ends of her fingers.

Hickman stared at Rampling, then at Meade. He prayed he could get his attention, that Meade would look up. That stupid bitch! That stupid bitch! What in the hell was she doing in there?

The cry was loud and painful.

Suddenly Meade's eyes widened and shot over to Hickman. A look of horror swept over the president's face. What in God's name is the problem? he asked silently.

Hickman shook his head, silently replying, How do I know? He decided it was time to end the president's meeting. He stood up.

Maria was finally sucked in. She tumbled into the pit and fell deep into a coffin. She shut her eyes and her mind circled in an endless maze of horrors. High above her she could see the bedroom chandelier. Hanging from it was the tiny black man. He leaned over and laughed at her.

HAHAHAHAHAHAHAHA! Chil', you done fo' now! Yes, Lawdy! HAHAHAHAHAHAHAHAHA!

The walls of the bedroom fell. The room seemed to implode. The chandelier came crashing down on her and the black man disappeared. Sobbing, Maria glanced up and saw unfamiliar people standing over her grave, mocking her, laughing at her as the black man had.

Then everything went dark. The coffin's lid had been shut. The hammering began.

Sobbing, Maria put her hands to her face and rocked in anguish. Her entire body was cold and aching. Above her she heard dirt pounding against the lid.

Thump! Thump! Thump! They were shoveling it on her.

She couldn't breathe. She was using up air. It can't be happening! This isn't real, is it? No! Stop it! Maria tore her hands from her face and suddenly thought, I've got to get out of here!

Everyone in the apartment could hear the crying and the pounding, but tried to follow protocol and ignore it.

"Gentlemen," began Hickman hurriedly, "I really hate to break this up, but it's very late and you, Mr. President, have only got a few hours to catch some sleep."

Meade took the cue. "Right, Howard, thank you." The president then quickly, but diplomatically, ushered Mario Cuomo to the front door and, just as it was shut, the crying turned into a shrill wail.

In the bedroom Maria was battering on the coffin lid with all her strength, feeling the wood practically split from her hysterical force. But there was no coffin, no pit, and no lid. What she was beating on were the bedroom doors.

Before anyone in the suite had time to rush the doors, they flew open and a nude Maria ran past several of the president's stunned agents and staffers toward Meade himself. Disoriented, she stumbled on the carpet and collapsed in Paul Rampling's arms. The agents rushed to subdue her.

"She's going through a severe withdrawal," the White House physician told Meade as he shut the bedroom doors.

"Withdrawal?" Meade asked. "From what? She's no drug addict."

The physician shook his head and said, "I'm afraid she is, and it's a most disturbing addiction at that."

They were the only ones remaining in the apartment besides

Hickman. Maria had just been put to sleep. They took seats on one of the couches.

"What do you mean? What kind of addiction?"

The physician sighed, "I'm still almost too stunned to believe it myself, but it's a number of things. Qaaludes, Valium, Seconal, phenobarbital, codeine, morphine, ethchlorvynol, amitriptyline—you name it, she's had it."

"Christ," sighed Meade. "Are you sure? How do you know?"

"Very sure. I suspected something of this sort from the moment I saw her, although I must confess I never expected it to be so severe. So I checked her purse."

"And?"

"And she has over a dozen different prescriptions from various D.C. and Maryland doctors, who, I'm sure, know nothing about the other prescriptions."

Meade was depressed, his breathing heavy. His eyes were sad. "I never even suspected . . . I mean, she's high strung sometimes and low sometimes, but really, I . . . "

Hickman, who'd been sitting in angry silence asked, "How could she've been on all this and the president not have noticed?"

The doctor turned. "Well, how long has she been employed by you people?"

"Less than six months or so," Meade mumbled.

"Well, there's your answer. She's been on half this junk for almost eight months. You've never seen her differently."

"But can prescription drugs do that?" asked Hickman in disbelief.

"Look what they did to Elvis Presley. And multiple withdrawal like that can cause enormous problems physiologically, even death. And did you see her fingernails?"

Meade nodded. "What a mess."

"So what do we do now?" asked Hickman.

"I suggest she get to a hospital immediately. We should transfer her tonight, but you're going to have to be careful. The press is everywhere."

"No joke," said Hickman.

"Can it wait until tomorrow morning?" asked Meade.

"Yes, she's sleeping now, and the injection will work for several hours. And I think she'll be safe for a while, but she needs to be somewhere where they can supervise the rest of her withdrawal."

"In New York? Don't tell me it has to be here," said Meade. "If she's going to spend some time someplace, it might as well be near her home."

"Mr. President, there are some good clinics all over the place where she can be rehabilitated. In fact, there's a very good one in Tennessee."

"I don't want one in Tennessee, I want one in D.C. Are there any there or not?"

"I know of one. It's in Maryland and very very expensive."

Meade stood up waving his arms. "I don't care what it costs! If she needs it, hell, I'll pay for it. But let's just get her there and keep this thing quiet. We'll fly her out in the morning."

Meade was at the door thanking the White House physician for acting so quickly, and when it closed, only he and Hickman were in the living room.

"We need to talk."

"Not now, Howard. It's been a bitch of a day."

"We've got to!"

"For how long?"

"I don't know, but it doesn't matter. Some things can't wait.

Meade asked him if he wanted a drink, and Hickman said no. The president went to the bar and poured a strong scotch.

"All right," he said, taking a drink, "what is it?"

"You know what it is . . . "

"What do you want me to do? How did I know she was going to go haywire on us? Do you think I wanted this to happen? Come on, Howard, don't throw this on me."

Hickman was mad, but tried to control it. "What'd you bring her along for anyway? I mean, can't you stay out of her pants for one week?"

Meade's eyes flashed with anger—insubordination. Howard could only go so far. "That's none of your fucking business. You hear me? I won't tolerate you sticking your nose in my business. I *am* the president."

"So you keep telling me."

Meade slammed his glass down on the bar. "Damn it, Howard, don't give me any shit now. I brought her along because she threw a damn fit one afternoon last week after I'd seen her and didn't say hello. Can you imagine? Just because I didn't say hello, she gets all bent out of shape."

"So you bring her to New York?"

"It was an easy way to mend things. And besides, Kat sure as hell wasn't going to be here. She's off in Wisconsin someplace doing her bit there."

Meade poured himself another drink.

"Well, it mended things all right. I just hope to God this doesn't get out."

Meade swallowed. "It better not."

Hickman finally exploded. "Well, it just might! You know how damn hard it is to trace those leaks. We can barely keep a lid on anything anymore and this is just the sort of thing the press would eat up. So what are we going to do? You tell me."

"I don't know! New York isn't our only primary. We'll pull things together and keep them together. Don't worry. We'll do something."

"Like what?" he pressed.

The president looked into his glass without answering.

22

WASHINGTON

In the morning their troubles continued. Although Maria had been flown out in a shroud of secrecy before dawn, several other problems cropped up. The president's episode with Hawkins the night before was still a lead story on the national news shows, complete with filmed coverage and reporters' commentaries. After many drinks Hickman convinced Meade at around four in the morning to explain himself on the matter in a written statement to the press, which the president did. He said he hadn't shaken Hawkins's hand because he'd received some very disturbing, highly sensitive intelligence reports over his limousine telephone just moments before. He was still trying to absorb the news when he encountered Hawkins, hence his "regrettable disorientation." They sent Krantz to the "Today" show and Rampling to "Good Morning America" to clarify the matter further, but, watching both men and hearing the questions fired at them, Hickman had the feeling the president's explanation wasn't going to wash.

Among their other problems McClellan brought Hickman his latest polls, confirming Gallup and Harris, and a new one showing Meade losing considerable support in traditional strongholds to Jackson Chambers. Also the latest unemployment figures had just been released and they showed the greatest increase in over a year.

Even worse, two of the nation's leading banks announced yet another increase in the prime lending rate, with other banks expected to follow suit, which meant higher inflation. To top it off, Francesco Gianni had called.

Yes, Francesco Gianni.

Hickman was watching Krantz on the "Today" show when the White House called the president's apartment asking for him. When Hickman got on the line, he recognized the voice immediately, but couldn't figure out how Gianni had gotten the call transferred to the president's suite. It was something very few staffers could have done.

"Howie, baby," he laughed, "how's our president's hand? Finicky, no?"

"Are you crazy?" Hickman whispered. "What are you doing calling here? How'd you get this put through?"

"Don't worry 'bout it, I've got plenty of tricks. Phone calls are a cinch."

"You know what the score is on making contact with us. It's out. Has been from the very start, or did you forget?"

"No," the voice said angrily. "No, I didn't forget. But you people—you're making me mad, Howie. Not keeping up your end of the bargain. Not keeping me informed. I don't like that. I need money. Or a construction contract."

"There's neither right now. We're still negotiating on the pipeline and we're spending cash as carefully as we can. Things are all screwed up."

"You're telling me. Jeez, it's bad enough he's got that fucking Jackson Chambers in the race against him, no? But Cliff Hawkins?"

Hickman heard a wheezing, wicked laugh.

"God," Gianni continued, "that's really taking the cake." He laughed again, then suddenly changed his tone. "Look, no fucking around, Howie. How long's it gonna be? I've got obligations myself and I—"

"Look," Hickman said under his breath, "we're doing the best we can. If you need cash, the president can arrange some short-term loans. We have some friends with the banks we didn't have four years ago and . . . "

Hickman was interrupted by another burst of wheezing laughter.

"Short-term loans!" he roared. "You asshole, I'm supposed to be in jail! Now get me that contract or . . . oh, fuck it. You know what to do."

The phone went dead.

Two days later, while campaigning in Wisconsin, Cliff Hawkins was en route to a political rally given by a group called Christians for Godly Government, which promised good media coverage. When he looked up from a report Randy Perrin had given him, Hawkins said, smiling, "I think we've got him."

He was right.

If Howard Hickman thought the president's explanation wouldn't wash, he wasn't the only one. Hawkins and his strategists wondered how Meade was going to get himself out of the Waldorf-Astoria affair, but couldn't believe the statement Meade had issued. Neither, it seemed, could anybody else. The statement not only caused a furor of speculation among the press, as well as America's foreign allies, about the nature of a "highly sensitive intelligence report" that could so disorient the president, but also brought an onslaught of new questions concerning the president's ability to withstand pressure. The explanation unraveled even further when it was noted by various journalists that in slow-motion video playbacks Meade seemed completely in control of himself; he was smiling and not the least bit worried about anything until *after* he had seen Hawkins.

Hawkins finished reading the report Perrin had given him, a confidential report that Joseph Atwood, a friendly nationally syndicated columnist, had sent to them by courier. The columnist had discovered that "highly placed White House sources with access to the president's telephone logs have no record of any communication being transmitted to his limousine on the evening in question." The report also quoted an anonymous individual, who had been present in the president's apartment after the incident, describe Meade's four-letter tirade about Hawkins, calling him a son of a bitch and saying, "I send money to preachers, not shake their hands." The crowning point was when the president was quoted as saying he didn't consider Hawkins a "serious candidate."

The column would run the next day.

"So he doesn't think I'm a serious candidate?"

"What do you expect from him?" Perrin asked.

"You're right," Hawkins said, suddenly laughing, "but this comment about sending money to preachers . . . I wonder if he really meant it."

Perrin laughed too. "I wouldn't ask him for a contribution if that's what you're after."

"That's okay," Hawkins said. "As soon as this column runs, the American people will see what their president is really like."

The next day, when Cliff Hawkins stepped before the cameras for his press conference, it had already been agreed upon by his strategists that he should be careful in his attack on Meade. Appear neither vicious nor malicious, but simply righteously indignant. Careful not to feed the public's stereotypical image of an evangelist, Hawkins was determined to keep cool.

"Reverend! Reverend!" more than two dozen voices called out.

"The gentleman in the back," said Hawkins, pointing.

"Reverend, the White House is calling Atwood's column a complete falsification and is standing by the president's story concerning the telephone call. Which story, sir, do you believe?"

Cameras fired away, microphones came in closer, ears perked up.

"Ladies and gentlemen, I am not about to stand here and call the president of the United States a liar, I have more respect for him than that. I would like to believe his story, and will if for no other reason than Christian charity, However, I think the evidence is overwhelmingly against his version ... "

Hawkins paused, knowing they were expecting more, but hoped he would get a follow-up question that would allow him more effective histrionics. After all, this was good television and he might as well make the most of it.

"Reverend," CBS asked quickly, "what evidence are you referring to?"

Hawkins smiled ... said mildly, "You've all seen the videotapes of the incident, as have the American people. From the moment the president stepped out of his limousine and walked through the Waldorf-Astoria's lobby, he seemed to be in a fairly good mood." Hawkins chuckled, "Until he saw me!"

Everyone cracked up.

"Reverend," *The New York Times* asked, "do you feel his response to you was a personal affront or one reflecting his political feelings toward your candidacy?"

"I think we all know how the president feels about me personally," laughed Hawkins, referring to the Atwood column. The journalists laughed with him. "However," he said more seriously, "I was nevertheless shocked, as I'm sure the American people were, by the president's actions."

Hawkins paused and looked straight into the cameras.

"Shocked because I believe the president's refusal to shake my hand was a personal affront to me, and such actions are an insult to the office he holds. Regardless of whether or not Otis Meade likes me, the president of the United States is supposed to represent himself before others with the same respect and dignity we afford him—and not mock any individual, whether or not he's a political opponent."

"Reverend! Reverend!"

"Ladies and gentlemen, I'm not through. What disturbs me most about this incident, though, isn't the president's personal affront to me, but rather his affront to the American people. By not shaking my hand, Otis Meade turned his back on every individual who disagrees with him, be they black, white, Democrat, Republican, Christian, Jew, atheist, young, or old. He doesn't have to like what we say, but he should afford us the same respect we've given him. If he isn't willing to do that, if he wants to turn his back on the American people, then it's time we turned our backs on him."

This was making good television. Another flurry of voices called for his attention.

"Yes, Jim?"

"It's been quoted in Mr. Atwood's column that the president doesn't consider you a serious candidate. How do you respond to that?"

Hawkins smiled. "Obviously the president hasn't seen our latest polls or else he was being facetious. I would assume the latter since he has access to the same polling information we do and *knows* just how serious this campaign is. We're gaining in almost every state. My opponents, Larry Broder and Sheldon Roberts know this, as does the president himself. People know that things in this country could be a lot better than they are. They don't need me to tell them. They can look around and see the decay in our cities, the crime in our streets, the pornography in our theaters. When they go home at night, they know what it's like to face a broken home or marriage, know how hard it is to try and do something only to get entangled in some confounded government regulation. They know how effective Otis Meade has been when they check out at the grocery store and their bill is higher than the previous week's, when their gasoline bill goes higher and higher even though—thanks to our gas allocations—they're getting the same amount as the week before."

Hawkins took a breath and again was confronted by "Reverend! Reverend!"

"Frank?"

The man from the *Los Angeles Times* asked, "Sir, are you seeking vindication for the Waldorf incident?"

Hawkins looked genuinely hurt and the cameras captured it beautifully.

"No, not at all. I don't want vindication. I've forgiven him. The American people might, but they'll get it at the polls."

"Reverend!" another dozen voices shouted. Randy Perrin stepped up to the podium and said, "Ladies and gentlemen, this will have to be the last question."

Another dozen shouts for Hawkins's attention.

"Yes, Gloria?"

The crack correspondent for ABC asked boldly, "Reverend, if the president released his telephone logs and they did indeed show a transmission had been made to his limousine, would you retract the statements you've made here today?"

Hawkins smiled, already trying to decide how best to answer the question. If he said no, then he would appear as callous and disrespectful as Meade, but if he said yes, then they would be left with their pants down. The correspondent waited. Quickly he thought about Atwood, about the column, and then about Meade. He decided to take a gamble. He cleared his throat.

"To tell you the truth, I don't think the president *can* release those records."

"Why?"

"He's got too much to lose."

WASHINGTON/The White House

"Of course, I've got too much to lose," snapped Meade to his immediate campaign aides. "And that sonofabitch knows it. Why did we ever have to be in that fucking hotel the same time he was? Why in God's name wasn't he out of there? I swear, if that ever—*ever*—happens again I'm going to cut the balls off every one of you!"

"Don't worry," Howard Hickman said wearily, "it won't."

"It better not. That still doesn't help us now, does it? He's got us right where he's had us before—cornered—and we're left holding the fucking ball." Meade was chewing so nervously on his pipe that Hickman thought he would bite the end off.

"What if . . . " Paul Rampling said reflectively, "we released a copy of the telephone logs that *proved* you were right?"

"You mean alter them?" asked Meade.

"Well ... "

"No," Joseph Krantz said immediately. "They'd spot the altera-
tion in a minute. And if Atwood's got a copy of the original record,
we'd be even farther up shit creek than we are now."

"I still don't know how he got the original," piped in Jerry Ecklecamp.

"It's these fucking leaks!" Meade roared. "Howard, you initiated
an internal investigation into the thing back at the Sherry-Netherland. Have you found anything?"

Hickman hated to fail the president, but he couldn't lie. "No, sir,
we haven't found anything yet. But we're still investigating ... "

"Good! Good! I swear, if we ever turn up the people or person responsible for this ... "

"They'll never work in this town again," said Hickman.

"Damned right."

"Mr. President," Paul Rampling said, "I think we're straying off
the subject of Cliff Hawkins."

Meade shook his head in disgust. "Hawkins? Hawkins! I thought
Chambers was bad enough, but I'm so fucking tired of hearing
Hawkins's name, I could scream."

"He's giving us all migraines, Mr. President, but the problem remains," said Reed McClellan.

"Well," the president said, "what are we going to do? What can
we do?"

"Why not plead executive privilege?"

"No," said Meade shaking his head. "Shades of Nixon. People
still hate the term, let alone the meaning behind it."

"Then why not refuse to release them on the grounds of national
security?" asked Paul Rampling.

"Because," Meade said in an exasperated tone, "there are no
grounds for national security. Granted, there could be, but since
that damn phone call was never made, you can bet your life Atwood
will counter anything we say."

"Great," moaned Joseph Krantz. "That's all we need is another
knock-down-and-drag-out in the papers."

"No way can we afford that," said Hickman. "No way. You know
that, Mr. President. Our press is bad enough as it is."

"I know," said Meade bitterly. "It looks like it's going to stay that
way."

"At least Hawkins's press isn't much better," offered Ecklecamp.

"No, but he's finally got us by the balls, hasn't he? And he hasn't even won a primary."

Hickman turned to Reed McClellan. "How do his figures look?"

"Strong," McClellan told them all. "Stronger than I imagined they would, and this New York thing is only going to help him."

"How strong?" demanded Meade.

McClellan looked at the president. "He could win New York *and* Wisconsin."

Everyone moaned in unison.

23

IN FLIGHT

Seven days later, primary election day in both New York and Wisconsin, Cliff Hawkins sat in his campaign plane's cabin office not believing the figures he was reading. Randy Perrin had brought in the first set of exit-poll results from both states shortly after takeoff. The polls hadn't been open long, but the figures weren't good. Not at all.

Hawkins looked up from the yellow legal pad on which the numbers were written out in long columns. He put his hand to his face and wiped it slowly. "What's happening to us? Yesterday we were predicted to win, but today . . . "

"Cliff," Perrin said slowly, "it's still early. New York's only been three hours and Wisconsin only two."

"But everyone—Gallup, Harris, PollWatch—said we were going to pull it off this time."

Perrin tried to explain to him again that these were the first set of results. There were still nine or ten hours of voting left, anything could change. Hawkins barely listened. The voting had been expected to start off strongly in his favor as soon as the polls opened. Things couldn't have been better politically, yet everything was wrong. He gambled that Meade couldn't produce his telephone logs, and the White House had been forced to admit sheepishly that this was the case. Larry Broder's polls had dropped suddenly after several major tactical errors, while Sheldon Roberts's campaign faded into obscurity after the Meade-Hawkins hotel controversy.

Hawkins thanked Perrin for the information and told him to keep bringing him the results. It was going to be a long flight.

An hour later Perrin stepped back into the cabin office, this time with Gordon Wade, and gave him the latest exit-poll results. Hawkins read them and looked up at both men. "It's not getting any better, is it?"

"Not yet," Wade said. "But it's still early. Most of the voters are still in their offices. It should pick up around lunchtime, then right after work."

Hawkins wanted to believe him, but couldn't. After both men had gone back to their desks outside his office, he leaned back and feared his faith was going to crack. He could feel it. It had begun with the defeat in North Carolina. Hawkins knew that somehow his faith wasn't as strong as it used to be. That he, a man whose life for thirty years had been devoted to witnessing the power of faith in the Lord come to others, had finally allowed his to falter. They had said he would lose from the very beginning, had called his candidacy unacceptable, had regarded him as a novelty, had used him as someone to chastise and criticize, and he had never let it bother him, had always stood firm in his belief that eventually he would be victorious. But he hadn't been and now fear crept into him. Fear that ate at his faith like a cancer. Sitting there, he felt there was no stopping it.

He prayed.

Several minutes later he pulled out his Bible and opened it to Psalms. His eyes immediately fell upon Psalm 71.

> *Though you have made me see*
> *troubles, many and bitter,*
> *you will restore my life again;*
> *from the depths of the earth*
> *you will again bring me up.*

For a moment he stared at the words, then he began reading them. Suddenly he laughed. What was he doing? What had he been doing? He was Clifford Hawkins, a man who was a source of strength to millions, and yet a man who was suddenly weak. Hawkins looked at the words again, reflected on them, and softly laughed again. Of course, you're going to bring me up, my Lord. Of course, you are.

And he believed it.

Two hours later, just before they touched down in Kansas City, Kansas, Perrin opened the door once again, this time with a smile. Cliff looked up from a speech he was working on.

"It's getting better?"

Perrin nodded and stepped in. Gordon Wade came in behind him. "We're pulling them in. The figures look good."

"Very good," added Wade. "And the number of voters has doubled since this morning. We're moving ahead. There's no mistake this time."

Hawkins beamed. Could it be?

Wade said, "The pollsters are coming damn close to their original projected figures."

"What's Winny say?" asked Hawkins.

"Same thing. He's on the phone with his Boston office. ABC and CBS are tilting both elections in our favor."

"But it's still early," said Hawkins. "We've got seven hours of voting left."

"Seven hours to come out with a solid win," said Perrin.

"Two wins," corrected Wade. "And we just may do it."

But by midafternoon, as Hawkins's motorcade was leaving the University of Missouri at Kansas City en route to the Harry S Truman Library in nearby Independence, Broder was moving out ahead. By the time the motorcade stopped the press had received the same news. Nobody knew what was going on. Hawkins was inundated by questions, but he couldn't give them any answers. Instead he professed his faith that the vote would eventually turn around in his favor and went into the library, wondering if it really would.

Then in the early evening, when they were airborne for Dallas, it began to happen. Since late in the afternoon the tide had turned again in Hawkins's favor and, as Perrin and Wade continued to monitor the polls taken as voters left the booths, the pattern held. Now that the voting was over, it continued to hold—in their favor. At first the precinct results from both states came in a trickle, but the trickle turned toward Hawkins. Then the trickle became a flow. A steady flow. For the past hour it had been an all-out flood. It *was* happening. They were pulling out ahead. Easily moving past Roberts, and now Broder. With each passing minute, with each new precinct result, their lead was solidifying.

"We're actually winning?" Hawkins asked.

"You better believe it!" said Gordon Wade, beaming.

"It's holding, Cliff. It's finally holding. ABC and CBS are both saying it's going to stay."

"What's Winny say?"

"Same thing. He thought it would happen all along."

"Cliff, relax," Wade said. "You're going to win!"

Hawkins stared at him, eyes sparkling like a child's. The words seemed so definite, so positive. Win. Winning. Won. "You're going to win," he had said. "You're going to win." Again and again the words repeated themselves. Things had changed. The more he thought about it the faster his heart beat, the more excited he became. He pushed his chair back from his desk and fumbled around looking for a pen and paper, though why he needed them he didn't know. Then, realizing how nervous he was, he set the paper down and looked up at the two men before him. His best friends. He folded his hands and smiled. Finally Hawkins leaned back in his chair and threw his head back laughing. He laughed louder and longer than he had in a very long time, and Perrin and Wade joined him.

Laughter and the freshness of joy echoed through the cabin like a song of absolute happiness. Victory! Victory at last!

Laughter broke out among the dozen or so members of his traveling staff as they began hugging one another. Tears of joy flowed throughout the staff. Even the usually ambivalent press corps that now traveled with them seemed caught up in the excitement.

TEXAS/Dallas

By the time Hawkins's plane arrived in Dallas he was not only leading in New York and Wisconsin, but surging ahead with comfortable margins.

Police estimated that over seven thousand people showed up to greet the candidate. When the plane finally rolled to a stop at Love Field, the tumultuous welcome started. Hawkins bounded down the steps to an array of flashing cameras and television lights and was greeted by a wave of ecstatic cheers. People were waving placards and banners and flags everywhere. They were reaching out to hug him, kiss him, shake his hand. A band was playing "The Eyes of Texas." His Secret Service agents guided him to a set of microphones facing the crowds and cameras, and he stepped forward. His voice was so choked with emotion that at first he didn't know whether he could speak. Gazing out into the crowd, with cameras and lights beaming on him, his eyes grew misty. He gave the cameras a huge grin and waved to the crowds once more.

"I want to thank all of you and the people of Wisconsin and New York for showing us the faith you have in our efforts. And I also wish to thank my Lord, without whom this entire race would not have been possible." The crowds cheered and Hawkins paused to look around. "With these two victories, we're telling the rest of the world that we're not going to stand by idly any longer and let America continue down the path it's been going. With these two victories we've begun the long process of turning this country back to the good, righteous people who helped build it! We're not going to stop until we've reached the White House!"

The crowds roared their approval. He was finally home, a loser no more.

Charlotte Hawkins hurried down their mansion's staircase, adjusting her expensive blouse and skirt and hoping she didn't look too drained from her own flight from New York. Having arrived in Dallas just two hours ago, after some last-ditch campaigning for Cliff in Buffalo, she had wanted to be at Love Field when Cliff flew in. But because they were his first victories, she had been detained by last-minute interviews her staff insisted she simply had to give. The reporters had now left, and the Secret Service had rushed upstairs to tell her Cliff's limousine was turning in through the main gate. Charlotte was determined to be at the front door the moment he walked in.

Stepping into the main foyer, she moved to the powder room across from the library and checked her appearance. Examining herself in the bright mirror, she smoothed a smudge of makeup with one hand and puffed up her stylish coiffure with the other. She smiled to herself, satisfied that Cliff would be happy with what he saw. She flipped off the light in the powder room and went back into the foyer. She paused in front of the library. One low light was burning next to Cliff's favorite wingback chair as she slipped in, the stillness of the room enveloping her. Her eyes went to one of three hollow books placed secretly on the shelves across from the fireplace. Within its covers was a flask full of liquor. She felt extremely proud that she didn't want a drink. She hadn't felt so secure in a long time. Today, when reports had filtered out that Cliff was unexpectedly trailing, and trailing badly behind Broder and Roberts, she would have given in to the need. In fact, had she not been in the middle of campaign stops in Buffalo and then confined with her staff on the small jet that brought them back to Texas, she would have drunk herself silly. It was horrible to lose, especially to lose with such consistency over so many months. There was a time, even a few weeks ago, when the losing had gotten so humiliating, when the attention and lies and distortions thrown at them by the press and their opponents had gotten so degrading, that she couldn't face the crowds anymore. And then she had tripped—in front of all those people. When she stepped back and looked at herself, she didn't like what she had seen. She had become bitter toward the campaign and Cliff. Suspicious, jealous, and, most of all, angry. She felt as though he were trying to live out his pipe dream at her emotional and physical expense. It seemed that at every step they took forward, the campaign went two steps back.

But then came the change: rising polls, less hostile press coverage, more welcoming audiences. To top it all off, Cliff had turned the most controversial moment of his campaign at the Waldorf into a very embarrassing situation for the president and an effective image booster for himself.

And now, she thought, moving down the hall, he's actually done it, hasn't he? Broken the barriers. When Cliff stepped inside and saw her standing there, Charlotte's face was as bright and as happy as he had ever seen it.

"Honey," she said as tears welled up, "I'm so happy for you!"

And for the time being, she was.

COLORADO/Boulder

Larry Broder stared at the television screens. "We repeat, Cliff Hawkins has won the Wisconsin primary in a smashing upset over the former Colorado governor Larry Broder and Senator Sheldon Roberts, the other two contestants in that race. This marks the first victory in the Republican primary sweepstakes for the evangelist and, while there are still late returns coming in from New York state's voting, NBC is projecting another victory for Cliff Hawkins in that primary. As you can see by the figures on your screen, Hawkins is already a good distance ahead of Broder in that race, giving him . . . "

Broder grabbed his remote control and punched off the television. He sat in the vast comfortable den of his home in silence. It was two in the morning and he had left his downtown offices thirty minutes before, leaving his staff, though still numb from defeat, to begin plotting out new strategies for his race. Now with his girlfriend already in bed, exhausted from their flight from New York earlier in the day, and his telephone off the hook, Larry Broder had some thinking to do. The fact that he'd lost to Cliff Hawkins hadn't sunk in yet. Yes, pollsters had been predicting his defeat, but Broder had never paid them as much attention as his staff said he should, relying instead on "vibrations" he received from the voters themselves. Granted, such an esoteric method of reading the electorate's mind was about as intangible as one could get, but it was one of the many means Broder had successfully used in the past in his political maneuvers, and the methods had given him a quirky, almost mysterious, aura lacking in most other nationally known politicians. It was precisely this aura that attracted many of his supporters, who, during the resurgence of Republicanism in the 1980s, had aligned themselves with conservative Republicans, but now had become disenchanted. Instead of defecting from the party, they shifted to Larry Broder, one of the few Republican politicians they thought had original ideas. Broder appreciated their approval, manipulating their responses so successfully that he rode into the 1988 convention like the pied piper, his followers marching behind him. He eventually lost the Republican nomination, but his popularity among the younger party members was beyond question. They liked his youthfulness, energy, and dedication, they liked his sincerity. But most of all, they liked him because he was such a contrast to the stereotypical conservative Republican, and so were they. This was to be their year, reflected Broder, our year! We've got the members, we've got the support, and all we had to do was convince the voters that a Broder administration was better than anything else they were being offered. Now, he reminded himself bitterly, everything had been turned upside down by Cliff Hawkins. Two damn primaries in a row. And New York, one of the biggest prizes in the entire sweepstakes! The delegates Hawkins would receive from New York alone were almost as many as Broder had won in both Illinois and North Carolina. And there were more to come—big ones. Hawkins would be there, fighting him every step of the way. Broder knew the power these two victories had given the evangelist. Hawkins had finally broken the voters' psychological resistance, which said it couldn't be done, that a religious leader couldn't enter a presidential race and be taken seriously. It's frightening, he thought. The man's a fascist. A fucking fascist religious leader who's actually getting these old, dying conservatives to listen to him. There was a poll released a couple of weeks ago that showed that conservatism was swinging back into its own. It could be bullshit, since most polls generally are if you ask me, but still . . .

Broder, getting up from the couch and stretching, began to consider the effect Cliff Hawkins might now have on his own political future. He was tired and sleepy, but by no means incoherent. He knew how rough it was going to be, that Hawkins would have the psychological edge, and Larry Broder was going to have to fight it. Fight it as long as he could if he wanted to survive this race . . .

24

PENNSYLVANIA

The president lost in the Wisconsin and New York primaries to his Democratic challenger, Senator Jackson Chambers, though Wisconsin was lost by a smaller percentage than predicted. The weeks following those contests were frantic, as Meade stumped Pennsylvania trying to win back some of the support Chambers had taken.

Meade had told his staff a month before that, in order to hold onto the nomination, they would have to concentrate on the big primaries, those with the largest delegate prizes. Pennsylvania offered him one of the biggest delegate purses in the race. While the other candidates had taken breathers before hitting the state, Meade had been stumping it since they flew out of New York.

As is generally the case in an election, a president's actual presence in the state can do more for him politically than anything the best PR firms could generate. But Pennsylvania was an industrial state, part of a region that had given him considerable trouble during the past four years. Convincing these voters to forget much of his past record was not easy. During his first week in the state attendance at his rallies was less than spectacular, fund-raising dinners didn't sell out, and many of the crowds he encountered were openly hostile. But as his television and print coverage rose, so too did the Pennsylvania polls. Slowly at first, but the changes were significant enough for many political scientists to reassess his chances.

Nevertheless, the president was still not without his problems. While his projections in the state looked brighter than they had in months, there always seemed to be something ominous in the background. Initially the important issues had been commerce and industry and the latest downturn of the economy. Now little things began to pick away at him too.

When Meade was posing for pictures with the state's oldest resident, a 112-year-old black man in Harrisburg, the man fell to the ground, dead of a heart attack.

In Norristown Meade stepped out of his limousine and slid in a pile of dog turds.

At a Daughters of the American Revolution luncheon the platform on which he was eating collapsed, sending him, his lunch, and a dozen women to the floor.

In Pittsburgh, when Meade's pace car was circling Blissman Speedway before thousands of supporters, all three fanbelts snapped and the automobile died in the middle of the track.

At Carnegie-Mellon University he said he was proud to be there with the fine people of Penn State.

At Penn State he said he was more than proud to be with the people of Carnegie-Mellon.

They were small gaffes, minor when one considers the breadth of the whirlwind tour Meade made of the state. Thirty-nine towns and cities and seventy-nine speeches within sixteen days. But Meade didn't like mistakes, especially when he made them. His patience was dwindling. He had been without proper sleep, food, and relaxation far too long. What bothered him most was all the shit he had to go through simply to win the primaries. If a new projection or set of economic figures didn't throw his staff into a tizzy, something else did. In New York it had been Maria Vásquez. Then, according to Hickman, it was Francesco Gianni. In Washington the pipeline talks themselves. In Pennsylvania the gaffes.

It was on the eve of the steel state's primary election ten days later that the final blow came . . .

Air Force One had just left Scranton, heading back to Washington, and Meade was discussing his Texas strategy with Paul Rampling and Reed McClellan when Howard Hickman stepped into his office. The chief of staff's face was void of color. He looked like a corpse in an old Vincent Price movie.

"Sir, I need to talk to you right away."

The president looked up and his other two advisers turned around. "Is it urgent, Howard? Paul and Reed were just—"

"Mr. President, I'm afraid it is."

Meade looked at Rampling and McClellan and said, "Gentlemen, I'm sorry. We'll have to continue this later."

Both men left. Hickman pulled a chair in front of the president's desk.

"Howard, what is it?"

Hickman sighed, "We may be up shit creek."

Meade leaned forward in his black leather chair and removed his reading glasses. "Why? They're not still riding you about that old nigger dying are they? Screw 'em, we sent flowers to the funeral."

"No, it's not that," he said, shaking his head. I just got through talking to Schwartz from the *Post*. It's Wallbanks, the Texas governor. He's finally gone off the deep end with those Mexican migrant workers."

"What's he doing now?"

"He's rounding them up. Every Mexican migrant worker he can find, like a witch-hunt. He's checking their visas, work permits, you name it, trying to send back as many as he can."

"You mean for violations?"

"I mean for anything—anything he can pin on them. Schwartz said it's harassment, pure and simple. He's nailing some for labor violations, some for charges as obscure as vagrancy."

Meade leaned back in his chair. "Vagrancy? What kind of charge is that?"

"One typical of Wallbanks."

"Christ, I wish he'd get off their asses."

"Portillo's going to blow a gasket, I can see it now. Subtle harassment is one thing, but open-season hunting of illegal aliens and migrant workers with expired visas is something his pride—and political stability—won't allow him to tolerate."

"Howard," the president finally said, "this isn't going to help us at all with the pipeline talks. Not one damn bit. I mean, Christ, do you realize the position this could put us in? The whole thing's been on tenterhooks since we began."

"That's what I'm afraid of," Meade said gravely. "That stupid sonofabitch Wallbanks. He's got to throw his wrenches at us all the time."

Relations with Mexico had been precarious for years. The pipeline talks were the only solid thing holding them together. But over the years there had also been the problem of Slim Wallbanks, a belligerent Texas oilman who'd spent eight million dollars of his own money to get elected governor. Wallbanks was all but an open racist. He harassed the Mexicans working and living in Texas almost from the day he took office, but always under the guise of laws written on the books. Portillo hated Wallbanks and Meade could easily understand why, but Portillo also expected Meade to handle the governor, which was something the president couldn't do.

Meade took a few puffs from his pipe, then asked, "And the wire services? How are they handling it?"

"It's hot. People've been saying all along it was only a matter of time before we got into something with them."

"Shit. This is just the sort of thing Wallbanks would do to me. The Texas primary is less than two weeks away. He knows how much we need those delegates."

"And the farm vote," Hickman reminded him. "There's no way we can endorse something like this. It could really hurt us. Wallbanks claims he's doing it because the Mexicans are taking jobs from the American farm workers. If we don't endorse it, the labor and farm vote is going to say we're siding with the Mexicans. And if we do, Portillo will probably have the Federales incarcerate every American tourist down there."

"That sonofabitch!" snapped Meade. "God, how I hate Wallbanks. He kicked me in the face back in '88, then threw a fundraiser for my opponent the next week. Now he's trying to do it again."

"It's political," said Hickman. "The only thing is, he doesn't know the position we're in concerning the pipeline talks."

"No kidding. Thank God we've kept those secret."

"And if it isn't that . . . "

"Then it's got to be Chambers. He's probably supporting him. This is just the sort of thing that would give Chambers leverage."

"So how are we going to handle it?"

"How can we?" snapped Meade.

"You could call him."

"And tell him what? That there are highly classified negotiations going on and, if he goes through with this, he'll be putting the nation's ass on the line?"

"Exactly."

"Forget it. I don't trust him for a minute."

When Air Force One touched down at Andrews Air Force Base, Meade transferred to a waiting helicopter. Within minutes he was hovering over the South Lawn. The helicopter blades fanned the grassy expanse and the chopper set down. Tony LaCross ran toward it, holding his hair from the blasting winds. As soon as Meade stepped out, LaCross told him that there was some bad news concerning Mexico and the situation in Texas.

"Bad news? . . . Mexico?" Meade shouted.

"Go inside! They're in the Oval Office!"

Skipping the traditional red carpet and trying to avoid the usual corps of photographers and reporters on hand to cover his arrival, Meade, Hickman, and LaCross hastened across the lawn.

Inside Saul Berkowitz and Byron Knowles, two of the chief negotiators on the pipeline, who were seated on one of the president's couches, stood up when he entered. They told him the news: at two that afternoon the pipeline negotiations had been broken off indefinitely, and Mexico's three representatives, Juan Ortega, Eduardo de la Cruz, and Luis Pérez had been ordered back to Mexico City for immediate consultations with President Portillo.

"Christ," was Meade's only response.

"He's on the line, Mr. President."

"Thank you. Slim?"

"Mr. President?"

"Slim, good to hear your voice! It's been too long. Where on earth have you been hiding yourself?"

"The question is, where have you been, Mr. President? Ah've been trying to reach you for months on those welfare allocations. Fortunately we resolved the problem by ahselves."

Meade wished briefly that he was a scorpion so he could sting that sonofabitch but good. Instead he laughed. "Well, you know how it is around election time, Slim. In fact, I'm sure you do. But that's not really why I'm calling . . . "

There was silence.

"You see, Slim," Meade said slowly, calmly, "we heard news reports today about you rounding up all those migrant workers and . . ."

"Yes, sah, Mr. President, rounding 'em up like cattle."

"Right," Meade said tersely. "I thought there was a mistake—that all these news reports were exaggerations. That you weren't really going to . . . Hell, we heard one report that you wanted to put them in camps until Immigration could check them all. That must have been a mistake beca—"

"No, Mr. President. It wasn't any mistake. We're gonna check every single one of 'em if it takes two years."

"You are." It wasn't a question.

"Yes, sah," Wallbanks drawled, "every last one of 'em."

Meade swallowed hard. In a clipped, impatient tone he said, "Look, Slim, cutting out all the protocol crap, just what the hell are you doing down there?"

There was a startled cough on the other end.

"Mr. President, you seem rather unhappy."

"You could say that," snapped Meade.

"Well, ah'm sorry, but ah'm only doing my job. We've got Texas farm workers—Americans, mind you—that are stahving down here. Stahving, I tell ya, and these spi—Mexicans—are stripping 'em of their jobs. It's got to stop."

Meade searched out his pipe.

"Look, Slim, you and I have been old pros for a long time. We both know the seriousness of actions such as these. You know how strained our relations have been with Mexico. Christ, they've seemed like another Cuba at times. And this administration has been making a concerted effort this past year to strengthen our ties. But something like this . . . like what you're doing . . . could cause irreparable damage to our relations with them, not to mention our foreign policy in general."

"But, Mr. President," Wallbanks said quickly, "you yourself decreased the flow of Mexican agricultural imports by 35 percent back in '89 and you *still* haven't rescinded your actions."

Meade took a few drags from his pipe. "Right," he puffed, "I know that. That's going to change, I can assure you. As you know, I was under tremendous pressure from the farmers. But this is a different matter. My situation was purely economic. But this situation, even if it is economic, is also a matter of pride. Christ, Slim, it's as bad as our rounding up our Japanese citizens during World War II."

"With all due respect, Mr. President, ah disagree," Wallbanks said.

Meade could feel his blood pressure rising. "You just don't go in and decide to start harassing one particular group of people, regardless of what kind of economic impact they're having on your own citizens. It just isn't the American way to conduct state or national policy."

"And what is, Mr. President? Allowing American farm workers to stahve while foreigners take their jobs because they're willing to work for less? Is it educating these people at the expense of my state's taxpayers? Feeding 'em with American dollars? Is that the American way, Mr. President? Ah don't think so, and the farm workers in this state don't think so. The labor movement doesn't think so. Ah have to go by their dictates, Mr. President, and address this problem the best ah can."

Meade pressed the phone close to his mouth. "The best you can? By rounding them up like cattle? Herding them before a pile of red tape simply to make them show they're legitimate or not? I do believe you could come up with a better way of dealing with the problem than that."

Wallbanks said politely, "You're entitled to your opinion, Mr. President. After all, it's within your prerogative. But ah've got over ten million voters in this state to answer to, labor unions, lobbyists, and more farm workers than ah can piss on—'scuse the French."

"Look, Slim, you helped this country out last October when we had that migrant worker problem—the riots and all—in Brownsville. Can't you do it again?"

"That was over seven months ago, Mr. President. Things have changed."

"I realize that. Everything changes. And if you don't consider what you're doing very carefully, if you don't call off this . . . this damn roundup, then a lot of things could change between this country and Mexico for the worse."

"Mr. President—"

"Slim, listen to me. Do you remember those border clashes we had back in '88?"

"Yes," answered Wallbanks as slowly as if he were recalling a dry hole he'd drilled twenty years ago, "Ah believe ah do."

"Well, what are you going to do when they start again? When all those tourists want to hang you because they can't get into or out of Mexico? All those voters whose property's been seized down there? What are you going to do then? Think about it. Are the American farm workers and labor unions going to help you when the trouble begins? Think about it."

Silence on the other end.

"You see, Slim, I want you to consider those things for a reason. I want you to call off this thing on the grounds that it could be detrimental to our relations with Mexico. *Detrimental!*"

More silence, which only increased Meade's impatience.

"Mr. President, ah think you're overly concerned, don't you? Besides the decision has already been made. We've already got Texas Rangers and Immigration marshals out in the fields, in the towns—it's too late. There's absolutely no way I can call it off. Why, the voters would have my hide."

Absolutely no way ... Meade couldn't believe it. That two-bit sonofabitch was doing this to him on purpose. God, he'd like to cut every fucking allocation he could from that state. He'd find a million reasons to do so. "I've got every reason to be overly concerned and I'm trying to tell you why! This is a horrifying act and you know it! Now why can't you call the damn thing off? These aren't rodeo roundup days, you know."

"Because, for one, ah *never* go back on my word. Ah promised the people ah'd do something about this horrible situation. And the program hasn't been in effect twelve hours and ah'm already getting glowing reports. We're getting illegal aliens by the hundreds, and migrant workers with expired visas by the dozens. You see, it's working. In two months we should have almost all of 'em on their way home."

Meade took several drags from his pipe. He tried to control himself. He wasn't getting anywhere. He could see that. What next? He thought about it for a moment, then, biting his lip, said, "So I guess your decision's final?"

"Yes sir." His voice was firm.

"All right, Slim, if you're not willing to cooperate, we'll have to reassess the situation from that perspective and, let me tell you, I'm going to fight this all the way. Mexico's going to be our biggest adversary and there's going to be trouble and you're going to be the one with bloody hands. Don't say I didn't warn you."

On the other end in Austin Wallbanks said, "Yes, you've done all you can do. Don't worry about my hands. Ah always keep 'em clean. Keep in touch now ... "

Meade was about to hang up when Wallbanks added, "Oh, yes, please do give my condolences to that black man's family. You know, the one that died on you."

Meade slammed down the phone.

* * *

Evening. Katherine was curled up on a chintz sofa in the West Sitting Hall in her nightgown trying to watch television. The hall itself, which wasn't really a hall at all but an informal living area designed for the president and his family in 1902, was completely dark save for the light from the television screen. Behind her were sweeping swag curtains draping the French bow window she had admired so often, below which one could see the rooftops of the West Wing offices and the Rose Garden. At each end of the sofa was a Sheraton-style mahogany drum table. One of them was covered with photographs of the presidential family, and the other displayed Katherine's small collection of porcelain rabbits. In the dark shadows against one wall was a beautiful Federal-style mahogany secretary-bookcase inlaid with satinwood accents and with tiny glass doors. Beside it hung the *Isle of Shoals* by Childe Hassam. Against the opposite wall beneath another painting was the television set, enclosed in a richly designed custom cabinet.

Katherine sat staring at it. The Pennsylvania returns were coming in slowly and one of the anchormen was discussing the early figures with a nationally known columnist. Whatever they were saying didn't register with Katherine. Her mind was in another world, a world of pain and anger.

She knew something, actually had something concrete this time. She had hoped and prayed she would never find out, but she had. Suspicions were one thing, but knowing was much harder to deal with. It wasn't surprising, just painful. Painful because she loved him so much and, though she had been almost a hundred percent sure of what was going on, had held onto that one percent of doubt. She wanted, more than anything else, to keep their marriage going. Now the illusion had been stripped away and there was hurt and fury.

Katherine had stopped by the White House physician's office for her periodic breast examination. She was sitting in the small examining room, breasts bared, when the telephone rang.

"It always rings at the worst time," the nurse said, stopping the examination. "You and I in here and Dr. Walsh on the tennis courts. Will you excuse me for a second?"

"Of course," Katherine said.

Minutes passed. When she came back in, she was flushed and very apologetic. "Terribly sorry, Mrs. Meade, but I couldn't hang up. I had to write down some information for the president and Dr. Walsh."

"For Otis? Nothing serious, I hope."

"Oh, no," the nurse laughed, beginning the examination over. "Not at all. It was just the clinic calling in their daily report on Maria Vásquez."

"Who?"

"You know," she said casually, continuing the exam, "the tour guide." Katherine frowned and the nurse elaborated. "The one who got so sick on the president's trip to New York. It was such a horrible thing from what Dr. Walsh said. The president, he's so nice to keep tabs on her, considering everything else on his mind. Why, he must call at least every other day to see how she's doing."

"He does?" Katherine felt a squeeze on her breast.

The nurse pulled her hand away, aware that she had told the First Lady something she shouldn't have. She blushed and tried to evade the question with an inadequate remark.

"But, Mrs. Meade!" protested Secret Service chief Charlie O'Rourke. "Why do you want to see our logs on the private residence?"

"It's my business, Charlie," said Katherine from behind her East Wing office desk. "Now if you please . . . hand me those logs."

O'Rourke handed them to her. "I really don't understand this. I think the president would want to know about it."

Katherine leaned forward. "Charles, if one word is mentioned to the president about this, I'll personally request your transfer off the White House detail. Is that clear?"

O'Rourke nodded sadly and Katherine opened the logs.

Katherine saw a figure moving toward her in the darkness. It was Otis. He had phoned a few minutes earlier from the office, where he'd been working on the Texas problem with some of his staff, and said he'd be up in a few minutes.

He walked in front of the television and went over to the couch where she was sitting, leaned over and kissed her. He eased himself down next to her. He hadn't really wanted to watch the Pennsylvania returns since his campaign office had been keeping him informed. It didn't look good, but she had asked and he said he would.

If things weren't bad enough in Pennsylvania, Wallbanks had

stepped up his efforts to round up workers with expired visas and illegal aliens. The national networks had shown film clips of Texas Rangers on horses chasing the workers through fields and herding them together until Immigration and Naturalization officials could reach them by car. It was humiliating. Meade had spent over an hour with the Attorney General and heads of both Justice and Immigration trying to figure out how to resolve the situation. His advisers had only ended up bickering and offered him no immediate answers. Meanwhile, the White House had been besieged with protests over the situation in Mexico.

He always felt uncomfortable around his wife when crises erupted, but, if she wanted him to join her in watching the returns, he'd oblige. It was the least he could do after she'd been out campaigning for him for the past two weeks.

"It's not looking the greatest, is it?" he said.

"No," she said coolly, "they just said you're losing four major counties, and your exit polls look horrible."

Meade let out a sigh. "Shit, they've been saying it'd be this way for the past three days. Right after the new polls came out."

He leaned back on the sofa, resting his head, and spoke toward the ceiling. "We needed a solid win to go into Texas, but with the new polls and those accidents that happened in Pennsylvania I should've known." He sighed again. "Of all the times for an old geezer to die, he dies on me!"

"That *was* unfortunate," she said, then nothing more. She was still trying to collect her thoughts. Meade noticed the distance between them, knew when Katherine was bothered, but said nothing.

He began switching channels and taking calls from his staff. They were still behind. Chambers was again successfully challenging him and winning.

"Damn him" Meade growled, looking at the figures on the screen. "He's forcing me to play a frigging cat-and-mouse game with him through every primary and it's going to be like this until the convention. God, we've got to turn things around. Those gaffes in Pennsylvania didn't help."

"Things like that didn't happen in New York?" Katherine asked.

"Not really. Not with Chambers anyway. That crap with Hawkins was the worst thing."

Katherine drew her knees up under her chin, clutching them with her arms and stared at the screen, her eyes never moving. "I guess. I thought ... perhaps something might have happened that you hadn't expected, like in Pennsylvania. But if you say it didn't ... "

Meade was puzzled. Her phrasing wasn't right. She was leading him into something. His instincts told him so. "What else would have happened?"

She turned and stared at him. It was a cold, infuriated stare, one he hadn't seen in years. "Oh, I don't know," she said through clenched teeth, "I thought maybe someone had given you more trouble than you could handle ... and not Cliff Hawkins—Maria Vásquez."

His mouth dropped. Then he leaned over to her, "Oh, Kat ... "

"Don't 'Oh, Kat' me, you son of a bitch. You've lied to me, Otis. Lied from the very start!"

He ran his hand through his hair, not knowing how to handle her. "Kat, that's not true. I ... I ... "

"Oh, God, you're disgusting," she snapped. "How long did you think it would take before I found out? A few months? A year? Maybe after I read you memoirs?"

"How long for what?" he cried.

"Don't play innocent with me, you bastard, I know everything there is to know about your little escapades. How you humped every piece of ass you could get your hands on. I know, Otis, I know!"

She got up and began pacing the area in front of the couch. Meade thought she looked like a tiger on the prowl. She stopped and turned to him. "God, you had some nerve! Trying to pull this off right under my nose. Everyone else knew but me ... or so you thought. But I've known, Otis. I've known for months. Maybe not the whole story, but I've had my share of suspicions, my doubts and suffering because of you."

She began pacing again, her voice losing more of its control. "But for some reason I refused to believe it. I ... " She stopped. I can't do this. I've got to keep myself together. If I crack, he'll move in on me. I can't do it!

She straightened herself, cleared her throat. "I held out until the very last minute. I tried to make myself believe it wasn't happening, even when the evidence was all around me. But now—" she said, waving one hand out in front of her, "—now everyone knows!"

"Kat—" he was getting up.

"No, please!" she said backing away. "Don't say anything. I don't want to hear it. I just want to get this over with." She folded her arms and, placing one hand to her forehead, she looked up. She was trembling, her lips quivered. "I couldn't believe it was them, though. Tour guides, lower aides, secretaries. And New York, that was the worst. That poor girl." She choked. "That poor girl just happened to be addicted to everything in the book and you took her to New York." She tried to continue looking at him, but her eyes filled. She was going to cry. I can't let this happen. The room was growing cold now, the temperature feeling as if it had suddenly dropped thirty degrees. "How could you do this? After all I've tried to do for you?" She was trembling more now. "And right in the middle of a campaign? Right when the attention's really focused on you. Why, Otis? What's wrong with me? Am I that pitiful in bed? Did they all do the things I wouldn't do? I thought we had more than that. I know there've been problems, but . . . "

Meade went to her. "Kat, please. Let me . . . "

"No!" she cried, backing off, moving farther into the darkness. " . . . explain."

"No! don't speak. I don't want to hear you. Not now. Don't you see? This is very hard for me." Tears streamed down her face. "I'm trying to handle this the best way I can," she cried. "Who are you, Otis? What have I done to you? You're not the man I married. This isn't the marriage I wanted. It's a marriage of convenience. I'm seeing that it's always been that way."

He was standing in front of her. She looked up. "I wanted you to love me!"

She was crying openly now, shaking, gasping for air. Meade lifted her up against him. His shoulder grew wet from her sobbing. He wanted to say, "I do love you," but he couldn't.

Moments later, still holding her, he cupped her chin and made her look at him. Her eyes were red and swollen. Her cheeks were streaked with wet mascara. What was there behind those eyes? What was there so many years ago? Where had it gone? Meade wondered. He tried to kiss her.

"No," she murmured.

He shut his eyes and felt numb. He opened them again and she was gazing at him. There was pain behind those eyes of hers . . . and also love. This time he did kiss her. And kissed her again. She trembled.

"It's too late," she whispered, another tear running down her cheek.

"No ... it's not too late," he said, kissing her once more. She clutched him with all her strength. They stood there for a moment longer, holding each other in darkness except for the glow of the television screen. The world about them—the election returns, Washington, the White House—became still.

It was three in the morning. They had been awake for the past ten or fifteen minutes, not saying anything, just holding each other. Silence broke when Katherine said, "I didn't handle it very well tonight. I guess most women never do. I gave in too easily ... "

"It doesn't have anything to do with giving in, it's what you feel."

She sighed. "It's not over, Otis. But it's not going to last unless some things change." She turned to him. "We've got to talk. It's something we haven't done in a while."

"Okay."

She turned away and lay on her back, staring at the ceiling. "This is going to sound ridiculous, but, if I didn't know it was the truth, I wouldn't say it."

"Fine," he said, running his smooth hand over her shoulder, then her breast.

"Don't."

He retreated.

"You need me, Otis. You need me just as much as you need your cabinet or Howard Hickman or anyone else around here. This whole country knows it. Without me you're doomed. Your career will be over. The country, the people have given me this position, Otis. And they'd never stand by a leader whose own wife won't stand by him. It says something about a man."

"I know that, Kat."

"Do you?" she asked him. "I don't think you do. There was a time when you *could* have done without me, and it probably wouldn't have made much difference. But that's in the past. This is now, and your future's on the line. Your job, and your marriage, and we've got to get some things straight or you're going to be in even greater jeopardy."

Meade didn't like the way she was talking.

"Such as?"

"For one thing, Otis, realizing some things that should already be obvious. I don't like what I'm doing, Otis. This role I have to play. In fact, I'll be damned if I don't hate everything about it. But I love you. And because I love you, I've put up with a lot. So I've not only learned to bear it, but actually like certain aspects of my life here. Not many, but some. However, if you want me by your side, out there plugging for you, then you're going to have to put your life in gear instead of your cock. It's as simple as that."

She went on. "I'll be damned if I'm going to put up with this anymore. You may have a need to prove yourself, but you're also married and the president of the United States and I'm not going to be used like this. Do you understand?"

He said nothing, remaining motionless.

"Well, if you don't like the options, I'm sorry. If you want it some other way, I'll call the *Post* or the *Times* and tell them I'm leaving. I've invested all I can into this marriage and received very few returns. It's time that changed."

He still said nothing.

"Otis?"

Meade turned and said, "Okay."

Outside their bedroom the television was still on. An anchorman for CBS was telling America about the Pennsylvania primary. Through the cracked door Meade could hear that he was still losing.

"Our latest CBS election returns show the president still far behind in his race against Senator Jackson Chambers. As more counties from across the state come in, we're predicting another defeat for the incumbent president. Right now, as you can see on your screen, Chambers has a six-point lead and we expect that to hold throughout the rest of the night.

"On the Republican side Cliff Hawkins, a man who made a most remarkable turnaround in his fortunes by winning the New York and Wisconsin primaries, is running neck and neck with the former governor from Colorado, Larry Broder. Our projections give the religious leader a very good chance of pulling out ahead of the former governor before the night is out.... In other election news ... "

Losing. Not only was he losing on the political scoreboard, but the scoreboard of his life as well. He looked at Katherine, lying silently, her nose and chin silhouetted against the moonlit room, her eyes staring into space. She had been with him through it all. So long ... so long for a man who never wanted to be tied down. And yet he had been, and somewhere along the way whatever love he'd had for her had been displaced, going from Kat to their daughter, Alexandra. Still he had stayed with her, or rather, she with him. Almost a quarter of a century. A long time for a man like him. But what she'd said was true. He needed her. Now just as he had then.

Lying there, he remembered how it all began. He had, in fact, recounted it to various reporters many times, but what he'd told them and what had actually gone through his mind when they met were two different things. The reporters heard how they'd grown up in the same town, how he'd known her brother and through him Katherine, and how, after being away from Indiana many years, he had met her again. But what they didn't know was how totally captivated Meade had been when he first saw her the night of the fundraiser, how her presence mesmerized him in a way no other woman's had. She had an aura that was far more beautiful, far more alluring than newspaper photographs ever captured. Her skin was like porcelain, yet with a faint pinkness in her cheeks. And her lips ... her eyes ... all aroused something within him that quickened his heartbeat and excited his groin. If anyone had pointed her out on the street and told him who she was, Meade would have called him a liar. If this was the same girl, he'd told himself then, that he had ridden home with so many years ago, he had missed something in between. It was then that Meade knew he had to have her.

And he did.

But he didn't want to marry her. Other people said he did. The campaign people told him if he was going to survive, he would have to get married to clean up his image. Money and support didn't come easily in those days and it took both to win elections. At the time that he became reacquainted with Katherine he had an image so randy that it wasn't just the older, more conservative voters who'd grown weary of him, but a vast cross section of people who could destroy him politically. But he fought his staff's advice, remembering all too well the position his father had been in, one Meade had sworn he would never place himself in. His father had relied so heavily on his mother that it was pathetic. Fired from one job after another for incompetence, he moved his family to Evansville hoping to find employment, but his previous work record was like a communicable disease and nobody would touch him. The family was forced to live off his mother's inheritance until he died, and the old man left enough scars and memories behind to remind his son forever of the price of being dependent. His father had been degraded, belittled, ostracized, and ridiculed for years by his mother. She had slept with his friends and humiliated him before her own. She never let the old man forget where the money came from. It was her food he ate, her bed he slept in, her house he lived in. Otis had thought many times that his father's death must have been a welcome release. The poor bastard had been dependent because he couldn't make it on his own, and Otis swore that it wouldn't happen to him.

But it did.

To save himself and his career, Meade was forced to go after Katherine with marriage in mind and not, as had been his initial inclination, just sex. Her influence and resources in Indiana were considerable and she was the hometown favorite, the darling of his constituency. She held the key to the city—and to him.

He shut his eyes and took a deep breath, wishing sleep would come but knowing it wouldn't. Thoughts of her kept running through his mind. It wasn't, he told himself, that he didn't enjoy Katherine. He guessed he did. She was peaceful and honest, qualities he had missed in his early life, but the sense of his father's failures was still with him. And the fact that his congressional district could have forced a relationship on him simply to make him look respectable still disgusted him. But he had needed her to help him realize his ambitions and she had done it. He was now president of the United States and liked it. She was the First Lady and hated it.

Meade opened his eyes and stared into the darkness. God, why did he ever choose politics in the first place? He had never really liked people, and politics dealt almost exclusively with people. All kinds of them. It was a curious juxtaposition and one he'd never understood. Politics was a life meant for unencumbered men, one that required long hours and very little sleep, but all politicians had the responsibility of a family. You were expected to have a family, or at least a wife. Then, once you were in, you ended up without one. You were completely alone, married to the system.

That's just how Katherine had been for so many years now, he thought. Alone yet married, and married to a man who was married to the system. What a pity to waste a life as beautiful as hers on his dreams. She loved him and, though he didn't really love her, he knew he had to stay with her. She wanted a husband, but could he ever really be one?

Otis Meade knew he couldn't. It was a shame. But for tonight at least, and for the days ahead, he would try to be the husband Katherine wanted, the husband she needed—the husband she would never have.

INTERLUDE

DALLAS/Christ Church Plaza

It was almost too quiet. Between the bottom of the door and the floor there was total darkness—a good omen, the room was empty. He gave the doorknob a slight turn with his gloved hand, but stopped when he realized it was locked. Quietly, but quickly, he produced from his jacket pocket a palm-sized case. He removed the rubber coating surrounding it which had allowed him to pass through the upstairs entrance undetected. He opened the case now and, glancing over an assortment of miniature locksmith's tools, he chose one, hoping it was the right size, and inserted it into the lock. His heart quickened as the lock's chambers made small distinct sounds—sounds that seemed magnified ten times in the stillness of the hallway.

As he continued to work with the lock, he felt his hands perspiring, their wetness absorbed by his pigskin gloves. A trickle of sweat rolled down from the top of his forehead past the crevice between his eyes and the bridge of his nose. It came to rest at the top of his upper lip. His tongue darted up and caught the sweat and he went on working with the lock.

After another minute he turned the doorknob, but still it was locked. His anxiety worsened. For an instant he thought he saw something out of the corner of his eye. He tensed. More sweat rose up on his forehead. He glanced over his shoulder and looked down the sterile tiled hall but saw nothing.

Suddenly he felt it. It had worked. Blinking sweat away from his eyes, he left the instrument in the lock and gently turned the knob. He pushed the door open, stepped inside, took the protruding pick out of the lock, and shut the door behind him. Moving his hand up and down the wall, he found the light switch and flipped it on. At last he could get to work.

Scott Houghlin was an ambitious reporter whose most immediate goal was to elevate himself to the ranks of Woodward and Bernstein. Having been with the *Dallas Times Herald* for just under three years, he had systematically worked his way up from obituaries and live births to the police beat. That wasn't enough. He wanted more and planned to get it. The most obvious way to begin, he had decided, was to use his police beat connections to do investigative work. So far he had been fairly successful. In the past year alone he had penetrated a male prostitution ring, uncovered a drug-smuggling operation, and exposed a small but significant pornography ring. But Houghlin needed something bigger, a story that would keep him out of the police beat forever. And he looked for it in Francesco Gianni.

Gianni was virtually an institution in the South, a man whose syndicate of organized crime stretched from El Paso to Atlanta and whose influence, it was suspected, went even further. Some speculated it went as high as the White House. One thing that everyone agreed on was that no one knew for sure. Which was why Scott Houghlin was now standing in the accounting file room of Christ Church Worldwide's main offices. Several months ago another don, who was bent on exposing—and thereby destroying—Gianni's empire, told Houghlin that if he could establish a direct link between Gianni and just one national figure, other sources—eager to destroy him as well—would step forward. Houghlin listened as the don told him where to begin. Thus he found himself breaking into the accounting file room of Hawkins's offices.

Why? Because, the don said, one of Cliff Hawkins's most loyal financial supporters was a man named Francis Gear, alias for Francesco Gianni. Looking around the room at the rows and rows of file cabinets, Houghlin began his search.

25

Two weeks and five primaries after Cliff Hawkins won Pennsylvania, Tennessee handed him yet another victory, assurance that millions of Americans were throwing their support behind one very determined man. Four months before, the public had been skeptical of Hawkins's entrance into the race. Many still were—and said so loud and clear—but the silent majority of supporters Hawkins had always insisted were out there were now coming forth. Construction workers, housewives, truck drivers, businessmen, factory workers, and many other groups of Americans found a place within the ranks of his supporters. He was one of the nation's most familiar faces, a religious leader trying to enter a world where the experts said he didn't belong.

The experts and his critics had tried to mold him into an image that the American public wouldn't buy. Cliff Hawkins was not the man they claimed he was, was not a megalomaniac bent on reshaping the Constitution, not a demagogue or a fascist, but a loyal citizen who had witnessed the decline of America and had decided to do something about it. His supporters knew, perhaps better than anyone, what Hawkins was talking about, and their votes said so. Now he was beating them all: a former governor, a senator, the columnists, the polls, and the odds. Living proof that even the most extraordinary dreams can still come true.

Hawkins's limousine, turning into the crowded gates of the Christ Church complex, passed hundreds of supporters and journalists and rolled slowly through the grounds toward the lighted plaza, where even larger throngs were awaiting him. AP and UPI had given him Tennessee as early as nine that evening and he'd flown back as quickly as possible for the victory celebration.

As the limousine moved down the long winding drive, the crowds multiplied. The hundreds became thousands and, as the limousine passed, bodies leaned toward Hawkins's window with waving hands and beaming faces. Gordon Wade had told him it would be his most victorious homecoming yet and it was.

Around the brightly lit outdoor stage, where he would speak, streamers were tossed through the air, balloons drifted up into the night sky, placards reading "Hawkins In '92" were everywhere, and nearby a band began playing. He had seen welcomes like this on the night he won Wisconsin and New York, but never one so elaborate. Lights, cameras, people, surrounded him. When the limousine stopped, the crowd encircled it and Hawkins knew he was home. Cheers and squeals of joy could be heard, and he realized there was more than just a church and its followers behind him, there was a city, a people, as well as many states. Soon perhaps a nation . . .

Hawkins smiled at the cameras and turned to Charlotte, who had met him at the airport. He kissed her. When he pulled away, he saw her eyes were moist. He was moved beyond words. He raised one hand to her cheek and kissed her again, wanting to say something, but not knowing what. For the first time in a long while she looked happy. Not pleasant, as she usually looked, but happy—as if this happiness had sprung up from deep within her after being locked away. He clasped her hand in his and smiled, and she smiled back. Then the doors opened and they met the crowds.

"Welcome back!" a local reporter shouted over the cheers and screams.

"Thanks!" he shouted back.

"Do you feel Tennessee's going to help you snowball through the other primaries?"

"I hope so!"

"How 'bout a smile? Look this way, please. That's right . . . great!"

"Here's a campaign hat for you! Can we get you to put it on?"
Hawkins obliged.

"How about a kiss from the missus for AP!"

"What? You'll have to speak up!"

"A kiss! A kiss!" the photographer cried.

"Mrs. Hawkins, how do you feel about this wave of success?"

"Do you expect your husband to get the nomination?"

"Well, I—"

"Reverend, do you know you're leading the West Virginia polls?"

"And what about Nebraska? Isn't that next on your schedule?"

"Reverend, have you thought about your strategy after the nomination? Against the president, that is . . ."

The group moved toward the stage and the throngs pushed closer, squeezing them in.

"Is it true your contributions are at an all-time high?"

"That your volunteers have doubled?"

So it went. Hawkins had come back to a people he'd left in doubt, but who were now full of the same excitement, enthusiasm, and anticipation that he had had for this race from the beginning. Moving rapidly up to the heavily guarded stage, he could see supporters and well-wishers stretching out onto the lawns deep into the night's darkness. Many people were perched on friends' shoulders, some had climbed the huge oaks anchored in the lawns, while still others stood atop their automobiles, all hoping for the best possible view.

When he stepped up to the microphones, there was an explosion of applause and cheers. He felt a lump in his throat and his vision blurred.

"We just wrapped up Tennessee and we're going stronger than ever!" Another round of cheers. "Do you realize," he said almost with an incredulous laugh, "that this is the *ninth* straight primary win we've had?"

The band struck up another fanfare and the crowds went wild. Hawkins threw his head back and laughed with the happiness and delight of a child. Then he grabbed Charlotte by the hand and brought her before the crowds. They roared their approval. The cameras zoomed in and caught them both, with their hands clasped and tears streaming down Hawkins's face. The moment would be frozen on the upcoming covers of *Time* and *Newsweek*.

Charlotte lifted her head from her haven of pillows and scrutinized the clock: seven fifteen. It couldn't be right. She glanced over at the windows, where the spring morning's brilliant sun was pouring in. It had to be at least an hour off. The batteries. Must be the batteries in the clock. Time. A long time. It'd been a long time since they'd replaced them. What was she thinking about—clocks, batteries? She didn't care about the time and neither did Cliff. Not this morning—a well-deserved day off. She shook her head, not believing how conscious she'd become about time since campaigning for him, then rolled on her side, snuggling closer into the depths of his arms. She thought about last night. Ah, she hadn't seen a production like that in years. And it was a production. Like something out of Hollywood. Four months ago, even last month, she would have hated it. Rallies had always seemed like circuses, ridiculous in their noise and the kinds of people they brought out. And the press. Always buzzing around her, asking questions, taking dozens of pictures, trying to get her to say something they could use—either for Cliff *or* against him. She had always feared them. Worried that they would tear up her privacy—which they had—and expose her for what she really was—which, thank God, they hadn't. Then . . . then Cliff would know the truth and everything would be over.

"Reverend, do you consider your wife a problem?"

"Yes, the drinking thing . . . doesn't that contradict your religious beliefs?"

"You did know she drinks, didn't you?"

"Oh, yes, it's true. We've known for some time."

"Actually fell in public once."

"What? You didn't realize she'd been drinking then? Oh, come on, Reverend . . ."

"This surprises you? Shocks you?"

"We do have our sources . . ."

"The flasks. She keeps them hidden from you, prays you won't find them."

"Has for some time."

"Will this affect your marriage?"

"Oh—well, you'll still love her anyway, won't you?"

But her secret was safe. There had been nothing like that last night, and she hoped there wouldn't be. No nasty questions and no insinuations. It had all been glorious, in fact, overwhelming. And they had been kind to her. Hadn't exposed her, subjected her to humiliation. On the morning of his announcement she remembered that Cliff had told her, "I'm not going to fail," and he hadn't. He had made a believer out of her, when just a few weeks ago she was still a nonbeliever.

He had won.

Wisconsin . . .

New York . . .

Pennsylvania . . .

Alabama . . .

D.C. . . .

Then it jolted her.

Georgia!

Texas!

Indiana!

Tennessee!

It was all coming together. My God, she thought, he just might make it! She felt wonderful. Cliff was soaring. He'd taken the risk and was winning! There was the nomination. Then the campaign. Then the election. And . . . the presidency. The *presidency?*

Charlotte giggled. It startled her so that she wasn't sure she had done it. But—there it was again. A silly giggle, like that of a little girl. Heat flushed her cheeks. She smiled to herself and did it again. It tickled her body. She shivered . . . another one?

No, a laugh!

She covered her mouth. Oh, I've got to stifle this. But she couldn't. Laughter and giggles! Childish delight! Tiny little giggles that went from her throat to the tingling nerves of her cheeks. They wouldn't stop. It had been years. Roaring down the country roads outside Austin in college. Her head was bursting with joy! Unrestrained happiness she hadn't felt in ages. Freedom.

Cliff raised his sleepy head. "What's so funny?"

"Nothing, absolutely nothing!" But everything was, and she laughed even harder, doubling up in delight. It was ricidulous. Tears coming from her eyes while she held her sides. The whole bed shook.

"Aren't you the happy one this morning?"

"Oh, Cliff, this is so silly. So unlike me. But, really, I'll be okay."

"Then what are you laughing at?"

"Oh, nothing. Nothing in particular. It's just that . . . well, me, I guess. I feel so . . . oh, I love you. I love you so much. Can you believe that?"

She wiped her eyes and rolled into his arms, still trembling from her brief excursion. She kissed him. Kissed him again and again. His forehead, his nose, eyelids, lips. She clutched him. Needed him. Her love for him was like the love she'd had for him back in college. Unleashed and totally consuming. All she wanted was him—his warmth, his love, his body.

Sometime later, though, while they were still in bed, Charlotte stirred uneasily. Why had she been acting so absurdly? It was juvenile. She giggled again and suddenly felt a sharp pain. The realization was so devastating and sweeping that she shivered in his arms. The pain intensified, the revelations became clearer. She knew why she had been laughing so hard, it hadn't been joy or his success or her love for him. She had been laughing at herself. Laughing at what she had become . . . the wife who went behind her husband's back to drink, hoping secretly that she could survive and find fulfillment with drink because she hadn't found fulfillment with him. Realizing this, she felt great torment.

"Will this affect your marriage?"

"Oh—well, you'll still love her anyway, won't you?"

She couldn't handle this, could she? None of it. She loved him so much, she couldn't handle what was happening. God knows, she wanted to. Oh, how she hated herself! What was wrong with her? Couldn't she see that this would destroy him if he ever found out? Yes . . . oh, yes . . . but . . .

Tears welled up in her eyes. She began crying.

You're so foolish. A foolish little girl!

26

MEXICO/Acapulco

Yesterday it had been perfected. It had taken a week to iron out the details until they were flawless. The site had been surveyed and their observations recorded. The munitions and equipment secured without suspicion, their weapons cleaned, the timing synchronized. Their movements were as automatic as their reflexes. They had given the United States imperialists two weeks to retract their expulsion of Mexican farm workers, and the Americans had not done it. It had taken them another week to prepare, but now they were ready. This was revenge.

The four boats moved swiftly through the calm waters of Acapulco Bay. Disguised as sporting yachts, they drew little attention passing the private boats anchored in the bay. In the leading craft General Carlos Martínez spoke to his crew in the cabin, his voice being transmitted simultaneously to the other boats via high-frequency radio. They couldn't risk the shortwave. In a self-assured voice he told them in his native Spanish: "Tonight is our only chance. To succeed is everything, to fail is your own death. It is entirely up to you, comrades."

The boats picked up speed. Carlos Martínez went up on deck. Gazing out at the magnificent shoreline, he understood why so many Americans came here. So beautiful it was, just like the hotel beyond it.

"It is excellent," he said to a troop that had followed him on deck. "Our chances of survival and success are much better here. More realistic. It will take the authorities time to get from the city. And then . . ." he laughed wickedly, "we will have finished, no?"

Martínez turned from the shoreline to his troop. His head was covered with thick black hair, framing a moustached face with stubbled cheeks. He slapped his hand on the comrades' back and went back into the cabin. "It is time!" he barked. Immediately the men grabbed their shoulder bags and machine guns.

Ashore, not less than a mile from the hotel, five identical jeeps rumbled down one of the few good roads leading to the hotel. As they picked up speed, the Pacific tradewinds rushed a scent of fresh flowers beneath the noses of the occupants, blending with a mélange of insect noises and the whoosh of swaying palm trees now waltzing beneath the tropic's full moon. The caravan's leader, Diego Rosales, glanced at his watch and nudged his driver. "Perfect timing." He picked up a large flashlight resting on the floorboard and turned around, flicking it on and off three times. The message would be relayed to each succeeding jeep: get ready.

Rosales's driver flipped off his headlights and the jeeps coasted silently down the winding drive and past the hotel's main entrance. They were nervous. Passing beneath the jungle of overhanging plants and trees, several made the sign of the cross while their eyes darted about. So far they had seen neither guests nor management. All was well.

The four boats sped toward the shore, quickly passing a few predawn swimmers, who cast them curious stares, and when they hit upon the sand, the men onboard jumped off and waded quickly through the splashing waters toward the beach. General Carlos Martínez was ahead of the small group. He reached the shore first, then he turned and waved his arms. When the last of them had made it ashore, Martínez glanced toward the hotel and began the ascent.

At the top, only yards away from the hotel's lobby, Martínez and his men were shielded from view by an overgrowth of bushes and plants. He pointed toward two couples talking by one of the pools. They would be the first. Complete surprise. Death to the imperialist pigs. With the prowess of a panther Martínez inched forward. He stopped, then he raised his hand in the air and sliced the night in one swift downward movement: attack.

It was 5:45 A.M.

For many of the world's celebrities there is no finer hotel in Mexico than the Acapulco Princess. Sitting on acres of lush tropical oceanfront, it is a half hour's drive from downtown Acapulco. Styled after the Mayan pyramids, its soaring open-air court welcomes the visitor as he steps into the lobby, dazzling him with its magnificent hanging gardens; five swimming pools, six tennis courts, thirty-six holes of golf, horse stables, health spas, backgammon rooms, and clubs. An emaciated Howard Hughes spent his last dying days here watching old movies. Within the hotel's five dining rooms and countless bars are found some of the world's most fun-loving people.

It was indeed unfortunate that the Acapulco Princess was completely occupied that warm summer night. Every room was booked and, even though there wasn't a rocker or movie star in the place, there were plenty of tourists—ordinary people—and on the top two floors of the hotel they were almost all American. Unfortunate, yes, but then that's the way Carlos Martínez and Diego Rosales wanted it to be.

Rosales's driver floored his jeep as he was told, and the following caravan swung around the final curve and braked abruptly. Jumping out of their jeeps, the guerrillas opened fire, sending a hail of machine-gun blasts across the hotel's entrance, splintering glass, lights, and tile. A doorman came running out to investigate the commotion. Rosales opened up his carbine, pelting the man until blood gushed from his mouth, ears, and nose. Just yards away an elderly couple returning from a walk froze in horror at the attack. A guerrilla turned on them and riddled them with bullets as well. The old man danced a deathly spin and, falling, saw his wife's white head explode. A young woman coming out of one of the gardens with her boyfriend screamed and started to run. Another of Rosales's men spun around and pulled his trigger. Her back erupted into bloody flesh, blowing her into her boyfriend's arms. He was next.

Moving through the open-air entrance, Rosales didn't stop to think—his actions were automatic. Carlos would be coming through the back and they had to work fast. Guests cried out in terror as they realized what was happening. Rosales shouted a command in Spanish as his troops stormed past him, and the beautiful open-air court erupted in gunfire.

By the reservations desk a night clerk threw up his hands, thinking it was a robbery. His head was blown off. A large confused assistant dashed behind him for the office door, but was slammed into the wall by gunfire before he could even open it. He slid to the floor, his blood smearing the wall.

When the elevator doors opened, a guerrilla turned and fired automatically, blasting a woman and her husband against the back of the cab. As they lay in a pool of their own blood, other guerrillas rushed in and took the elevator up. They were headed for the top two floors.

Two women strolled through an entrance unaware of the chaos, stared in disbelief, and turned to run. Before they could flee, their tan slender bodies were blistered by a hail of bullets. A violent pandemonium erupted where only moments before a hotel full of people were dancing and drinking and making love to the good life.

Carlos Martínez and his troops crashed through several beach-front entrances into the lobby and found themselves in the midst of their own planned chaos. Martínez shouted some orders, then darted across to Diego Rosales.

"Going okay?"

"Just as planned. They're hitting the nightclubs and the disco now . . ."

In one of the few nightclubs remaining open Rosales's troops surveyed the room, took a fast inventory of their potential victims and released a wave of ammunition. Many of the guests had already overturned tables and chairs and leaped beneath them at the first sound of gunfire in the court, but even then they weren't safe. The tables disintegrated, tile burst from the walls, bottles of liquor shattered, lights exploded, and the mirror balls on the ceiling crashed to the floor.

Outside in the open court Martínez stood with hands on hips, staring up at the walls of the pyramid. Guests who had awakened to the screams and gunfire stumbled to the edge of the balcony railings, looked down at the tangle of bodies and armed men, and jumped back into their rooms slamming the doors behind them. Others, still half-asleep or too confused, lingered too long and Martínez saw them. One gay Brazilian and his American lover, finding the men in fatigues so butch, gave a friendly wave. Martínez eyed them first. His machine gun dropped from his shoulder so rapidly the men didn't have a chance to move before he fired.

Amid screams of anguish, Martínez turned a complete 360 degrees as he emptied his cartridge, then grabbed one of his troops' machine guns and continued firing. A mad, sick delight swept over him as bodies jolted with bullets and tumbled over the railings or fell back out of sight. Blood burst in the air like a fountain and, hearing the screams of death, Carlos Martínez let out a chilling laugh.

They had only begun.

27

"What? . . . Oh, God. How many casualties? . . . What do you mean, you don't know? Can't you do better than that? . . . What? . . . I know that already . . . No, but find out what in God's name is going on there . . . Right, you do that. Let me know the instant you hear anything."

The president put down the telephone and glanced at his watch: 8:30 A.M. That would make it 6:30 Mexico time. The attack was less than forty-five minutes old.

"Something wrong?" asked Katherine.

"Yes, a lot," he snapped.

"What?"

"They've raided a resort hotel down in Mexico. Some fucking terrorists! Christ, of all things . . ."

Katherine placed her hand to her mouth. "A resort hotel? That means . . ."

"Right. At least half the hotel's guests are American."

"Oh, Otis . . ."

While information was sketchy, the Company's closest contacts were in Puerto Vallarta and were flying into Acapulco's Los Amates Airport to get some solid facts. They should have them in the White

House within the next three hours, relayed to the president through the Situation Room's RYBAT cables.

At noon Meade sat behind his desk in the Oval Office and said, "So that's all I know. I'm just waiting till we get something else." He was speaking to two National Security Council advisers, Secretary of State Jeffrey Jong, Howard Hickman, and his press secretary. They were seated in a semicircle around his desk.

"Do we know how many were killed?" asked Secretary Jong.

"No, we hardly know anything. Our RYBAT's late. It should have been cabled fifteen minutes ago, but Situation hasn't heard from them. Nevertheless," said Meade wearily, "I bet it's going to be messy. Preliminary reports have said it was a bloodbath."

"How close have our operatives gotten to the hotel?" asked Hickman.

"I don't know that either. Langley said our task force was supposed to be interviewing some of the people who got away, but I don't know. Whatever they're doing, our people are going to try to get as close to the place as possible. How close it'll be, is up in the air. That's Mexican territory, remember, and we've got to walk softly."

"No clues on their motives?" asked Jong.

"Nothing, we don't even know if the United States is involved or not. Hell, this attack may have been directed toward the Mexicans, the Cubans, or some damn country in South America. We just don't know."

One of the men from the National Security Council said, "But if we're a target, Mr. President, and if they've taken any of those Americans as hostages . . . then, Lord, I hate to even think about it."

"Well, let's not," suggested Hickman. "The last thing we need is speculation."

"True," agreed Meade, "but he's got a point. The possibility is very real. But if they have taken some of our people, I don't know what their motives could be . . ."

"Do you think it could be related to Wallbanks's decision a couple of weeks ago, Mr. President—herding up those migrant workers?" asked Jong.

"I don't doubt it. This whole thing could be directed toward us because of the shit that bastard's pulled. That'd be just my luck, wouldn't it?"

No one spoke, Meade's intercom buzzed. He picked it up and was immediately connected to the Situation Room.

"Yeah? . . . Oh, that so? . . . Thanks, we'll be right down." Meade hung up. He looked at his advisers. "Let's go downstairs, it looks like we've got something."

Walking down the stairs that led from the side door in the Oval Office to the basement, Meade cocked his head toward one of the Security Council advisers behind him and said, as they descended, "Jarvis, you might just come in handy, you know? I understand you've studied these terrorists before haven't you? Worked in Beirut, wasn't it?"

"Tel Aviv."

"Whatever," Meade grumbled, not giving a damn where the man worked.

For all that had been written about the Situation Room and the speculation about what went on in the place, it was in reality nothing more than an ordinary paneled office, cluttered with desks representing the various armed services and small intelligence computers and communications equipment capable of receiving the security network's most advanced reports as they were filed. When the president walked in, the room snapped to attention.

"What've you got?" asked Meade greeting a military aide.

"Some bad news, I'm afraid. The United States is involved."

"How do you know?"

"Our people in Acapulco set up some microwave eavesdropping equipment at a neighboring hotel, the Pierre Marqués, and aimed it at the Princess. They've picked up some conversations between what appear to be the terrorists and guests. They kept repeating the United States by name, but we couldn't figure out all they were saying."

"I should've known," said Meade. "God only knows what they're after. Did we catch anything about motives?"

"No, sir, I'm afraid not."

"How about the Americans down there. Are they safe?"

"We don't know. From the converations we picked up, it sounds like more than a few were shot."

Meade was visibly irritated. "Well, for godsakes, when are you people going to find out something?"

"As soon as we can, Mr. President," the aide said, somewhat flustered, "but until they communicate with us—if they do—it's going to be hard. At present they've got guerrillas patrolling the grounds, explosives wired throughout the gardens and beach areas, and sharpshooters on the roof. Until they want to talk, there's not much we can do but wait. The Mexican Federales tried to fly a chopper overhead, but they shot him down."

"A bazooka," added another aide.

"What've they got? A whole army up there?" snapped Meade. Both aides flushed.

Secretary of State Jong tried to relieve the situation. "Do you know who they are? Or how many men they have?"

"We've identified at least two of their leaders and have a conservative estimate on their number."

"Oh?" said Meade.

"Yes, sir. One of the men is Jesus Carlos Martínez. He is a self-appointed general and belongs to a radical wing of the National Action Party. We don't know about his men, but we assume they're in his faction too. He's also got a partner." He looked down at a sheet of paper before him. "One Diego Rosales, a Mexican national, but at current there's no information available on him either. All we know is both are very anti-American terrorists. This coming, of course, from the file the Federales have on Rosales and Jesus Martínez."

Meade was pissed. He glared at the aide and asked, *"Jesus?* What kind of name is that? Is he some sort of religious nut or something? Heaven forbid a Mexican Cliff Hawkins . . ."

Secretary Jong again broke in. "Mr. President, I think he's mispronouncing the name. In Spanish it's 'Hey-zoos' not 'JEE-zus.' "

Meade rolled his eyes. "They're still weird names. Christ, what a mess." He turned and glanced around the room, then another question came to mind. "How many men do they have?"

The aide looked down at his sheet of paper and said, "Our RYBAT says at least thirty-two and that's being conservative."

"Thirty-two. . . ?" Meade said, appalled.

"Must be a dedicated bunch," his press secretary remarked.

"No wonder they could storm the place. Have you ever seen it? Looks like one of those huge Mexican pyramids, but a helluva lot nicer. With our luck they're probably right at the height of their season."

"Actually they're not, but the hotel was fully booked," said the aide.

Meade turned to leave. "If there's nothing else, we're going. Keep me informed at all times."

"Yes, sir," he said saluting.

They were back in the Oval Office and Meade was leaning back in his leather chair, feet on the desk. "Well, I guess there's nothing more we can do about this thing except wait, right Jarvis? You're the expert."

"That's right, waiting is our only alternative."

"So, we'll wait and just hope those idiots decide to talk before they kill off the whole damn bunch."

'It's really rather intriguing," said Secretary Jong philosophically. "I mean, this is such a radical diversion from the norm. It has to be something big."

"Oh, it's something big all right," sighed Meade. "That's what scares me. I warned Wallbanks three weeks ago that something like this might happen, but did he listen? Does he ever listen? Bastard! To deliberately ignore the pleas of the president of the United States just to save his own political ass is unconscionable and you better believe the people are going to be made fully aware of this."

"But, Mr. President," said his press secretary, "we don't know that's their reason for storming the hotel. It could be any number of things."

"Well, I'd put money on it that it's got to do with those humiliating, absolutely appalling witch-hunts down in Texas."

"What are we going to tell the press?" asked Hickman. "They've been running around here since early this morning . . ."

"Didn't you cancel the regular briefing?" Meade asked his press secretary.

"Yes, sir. But that won't hold them off. Howard's got a point—what do we tell them?"

"Nothing. We don't know anything."

So they kept things vague.

NEBRASKA/Lincoln

Senator Jackson Chambers's limousine pulled away from the Nebraska Wesleyan University campus and flowed quickly into the Fifty-sixth Street traffic.

"Did we do all right back there?" asked the Democratic candidate.

"Okay," replied one of his aides. "Better than we'd expected for that kind of audience."

Chambers seemed pleased with the news. Any politician challenging the president for the nomination as successfully as Chambers was would be pleased by signs of progress. After all, they were ahead and knew it. If matters continued as they had been, it looked as though they would stay ahead and steal Meade's nomination right out from under his nose. Yes, Chambers was definitely pleased. He had worked long and hard over the years to get this far.

"What's next?" he asked his scheduling director.

"Veterans Hospital."

"Great," he sneered. "Just what I need—old men drooling on me for the cameras."

"I wouldn't worry about it unless they die on you," the director joked and everyone in the limousine laughed, particularly Chambers.

"No kidding," he snorted. "What luck. Sometimes I almost feel sorry for the president. Seems like all he ever has is trouble. And that, fortunately, is what's going to put us in the White House."

"Take this thing in Acapulco, that's going to be something to watch," said his press secretary.

Chambers frowned. "Acapulco? Frank, what are you talking about?"

"You didn't hear?" another aide asked.

"How can I hear if you don't tell me anything?" he growled. "I've got to be the only candidate running that gets news after the rest of the public!"

"What?"

"We just heard it ourselves. Terrorists seized a hotel down in Acapulco last night. There are a lot of Americans trapped in the place."

Chambers raised his eyebrows. "Did they say how many?"

"Maybe two hundred, they're not sure."

"Two hundred?" It took him a few seconds to comprehend the significance of the number. "Did they say why they raided the place?"

"No, but everyone's speculating it's connected to all that crap the Texas governor's been giving those Mexicans. Others are saying it's got to do with Meade's policies toward the government of Mexico. Could be a combination of both."

"Ummmm," Chambers purred reflectively. "If that's true, something like this could get real sticky."

"Real sticky," his other aide said. "Remember the American embassy in Tehran?"

"Right, and then even further back was the Mayagüez incident . . ."

"Things like this can always go either way politically," his press secretary said. "Depending on what the president does . . . if he has to do anything at all."

"Yeah," Chambers mused, "but one way or another I'll bet you we can use something like this against him. That is, if we play our cards right. Let's see what happens."

TEXAS/Dallas

Cliff Hawkins stood on the steps of their mansion, saying good-bye to Charlotte before hitting the campaign trail once again.

"You'll be joining me in two days, right?" he asked her.

"Right," she nodded.

He looked at her. Her response had been perfunctory, as if she didn't really want to go at all.

"You feeling okay, hon?"

"Of course."

"Good," he said, satisfied. He kissed her and said, "I love you."

"I love you too."

She watched him go down the steps and ease into his limousine, then gazed as the long black automobile rolled down the driveway, moved past the guardhouse, and then turned out from the compound, its taillights blinking a final good-bye.

After the electronically operated gates had closed, she stood alone on the steps, looking out at the vast front lawn of their mansion. She felt a twinge of guilt at having lied to him. She wasn't all right. For the first time since the campaign began, she realized just how real the possibility was of Cliff's getting the Republican nomination. The support that was gathering among the ranks of the party and the voters was at once overwhelming and frightening. The fact that he had been able to transcend the realm of religion into the realm of politics so quickly was even more frightening. What did the people want from him? What were they expecting of him? They had turned so quickly from opposition to support. It scared her. Cliff's success had made them both more vulnerable than before. People were giving him more, but they expected more too. From him—and from her. Where did Charlotte Hawkins fit into all of this? Her life was becoming a fishbowl . . .

Yes, she said to herself, pouring a scotch in the library, it's becoming a fishbowl. It's worse than I thought it could be, and it won't get better. The more visible Cliff becomes and the more he continues to win, the worse it's going to get. I've got to be able to handle that . . . got to be able to accept that . . . but, O God, I'm frightened. She drained her scotch and poured another and then another. There are millions of people out there! Millions! They're watching me. Everywhere. Everywhere I turn they've got their eyes on me. Making comments. Taking pictures . . . writing down thoughts . . . every move I make . . . every single move . . .

Charlotte shook her head, tears coming to her eyes.

What am I going to do?

28

Information was still vague the next morning. Meade had waited throughout the afternoon and into the evening for further word from the Company's operatives in Mexico, but there were no substantial reports. The conversations still came in in bits and pieces over the microwave surveillance they'd set up, but the voices were too jumbled with crying, screaming, and occasional gunshots to be intelligible. Meade had spoken with President Portillo last night and, while Portillo was apologetic and full of promises, Meade gave the Mexican president's grip on the situation a poor rating. It was quickly building into a crisis and Meade knew it. Not knowing the terrorists' motives or why they hadn't issued a communiqué was as taxing as the knowledge that the lives of possibly two hundred Americans were in their hands. Meade had never had a crisis of this dimension before and sure as hell he didn't need one now. The campaign, his presidency, Gianni, Maria, Katherine . . . a hundred streams flowing into a great river of darkness, a river that Meade knew could easily drown them. And all they could do was play a waiting game . . . wait for a communiqué . . . a movement . . . a sign . . . anything!

By noon of the second day there was still nothing.

MEXICO/Acapulco

Carlos Martínez pointed to a pretty sandy-haired American girl with petite breasts and a deep tan and said in Spanish, "That's the one. I want her."

The girl saw Martínez pointing at her. She was filled with terror. She had lived in fear for the past thirty hours, like everyone else crowded in the top two floors of the hotel, not understanding a word being said, not knowing who would be next to die or whether they would ever get out alive.

A soldier breathed down on her face. "Get up," he said in broken English, "Generale Martínez want you."

The girl was crying, she didn't want to go, she begged them not to take her. Other guests, huddled in the suite, looked on with sympathy.

"Get up!" he shouted, jerking her to her feet.

"No, please! I have a husband! . . . I . . ."

The soldier shoved her toward Martínez, who grabbed her by the arms and smiled.

"Eric!" she cried out looking back at her husband.

"Angie!"

Martínez, annoyed, whipped out his revolver and aimed it at the young man's forehead. Eric froze and the newlyweds stared at each other hopelessly. Five others from this room had been killed. He watched them lead her away.

They took her to one of the more luxurious suites and sat her down at a desk. She had been there for the past hour with Martínez, Diego Rosales, and three of their men. A tape recorder lay on the desk.

"Read it again!" snapped one of the men.

Angie broke down. "I've read it twenty times! Isn't that enough? Please, I just want to . . ."

Rosales grabbed her hair and snapped her head backward. Her eyes were red-rimmed, her mouth was open, but her crying made no sound. She was beyond that. He shoved her head forward, jerked it back again, and slapped her furiously.

"Motherfucking bitch! Cunt! Read it again!"

"Please . . ." she begged, "I just . . . want . . . to . . . see . . . my . . . husband . . ."

Rosales's hand moved so swiftly Angie didn't see it. Blood trickled from her nose and mouth. "Fuck your husband! You read or you both die!"

She took the piece of paper and began to read.

"Very good, play that back," Martínez said in Spanish to Rosales. He did and they listened to the entire message. "It's just right, no?

"Plenty of emotion on this thing. Shows them we mean business." Rosales agreed.

"Good," said Martínez, "tell that bitch we're through."

Angie let out a sigh of exhausted relief.

Martínez turned to one of his men. "Rolando, go get your men and deliver this to the journalists up on the frontage road. Tell 'em it's an official statement."

Rolando took the cassette and left the suite, shutting the door behind him.

Angie began crying again. "Can I leave now? You said we're through."

Martínez and Rosales exchanged glances with the other men.

Angie realized something was wrong. Now, more terrified than ever, she said, "Please ... you said ... I'd be able to ... leave ... I've done everything you asked ..."

"Not everything," Rosales said, jerking her up from the desk's chair and standing her before the men. He looked at her, then spit in her face. She cried out when he ripped off her blouse. The men howled in excitement as Rosales threw her on the bed, ignoring her kicking and clawing. The other men held her while Rosales pulled down her pants.

"No ... please ... I haven't done anything to you ... I ..." One of the men covered her mouth with his hand. She could taste its foulness. Someone stuffed a pillow under her buttocks and she could see Rosales at the foot of the bed stroking his stiff cock and eyeing her spread legs. Tears filled her eyes and she turned her head away. On one side of the bed another of the men unzipped his pants and tugged at his member. On the other side Carlos Martínez was laughing at her as he fumbled with his own zipper. Then they all laughed together. All but Angie.

Rosales said, "The fun's only beginning, bitch ...." And he was in her.

NEBRASKA/Lincoln

Cliff had told Charlotte they were giving Larry Broder a run for his money, and they were—but not in Nebraska. They didn't need to. Dynamic, unabashed in his conservatism, and completely in accord with Nebraskans religiously, Hawkins had made a splash in American politics unlike anything they'd seen. As his support grew after his first primaries, Nebraskan voters liked him more and more. They were aware of his controversial image, and some were worried openly by his power and popularity as a religious leader, but they reminded themselves that the people who criticized him so vehemently were, for the most part, the same people whose liberal feminist homosexual communist smut-peddling pornography attitudes had helped bring the country to the position it was now in. They were God-fearing people. They had witnessed America's decline in prestige and power, had seen the reality of the Soviet threat, and knew that people like Otis Meade and Larry Broder and Sheldon Roberts weren't going to do a damn thing about it. These voters believed Ronald Reagan had been God's gift to America, fondly remembered John Wayne's stand on Vietnam as the right one, and still believed Nixon got a bum rap.

Hawkins had known the state would be his even before they flew into Lincoln's Municipal Airport, but he wasn't going to take any chances.

His first stop at the state capitol got excellent media coverage and went off flawlessly. Party leaders and top-ranking legislators—like so many others who three or four months ago wouldn't even have met him at their city's airport, let alone their offices—now greeted him with a hand and a smile in front of the cameras. Hawkins took advantage of this warm reception, milking it for all he could.

His second stop, at the home of William Jennings Bryan, was made simply out of historical courtesy. He toured the building quickly, and the usually leery press corps traveling with him kept their questions light and frivolous. It looked as if the swing through the state was going to be a snap.

It was.

29

WASHINGTON/The White House

The communiqué that Rosales and Martínez sent the White House
was explicit, interrupted only by Angie's crying. The terrorists de-
nounced the self-serving, politically motivated fascist actions recently taken by the state of Texas and the American people with
regard to the Mexican migrant workers and illegal aliens living in
the United States. They were particularly incensed over Governor
Slim Wallbanks's roundup and incarceration of every Mexican migrant worker or alien he and the Immigration and Naturalization
Service could find. Wallbanks's actions were a climax to a succession of aggressions against the Mexican people by the governor,
which only furthered their belief that he was a vicious and self-serving bigot. In retaliation they were holding 213 Americans, to be released only when Wallbanks called off his roundup. If the governor
refused, they would hold President Otis Meade personally responsible for the lives of all concerned. The time limit for a response was
twenty-four hours. After that, or on any attempt to enter the hotel or
sabotage these demands, all concerned would be immediately executed.

Standing behind a podium in the press room, the president's press
secretary faced a barrage of popping flashbulbs and a sea of White
House correspondents.

". . . I repeat, the president can in no way condone the actions that have taken place in Acapulco within the past forty-eight hours. He feels that placing the lives of innocent people in danger as Jesús Carlos Martínez and Diego Rosales have done is completely uncalled for and totally irresponsible. He has listened carefully to the communiqué and is at this moment trying to contact the governor of Texas . . ."

"What do you mean you can't locate him?" Meade howled into his telephone.

"I'm sorry, Mr. President," the White House operator said, "but he's been on a fishing trip in Canada for the past three days."

"*Canada?* Do you realize how many heads of state have phoned me within the past hour? You put me through to him if you have to go through Timbuktu!"

"But, Mr. President, his staff said he can't be reached—he's up in some uninhabited region of the—"

"Uninhabited? What about the lieutenant governor? Get him on the phone!"

"I've tried, Mr. President, but he's on a yacht off Saint Croix with the Texas state attorney general."

"Jesus H. Christ! Doesn't anybody down there work?"

"The governor's staff said they're all gone because the legislature's out of session. Would you like me to keep trying Saint Croix?"

"Yes, and, when you get hold of him, let me know."

Meade hung up. He looked at Howard Hickman. "They can't find any of them. Can you believe it? Everyone's left the state!"

"I believe it."

"Has everyone arrived for the meeting?"

"Yes, sir. They're all waiting for you in the Cabinet Room."

Once Meade's top foreign affairs and domestic advisers were assembled, it took them less than twenty minutes to decide what to do. If the governor or lieutenant governor couldn't be reached, the president would announce a halt to the roundups himself by executive order and worry about the constitutionality of it later. They had all heard Angie's tape and were sickened by it. They agreed something had to be done but their agreement wasn't reached without considerable discussion.

Secretary of State Jeffrey Jong, a rather frumpish-looking Asian-American scholar, wanted an extended deadline to consider other possibilities. He told the president he thought they were rushing things.

"You've got to," said Meade. "You don't play games with these people. They set the deadlines, not us."

"I realize that, but I wish we had some other alternatives. I don't particularly like overriding another man's policies—even if he is Slim Wallbanks. And I don't like us being forced into anything by a bunch of fanatics. Making concessions to these people will set a precedent for future retaliations like this, and that's just what we don't need."

"I agree," said Jarvis, one of Meade's National Security advisers.

"So do I," added the attorney general. "And Jeffrey picked up a good point about overriding Wallbanks's policies. Ever since the laws were changed in '89, superseding a governor's state actions could place you in a precarious position if you go ahead and invoke executive order or presidential decree or whatever you plan on calling it. I think you should be aware of that."

Meade tapped a pencil impatiently on the long cabinet table. "I'm aware of it, and it's not as though I haven't given it some thought. But I've got 213 Americans down there with guns pointed at their heads and, unless we do something, the Mexican police are going to be dragging them out in body bags. Now I've got half the leaders in the world on my ass to do something and the man that caused all this can't even be found! So, unless they find him or his lieutenant governor by midnight tonight, I'm going to retract this idiotic witch-hunt of his."

Meade folded his arms and waited for their reactions. Then, as an afterthought, added. "I mean, you all heard the tape. It's disgusting! We . . . we don't have a choice."

"What do you think Wallbanks will say?" the attorney general asked.

Meade's face grew flush. "I don't give a damn what he says! Just let him try to raise a flap about this. That sonofabitch's to blame for this anyway, and don't think for a minute he's not going to have some explaining to do when he gets back. Oh, just wait until they get him before a Senate committee!"

Secretary Jong threw up his hands. "All right then, I move that we all back the president's decision. It's hard to believe—a national crisis erupts over some migrant workers. Astounding!"

"It's not astounding," said Meade. "It's fucking ridiculous. Look what happened over a bunch of diplomats in Iran twelve years ago."

*   *   *

After Otis Meade and Katherine finished dinner that evening in the President's Dining Room on the second floor of the residence, he pushed his chair back and walked over to the wall phone. He glanced at his watch: eight ten.

"Anything?" he asked the operator, when she came on the line.

"No, sir. We're ringing Saint Croix every few minutes, but the lieutenant governor's still out on his yacht with the Texas attorney general. They've sent a messenger out by boat, though . . ."

"All right," he said dejectedly, "keep trying."

When he hung up, Katherine was standing behind him. Meade felt her arms encircle his waist and her body press against his. He turned around.

"They still haven't reached either of them, darling?"

"No, neither one."

"Well, if you've got to retract his actions, you've got to. There's no use letting it bother you. You've survived worse times than this. You'll get through this too."

"I know that," he said, not at all comforted by her presence.

"Then why not try to forget about these things for a while? We're through with dinner, let's slip away and . . ."

Meade pulled away and turned around. "Kat, please. Don't ride me about that now. I'm not in the mood. I've got too many other things on my mind."

She looked hurt. "I'm not riding you. I just thought perhaps you'd like to . . ."

"No," he said, heading toward the door. He didn't want to make love to her and thought he might as well quit trying to fool both of them. For three weeks now he'd played the role of caring husband. He'd slept with her, taken meals with her, even exercised with her. But it wasn't working. The shoes he was wearing in this marriage were getting more pinched by the hour and he'd be damned if he would keep it up much longer. Not that he was going to do anything drastic, just that he'd worn the other shoes far too long . . .

Minutes after mighnight, Meade's self-appointed deadline, the telephone rang in the penthouse, where he had retreated. Meade rarely ventured up there, leaving it to Katherine for her teas and press interviews. But tonight he found himself longing to escape from the lower residence and the confines of his life there. Katherine must have assumed he was working diligently in his study, but that was fine, let her think what she wanted.

"Yes?" Meade said.

"I'm sorry, Mr. President. The people in Saint Croix still haven't reached the lieutenant governor, and the roads up to the region in Canada where Governor Wallbanks is fishing have been washed out."

"Shit. All right, connect me with my press secretary's office."

Meade, drumming his fingers on a small table next to his chair, regarded the room—simple, octagonal in shape, and splashed with a rainbow of delicate cheerful colors.

"Hello," his press secretary answered.

"Listen, those sonofabitches are still on their damn vacations. So go ahead with our plan and call the thing off. Also give Hickman a call. I want him to keep me updated throughout the night, understand?"

"Yes, sir. And I'll tell Howard. He's been down here with the press for the past couple of hours."

Meade almost hung up when he heard, "Oh, Mr. President?"

"Yes?"

"I think you've made a courageous move."

"Well, we had no choice, did we?"

NEBRASKA/Omaha

Half a continent away Cliff Hawkins was seated on the edge of his hotel bed, telephone in hand, talking with Charlotte. Hawkins had been afraid from the sound of her voice that he had awakened her, but she didn't mention it, so neither did he.

"Sorry this is such a late call, but we just got in. I've been in the studio for the past hour recording some new television spots Coco wanted me to do."

"It's okay . . ." she said. And then, a bit louder than usual for her, she added, "I was just getting ready for bed. You know, have to get my sleep for you! Flying up tomorrow and all." Her voice had a giddy ring to it.

This didn't sound like her. Cliff coughed, disturbed. "Ummm . . . are you all right?"

"Yes, of course, darling," she said quickly. Almost too quickly. "Why do you ask?"

Embarrassed, realizing it must be his own fatigue playing tricks on him, he said, "I'm just tired, that's all. We've had a rough day."

"I . . ." her voice suspended, and then she cleared her throat. "Well, how are things otherwise?"

"Nebraska's beautiful as far as farmland. More than I've ever seen in my life. But you'll see it tomorrow when you fly up." He was going to say more, but didn't really know what to say. Something was off and it had nothing to do with fatigue. Charlotte wasn't herself. There was a separation between them that went beyond mere physical distance.

The brief pause was interrupted by a muffled sound that Hawkins could have sworn was crying.

"Charlotte, are you sure you're okay?"

"I'm fine!" she chirped.

But he knew she wasn't and, for a long time after he had hung up, Hawkins tried to unravel the puzzle of that brief but revealing impasse. Something was wrong. He couldn't put his finger on it, didn't even know what it was, but it was there. He could feel it. Now. And the other day as he was leaving. On the morning of his Tennessee victory, three weeks ago, when she had laughed and cried. A year, ten years, twenty years ago . . .

There was a problem.

What perplexed him the most was whether the problem lay with her or with him.

He sat on the edge of the bed, staring at the telephone. He had almost asked her the one question he knew he should never ask her— the one question whose answer he didn't want to hear. He hadn't asked her in almost twenty-five years . . . but he could have sworn it sounded as if she had been . . . drinking. Instinct told him it wasn't beyond reason. Not with the pressure she was under, they were both under. And yet . . . she just couldn't be. Not after so many many years.

No. Not now. Not when I need her.

Hawkins shook his head, not wanting to consider it further. She had sounded unusual tonight, true, but that didn't mean she'd been drinking. He knew Charlotte would never stop surprising him . . . that for all he knew about her there was still a great deal he didn't know. But he couldn't think or concern himself with what he didn't know. Right now he knew that Charlotte wasn't ready. Not for him, or the campaign, or even herself. But the campaign couldn't wait—they needed her.

TEXAS/Dallas

Charlotte fell back into one of the Queen Anne chairs in front of the fireplace in their bedroom, letting the telephone fall from one hand, hitting the carpet, and her highball glass fall from the other. Ice scattered like dice, but she didn't care. She was too drunk to care. She put her hands to her face and cried. He had to know. There was no way he couldn't. There were too many awkward pauses, too many rambling sentences. What could she do? She couldn't face it anymore. She didn't like it out there. She didn't like the attention, the questions, the obligations. It was getting to a point where simply shaking the crowds' hands terrified her. The people didn't like her, she could tell. Some probably hated her. They hated her and, because they hated her, they were capable of doing bad things to her. They were vicious. They were vengeful. They were slowly moving against her. Little by little they were coming after her . . .

"No!" Charlotte cried out to no one but herself. "What am I saying? What's happening to me? They're not that way . . . they love us! They love Cliff . . ." She doubled up crying. "They just can't be . . . that bad . . ."

WASHINGTON/The White House

It was two in the morning and Meade sat restlessly in a rose velvet chair, flipping through intelligence reports while his mind drifted back to the crisis at hand. It had been almost two hours since they'd announced a halt to Wallbanks's roundups. Although most of America was asleep or going to bed at this hour, the announcement brought a flood of supportive telephone calls and telegrams to the White House. But there had been no acknowledgment from the Acapulco Princess. No movement from the hotel had been observed and no further communiqués released.

Why?

Meade had done as they'd demanded sixteen hours before their deadline. So why the delay? Why hadn't they at least given word that they were aware of Meade's actions? Nobody knew. Not the Company . . . nor the Mexican Federales.

Meade threw down the intelligence reports and rubbed his eyes. He didn't feel well.

WEST VIRGINIA/Morgantown

Two hours later, after the president had finally gone to bed, Senator Jackson Chambers arrived at his hotel following a late grueling flight from Nebraska. What he wanted more than anything was a tranquilizer and some sleep. He was a nervous wreck, had been throughout the entire flight. Airplanes always affected him this way and the early morning hours certainly didn't help matters.

They moved through the hotel lobby, heading toward the elevators accompanied by a bedraggled and cranky press corps. One of Chambers's advance men came up, greeted the candidate, then stepped into the elevator with him and his aides and Secret Service people. As soon as the doors closed, the man turned and said, "Senator, we just got word from Washington about the situation in Acapulco . . ."

At first it appeared as though Chambers hadn't heard him. Then he gave the aide a quizzical stare. "Acapulco?" he said, uncomprehending. "What in the hell are you talking about? We're in West Virginia, right?" He turned to his Secret Service, "We're in West Virginia, aren't we? This isn't Acapulco."

Everyone in the elevator exchanged glances. They knew flights did this to him.

"The siege in Acapulco," the advance man reminded him.

"Right," Chambers said finally. "So what about it?"

"We just got word that the terrorists have decided to go ahead and release the hostages."

"When?"

"Now. Seventy-five people every thirty minutes."

Someone else in the elevator said, "No one thought they would. Meade supposedly went to bed a couple of hours ago still not knowing . . ."

"Well," Chambers sneered, "he knows now, doesn't he?"

". . . at least they're being released. We've got to give him credit for that."

"Right," said Chambers. Everyone remained silent. When the elevator doors opened, he added, "I'm glad to know the president can do something for this nation besides screwing it."

30

WASHINGTON/The White House

The telephone rang—again.

The president took a deep breath, then rolled over into a mound of pillows and tangled sheets, trying to ignore it. It was useless. The Signal Corps never gave up. He turned back on his side, and on the third ring, through a glaze of early morning lethargy, peered at the clock on his nightstand: 5:47 A.M. It was less than two hours since they had phoned him from the Situation Room telling him the hostages were being released. He'd slept maybe a total of three hours since yesterday.

The phone rang again.

"Yes?"

"Mr. President, this is Lieutenant Mawson down in Situation. We've got some trouble."

Meade snapped out of his stupor and sat up. "What is it, Lieutenant?"

"We got word from Acapulco that Martínez and Rosales haven't released the last fifty Americans."

"Why?"

"They've issued another communiqué"

Meade reached for his robe and slippers. "Oh, Christ. What are they waiting for?"

"They're now demanding that the United States reestablish the Mexican agricultural import quotas to pre-October 1989 levels."

"The pre-October levels?"

"Yes, sir."

He'd heard him all right. "Are they crazy?"

"Seems that way, sir."

Meade tightened his robe and sat down on his bed, letting the words sink in . . . pre-October quotas. "Damn them!" he said after a moment. "I should've known things wouldn't be so simple. What other information do you have? Have they given us a new time limit, Lieutenant? Or are they just going to blow the hell out of our people without giving us some more time to think?"

"No, sir. They've given us a limit. Same as before—twenty-four hours."

"All right, Mawson, thank you for calling." He hung up.

So we've finally got a crisis after all.

Howard Hickman stepped into the Oval Office. The president sat behind his massive desk, absorbed in a stack of papers. Normally Hickman would have entered without hesitation, but this morning he sensed an eerie stillness in the room, so he crept in. Meade brought a powerful presence to the Oval Office that Hickman believed no other president had since Theodore Roosevelt. It lingered, told you he had been there even though the room was empty. But the stillness today was like the eye of a hurricane. Meade looked up from his papers.

"Mr. President," Hickman said.

Meade removed his reading glasses and waved him in. "Sorry you had to come in so early this morning, but . . ."

"I'm glad you called."

Meade fumbled for his pipe, found it, and began packing a blend. "Did you stop by the Situation Room yet and get a copy of the communiqué?"

"No, sir. I came straight up. I'm not even sure I want to."

Meade lit up and inhaled. "Well, you might as well. Everyone in God's creation is going to know about it. Here," he said, tossing him a manila folder, "go ahead and glance over it."

Hickman picked up the folder and opened it. Inside was one photocopy of the communiqué, nothing else. He tried to read as Meade explained.

"They want everything, Howard. The whole fucking world.

Everything that could ruin us. They're playing with the lives of our citizens like a Monopoly game for a bunch of tomato and lettuce crops."

Hickman looked up from the communiqué "You're not kidding, are you?" He looked down at the paper. *"Pre-October '89* quotas? They can't be serious. That would mean . . . would mean the quotas would be—"

"—a full 100 percent."

Hickman sighed and handed the folder back to him. "Do you realize what kind of position that—of course you do. That import restriction is—"

"—our only leverage. If we lost that, we've lost our oil pipeline. But they need those agri-dollars just as we need our oil. Hell, ten years from now they won't need to send us any produce goods. They'll have more oil revenues then they can keep track of. But if the balance is tilted either way, we might as well call it quits."

"This thing is dynamite," Hickman said.

"It scares the hell out of me. Dealing on this isn't going to be half as easy as it was on the other thing last night. This," Meade said, waving his pipe, "is another ball game. There are so many factors involved now."

Hickman agreed.

"Not just that last bunch of hostages down there, but hundreds of things. Voters, farmers, and the negotiations. Christ, Howard, what are we going to do?"

But before Hickman could answer, Meade was already on the phone to the National Security Council members.

Two hours later the NSC was gathering in the Cabinet room, its members taking their chairs to wait for the president. The tension was palpable, and the thoughts running through their minds were synonymous with the president's. They had a formidable crisis on their hands. A situation as alarming as the seizure of the American embassy in Tehran or the Cuban missile crisis now confronted them. They had prayed something like this would never happen in this administration. They knew they were being challenged on major American policy. The secretary of agriculture had phoned each of them personally. Not only were the lives of American citizens at stake, but hundreds of millions of dollars in agricultural revenues for thousands of American farmers as well. With the economy what it was, the secretary said, such a rise of import quotas could cripple small farming communities across the nation indefinitely. And what about the hostages? Even as the members waited for the president, they could sense the conflict before them. How could they save those people and American farm interests as well? Meeting the demands would save the hostages, but at the same time would kill a large share of the nation's farm interests. But ignoring those demands would mean death for the captive Americans.

Someone said, "They've finally put this administration on the line. This could be a turning point, a big turning point."

"Yes," another said, "but which way?"

When Meade came in five minutes later with Howard Hickman, the official White House photographer, and the director of the CIA at his heels, everyone rose. Meade waved them back to their seats.

"Gentlemen, you need no explanation for being here. I presume you've heard the latest news and have all had preliminary briefings. I'm going to ask Frank to elaborate a bit on the situation and then we'll have your comments and questions."

Meade turned to CIA Director Frank Phillips. "Well, for those of you who may have missed what was supposed to have happened down there last night, we assumed the Mexicans were going to release their hostages as they promised. However, at approximately three thirty this morning their time, five thirty our time, after all but fifty of the hostages had been released, Martínez sent the journalists another communiqué . . ."

During the fifteen minutes Phillips spoke, he passed out copies of Martínez's demands, explained various points in the wording and their possible implications, and reiterated the seriousness of the situation they were in. But he found himself unable to offer any solutions. All he could say was, "I can't emphasize to you enough just how dangerous these idiots are. We've already seen that in their last communiqué, and you know their modus operandi—they think of killing as casually as they think of urinating."

An hour later they were still floundering, without an answer, a plan, a decision. Secretary of State Jeffrey Jong had just finished a long soliloquy on subversive foreign interests manipulating American policy. He directed his last words to the president himself. "So I don't think we should give these bloodthirsty bastards a thing, not one, Mr. President. Those import restrictions are between the United States and official Mexico—which these renegades are not. We should do something, but not what they want."

"Jeffrey's absolutely right," said Meade's hawkish deputy defense secretary from the other end of the table. "They're blackmailing us and we shouldn't stand for it."

The vice president said, "I don't like any of it. But the situation stands as it is, whether we like it or not, and right now I don't see any alternatives."

The president nodded wearily. "That's the Catch-22 of this thing, isn't it? It's more than simply deciding our course of action, it's deciding what our course of action is. Who wins, who loses. How much we'll take and who's going to take it and who isn't. That's what it ultimately comes down to, right?"

They said nothing, thinking perhaps he wasn't through. "Right?" he thundered.

"I'm afraid so, Mr. President," the chairman of the joint chiefs of staff said. "And in the end, I think we all agree that the decision is going to have to be yours."

Meade stared at him, surprised by his candor, but realizing he had spoken for them all.

By noon the president had decided. He had recessed the National Security Council meeting until later in the afternoon and was lunching privately with Hickman in the Oval Office. The two of them had been skirting the issue for almost a half hour when a lag in the conversation finally prompted Meade to say, "Howard, I just can't do it."

"Do what?"

"Give in. I just can't give them what they want and raise our import quotas."

"I was afraid of that."

"Why?"

Hickman rubbed his face, "Because it makes whatever we do that much harder. We're already in a no-win situation with the pluses and minuses balanced, but the minuses are going to weigh much more heavily against us."

Meade's face showed the strain. "Howard, I don't have any choice. I've thought about it ever since we left that meeting. Their demands are impossible. We've got too many things at stake. That quota's all we've got to bargain with. It's our only chance to . . . to establish something in the annals of my presidency other than ineffective economic programs and a dozen other things that have failed miserably."

Meade's eyes pleaded, as if he were asking for Hickman's sympathy. "You see what I'm saying, don't you, Howard? If we give up that quota, we'll have lost our only bargaining tool."

Hickman leaned forward. "Mr. President, you don't have to convince me. I know what we're facing. But I hope you realize what you're setting yourself up for by not giving in. The minuses will pile up so high you won't know what's happened. Think about the NSC, for instance. How are you going to justify your decision to them? They don't know about the pipeline and they'll want some rationale or else you'll have a slew of resignations."

"The farmers," said Meade. "The fucking farmers. They're my rationale. I'll say we simply can't afford to jeopardize the livelihood of so many American farming households dependent on our maintaining that quota simply to placate a bunch of renegade Mexicans. That without the quotas being kept at their present levels, half the farmers in Texas alone would go bankrupt. Agriculture will back me up on it. So will the farmers. The NSC will accept it, they're not naive. They know how limited our choices are in this thing."

"And the hostages," said Hickman, "what about them? You simply can't leave them down there at the mercy of those people. Christ, that'd be worse than anything you did for the farmers. Those people are helpless, the farmers aren't. That's something you've got to consider."

Meade's face lost some of its anxiety. "Howard, I've considered them, believe me. Do you honestly think I'm such a coldhearted bastard and I would risk getting fifty corpses back just because of this pipeline? No, nobody's ignoring those people, especially me. I'm not going to leave them down there—"

"Then what are you going to do?"

"Well," he said, "I've got an idea . . ."

Operation Amates—that was the title Meade gave his plan after explaining it to Hickman. Together with several of the administration's top military and intelligence strategists they spent hours in the Oval Office working out the details through a meticulous step-by-step process before presenting the plan to the NSC when it reconvened. The plan was simple: a surprise predawn rescue mission on the Princess Hotel by a crack team of the government's antiterrorist unit, flying first into Acapulco's Los Amates Airport from Brownsville, Texas, and then moving with great speed over land and air to recapture the nearby hotel and rescue the Americans. He believed such a mission would be the captives' only hope for deliverance. But his most immediate concern was to refine the plan quickly so that he could convince the NSC—and himself—that there would be a minimum amount of bloodshed and that ultimately this was their only alternative.

Meade reconvened the NSC shortly before five thirty that afternoon to a packed Cabinet Room. His presentation took less than fifteen minutes. When he finished, there was a stunned silence, and then applause that climaxed with a standing ovation.

But the applause and ovation were quickly forgotten when the questions began to fly. The president's men wanted to know more about the plan. Some sought further details while others were content with his clarifying only a few points. Meade took the questions in stride, answering each as best he could, and turned frequently to the director of the CIA and the government's antiterrorist unit for help.

Finally the one question on everyone's mind was fired at Meade from a low-level NSC staffer.

"Can it work?"

Meade hesitated uneasily, smiled, and said, "What do you mean? Of course it can work."

The staffer persisted. "But, Mr. President, are you absolutely sure? Is the Company sure? And our antiterrorist unit?"

Meade felt his blood pressure rise. He knew everyone in the room expected an answer. Deserved one.

"No, young man, we can't be sure. No one can."

The room was hushed.

The NSC wanted to give Meade a vote of approval but couldn't. They split down the middle. After haggling over other alternatives and deciding there really were none, they left the final decision to Meade. In essence they washed the blood off their hands.

Immediately after the meeting Meade headed back to the Oval Office. He had a call placed to Mexico City. At the American embassy on the Paseo de la Reforma near the Monumento a la Independencia it took them less than a minute to connect him with the American ambassador, Alfred Higginbothem. Speaking over a scrambler phone, Meade informed the ambassador of Operation Amates.

For a moment the ambassador sat stunned. Then, after popping two Valiums he'd taken from his desk drawer, he asked Meade, "It's the pipeline, isn't it?"

"Yes, Al, it is."

"But why?"

"It's our only alternative, Al, our only one—"

"Well, Mr. President, what can I do to help?"

"I want you to get an audience with Portillo as quickly as possible. I'm sure he's expecting a call from us. Once you get in to see him, tell him about Amates, but do it gently. Ask him for support, tell him that such an operation is our only alternative and that we'll need his Federales to help us."

"But what if he doesn't buy it?" asked Higginbothem. "I can tell you right now he isn't going to like a bunch of commandos coming into his country."

"Well, I wouldn't either, but that's beside the point. They've got to be allowed in. You've got to convince him of that. Convince him that we're without alternatives ..." Meade paused, then said, "Surely he doesn't think his Federales are more capable of pulling something like this off than we are. The Company says they don't even have an organized antiterrorist policy down there."

"They don't," said Higginbothem. "But even if he does give us the okay, do you think he'll support the hostages' liberation? Pulling back those import quotas would only help him. Even if it is being done through violent means—"

"He wouldn't be that stupid. He'd be supporting the making of foreign policy through terrorism and he knows there's no way we'd stand for that. After all, we're right next door and we could blow them away in a minute."

Higginbothem conceded. Meade was going to get what he wanted one way or another, even if he killed everybody in the process. "I'll talk to him. And let's just hope this thing works."

"It's got to," said Meade.

Howard Hickman, having returned to his office when the president went to phone Mexico City, settled into his chair, noticed a pile of "While You Were Out" messages, ignored them, and spied a confidential note from Reed McClellan.

Howard,

Here are the latest figures on the race between the president and Chambers. As you can see by the percentages, the president is slipping fast. Chambers's support continues to build every day, ours continues to decline.

I also want to direct your attention to the preference polls between the president and Cliff Hawkins. Hawkins's appeal to Democratic voters is also spreading. He has finally begun to make a marked crossover impact, which is disturbing. Quite a large number of voters within our own party are beginning to favor Hawkins over *either* the president or Chambers. Both situations spell trouble for us. Unless we turn this around, it won't be long before the president is shoved right out of the race.

Hickman stared at the figures. The shifts to Chambers and Hawkins were astounding. They were falling behind too quickly. Hickman loosened his tie and looked at the figures again. Christ, what was happening?

To cap off the report, McClellan had scrawled at the bottom of the page, "H—These are pre-Acapulco figures. A copy has already been given to the Pres."

Terrific. Just what Meade needed.

MARYLAND

For the first time since he had unexpectedly run into the president, Cliff Hawkins had been given a situation that could either elevate his political standing or tear it down. Although less than forty-eight hours old, the crisis in Acapulco was developing into a formidable test of the president's abilities as a leader under stress.

Hawkins's camp was well aware of the consequences for Meade. They debated what to do at length. If Hawkins attacked the president, then he would be seen as the opportunistic demagogue his critics claimed he was. If he kept quiet until events in Acapulco were in some way resolved, he might lose a chance to square off with Meade with maximum visibility. Hawkins decided that, in the end, the risks of attacking the president at so vulnerable a time weren't worth the gains. So he kept quiet.

One man who wasn't content to keep quiet was Senator Jackson Chambers. He knew his lead was growing every day, and looked upon the situation in Acapulco as an excellent chance to show the president up for what he really was: a vacillating man whose foreign policies had brought embarrassment and humiliation to the United States and, as could be seen in Acapulco, danger to the lives of its people.

His aides and advisers begged the senator not to say anything derogatory about the president because public sympathy would most assuredly be with Meade. But Chambers felt his own instincts on handling the matter were to be trusted over his aides—his track record proved it.

So, as the worry over the fate of the captive Americans grew in the public's mind with each hour, Chambers called a press conference to offer his own thoughts on what should be done.

"I want you all to know that I deeply regret calling this press conference—regret that for the past twelve hours of this horrifying event neither the candidates nor the public have been adequately informed on the situation in Mexico."

"Throughout the day I've tried in vain to speak to someone on the president's staff. I have been totally ignored and I think I, as well as the other candidates and the American public, deserve to know what actions the president plans to take to secure the release of our citizens."

Chambers looked straight into the cameras with a pleading look and asked viewers, "Is this the sort of response the American people are going to get from the White House in times of crisis? Silence and indecision? Why hasn't the president spoken to us? We've been told he's working on the situation, but what is he doing? Why hasn't he already rescinded our pre-October '81 agricultural import quotas? Could it be that the president feels the expected losses to our farmers are far greater than the loss of fifty or more American lives? Certainly there must be enough money in this vast economy of ours to subsidize any losses the farmers might incur, and certainly the president realizes this . . ."

Howard Hickman sat in his office, glaring at the television across from his desk. Adrenaline flooded his body. His systems were shifting into overload. He couldn't believe what Chambers was doing . . . was saying . . .

"We have fifty Americans down there with guns at their heads. Fifty people just like you and me, with relatives and family waiting all over the country in anguish, waiting for the president to take some sort of action, and yet we don't know if he's going to let them live or die!"

Chambers lowered his head, eyes averted, and said slowly, "This is just one more example of the administration's complete and total indecisiveness . . ."

When Hickman threw a crystal ashtray at the set, the screen exploded. Circuits popped, wires crackled, and sparks flew as the ashtray smashed through the televison screen. The fireworks generated a delight in Hickman. He was breathing hard, nostrils flared, his cheeks red. Standing there with clenched fists, Hickman knew he hadn't been so fucking mad in years.

Shortly after 8:00 P.M. Meade received an urgent phone call from Mexico City. He took it in the private quarters.

"Yes?"

"Ambassador Higginbothem on the line, Mr. President."

"Al?"

"Yes, Mr. President."

"What's the news? Did you see Portillo?"

"Yes, sir, I did."

"And what's the word?"

"The word is go ahead. Portillo doesn't like it. In fact, he's still pretty pissed off about the whole thing concerning Wallbanks—"

"Christ, we got rid of Wallbanks's roundup," interrupted Meade.

"I know, but he bitched about this mess for over half an hour. I convinced him that the U.S. could never, under any circumstances, pull back those quotas under terrorist threats. I also told him that if he didn't help us, we'd consider that a clear indication he was willing to shape U.S.-Mexico policy through terrorism and that would destroy whatever relations he now enjoys with us."

"So the word's still go ahead, right?"

"Right, and he's pledged as much help from the Federales as we need."

"Good," said Meade. "I'll call Langley."

31

MEXICO/Acapulco

The landing was swift. Breaking through a predawn mist hanging over the airport, the American C-130 transport plane roared down the deserted runway, its wheels smoking. It was followed by another almost immediately.

Near the Los Amates terminal three jeeps filled with Federales and two unmarked American automobiles with plainclothes men moved toward the planes.

The transports came to a stop at the end of the runways, and the jeeps and cars moved across the pavement to meet them. Two helicopters, which had waited over an hour for the planes' arrival, started their engines. Slowly the chopper blades began to turn. The operation had to move with precision.

As the chopper blades picked up speed, the tail exits of both planes lowered and two long steel rampways were thrust from their bowels. The caravan of jeeps and cars came to a halt nearby. A truckload of commandos rolled down the ramp of each plane, followed by groups of men in army fatigues. Both groups were led by an American colonel in his early forties. He was trim, with a face that seemed chiseled out of granite. As he moved toward the lead car, several men got out.

The choppers' blades thrashed violently in the predawn air, raising the noise level on the runway to an uncomfortable pitch. Behind the colonel his men split off and rushed toward the waiting choppers.

"General?" shouted one of the men to the American leader in Spanish, "I'm Xavier Santos." He extended his hand to the American, who gave him a firm grasp in return.

"Not a general," the colonel shouted back in fluent Spanish over the roar of the helicopters. "Colonel Tom Harrison."

"Whatever," said Santos, smiling, and introduced Harrison to the men with him. The American could barely hear any of the names Santos rattled off—nor did he care. His mind was on his men, the trucks, those choppers, and, most important, the hotel.

Santos turned to his men. "Let's go!" Quickly the men got back into their cars and Harrison gave them a thumbs-up signal. He sprinted toward one of the choppers. As it lifted off the ground, the jeeps and trucks headed toward the main road that would take them to the Princess. Harrison looked at the faintly glowing horizon, felt the copter gently rocking and swaying, wind blowing dust everywhere.

Operation Amates was under way.

Aware of the newsworthiness of the recent events, journalists had been covering the Princess since the hotel had been taken two and a half days before. Waiting for new developments, most of the journalists had retired for the night to their rooms at the Pierre Marqués, the Princess's sister hotel nearby. But one small group of journalists were not staying at the Marqués. Instead they had opted to camp out on the golf course next to the long drive leading to the Princess, in case anything extraordinary happened. By forsaking the comfort of a first-class hotel for the damp golf course, it was these journalists who would witness a spectacle this morning—which would be the envy of every other journalist in the world.

"*Pronto! Pronto!*" a city policeman was saying as he and several of his colleagues walked around the group of sleeping journalists, poking them with their nightsticks. "Get up, Get up! We moving you out."

Several reporters sat up, rubbing their eyes. Some of the policemen were pulling other journalists to their feet, grabbing their equipment as they did so.

"Up! Up! We moving out!"

Immediately the group began demanding an explanation. Why were they being roused?—it wasn't even light. What happened? Had there been a break? Were the hostages being released? A dozen questions in a half dozen languages besieged the policemen.

"Orders!" replied one, jerking a photographer to his feet. "We have orders to get you peoples outta here."

The journalists swore. A scuffle erupted, nightsticks were raised, shouts rose up.

"Quiet, *por favor!* We've got to have quiet! No noise."

What the hell was going on?

The policemen, trying to round the reporters up and steer them toward the road and the waiting cars, were by now clearly anxious. Several glanced nervously at their watches and each other.

Something was up. Big time. The journalists knew it. Like hell they were going to move. They hadn't spent the last two nights under a muggy Acapulco sky for nothing.

Then they did a double take. Turning in off the frontage road was a line of unmarked cars and jeeps, and behind the jeeps a large U.S. Army truck. Everyone grew quiet. As they watched the silent procession, they heard a noise in the distance. A look of disappointment swept over the Mexican police. They had failed to evacuate the journalists on time and now it was going to be their ass. Heads turned up to the sky as the noise became clearer. Then the two choppers appeared on the horizon, moving rapidly toward the group.

As the choppers swept over them, their mouths dropped open with the sudden realization of what was happening. They watched as the choppers roared by, crossing into the airspace surrounding the Princess. The motorcade that had turned off the frontage road sped up, roaring by with jeeps full of commandos. They were going to raid the fucking place.

The choppers brushed over treetops and headed straight toward the magnificent pyramidal structure. Illumined by the early dawn sky, the Princess looked like an elaborate shrine about to be vandalized. As the choppers closed in on the hotel, their searchlights began sweeping over the building's side, crisscrossing back and forth, searching for God knows what.

The journalists moved toward the hotel as if hypnotized, stumbling over dips in the green, all the while watching as the choppers circled the main structure and its two adjacent buildings. Gently they were pushed back by the Mexican police, who were themselves fascinated. Then the choppers rose and hovered over the flat top on the pyramid.

Suddenly there was machine-gun fire. Short, rapid bursts followed by a succession of more quick bursts. Ignoring the shouts of the Mexican police, several journalists sprinted down the drive toward the hotel, followed by several photographers.

There were several small explosions, like those a hand grenade makes. Then more gunfire, followed by more small explosions.

As the journalists ran down the drive, they lifted their Minicams onto their shoulders, pulled their microphones from their tape recorder cases, flipped open their notebooks, jerked their pens out of their shirt pockets. They were ready: shutters, eyes, hands, feet.

Ahead of them the choppers dipped down to the roof. They were landing. There were several more bursts of machine-gun fire, and nobody could tell whether the shots came from the commandos or terrorists. Over by the golf club they heard a much louder explosion, followed by screams and more gunfire. There were other blasts, followed again by screams, this time up at the front of the drive. Orders were shouted in Spanish and English while the gunfire was going off, and in the distance sirens pierced the dawn's air.

Then it happened—a series of volcanic explosions that sent tremors rumbling beneath the hotel's grounds, the drive, and beyond. The eyes of the journalists and Mexican police were riveted on the hotel, witnessing a horror that would live with them for the rest of their lives. The upper floors of the Princess—floors where many of the hostages were held—were blowing apart. The choppers on the roof soared into the sky in a holocaust of flames. The entire horizon lit up in a sunburst of orange and yellow fire. Screams mixed with explosions and gunfire. Tile and concrete showered over the grounds like a waterfall. A final round of explosions erupted, sending the rest of the roof disintegrating in every direction.

Those watching stared in disbelief. The Princess was engulfed in flames. Eyes still frozen on the hotel, the Mexican police made spasmodic attempts to move the journalists toward their cars, but all of them were too numb to do anything but stare . . .

32

Senator Jackson Chambers, unaware of what was happening at that moment in Acapulco, opened the news summary folder he read every morning and knew his instincts had been wrong.

In virtually every clipping or summary of yesterday's late-edition newspapers as well as in the editorials in the morning papers, he was being raked over the coals. The outcry against his press conference was unanimous. *The Washington Post* called him "an opportunist with an unconscionable sense of timing" while *The New York Times* said that "this should be a clear indication of Senator Chambers's lack of political ethics." *The Wall Street Journal* said that "he seems to have the scruples of a weasel." He flipped through some more summaries and they were worse.

Chambers put down the folder and rubbed his forehead. His press conference would be in the news for weeks, getting the kind of coverage no politician needs ... unless something worse happened to one of the other candidates.

God, how he prayed it would.

Cliff Hawkins had seen his own clippings that morning and was glad he had opted to remain silent on the situation in Acapulco. Only two papers so far, *The Dallas Morning News* and *The Orlando*

Sentinel, praised him for keeping silent and not making a spectacle of himself as Chambers had. The others didn't even acknowledge his handling of the issue.

Love and forgiveness weren't coming as easily as they had before. Christian charity was slowly giving way to a growing bitterness and resentment toward those who were out to stop him, those who smeared him, misquoted him, and deliberately misconstrued his ideas. He knew that, if anyone learned of these innermost feelings, he would call him hypocritical and pious, which was exactly opposite from the truth. The campaign was getting harder, the demands more taxing, the criticisms more pointed, but it made Hawkins even more determined to win the nomination and the presidency.

Yes, he was changing, and somewhere within him instinct told him it wasn't like him. Too much was being placed on him too quickly. He was glad he hadn't spoken out on Acapulco as Chambers had, and glad that he wasn't getting that kind of coverage. He was not sorry to see it tearing Chambers down. Chambers would be a lot more difficult to take on in November than Meade, and it was Meade who should pay the price for bringing God's country to its knees, Meade who should face what he had done.

Meade—his nemesis—and the one man Cliff Hawkins now wanted to see fall.

Yes, it wasn't what most people would perceive as a Christian thought. Nevertheless, Hawkins still wanted to see him fall. He hated himself and yearned for it at the same time.

33

It had happened too quickly—all of it. Eight hours after the raid Otis Meade still had trouble grasping the mission's failure. Outside his office congressional leaders were waiting to confer with him, the Mexican ambassador was due in an hour, and the third National Security Council meeting of the day had been called. But they could wait. Meade had been alone in his office for the past half hour and wanted to stay there. He needed more time alone to think, to absorb as much of it as he could, and let his system get over the shock. But how could he?

Everytime he tried to think things out, began to rationalize, all he could see before him were the film clips the national networks had shown during their noon broadcasts. They haunted him. Over and over the footage rolled before him. He leaned forward and propped his elbows on his desk and stared at the television screen—blank, but alive.

There was the Princess slightly in the distance, looking peaceful, almost majestic, in the awakening day. The camera moved upward toward the sky and two helicopters flew directly over the hotel. They were not American, but Mexico's. Still nobody had to tell Meade who was in them: American servicemen. He watched as the choppers moved in on the hotel like two giant birds swooping down on their prey. Then he saw the armed caravan rush down a long drive leading toward the hotel. There was a break in the film, a splice.

Meade rested his forehead in the palm of his hands. He was sweating.

Now the choppers were much closer, directly over the hotel. They hovered momentarily, and then set down on top of the roof. There was another splice, the camera jerked as if something had jolted it. Another explosion? Meade wondered. Then it happened: the camera zoomed in on the hotel and Meade could see the top floors erupt in one huge series of explosions and flames. The camera jolted again several times and Meade watched in horror as the roof of the hotel blew into the sky, spewing the choppers and entire sections of wall and flooring into the dawn light. There were also flaming bits of . . .

. . . *of what? Bodies?*

Meade felt sick, but his eyes stayed on the screen and he saw the film clip in his mind's eye again. And then once more.

Oh, Christ, what have I done?

What had gone wrong? Was it the timing? The men? Or the whole operation? How was he going to explain it? Attempt to? Thirty-two known dead. Many still unaccounted for, their bodies scattered about the grounds like litter.

Blown to pieces because of a decision he made.

Just one decision.

His brainchild, his answer to these terrorists.

And none of it, none of it should have happened.

Twenty minutes later Meade's intercom buzzed. Slowly he picked it up.

"Yeah?"

"Mr. President, the congressional leaders are still here and would like to know if you're going to meet with them or if they should return to the Hill."

Meade sighed. He didn't want to see anyone. He broke all protocol and told her, "Let them meet with Hickman. Round him and Ecklecamp up, they can handle 'em."

"But, Mr. President—"

"Look, find Hickman and Eckelcamp. *I don't want to see them.*"

He hung up and sank deep into his leather chair. His eyes were fixed on the blank television screens across the room. His mind started to revert to the flim clips, but then he suddenly shook himself out of it.

Oh, God, what had he done?

He knew. Nobody had to tell him, he knew. And because he knew, his body, his soul, lay shocked and numb. All he could think about, had been able to think about since eight this morning when Intelligence had called him was the horror, the guilt, the uselessness of it all. It was so damn senseless, so fucking senseless. More Americans die everyday on the highways. But these people hadn't been in their cars. They had been vacationing in what was supposed to have been a safe resort in a safe country. Then paradise was blown up.

Meade lifted the reading glasses he'd had on for the past few hours and rubbed his eyes.

Why didn't we know? Why weren't we told the place was rigged to blow? Where were my experts when I needed them? Ten billion a year is spent on Intelligence and they couldn't—didn't—even tell me the place was wired!

Meade sighed. He looked over at a small chest beneath his bookshelves. It was a nicely concealed bar. He needed a drink, but didn't want to move. He wanted to sit there—and not face what was the biggest disaster of his political career. Why didn't he just give into their demands? Why couldn't the nation have gone without a pipeline for another few years in return for those lives? It would have been easy. But—Meade had to have the pipeline. A shrine for posterity. His ego needed it, his record needed it. Now it was all in jeopardy. Everything.

The election . . .

He didn't even want to think about it.

He'd taken complete responsibility from the beginning, but now there were other considerations at hand. Would the public allow him even to stay in office now? Surely there were going to be some sonofabitches out there who'd demand he resign. And what was he going to tell the press? The public? God, he'd like to run away and hide! The blame couldn't be placed on anyone else but him, which made the failure that much harder to take. When it boiled down to major decisions, to ultimatums and matters of life and death, it wasn't the people over at Justice or State or Congress—or even the Company—who decided. It was the president. And when the decisions resulted in failure, it was the president who had failed.

The president, no one else. The president, that's who had failed.

"I know," sighed Meade to no one but himself. "And how I've failed . . ."

Meade gazed listlessly at his bar, and then at the television screens.

Thirty-two dead, maybe more.
Blown to bits like common litter.
Thirty-two.
Who would be alive now had it not been for you.
Only you.
Meade could feel his eyes welling up. They were tears of self-pity more than sorrow. Recognizing this and welcoming it, he wept for the first time in years and years.

34

MARYLAND/Andrews Air Force Base

One week later the nation watched as casket after casket pelted by a steady stream of rain, moved down the conveyer belt of a government C-130. There were sixteen caskets in all, identical in size and color and each with the same contents: the remains of the commandos who died in Acapulco. As the caskets came to the end of the conveyer belt, they were silently loaded into waiting hearses, surrounded by newsmen armed with cameras as well as hundreds of huddled spectators. Nearby a line of limousines idled.

It was a cold homecoming and, accentuating the macabre atmosphere, the families of a dozen of the dead men had gathered beneath a green canvas awning not far from the planes to hear the president of the United States speak.

Otis Meade, looking as somber as they, stood before them. His eyes were lifeless, has face ashen. As the light wind carried the rain's mist under the awning, it gently tousled Meade's hair, completing the disheveled, bewildered appearance he exuded.

His comments were brief. Later many of the family members would remark that his words were empty, that the president had lacked emotion and at times was barely audible. Many would be bitter, would remember how strong and healthy their husbands or sons were the last time they saw them and what this man, this one man, had done to them.

Otis Meade, if not consciously aware of this, could sense the vibrations. Standing before them, reading from his prepared statement, he would glance up occasionally and in one instance his eyes locked onto a mourner, newly widowed. Her eyes were red. She wiped them, but then continued crying. When she and Meade looked at each other, there was such a total sense of understanding, mixed with anger, that Meade was forced to look away. The next person's eyes were just as haunting, and the next. Nothing he could say would alleviate their pain, their sense of loss, and he knew it. He had seen those caskets moving down the conveyer belt and, even from a distance, they, more than anything else, had brought the realization of what he had done—the death certificate he had signed in bloody ink.

Later he understood. Those men in Acapulco had paid as he would have to pay, and these people before him were going to make sure of that. Here and everywhere across the nation where other caskets had been sent, and even beyond, the bitterness and hatred toward him would be the same.

He was marked.

INTERLUDE

MEXICO CITY/Palacio Nacional

Mexico's president, José Portillo, second cousin to former president López Portillo, sat at a long dining table, eating his evening meal and watching Mexico's national news. The lead stories were those coming from the United States, where on this day America's president had received sixteen of the bodies of American commandos killed in Acapulco.

Picking up a fajita from his plate and taking a bite, Portillo watched with interest as a haggard Otis Meade eulogized the commandos who died. As Meade spoke, the cameras panned across a bitter audience. Portillo had phoned the president a few days earlier. He knew that Meade had appreciated the condolences and apologies, and he knew that Meade expected him to mention the possibility of resuming the pipeline talks. But even though Meade had stopped those idiotic roundups in Texas, Portillo wasn't about to mention the pipeline talks. First, Meade was in no condition to discuss the matter. His appearance on television now confirmed that. And second, Portillo wasn't sure he wanted the talks to resume.

Trying to live with the import quotas on Mexican crops was bad enough, and the American president was shrewd to use it as a bargaining tool. But who on earth could possibly expect a man of José

Portillo's stature, a man whose country might be sitting on the biggest oil deposits in the world, even to consider dealing with a man who was not in control of himself or his country?

It was absurd. Look at America's current political situation: a president who's just made one of the biggest political mistakes of his career; a fascist named Jackson Chambers opposing him; an evangelist running on the other side. Portillo had read the day before that Wallbanks was threatening to sue the federal government—and Meade—to reinstate the alien worker roundups, and several congressional committees were demanding to know what in the hell was going on in Washington. Portillo shook his head.

No, it was true that those import quotas were doing their damage to his country's economy, but José Portillo wasn't about to resume those pipeline talks. At least not until he was convinced that Meade had a better grip on things. After all, why talk to a man who might not be around next year to honor his agreements?

35

WASHINGTON/The White House

In the aftermath of Acapulco the average American had forgotten about the small but significant primaries in Nebraska and West Virginia until they were already over. But the White House had not, particularly Howard Hickman. Nine days after the failed rescue mission Hickman watched without surprise as Senator Jackson Chambers steamrolled over them.

Chambers's press conference seemed to have had little effect on the voters once the avalanche of media attention turned on the president. Shortly after the fiasco virtually every pollster from New York to Los Angeles predicted major victories for Chambers, and they were right. Not till after the votes were tallied, though, did Hickman realize how brutally accurate their predictions were. Chambers had slaughtered them. Those Democratic leaders still in Meade's camp warned Hickman and Hughes Martin, chairman of the President Meade Reelection Committee, just how dangerous the effects of Chambers's victories could be. Everyone wanted to avoid splitting the party—which would then split at the polls in November—but it was beginning to look as if that just might happen. Chambers was winning, and his taking the nomination was a real possibility. An incumbent president lose his own nomination? God forbid! They didn't want to think about it.

But Hickman couldn't help thinking about it. Two days after the West Virginia–Nebraska primaries he was still thinking about it. Meade was losing fast. And if their polls were bad, their media was worse. As McClellan had predicted right after the Acapulco fiasco, Meade's polls plummeted and with each succeeding day's news dropped even further. The evening news was dominated by stories stemming from Acapulco. Vengeful congressmen, eager to even the score with Meade, exploited the situation. A few called for across-the-board resignations. On national talk shows several survivors' families articulated their tearful thoughts on the raid and some did nothing to hide their bitterness toward the president and his administration. Several families filed suits against Meade and the government. One of the surviving commandos had been offered a six-figure advance to do a book. Another hostage had already signed with a major publisher for three hundred thousand dollars. A widow was shown placing flowers on the freshly dug grave of her husband. A military expert reflected on the situation while several syndicated columnists wrote about the fate of Meade's presidency and his chances, if any, of surviving the mess through the remaining primaries. Everyone in the nation suddenly had an interest in foreign and national affairs.

On the campaign front Hickman was informed that invitations for Meade to speak on behalf of senatorial and congressional candidates were being withdrawn. Party leaders pleaded with Howard Hickman and Hughes Martin to initiate a new media push on the president's behalf. A new tour. More staffers. New advisers. New commercials. Anything. State coordinators and steering committee members from all over the country were phoning the President Meade Reelection Committee daily, screaming for more positive news coverage, more phone banks, more air time. The Maryland–Michigan primaries were only a week away, and there was no way Meade could come close to winning either.

It all came back to Acapulco, Hickman mused over lunch at his desk. A beachfront hotel targeted like a sitting duck. One midnight raid by a bunch of fanatical terrorists and a failed rescue mission that could easily destroy the president of the United States. One mission, an attempt to save fifty American lives, and where the fuck did it get us? Nowhere. No-fucking-where but a pit of quicksand. The most powerful man in the world brought down by a series of explosions that didn't even occur in his own country. His entire career possibly blown asunder. Everything he's worked for, *strived for*. Everything he . . .

He? He? Everything *he* has worked for? What about me? If Meade goes, I go. All because of a fucking idea of his. I didn't have a damn thing to do with it and he's going to bring us all down because of it!

Everything will be gone. The power, the prestige, the privileges . . . everything. The Harvard degree won't do me a damned bit of good without this. I need this. I've earned it. And now . . . it might be taken away.

Hickman felt himself begin to quiver. His emotions were getting to him. His fears. He forced himself to think of how, if possible, he could save their asses.

Survival. That's the key. We've got to survive. Winning primaries isn't going to mean shit if we can't win the nomination. But we can't do that if we don't survive.

Meade had lost more than half the primaries he had entered and everyone knew there couldn't be an immediate reversal of the trend.

There've got to be alternatives. We can't let this one thing destroy the entire campaign. But what?

Hickman anxiously patted his shirt pocket for his cigarettes, took one out, and put it to his lips. I don't know. I just don't know. It wasn't supposed to be like this. We knew he was a weak incumbent from the beginning, but we were going to pull him through anyway . . . and probably could if every fucking thing in the world didn't go wrong.

He reached for his lighter and lit a cigarette.

But I've got to survive. This is where I belong. This is what I've earned. I deserve to stay here. Deserve it. It's what I busted my ass for in college. Its everything I need . . . the power . . . nobody has any idea of the magnitude of *power*—of absolute control—one can accumulate here. And I've got it.

Hickman's intercom buzzed.

"What?" he snapped.

"Reed McClellan's on line one, Mr. Hickman."

He punched line one and picked up the receiver.

"Howard?"

Hickman sighed. "Don't you have anything better to do than call me on my lunch hour?"

"Sorry. I forgot you were lunching with King Charles."

"Cute, Reed, now get to the point."

"The point is I've just gotten back this week's polling results."

"I don't want to hear them."

"You're going to sooner or later. I'm sending a messenger over this afternoon with a complete printout, but I thought I'd prepare you in advance."

"Your consideration astounds me. How bad are they?"

"Well, I don't think the president should see them right now."

"Christ."

"Chambers is . . ."

Chambers!

Hickman's heart skipped a beat. "What'd you say?"

"I said Chambers is . . ."

That was it. Of course. Jackson Chambers. America's number one son of a bitch. The one man who was doing them as much harm as the Acapulco thing.

Chambers.

That's it. Eliminate him and Meade's got a chance. I've known it all along, but why in the fuck am I just now realizing it? Chambers has always been our most immediate threat. Eliminate him and even with Acapulco we still might have a chance. Especially if that bastard Hawkins takes the nomination. And if he doesn't, all the better. Meade could easily take Broder in an election. And Sheldon Roberts too. But Chambers—that's our target. That's where our energies have got to go. Not on this Acapulco thing. We've said as much about it as we can say. But Chambers . . .

Hickman felt his adrenaline beginning to flow, his heart's pace quickening.

Chambers is the one we go after. Target him. Destroy the bastard. Eliminate him by ruining him and turning his whole fucking campaign into a little bitty pile of rubble.

"Hickman? Are you listening?"

"Yes," he lied, his mind already returning to Chambers and how they were going to get rid of him.

The afternoon sun sank slowly over Washington. The time alone had paid off. If his decision was carried out successfully, it would change the course of both Chambers's and the president's campaigns. Hickman knew that he held more power than any man in Washington except the president, and now he was willing to push it to the limit.

He picked up the phone. "Get me Ecklecamp."

In Washington at night it is not unusual to see government offices and building complexes lit up long after the horde of daytime workers have fled. Jerry Ecklecamp was alone in the West Wing office except for those few Secret Service agents assigned to night duty who wandered the halls or watched the monitor outside the Oval Office. On his desk were a stack of files, delivered via special courier from the CIA's headquarters at Langley. Hickman's order to Ecklecamp was simple: find anything at all on Chambers that might indicate a weakness—some point in his career where he faltered enough to be of national interest. Ecklecamp understood.

Thus far he had examined four files, containing Chambers's voting records, performance appraisals made by several political groups, surveillance notes taken at various rallies over the years, and a list of campaign contributors. Most of the material was public knowledge. There was nothing, as far as he could tell, that might be potentially damaging. He shut the fourth file, moved it aside, and picked up another file labeled:

CHAMBERS—PERSONAL
Classified Eyes Only
SEjsc File 1437
Updated: August 1991

Ecklecamp loosened his tie, and opened the file. He glanced through the first page, the second, then the third. At the fourth page he stopped. This was the beginning of a psychological profile compiled by the Company's own medical personnel. It was accompanied by copies of Chambers's medical records. He quickly scanned the profile, flipping page after page, passing a subsection entitled MEDICAL CONSULTATIONS. PERSONAL, and then stopped. He backtracked and, instead of scanning the text, read it with great care.

Within seconds he knew he'd found what he'd been looking for. Filled with nervous glee, he picked up the phone and dialed Hickman.

INTERLUDE

TEXAS/Dallas

Scott Houghlin wasn't a happy man. Sitting across from his editor's desk at the *Dallas Times Herald,* he decided that, if he had to listen to one more minute of this bullshit, he would leave.

". . . and, besides, it's too much of a risk. You know that."

"Why? Look at the copies of those checks. Look at those names. They're Gianni's aliases and you know it. Everyone knows it!"

"Wrong. Nobody does. They only assume they're his. And you know what happens when you assume, Houghlin. You make an ass out of you and me. Ass-U-Me, get it?"

"I don't believe this. I fucking don't believe it. I risk my life getting those checks and you don't even want to look at them! Even when they're staring you in the face! It's evidence pure and simple!"

His editor shook his head. "Evidence? You wanna know what evidence you got? You got evidence that shows you broke into a file room at Hawkins's organization. That's illegal entry in case you don't know it. Then you stole some photocopies of cashier's checks, which is theft in case you've forgotten. And the only thing you got to show for any of this are two names, one of which has been alleged to be one of Gianni's aliases."

Houghlin leaned over his editor's desk. "You know damn well that's who he is!"

His editor reared back, then leaned forward, his face three inches from Houghlin's. He gritted his teeth and said, "It's not his fucking alias. Not as far as we've been able to prove and this paper does not—repeat, does not—report underworld hearsay. Got it?"

Yeah, he got it. His own editor wasn't backing him up on the biggest story he'd had in months.

"So what are you going to do? Run it on the back page?"

"Back page?" he asked leaning back. "Who said anything about running it?"

"Wha . . ."

"I never promised you that."

"You fucker. Let some other asshole take this shit, I quit!"

Moments later Houghlin's editor was on the telephone.

"Frank?"

A coarse, wheezing voice replied, "No, Bugs Bunny. Who'd you think it was? Did you do it?"

"Yeah, but it cost me one helluva reporter. I could've used him."

"Yeah, well, too bad. Plenty other kids need jobs. What about the cashier's checks?"

"The copies are here. He was so mad when he left he forgot 'em. I just shredded them."

"Good, good," the voice replied in a hacking cough. "I'll see you're dropped the usual amount plus a little extra."

"Appreciate it."

"Anything else?"

"Just one question."

"What?"

"You're really not connected to Hawkins are you?"

"Christ, you kidding? Him? We just needed to get rid of some cash in a hurry. IRS and shit. One of the boys suggested him and I said, 'Why not?' It woulda made my mother proud."

"Did he ever know?"

"Fuck, no."

The editor was about to say thanks when the voice said, "Later," and hung up.

The man never talked long to anyone.

36

WASHINGTON

Two weeks after Acapulco massive suits against Mexico, the United States government, and Otis Meade were being filed. Two investigatory committees were set up in the House and Senate to hold hearings on the failed rescue attempt. It was generally acknowledged that Meade would be asked to testify in person. On the political front matters were looking worse. The president's polls were at their lowest point since taking office. Contributions were off heavily. And the previous day, when five states held their primaries, Meade carried only two: Arkansas and Nevada. Idaho, Kentucky, and Oregon went to Jackson Chambers.

As the president's troubles mounted, so did the talk that it would be Chambers heading up the Democrats' 1992 ticket. While Chambers's press conference at the height of the Acapulco crisis did not allay his image as a political opportunist, he was somewhat able to rectify this by later admitting to reporters that it was inappropriate at the time. However, he said, the criticisms that he launched against Meade stood, and he reiterated them during every stump speech he gave. The people, seeing the evidence, listened to his charges. Predictably Chambers's polls climbed.

Even more incredible than the fact that the incumbent president might lose his party's nomination was the possibility that an evangelist might be heading up the Republican ticket. Reed McClellan's warning about an ideological shift toward fundamental conservatism seemed prophetic. Hardcore conservative leaders, once hesitant to support Hawkins publically because of his religious ties, were now zealously campaigning for him, raising millions for his war chests. Hordes of Republican action groups were doing everything they could as well to get out the vote for Hawkins in the remaining round of primaries.

Hawkins's campaign, however, was not trouble-free. On the contrary, despite the fact that many Republicans had gotten over their fears about a presidential candidate so closely linked with religion and had joined Hawkins's ranks, a large number of Republican voters were becoming increasingly concerned that Hawkins might have a very good chance at winning the November election. This spawned various groups with names like Republicans for Religious Freedom, Anybody But Hawkins, Citizens Against Religious Intervention, and several committees bent on finding and running candidates on the Independent ticket.

Thus Cliff Hawkins needed to go into the final round with all his ammunition—and Charlotte was part of it. But at a time he needed her most Hawkins felt she might not be able to come through. He didn't know why; he simply had the feeling that something was tearing her down. Although she still projected herself well before the public, privately she had grown increasingly more irritable and capricious, would retreat to her hotel room early and leave it late, was often out of sorts. She also began to make more and more slips in print and television interviews.

He was determined to find out why.

He and Charlotte were both in Dallas for an evening before flying out to hit their respective campaign stops on this last leg of primaries. It was then that Cliff decided to try. They had just had dinner with Blair, who had given his father a full report on their evangelistic enterprises. After their son left, Cliff suggested to Charlotte that they go into the library. Once they'd both gotten comfortable and chatted for a while, he asked her what was wrong. He could have guessed what her reaction would be.

"What do you mean? Nothing. Everything's fine."

"Charlotte, I know better. I can tell. I want you to talk to me, tell me what's bothering you."

There was a nervous edge to Charlotte's laugh. "Cliff, nothing is bothering me. I'm telling you the truth."

She could be right. It might be that the pressures had gotten to her and she was simply responding to them. But Cliff didn't think so. There was more. He could feel it.

"Are you sure?"

"Of course, I'm sure, why would you . . . even think . . ."

"I don't know. I know you, know how you act, and I don't think you're leveling with me. What is it? The campaign? The pressures? Are they getting to be too much? If so, say so and we can . . ."

"No, no. It's not that, it's nothing. Nothing's wrong."

"Charlotte, you're not doing a very good job of hiding your nervousness . . ."

"Nervousness?" she snapped. "Cliff what is wrong with you? What brought this whole thing on? We had a nice dinner, saw Blair, came in here, and everything was fine. Then . . . then you start asking me these questions like a psychiatrist or something. What is it? What's gotten into you?"

"I'm asking *you.*"

Now Charlotte was angry. She shook her head, looking at the carpet. She was trapped. Caught in a situation where she would have to talk to him. This wasn't long distance now, no staff members waiting to consult with him, no polls he should read. Just the two of them. It scared her. She was vulnerable. It was too easy to slip up. She knew it. He knew it. That's why he wanted her here and why she wanted out.

"Cliff, look, it's been an exhausting week for both of us. Let's go to bed. We haven't slept together in weeks and . . ."

"Not until you give me the truth."

"Truth? What are you talking about? You're acting as though I'm on trial and I don't even know what the charge is!"

"It's about you! It's about reports I've been getting from the staff and Secret Service saying you're on edge, that you're uncommunicative with them. That you withdraw into yourself and aren't letting anyone else in. They say you're getting capricious, flippant, demanding. That you're doing your duty but that's about it. Like reading a script. Once it's over—bam!—you head straight to the hotel and don't come out till the next morning. And when you do, they say you're not yourself. That you don't look well, act well, or handle yourself well. Now, what is going on?"

"I didn't know you had my own staff and agents spying on me. If you were so damned concerned about me, why didn't you ask me instead of them? How dare you say I'm not handling myself well in front of people? I'm the same as I've always been and if you don't like it, if you think you'd be better off with someone else out there eighteen hours a day plugging for you, hitting who knows how many cities and eating who knows how many rubber chicken dinners, then fine—go right ahead. Get yourself a perky little Junior League wife who wants a hubby to win the presidency so she can redecorate the damn place. If that's what you want, then go for it. But don't come down on me about the way I'm handling myself when I'm out there using . . ."

She realized she was losing control.

God, how I wish I had a drink. I hate this. All of it! He's changing. He isn't the way he used to be . . . and neither am I. Politics is destroying us. I just want to cry and forget about all this. Blank it out of my mind . . .

"Were you going to say something?"

She cleared her throat. "It's becoming such a soap opera. And not a very nice one. This campaign, I mean."

"Nobody said it would be nice. But we have the Lord's blessings. He's turned the tables around, brought out the support we knew we had, and day after day the prospects grow better."

They certainly do, Charlotte thought.

"Six months ago nobody would have guessed things would be turning out this way, but I told you all along it's the Lord's will that I run."

"I know."

"You believe that don't you?"

Charlotte said nothing.

INTERLUDE

WASHINGTON/The White House

Howard Hickman never underestimated the impact Acapulco would have on Meade's campaign. If it didn't ruin the president outright, it would at least cripple him, bring him to his knees. Hickman pictured him like an animal caught in a metal trap, helpless and at the mercy of the one son of a bitch who was their most immediate threat—Jackson Chambers.

Reed McClellan had just sent over some more polling data. Not only was the president losing more and more of his core support within the Democratic party, he was losing heavily in areas that were once considered Meade strongholds, namely among blacks and other minority groups, as well as the elderly, the young uneducated, and the working class. Chambers was chipping away at every faction, using nothing but Meade's record and the fiasco in Acapulco. And it was working.

Which was why Howard Hickman was glad he'd called this meeting. Sitting behind Hughes Martin's desk in the director's office of the President Meade Reelection Committee, Hickman surveyed the four men sitting before him. For two hours they had discussed the problems the president was having in his reelection and how serious a threat Jackson Chambers had become. Hickman handed each of them a copy of the file Jerry Ecklecamp had come across while going over Chambers's records, and asked them to read it. He wanted to know whether they didn't think there was enough information there to do irreparable harm to Chambers's campaign if the right channels were used in releasing the information. They agreed, and Hickman was pleased, asking them then what specific information they thought should be concentrated on. The group said two things: Chambers's fear of flying and the fact that it had forced him to see a psychiatrist, and his contraction of syphilis when he was younger. Hickman smiled.

"Gentlemen, you realize that this meeting never occurred. I don't know you, never met you, and neither has Hughes. Got it?"

They nodded.

"All right. The money's to be drawn out by Mr. Ferrigo as you need it." He handed Ferrigo, the man in the middle, a slip of paper. "The expense records will be dropped in this locker at Dulles once everything's been done."

"Once the program's been put into action, we'll drop your payments in the same locker. Got it?"

Again they nodded.

Hickman stood up.

"Good. In two weeks the fireworks begin."

37

WASHINGTON

The warm, beautiful days of spring suddenly turned into the hot, sultry days of summer. Air conditioners ran full time, sprinkler systems quenched dry lawns, and the colorful flowers of Washington were quickly disappearing, heralding both the end of spring and the end of the primaries. There were only three left: Ohio, New Jersey, and California.

The Big Three.

Katherine Meade, standing on the Truman Balcony and gazing down at the Rose Garden, was thinking about these final three contests. She was alone; the president had retired to his bedroom for a badly needed nap. Standing there, watching a gardener work beyond one of the hedges, she knew the campaign was in critical condition. Otis had lost three of the last four primaries to Jackson Chambers, and although the races had been close, they had still ended in defeat. The negative sentiment against her husband had never been stronger, and the polls continued their decline every day. The White House had turned into a morgue with staffers and campaign personnel brooding as if Otis were already out of office. Even sadder was the condition of her husband, the man who was—either directly or indirectly—responsible for the situation.

Katherine was painfully aware of his condition. Besides not eating properly, Otis slept irregularly and got no exercise. For several nights, after the bodies had been returned from Mexico, Katherine heard and secretly observed him walking about their quarters at the most ungodly hours. He rattled around in the family kitchen, but not preparing anything, or left the television on in the West Sitting Room, but not watching it. At other times he drifted from room to room in silence—opening a door, looking in, then shutting it. As the weeks passed, he became worse. One night Katherine jumped up in bed when a glass shattered. The noise had come from the kitchen. She glanced at her clock: 5:00 A.M. She waited until she thought he had gone, then got up and went to the kitchen. On the floor was a broken glass in a puddle of scotch.

Katherine wasn't the only one to notice.

The Secret Service had come to her several times in the past few weeks about the president. On their last visit they brought their log books with them. Going over the entries, Katherine read a more painful story about her husband than she could have imagined. Twice the president had been dissuaded from walking about the darkened grounds. Once, at quarter to three in the morning, they found him floating on a raft in the White House pool. Other entries were just as revealing: the president was seen playing the piano in the dark in the East Room; flipping through—but never reading—numerous books in the library on the ground floor; sitting in the Blue Room with the lights out; gazing out at the Washington Monument from the penthouse before dawn. On other nights Meade, disheveled and attired in his pajamas, would retreat to the Oval Office and go over briefings, speeches, AP and UPI news-service reports, campaign material, and his mail. When he finished with one stack of papers, he would shuffle them off to the side, pause, rub his bloodshot eyes, and begin another. He seemed dazed by the effect Acapulco was having on his empire; he was like a man who knows he's dying and retreats into his own world to tie the loose ends together. But, unlike others who faced death, Meade could not make peace with himself.

And it showed.

At staff and Cabinet meetings he was half-attentive and, when prodded for an opinion, would bark out an irritable answer and then resume his silence. His once-firm handshake had become limp, his smile nonexistent. The cameramen who photographed him never ceased to be amazed at how frazzled and spent Meade looked. His usual healthy color now looked anemic, highlighted by dark circles under his eyes. One eyelid twitched incessantly, although no one mentioned it.

Many wondered how long would it be before he cracked. A week? Ten days? During the convention? Katherine hated to consider it, but she had, and she forced herself to confront Otis's physician, Dr. Walsh. Walsh had noticed the changes in Meade during his morning examinations of the president. He mentioned them to him, as had Katherine, but, often the case with victims of acute depression, Meade barely listened. Walsh suggested that he bring in a psychiatrist. Meade heard him, got up, and walked out.

What else can I do? Katherine asked herself still gazing at the gardener. I've done everything I can and things still haven't changed. In fact, they've gotten worse. He won't talk to me and won't let me talk to him. I've tried to sleep with him, but he just gets out of bed and leaves. I told him I'd go back out and campaign for him again, but he just laug' and says, "What campaign?"

What am I going to do?

Depressed herself, she turned to go back into the Oval Office when she saw a figure walking toward the Executive Wing. She leaned on the balcony railing to get a better look. It was Howard Hickman. Well, she thought, as much as I despise him, he might be able to change things around here. But I don't know.

Hickman knew.

Jackson Chambers's fear of flying was one of the best-kept secrets in politics. And one of the oldest. Plagued by the phobia since his teens, it was one of the reasons he had moved to New York after the death of his parents. Thanks to the commuter system, you could go up and down the eastern seaboard without ever having to step on a plane. In the early days Chambers had used the train constantly and, whenever they were on strike, he drove, rode with friends, or took the bus. Later, after he had made his millions in the export business, he hired a chauffeur, who drove him everywhere he needed to go, from city to city, state to state.

It was partly because he was constantly in an automobile that Chambers developed a penchant for picking up women. Although he certainly wasn't one to turn a woman's head, his limousine, chauffeur, fine clothes, and ever-ready cash were alluring enough. Soon Chambers found reasons to go out even when there was no business to attend to, other than appeasing his libido. After a while the first symptoms of syphilis appeared, but Chambers was too busy to take notice. He developed what looked like a fever blister on his lip, unaware that it was a chancre. Another appeared. Later they sprouted on the underside of his penis and then disappeared. Before long Jackson Chambers had spread his little gift to his wife and a dozen other women. A rash developed on his body and, when he realized what he might have, Chambers immediately went to the only man he ever discussed his medical or personal problems with, a Jewish general practitioner from Chambers's old neighborhood in Queens. The doctor treated Chambers successfully with penicillin, but the fact that he'd contracted the disease created havoc at home. Seeking something that would take him away from his home, he turned to politics. When he discovered he loved it and recognized his ambition, Chambers began to travel more and more. When urged to run for office, he knew he would have to start flying unless he wanted to limit his scope to New York state. Once again he went back to his Jewish doctor and the doctor recommended a psychiatrist in Manhattan. Reluctantly Chambers decided to go.

It took him only six weeks of therapy to decide the doctor was a quack. But, instead of going to another psychiatrist, he decided he'd just suffer through and rely on Valiums—and frequent shots of bourbon—to make his necessary plane trips bearable. But they rarely were.

Under the casual eye of the First Lady, who stood gazing down from the Truman Balcony, Hickman walked from the main mansion to the West Wing executive offices. Although Katherine was unaware of it, in a few days the entire nation would know about Jackson Chambers's problems. Thanks to Chambers, Hickman was able to plot what would become one of the most brutal smear campaigns in recent presidential politics. If everything worked, Chambers would be finished before the voting in the last round of primaries began.

For the past two weeks four operatives with contacts in several major cities worked on setting the "real" story behind Chambers into motion. They planned to show to a few select and highly influential people in the publishing and television industries copies of

Chambers's medical records: they were also prepared to produce a woman who would swear she'd had a syphilitic baby by Chambers, and, if necessary, show the nation her child. They were also prepared to produce flight attendants and crew members from some of Chambers's previous trips who would bear witness to his inability to cope with his mental anguish about flying. One of his past chauffeurs, out of patriotic duty, was willing to tell the public just what sort of philanderer Chambers was. And even a few disgruntled former congressional employeees had a score to settle with the senator.

When we finish with him, Hickman told himself, Chambers is going to wish he never entered the race. And all for the princely sum of $350,000. The only thing was that by day's end Hickman would have no need for all of this, but nobody knew it at the time.

INTERLUDE

Otis Meade sat up in bed sweating and breathing hard. It was useless to try to get any sleep. Every time he drifted off, the same haunted dreams came to him.

Jackson Chambers standing before him in the Oval Office, yelling, "Get out! This isn't your office anymore!"

Chambers turning and calling out, "Guards! Guards! Get rid of this pitiful excuse of a man!"

Then Cliff Hawkins bursting through the door, Bible in hand, shouting "Murderer! Sinner! You're going to die for what you've done! Die for your sins! Do you hear me, Mr. President? Die!"

Getting up, Meade wanted to flee as they moved toward him. But Hawkins disappeared and suddenly Chambers burst into flames. Coming toward him, Chambers began to laugh. Terrified, Meade could do nothing but watch as flaming skin dropped off him like melting wax and the body came closer and closer . . .

Meade took a deep breath and thought desperately.

I can't go on like this, he told himself. It's killing me.

He got up, went to the window, and looked out. Once again he felt tears rising. He had never been this depressed before, and he hated the feeling. But so much of what had brought it on was beyond his control, and the things that perpetuated it were even more so: the continual reminders of his actions—the newspapers, hate mail, commentators, and newscasts. His thoughts always went back to Acapulco. They're tearing me down, aren't they? The very people who elected me are tearing me down . . .

But . . .

He took a deep breath.

I . . . can't . . . let . . . them.

38

EN ROUTE TO CLEVELAND

Jackson Chambers's flight from Los Angeles, like all the others on the campaign, had been nerve-racking. By now the very idea of stepping on a plane made him shiver. Shut off in a specially built office at the rear of the plane, Chambers had been sick before take-off. Now, miles above the earth and rapidly approaching the state of Ohio, he thought he was going to die.

Mark Fisher, captain of Chambers's chartered DC-10, looked out at the beautiful blue sky before him, glanced at his copilot, then radioed Cleveland.

"Cleveland approach, this is November H-731 Hotel . . ."

A metallic voice, interspersed with static, replied, "November H-731 Hotel, this is Cleveland Hopkins, we read you."

"Cleveland approach, 31 Hotel is sixty miles southwest of airport, squawking 1200 with pappa . . ."

Keeping an easy grip on his control wheel and one eye on his altimeter, Fisher waited a few seconds and then heard, "Yes, 31 Hotel, this is approach—please ident."

Fisher glanced at his copilot, and she activated the transponder. A voice came back. "Okay, 31 Hotel, this is Cleveland approach, we have you on radar contact."

All was well.

When Jackson Chambers's assistant campaign director, Jeremy Rosenbaum, stepped into Chambers's converted office, the first thing he said was, "Jack, you look awful. Like something ran over you. You want me to get you something from up front?"

"No," Chambers sighed, "and get rid of this. It isn't worth shit." He tossed him a bottle of bourbon he'd pulled from his top desk drawer.

Rosenbaum caught it and looked up. "I thought you were laying off this stuff. You haven't been hitting it with the pills have you? The doctor—"

"The doctor doesn't have to fly in these fucking things. So how would he know what I should or shouldn't do when I'm in 'em?"

Before Rosenbaum could reply, Chambers clutched his stomach and winced. "God, I feel sick."

"Hey, pull yourself together. We'll be in Cleveland in less than fifteen minutes. The press'll be there and you've got to . . ."

"I know that already. You think I enjoy feeling like I'm going to puke? God, I must have been insane to let you guys put me on this thing."

He moaned again.

Rosenbaum leaned forward. "You want a sack?"

"Just sit down. I don't need you running around here like a Jewish mother."

"Look, you going to be okay?" asked Rosenbaum, sitting down.

"No. No, I'm not sure about anything. But for godsakes, quit asking me so many questions."

"Sure."

"Now," he said massaging his forehead, "give me a rundown on my itinerary and make it PDQ."

Rosenbaum began reading from a yellow legal pad while Chambers leaned back and listened. Rosenbaum was almost finished when the plane hit an air pocket and then moved downward. Chambers sat up and stiffened. His face went from pale green to powder white.

Rosenbaum looked up from his pad. "Jack, it's an air pocket. We're beginning the descent."

Chambers wasn't listening. Instead he was looking out one of the oval windows. Beyond the window everything was white. He couldn't see a thing.

"Clouds," explained Rosenbaum.

Chambers slowly turned back to him. "I know that. I'm not an idiot."

They hit another air pocket and the plane jerked. Almost immediately afterward they hit two more. The plane swayed and dipped. Its engines began whining much more loudly. Chambers broke out in a sweat. His eyes mirrored the hell he was going through and Rosenbaum was worried.

"Hey, come on, relax. We're almost there." Then as an afterthought, he said, "This isn't any time to fall apart, you know."

That did it. "Fall apart? Who's falling apart? What in the fuck are you talking about? You think I'm falling apart?"

Rosenbaum tried to clarify himself but Chambers cut him off. "Look, don't worry about me, Jerry, okay?" He ran his hand nervously through his hair. "Just get out there and see that those people up front aren't cracking up. They're the ones you oughta worry about. Now go on." He began shooing the air in front of him. "Go on, go on . . ."

Rosenbaum got up and went out.

The plane hit a cross current and took a violent dip. Vibrations trembled throughout the interior and the cabin moaned in a symphony of noises. For a few seconds it felt as though the plane might snap apart.

Chambers was breathing hard now and broke out in a heavy sweat. He glanced around nervously and gripped the sides of his chair. His body went rigid. Over and over he told himself, I can't flip. I can't flip. Air pockets. It's fucking air pockets, that's all. That's all.

Captain Mark Fisher, undeterred by the minor turbulence, looked several miles up ahead at the rapidly approaching metropolis and waited for a reply. In a few seconds it came.

"Okay, 31 Hotel, this is Cleveland approach. Change to tower frequency one-one-four-point-five."

"Switching frequencies," said Fisher. "Cleveland Tower, this is 31 Hotel. We're downwind for three six."

"Ten-four, 31 Hotel, we have you downwind for three-six."

* * *

In his back cabin office Chambers took deep breaths and tried not to think about the descent. But then the plane hit more turbulence, and vibrations ran from the tip of the nose to the rear of the fuselage. Then another air pocket. A jolt. Above his office door the FASTEN YOUR SEAT BELT sign was blinking on and off. If he'd had a gun, he would have blown the damn thing right off the wall. Instead he just swallowed hard. Jack, you've been through this a hundred times before. Just sit tight. Just sit tight. Nothing's going to happen. Turbulence and air pockets, that's all.

Mark Fisher's eyes kept moving from the altimeter to the TAI.

"Cleveland approach," he radioed, "this is 31 Hotel on base for three six." Fisher turned to his copilot. "Give me 25-degree flaps."

"Okay, 25 flaps."

"Gear down."

She activated the gear.

Nothing happened.

A small alarm went off in the cockpit telling them the gear had not been activated. Fisher glanced at the landing gear lights and confirmed it: they were all off.

"Christ, not again."

"I don't understand it," his copilot said. "Everything was okay on the preflight check."

"Go to auxiliary."

She did and beneath them they should have heard the backup hydraulic system shoving the gear down through the gear doors. But there was nothing.

"Manual."

Again, nothing.

Fisher and his copilot and navigator quickly glanced at each other. Something was wrong. This had never happened before. It wasn't supposed to happen. Your manual backup should *always* drop your gear.

"What in the hell's wrong with those wheels?"

In his back office Chambers was holding his stomach and trying hard not to throw up. He was also trying very hard to hold onto his sanity. His heart beat faster and faster. He was covered in sweat. Something's wrong. I know it I know it I know it. Don't ask me fucking how, sixth sense or whatever, but I know it. Never, never again am I going to get on these motherfucking planes. President or not, it just isn't worth it. Those bastards can come to me. No trips to Europe or the Middle East or Japan or anywhere. They're gonna come to me. To me to *me*.

Mark Fisher looked at the gear indicator lights and then at his fuel level indicator. They were in trouble. Their gear wouldn't drop and their fuel reserves wouldn't allow enough circling time even to attempt to correct the problem. They had bypassed their scheduled refueling stop and Fisher had been forced to do what no pilot ever likes to do: count on his reserves. If he wasn't making the money he was off these people, he would have insisted on stopping, but his passengers wouldn't hear of it. The senator had already been held up for three hours in a Los Angeles traffic jam and they'd be damned if they were going to have any more delays. Senator Chambers had to get to Cleveland on time, so they flew nonstop. And they were going to pay for that mistake.

Fisher picked up his intercom and called the head flight attendant. "Candy? Tell the campaign people we're having a minor problem and that we're trying to fix it as quickly as we can."

"I will, Captain."

After the announcement came over, Jackson Chambers popped two more Valiums and wished to hell he hadn't tossed Rosenbaum his bourbon. He was a wreck. An absolute wreck. Minor problems. I know a whole hell of a lot about minor problems on these things. And they never tell you until after you've landed just how minor the problems were . . . things like brakes failing, cargo doors flying off, landing gear that won't drop . . . minor problems? Fucking planes. Why did I ever get on this thing?

Back in the cockpit Fisher's copilot asked, "What about rocking it?"

"I dunno," he said nervously, looking out at the metropolis straight ahead, wondering just how long it would be before his colleagues realized they weren't going to be afforded the luxury of a holding pattern. "There isn't much else to do."

"What about a holdin—"

"I'll try rocking it."

He picked up his intercom again and told the head flight attendant to inform the passengers what was happening. "And warn them about the rocking."

She said she would.

Chambers ran his hand frantically through his hair and down his sweat-covered face. His body made little jerking movements to accommodate his rising blood pressure, heart rate, and overall panic. He wanted to get up, to run down and ask them if it was true, if the landing gear was really not dropping, but he could not move out of his seat. Instead he sat in an immobile hell, afraid to look out, afraid to look ahead, below, or above him. He just kept running his hand through his hair.

Gear ... the gear ... fucking gear ... rockitrockitrockitrockit ... the gear ... I knewitknewitknewitknewitknewit ... fucking p ... p ... p ... planes ... nevernevernever again ... be a beabeabea ... fucking cold ... day ... colddayinhellbeforeIflyagain ...

"Cleveland Hopkins, this is 31 Hotel, over."

"Go head, 31 Hotel, this is Cleveland."

"Uh, we're having a bit of trouble with our landing gear, Cleveland. Our wheels won't drop. Repeat, our wheels won't drop. Also ... uh, our backup isn't working either."

"Roger, 31 Hotel. Have you tried rocking your craft to help them fall? Over."

"We're going to do that now, over."

"Roger, 31 Hotel. Please keep us advised. Over."

Clutching his control wheel, Fisher gently tipped the plane from side to side like a seesaw. He watched the simulated plane in his artificial horizon do the same. Then he glanced over at the triangle of gear indicator lights. They were still off. He looked in front of him and could see they were coming up on Cleveland fast.

"Nothing's happening," his copilot said.

"I see it. Hang on, I'm gonna shake this baby good."

The plane dipped sharply from one side to the other.

Fisher gave it another good shake. Then another.

"Still hasn't dropped."

"Damn!"

Fisher tried it again, this time more anxiously. They were moving too quickly. The airport was already in view.

"It still hasn't."

Again, he tried.

"Damn it!"

"Mark, we've got to take into holding. Call Cleveland."

"We—" He picked up the mike and called without finishing the sentence. "Cleveland, this is 31 Hotel. Response on rocking is continually negative. Repeat, negative."

There was a pause. "Uh, roger, 31 Hotel. Obviously you can't—aren't capable of landing. Do you wish to establish a holding pattern?"

Fisher stared at his fuel reserves. He had thought they could go into a holding pattern for ten, maybe fifteen minutes, but now he even doubted that. They had tried everything they could and their reserves were almost gone. He looked at his copilot and navigator.

"Mark, aren't you going to tell them?"

Then slowly he turned away and said, "Cleveland, we can't go into a holding pattern. Repeat, can't go into a holding pattern."

Immediately his copilot and navigator turned in shock.

"What?"

"What, 31 Hotel? Did you say, 'Cannot go into holding'?"

"Ten-four."

A worried voice came back to him. "Is this going to be an emergency landing, 31 Hotel?"

Fisher swallowed hard. "Roger. We don't have any choice."

At Cleveland Hopkins there was considerable murmuring in the background.

"What is your ETA, 31 Hotel?"

Fisher glanced at his TAI, then said, "ETA is four minutes, maybe less."

"Roger, 31 Hotel. You have emergency clearance. We're getting rescue out on number 7. They'll try to get it foamed."

"Roger, Cleveland."

Fisher then decided to give the plane another shake. And then another.

"Captain," his copilot said bitterly, "it's not working."

They were moving too fast.

Too fast.

Fisher picked up the intercom again. "Candy, listen to what I have to say very carefully. I need you to tell the passengers that we're ..."

* * *

When Jeremy Rosenbaum heard the announcement, he ignored the flight attendant's orders to get into a crash position and rushed back to Chambers's office. When he opened the door, he saw the candidate sitting with his eyes shut, clutching the seat. Hearing the door open, Chambers looked at Rosenbaum and said with a frightened expression, "My mother. You're not my mother . . . where's my mother? I want to know!"

Rosenbaum went over to him and shook him. "Jack, look, you've got to pull yourself together for godsakes. It's gonna be all right, believe me. But hold together, Jack. Don't do this to me. Now now. Please, you'll lose everything!"

"My mother! I want her with me, you sonofabitch! Right now!"

"Jack, there are press out there. Keep it down and hold yourself together!"

Chambers looked at him, as if he didn't understand, and suddenly began to whimper. "I knew this would happen . . . knew it . . ."

Three minutes and fifty seconds later runway 7 was dead ahead.

Mark Fisher could feel his muscles tense as the jet began to lower for its final approach. His heart was beating furiously and his internal organs felt as though they were on fire.

This was it. They had prepared him for it, but nothing really prepares you when it happens . . .

He didn't want to move, didn't want to breathe. Before him lay the starkest reason for terror that he'd ever seen. Moving toward it, faster than they should, was number 7. A hot black slab. It went on for miles. He could feel it coming too quickly.

The foam! Where was the foam? The rescue squads? The fire trucks?

They were roaring toward it and Fisher's eyes locked straight ahead.

His copilot frantically called off their descending altitude. "One hundred feet . . . 90 . . . 80 . . . 70 . . . 60 . . ."

Numbers echoed throughout the cockpit.

" . . . 50 . . . 40 . . . 30 . . ."

"No . . . oh, God, no!"

In a blur of searing speed the runway passed beneath them.

Fisher's eyes riveted in horror as the black ocean of death swept up on them.

It was happening too fast! All of it was happening too fast!

Fisher screamed and his blood turned to ice.

39

CALIFORNIA/San Francisco

The sea battered the coast, sending waves high over the jagged rocks below. From the hotel's balcony it was awesome and magnificent. The waves were swift, strong, and ever changing.

Cliff Hawkins stood on the balcony of his hotel suite, watching the waves torture the rocks below, and thought about the sea and all its power, of how much he knew about the sea and how much he wished he knew, of how much he loved it. Another one of God's mighty creations.

Behind him a glass door slid back.

"Cliff?"

Hawkins didn't turn around. Instead he reached one hand out toward the sea as if to touch it.

"Isn't it beautiful, Randy? If we could only harness one-tenth of that energy, we'd never have to worry about OPEC again. The Lord's going to have to show us how."

Hawkins felt a hand on his shoulder. "Cliff, something's come up."

Hawkins looked away from the water. "What is it? You look tired."

"It's Chambers. We just got word that his plane crashed in Cleveland."

"What?" It was as if a bolt had hit him in the chest.

"Crashed. Coming in for a landing. Their wheels wouldn't come down."

Hawkins stared at him for a moment and then took a chair and sat down. He was having trouble registering Perrin's words.

"Crashed . . . is he—"

"No," Perrin said, lighting up a cigarette. "But it wouldn't make much difference if he was."

"He's . . . he's in critical condition then?"

Perrin shook his head. "No, I'm sorry. That's not what I meant. He didn't get hurt. Others did. The captain and copilot died, but Chambers got out of an emergency exit and . . ." his voice trailed off.

". . . and what?"

Perrin looked out at the sea, then turned back to Hawkins. "It's pretty bad, Cliff. He . . . when he . . . got out on the runway, he went berserk. Literally berserk. They said he was screaming and crying and yelling just like a little kid. He lunged at some firemen and newspeople and, when they tried to restrain him, he began kicking and biting."

Hawkins couldn't believe what he was hearing.

"Finally they restrained him, but he broke away and took off down the runway, tearing off his clothes. I told you, he just went berserk."

Hawkins loosened his tie and said slowly, "Oh, dear Lord, why?"

For a moment the two of them said nothing. Then Hawkins asked him, "Then . . . then what happened?"

It was so pathetic, Perrin thought, why do you ask? "Then they caught him again, but this time it took five medics and some Secret Service to hold him down."

"Anything else?"

"Yes—they took him away in a straitjacket."

Everything had changed. A series of events and now Chambers was out. A traffic jam in Los Angeles, a decision not to refuel, landing gear that wouldn't drop, and a plane that was forced to come in on its belly. As for Chambers, his career was finished. Nobody needed to tell Hawkins that. Reacting that way on the runway effectively destroyed everything he'd gained in politics, yet Hawkins knew he couldn't help it. Reports had begun to surface about his lifelong fear of flying and the evangelist was amazed that Chambers could have kept it a secret so long. But it was a mental problem and there was no way a man could expect to occupy the presidency and work with that disability. . . . The public tolerated very little when it came to the mental health of their politicians—remember Eagleton's problems in 1972. They would never stand for this, nor should they.

Hawkins stared out at the sea and knew that he or Larry Broder would be battling Meade in November. The president would get his nomination after all. It was amazing how life worked, he thought. For all of Meade's efforts to rally the people for all of his whistle-stops and pressing flesh to rectify his record and keep what little flock he had left from straying over to Chambers's camp, it had all been unnecessary. All of it. Meade would get what he wanted, whether he deserved it or not—and Hawkins knew it would change the course of the race even more. For Meade would be unable to use his record as a basis for reelection. So what would he use? Offensive methods. Fear. Mistrust. Suspicion. All directed at whomever he opposed. Hawkins's advisers and draft movement people had told him over a year and a half ago to expect this. During these primaries they had seen their predictions come true. And perhaps the voters had come to expect this from Meade. Perhaps that was why Christian evangelicals and even Mormons, Catholics, Orthodox Jews, and other religious groups who had been longing for conservative leadership within the Oval Office were now so openly rallying behind Hawkins. Although Hawkins's most ardent supporters, particularly conservative Baptists and Catholics, had supported his candidacy from the beginning, it was only lately that influential members from all the faiths realized he was the only man who would actually *work* for godly government and not just talk about it. They realized that he believed the law of God should have normative value in society, as implicitly stated in the Constitution and explicity stated in the Declaration of Independence. They knew he would bring intellectual conservatives into his cabinet to carry out his plans. There was no one else.

But Larry Broder was still a force to be reckoned with. So now the question was, who would oppose Meade?

Hawkins was within inches of having enough delegates to win. But the delegates weren't bound to vote for him on the first ballot. Historically they usually did, but if Broder pulled through in two of the three remaining primaries, there could be a floor fight for the nomination.

But the Lord wouldn't have brought me this far without giving me the nomination. I know he wouldn't. This is his race as much as it is mine.

Leaning on the edge of the balcony, he opened his hand and then quickly closed it as if he had seen something in the air and grabbed it.

The nomination?

Yes. I can feel it.

He turned to go in, glanced back briefly at the sea, restless in its attack upon the coast, and went inside.

40

WASHINGTON/The White House

Meade would never forget how he found out. It had been afternoon.
He was in a meeting in the Roosevelt Room. Although he was tired
and depressed and it showed, the people around him were getting
used to it. The room was filled with economic advisers, who took
forever to get their points across. Meade was looking for an excuse
to adjourn when Howard Hickman came in with the strangest look
on his face. Later Meade could have sworn it was a smile. Hickman
went over to him and whispered what had happened. Immediately
Meade adjourned the meeting.

He couldn't remember what he'd done the rest of the afternoon or
much of that evening. There had been phone calls to make and two
short emergency campaign meetings, but all of these were eclipsed
by the crash and what it had done to Chambers. He had watched all
three evening newscasts simultaneously. The stories were the same.
A plane without any visible wheels steadily approached the runway,
coming closer to the cameras with each frame. Then suddenly—impact. Sparks. Flames. The plane bounced and skidded along the hot
dry runway. It began to turn. A wing was ripped way. Fire engines,
ambulances, and television news trucks raced toward it. Eventually
the plane came to a halt. Emergency exits flew back and inflatable

slides appeared. One by one, the bodies came tumbling down. Then there was Chambers. The cameras zoomed in on him instinctively, and one could tell at once he was not the same. After he was helped to his feet at the bottom of the slide by the Secret Service and before they could hustle him off to safety, his mouth became a great screaming O. Several medics and firemen rushed forward. He lunged at them. The Secret Service tried to restrain him, but he broke away screaming. It ended with a long shot of a man running away from a burning plane tearing his clothes off.

Outwardly mesmerized by the footage, though inwardly unaffected by it, Meade knew that if anyone were to ask him for a reaction, he couldn't have given one. The pressures that had been plaguing him certainly weren't going to stop because of this, and the fact that the biggest obstacle blocking his renomination had now been eliminated didn't even occur to him. Instead his thoughts danced vaguely around other stories on the broadcasts: Acapulco, something about his campaign, and something on Cliff Hawkins. At the end of the eleven o'clock news he picked up the phone and ordered a chopper to the South Lawn. Although unsure why, he felt he had to get away from the White House. Forty minutes later he was flying toward Camp David—alone.

MARYLAND/Camp David

Meade's first night there was sleepless. He didn't think about the crash or about the campaign. Instead he lay in his bed, staring aimlessly at the ceiling.

The next morning he skipped breakfast and went out to walk through the woods and pathways surrounding Aspen Lodge, the comfortable presidential cabin. He walked through the woods like a ghost, not noticing the beauty around him. He simply walked. And walked.

Later in the afternoon Meade plunged into the swimming pool with such force that one would have thought he was on fire. The Secret Service agents watching discretely were amazed at the intensity of his swimming.

The president swam from one end of the pool to the other.

And then back again.

Over and over. Lap after lap.

With each movement, each stroke, each turn of the head, the muscles in his arms and shoulders and neck and the thrashing of his legs mirrored the strain he was feeling.

The pressure.

You're going to pay for this. More than you realize.

Lap after lap.

They're not going to let you forget what you've done. None of them.

Lap after lap.

It will be on your record, in the history books, they're not going to let you forget . . .

Over and over.

Not going to let you . . . not going to let you . . . not going . . .

Suddenly Meade stopped swimming, threw his head out of the water and cried, "Damnit, I'll make them forget!"

It was coming back. His motivation, his determination, his strength. He knew it. He could feel the depression that had been hanging over him leaving. He didn't know the psychological mechanics of why, but had no need to. He only knew he'd been living with a burden that he didn't have to carry anymore—as if he'd been required to walk up an enormously steep mountain with a fifty pound backpack tied on him, and then someone suddenly took it off. Acapulco was over. Jackson Chambers was out of the race and whatever energies he'd been channeling into the aftermath of Acapulco now had to be turned to the reality that the race had changed.

Yes, it was all coming back. He was beginning to feel again. The numbness had finally started to wear off. Fate plays such strange games, he thought, picking up the telephone in his cabin. It came close to destroying me, but it's destroyed Jackson Chambers instead.

A military aide answered. "Yes, sir?"

"Get my chopper ready. I want to get back to Washington."

"Yes, Mr. President. We'll have it ready in fifteen minutes."

"Thanks."

There was a knock on the front door. A military valet entered. "You're going to be leaving us, Mr. President?"

"Yes, got to get back."

"I'll go ahead and pack up your things, sir."

"Fine," Meade nodded, and the valet disappeared into his bedroom.

Meade was about to get up from his desk and gather up the few papers he'd brought with him when the telephone rang.

"Yes?"

"Mr. President, Mrs. Meade is on line 1."

He hesitated before answering. He would rather have talked to Kat when he got back to Washington, but he knew she had called several times today and yesterday. So had Hickman, his press secretary—Jody Allen—and half a dozen others.

He punched line 1. "Kat?"

"Otis, how do you feel?"

"Better."

"I've been worried about you. Why didn't you tell me you wanted to fly up there? I would have come if for no other reason than to be there with you."

"I needed to come up on my own. I had a lot of thinking to do. I'm sorry, but I was not in the best state to say anything. Anyway the Secret Service should have told you."

"They did, but I . . . well, you are feeling better?"

"Yes, and we're leaving in a few minutes. They're getting things together now."

Katherine sounded relieved. "Good. Howard's been trying to get through to you and so has Jody. This place is coming apart. Everyone wants to know why you took off in the middle of the night."

"It's none of their damn business."

"I know, but everything's up in the air over this accident. Jody says the press is screaming for a news conference, and Howard's got half the top party brass pounding on his door trying to see you."

"They don't know I'm up here, do they?"

"I don't know. You know how leaks have been, but Howard's trying to cover up as best he can."

"Do you have any good news?" he asked tiredly.

"Yes. Jody phoned me and said if I talked to you to tell you none of the networks carried anything on Acapulco this morning."

Meade couldn't believe what he'd heard. "Are you sure?"

"That's what he said. None of them."

"Then he's sure?"

"He said he phoned the networks for confirmation and they gave it. Everything's centering on the plane crash."

Meade felt as if someone had pulled a plug and let all the turbulent water surrounding him drain away. Nothing mentioned about Acapulco. Nothing. He felt relief, almost gratitude.

* * *

Ten minutes later the president's chopper lifted up, hovered momentarily over the beautiful pine trees, and then flew away from Camp David. It really was over. He knew he had almost lost the presidency and himself, but that was in the past. What had happened had happened. And while Chambers and Acapulco were tragic, neither would keep him down anymore. Two days ago he had arrived with nothing but depression. He was leaving with the self he had lost. He had an election to win and remorse and sorrow wouldn't help him win it. He had to lift himself up, go on, push himself harder than ever before. No one knew this better than he did.

41

What had done it? Katherine brushed her hair before her dressing room mirror and wondered. What had jolted him out of almost a month of brooding? Had his system been pushed to its tolerance level by the crash, then subconsciously boomeranged as an act of self-preservation?

Katherine laid down her brush and sighed happily. The reasons were unimportant. It didn't matter what had done it for him, she was simply thankful it had happened. She'd noticed the change in his eyes that morning as he came out of the helicopter. His color was back, his eyes were full of life, and his walk was straight and steady, not slumped and beaten as it had been. Within him there was a . . . a certain determination, a fierceness, that she hadn't seen in ages. As if he couldn't wait to get back to the work he had been doing so mechanically before. She had hugged and kissed him, and he had pressed his body close to hers and . . . and there was something else.

There was, I know there was. I'm not imagining it. Otis's message was clear. *I want you.* If not now, then later. But I want you.

So Katherine waited for later to come. Meade spent the entire day either in meetings or on the telephone, not even breaking for lunch and barely stopping for dinner. Early in the evening he held a televised press conference, his first in what seemed like years, and it was carried by all the networks.

Standing in the back of the East Room, Katherine watched her husband handle the conference with more mastery than she remembered his displaying in a long time. He began with an opening statement about the crash, calling it a "cruel tragedy," and expressed his sympathy for the families of the pilot and copilot and wished Jackson Chambers "a speedy recovery." Then he opened himself up for questions. By now it was well known that the president had sneaked off to Camp David for a few days and the questions centered around that. He handled them, as he did the rest of the news conference, with aplomb, saying the crash had left him "very disturbed" and he felt the need to get away and "reflect on a lot of things." When the press conference turned to foreign and domestic matters, Meade handled those questions just as expertly and, when it began to move away from the direction he wanted it to take, he skillfully moved it back on track.

Concerning the election, Meade told them that it looked as though the race might be between himself and Cliff Hawkins, incredible as that sounded. "I, as much as anyone, am surprised that a man of Reverend Hawkins's background could come this far, but I do realize the very large number of people who believe in his candidacy and are working for his election and I respect their efforts. But, of course, I don't support them." Everyone laughed. He went on to say that once the conventions were over and the campaigns kicked off on Labor Day, it would be a race unique in American history. Meade felt strong and said so, making it clear he was determined to meet Hawkins head on.

Katherine gazed into the mirror and allowed a smile. Somewhere deep within her, even when she considered all of their problems, the mistakes and sacrifices they'd both made, at bottom she was very proud of her husband. Yes, he'd made it hard on her. At times she thought she would scream out of the frustration and pain she felt, and even now she would leave him if forced to, but the circumstances and events that brought those troubles into being seemed so long ago. The incident in New York was behind them. So were the days of coming in and finding his bed sheets rumpled, perfume-scented towels hanging in the bathroom, and the many other irritations that reminded her she wasn't the only one. But that was in the past, she was sure of it. He needed her now. She had seen it in his eyes this morning when he flew back. They were hungry eyes. Hungry for love and passion and everything she wanted to give him. Months ago she had been sitting in this same room, trying to read a magazine, and thinking, he's never loved you. He only married you for your money, your name. You're nothing to him. A mannequin. Someone to pull out at state dinners. But to make love to? Oh, Katherine, how can you be so naive?"

And yet she wasn't, was she? She knew where the cards lay all the time and where they would be two, three years from now, God willing. No, maybe he didn't love her as she loved him, maybe that was true. But if anyone else had seen what she had seen in his eyes today, there wouldn't be any doubt. He needed her. His eyes told her so.

The president was in his wingback chair, in his pajamas with reading glasses on, as he worked on some papers, when she entered his bedroom. He was absorbed in his work and didn't look up. Undeterred, Katherine ran her hands down her nightgown to make certain it was smooth and went over and knelt beside him. He tilted his head and peered at her through his glasses.

"The First Lady."

"Yes, and the very busy president."

"Have to work," he said, removing his glasses. "So far behind I don't know when I'll ever catch up."

Katherine rested one arm on his leg. "Don't overdo it, Otis. You don't have to. Nobody expects it."

"Oh, yes, they do," he said, putting his glasses back on. "The public expects it. We're never supposed to rest, didn't you know that?"

She gently squeezed his knee and smiled, "No, I didn't."

Meade shifted uncomfortably.

"The press conference—do you think it went well?"

"Very," she said, slowly moving her hand up and down his leg. "Very, very well."

Meade tried to ignore the signals she was sending him and turned back to his paperwork, muttering, "Well, I'm glad, Kat ... really glad."

Katherine continued to rub his leg, moving her hand farther up toward his groin with each stroke.

He shifted again and Katherine thought: It's going to take time.

This past month has been hell for him and it's going to take time. He hasn't wanted to in so long. But that's understandable.

Katherine persisted, her eyes following the movements of her hand until she felt warmth flooding between her own legs. She placed her free hand down there. She was burning up. Her mouth went dry and her heart fluttered and she felt faint.

Her breath quickened and her heart pounded furiously. She rubbed his leg harder and harder, faster and faster, until suddenly, unexpectedly, shockingly, Meade laid down his papers, took off his glasses, ran his hand through his hair and said, "Kat, why are you doing this? Now? Now, when I've got a hundred other things on my mind?"

Katherine pulled her hand away and stammered, "I—I—I thought you, that you wanted to, that, well, this morning when you got off the plane and hugged me and looked at me and gave me that look or what I thought was, was that look that you wanted, needed . . ."

She stopped and stared at him, reading his thoughts. She understood.

"Kat, I'm sorry, but . . . you made a mistake. I don't want you. Haven't in ages. Why in the hell can't you get that through your head? . . . I've got too many things on my mind right now. I feel as if I'm on overload and this just isn't the time or place."

Her eyes grew large and her lips trembled. "Nothing's changed, has it? I thought somehow it would, but . . ."

"Kat, it's not like that. Honestly. It's just that—"

"Nothing's changed, has it?" she cried even louder. "Not a damn thing!"

He started to speak but couldn't. Using every bit of strength she had, she pulled herself up from the floor. Her tears smeared her mascara, painting two black daggers on her face. Trembling, she wiped her cheeks and backed away.

Meade got up. "Kat—"

She took one long look at him, then turned and went out.

Meade stood in front of his bathroom mirror, mesmerized by his own reflection. He leaned forward and studied his face—the thin lines etched down and across it; the shadow of a beard that had cropped up since he'd shaved this morning; the dryness of his lips; the tiny blood vessels in his eyes. It was not the face of a man he might, upon meeting, particularly like. This was the face of a hard man, calculating, even destructive. A face that needed no accompanying voice since its contour told everything one needed to know.

It was a face that hurt others.

Why?

Why had he handled her the way he did? Why couldn't he have given in to her, satisfied so small a need? Yet how could he without her knowing? She was so naive, even now. So damn blind. This morning—what was that crap about the way I looked this morning when I got off the chopper? God, I don't even know what's running through her mind half the time—and now tonight. But, had he done it, she would have known. She would have guessed, as he went through the motions, he wasn't thinking of her.

It was after 9:00 P.M. and Meade was nervous as he spoke into the phone. He hoped to God his voice wasn't recognizable. But then you never know. Those damned impersonators forever seemed to be taking potshots at him.

"Maria Vásquez?" the nurse asked, obviously surprised.

"Uh, right. It's rather urgent."

"Need I remind you what time it is?" she asked curtly.

"Uh, like I said, it *is* urgent."

"Well, she's probably in bed by now, but if you really think this warrants such an interruption ..."

"Yes. Yes, I do."

The nurse sighed. Meade could picture her filing her nails as she talked.

"All right, I'll go get her. No phone in her room, you know. So I'll have to walk all the way down to her room. It will take a minute or so."

"Fine, just—" The nurse was already gone. "Just don't strain your fucking self."

The longer Meade waited, the more he questioned the wisdom of phoning her. It had been an impulse—one of those rare moments when he had allowed emotion to take over. But what was the point? Why bring up old memories? Why bother? She was a tour guide who had serviced him. Nothing more. There were so many other things he needed to think about. She was well on her way to being fully recovered, or so the last report had indicated. But that had been a couple of months ago. What further progress had she made? At one point he'd heard she had begun counseling other addicts. But now?

Meade pressed his ear closer to the phone. The nurse had laid it down, probably on the counter at the nurses' station, and he could hear approaching footsteps. Then several women's voices. Maria's? He couldn't be sure. They came closer. Someone picked up the phone. There was a pause, and then the voice said, "Hello?"

Meade wet his lips. His mouth opened, but—

It was Maria all right. Meade tightened his grip on the receiver and took a deep breath. He tried again to speak, wanted to speak, but something stopped him.

"Hello? Hello?" the voice repeated.

Meade pulled the phone away from his ear and held it out before him. He could hear the alarmed voice drifting up from the phone. "Who is this? Hello? What do you want? Otis? Otis, is that you?"

His name! She said his name!

Meade held the phone farther away from him and wiped his brow. What was she doing? What was he doing? Why had he done this?

I've got to do something! Speak to her or hang up the phone or something!

And he did. Meade dropped the receiver on the floor and walked away.

INTERLUDE

WASHINGTON/Georgetown

Deep in Georgetown, where so many of the politically and socially prominent live, on O Street NW between Thirtieth and Thirty-first streets, there is a three-story townhouse known as the Crawford-Cassin House. Brick with a small garden in the back and neatly trimmed shrubs, it has a unique two-story porch on one side. The house is elegant without being pretentious, beautiful without being elaborate.

Howard Hickman began renting the Crawford-Cassin House from one of the president's biggest supporters right after the 1989 inauguration. Although he got the home at a fraction of the going rate, it still consumed more than half his salary. But for Hickman the price—as well as the sacrifice—was worth it. He was close to the heart of Washington and the address alone spoke authority, power, and, most of all, prestige.

On the eve of the New Jersey primary, when the lights of his neighbors' homes went out, Hickman's burned throughout the house. It was almost three in the morning and he had just returned home, having stayed at the White House after a state dinner to go over some last-minute primary details with the president. The four men sitting with him in his library hadn't been there long either, and Hickman wanted their meeting to move quickly. He was damn tired.

"All right," he said, pulling a chair away from his desk and taking a seat. "I'm sorry we weren't able to get together sooner than this—Ferrigo, I know you wanted to—but with the crash everyone over at 1600 Pennsylvania's been going crazy trying to sort things out." He looked down at a yellow legal pad in front of him. "Now, according to my figures you've had expenditures of $189,000 or thereabouts and, since we can't use any of that crap now, we're going to have to write the whole thing off. Obviously you're still getting your pay since it's already been deducted from this sheet, but that leaves us with $120,000 that went straight down the tube."

"Hickman, look," Ferrigo said, "I don't see why you still can't release that as additional information anyway. It'd cover your losses and rub his nose in his own shit."

Hickman took a deep breath. Christ, how he hated dealing with people who had room temperature IQs. "Because I think it'd look just a little too suspicious if your sources were handed classified information dealing directly with Chambers's fear of flying right after his plane crashed. Don't you think the crash would look premeditated? Besides, there's no reason to rub his nose in it. The man's in a rubber room as it is."

"Then why did you want this meeting?" asked Ferrigo.

"Because," Hickman said looking at the men, "we still have $161,000 left from the funds Martin gave us and I want to put it to use. The question is: do you think you can do something for that amount?"

Ferrigo glanced at his colleagues and then at Hickman. "That depends. How extensive an operation do you want?"

"How do I know? I don't even know what I want done or what you can do beyond what've you told me. All I'm saying is this: the president is going to face a very difficult reelection and we may need to call on your services. We have the money, but we're going to need assurance that we can count on you to come through."

"Didn't we come through on this last job?"

Hickman nodded, "Yes, but last time I handled the research end. This time I'm not going to have time. We've got a fucking convention coming up and then the general election. So are you willing to take on research and operation? Or shall we just part ways now?"

Ferrigo and the others looked at each other, and then Ferrigo said, "We'll do whatever you need us to. It's Hawkins, isn't it?"

"It is if he gets the nomination."

"Do you think he will?"

"God, I hope not."

MARYLAND/The Hampton Clinic

Maria Vásquez sat at one of the small partitioned telephone tables down the hall from the nurses' station and dialed a private line to the White House.

A few seconds later she heard, "Oval Office, this is Marge."

She took a deep breath. Her body was trembling. "Yes, this is . . . this is Maria Vásquez. I'm returning a telephone call that Ot—the president—made to me late last night. I'm . . . I'm afraid we weren't able to talk then."

"All right, Miss Vásquez," Marge said politely, thinking she had another nut on the line. How they ever got this number, she'd never figure out. "Just let me have your name and telephone number and I'll tell the president you called."

"No!" she whispered urgently. "No, I . . . I must speak to him now! As soon as possible! He needed to talk to me about something urgent, and I—"

"Now, Miss Vásquez," Marge interrupted, "you know the president's quite busy and it would be impossible for him to come to the phone right now. Now, please, just let me get your number and I'm sure he'll get back to you as soon—"

The line went dead. Maria had hung up. She was crying.

BOOK THREE

THE CONVENTIONS

42

TEXAS/Dallas

Before the three final primaries the pollsters, political scientists, and election analysts gave Cliff Hawkins only one state—New Jersey—with Sheldon Roberts taking Ohio and Larry Broder California. The more the analysts talked, the more apparent it became that Larry Broder might very well win the nomination over Hawkins. For Broder's supporters, who'd seen their candidate hold his own after announcing a woman, Alice Germond, as his running mate, the news was encouraging, and more money and volunteers poured into his campaign offices around the nation.

But if Broder's supporters were dedicated, Hawkins's supporters looked upon getting him elected as a mission of God. In all three states Christian fundamentalists, evangelicals, conservative Mormons, and even Orthodox Jews who had longed for a candidate like Hawkins turned out in record numbers and spent plenty of money to get the vote out. To them, this could well be the most important election year in the history of the United States, a watershed in American politics. Their political and religious zeal made them more determined than ever to see that their kind of candidate—a solid, intelligent, Christian candidate—won.

And in one clean sweep they turned the analysts' predictions upside down, handing Hawkins all three states, two by landslides, and with more than enough delegates to win the Republican party's nomination. Around the nation headlines screamed the news: HAWKINS WINS BIG THREE, LANDSLIDES FOR CLIFF, THREE STUNNING WINS FOR CLIFF, EVANGELIST TAKES ALL THREE, HAWKINS OVER THE TOP!, EVANGELIST GRABS ALL! Nowhere was it more evident that Hawkins was on his way to becoming a presidential nominee than on the campaign trail. His Secret Service agents were more nervous, crowds had tripled, his press had doubled. He had an army of new speech writers, pollsters, strategists, and accountants. Randy Perrin was now trailed by four assistants wherever he went. Political hopefuls and self-appointed advisers, who knew there was still a vice presidential running mate to consider, called him daily.

Hawkins had persisted, believing when most would have given up, and the people he'd said were out there, his "silent majority," began to come out and vote. In every state. The more other groups opposed him, the more they turned out. It came down to whether you wanted to leave America as it was, preserve it the way it used to be, or go the way of Rome. Enough people had now answered, "Preserve!" to give him the Republican party's nomination.

Outwardly Hawkins was the same as he'd been from the start. His speeches, goals, optimism, determination, and enthusiasm were the same. Nevertheless, if one looked for changes in him, one could find them: in his perceptions of people, his faith. The firm lines that separated pessimism and optimism, good and bad, right and wrong— which he'd used so often, with the Bible as the final word—were becoming less firm, replaced by a hardcore realism. For out there, touring the ghettos and seeing the poor, talking to the unemployed and those on welfare, he was not protected by the comfort of a television studio or an arena of eighteen thousand fervent supporters who'd come to hear him deliver the gospel. Surrounded by stark reality, he saw that it was going to take more than whatever he and Congress could do to change things. Perhaps even more than the Lord himself could do.

There were other changes too. Prayers and meditations, the foundation of his life, were getting shorter, his readings of the Scripture more hurried. There were factory lines to hit, fund-raising breakfasts to speak at, press conferences to hold, hospitals and clinics to tour, and nursing homes to canvas. A typical presidential candidate's itinerary left him with very little time for that one thing which had elevated him to where he was today: his religion.

For a man who had devoted almost his entire adult life to preaching the Gospel and witnessing his faith to others, he rarely quoted the Bible anymore in public. Issues were the password now, not deliverance.

Politically he was more aggressive, more calculating, more selfish. But, as he continually reminded himself, so much was at stake. Millions of people were putting their faith and money in his candidacy, believing it was truly sanctioned by the Lord. If he lost either the nomination or the election, where would he stand? *The Lord's candidate didn't lose!* His credibility and much of the support that had turned Christ Church Worldwide and Moral Americans, Inc., into an empire would be gone. Hawkins shuddered and pressed on, campaigning harder than ever.

If Cliff Hawkins's campaign was making him pay a price, the toll it took on Charlotte was even greater. The Republicans were going to nominate an evangelist for president because voters all over America had elected enough of his delegates to do it. And they wanted to do it right.

At the estate phones rang endlessly. Secret Service details prowled the grounds, and vice presidential contenders flew in daily for interviews with Hawkins and the party brass he'd invited to be a part of the process. With the press practically camping out on their front lawn, it had gotten to the point where Charlotte couldn't go from one room to another without bumping into someone.

Finally she had had enough. The place was worse than the Dallas-Fort Worth Airport. The constant activity and confusion stripped away whatever peace she had hoped for after the grueling primaries. So she threw her most casual clothes in a suitcase, grabbed her blow dryer and makeup, stuffing them in a matching carryon, and told Cliff she was going to their ranch outside Austin. Cliff protested. He needed her around the estate to entertain the wives of vice presidential aspirants who'd come to see him, to sit with people for photo sessions, to oversee their home generally. Charlotte refused. She had to get away. Cliff was still asking her not to go the afternoon she flew out with four Secret Service agents, her personal maid, and three bottles of Chivas Regal.

TEXAS/Austin

The moment she unlocked her suitcase Charlotte knew she shouldn't have brought the bottles, but she also knew she wouldn't have been able to endure without them. She was alone in her bedroom, one of five in the ranch's sprawling main house, with her door shut. It was almost three in the afternoon, her private jet having touched down at Austin's Ragsdale Aviation an hour before. As she stood at the foot of the queen-size bed staring at the bottles packed tightly under her clothes, the stillness of the room enveloped her. Looking at them, she felt pain and relief at the same time.

"Oh, God, why can't I just leave this alone?"

She picked up her purse and went into her bathroom. Opening the purse, she took out her flask and poured herself a drink. As she walked back into the bedroom, the tambour clock on her antique dresser was chiming three. Off to one side was a sliding glass door, which opened onto a patio. When Charlotte looked out, she jumped back in surprise. One of her Secret Service agents was looking right at her. Realizing that she had a drink in her hand, she turned quickly away and went back into the bathroom. When she came out, the agent's back was turned and he was standing at the opposite edge of the patio.

What had he been looking at? Did he see? No, this is ridiculous. He couldn't have known what it was. Besides, what was he doing looking in my bedroom? Maybe he was just . . . oh, hell.

She slid back the patio door and stepped out.

"Gary?"

The agent turned around.

"Mrs. Hawkins. Hope I hadn't startled you. I'd just walked up and thought I saw someone moving about . . . well, you see, this is part of my detail . . ."

She could tell the agent was genuinely embarrassed. They liked to keep their distance and be discreet.

"It's all right. I was just taking some aspirin and then . . . going down to the pool."

The agent glanced toward the swimming pool and guesthouse a distance from the patio and said, "Good day to go. It's got to be at least a hundred degrees out here."

Charlotte smiled. "Feels like it, doesn't it?" There was a pause, and then she said, "Well, guess I'd better go change."

The agent smiled and turned his attention back to the landscape as she went in.

"Damn it," she said under her breath in her bathroom. "This is the last thing I feel like doing."

Charlotte stepped into her one-piece bathing suit and pulled it up. She picked up her drink, took a hefty swallow, then examined herself in the mirror. Like most women whose husbands were in the income bracket hers was in, Charlotte had been able to keep herself in shape with regular workouts and a fairly good diet. A face-lift and tummy tuck had also helped considerably. Although she didn't consider herself photogenic, which fed her anxiety about the press, anyone looking at her pictures could see an attractive, even pretty woman with beautifully coiffed hair and a face that looked at least ten years younger than her actual age. Since her surgeon had told her that she shouldn't be in direct exposure to the sun, she grabbed a beach hat, sunglasses, and sunblock before going out. Stepping onto the patio again, she told the agent, "Well, I'll be down here for a while. Would you have Lucinda come down in a little bit? I may want something to eat."

The agent said he would, then spoke quietly into a hidden microphone in his sleeve as she walked away, informing the detail chief where Cowgirl—her code name—would be.

She had tried to read an article on the upcoming conventions in *Time,* but dozed off under the relentless Texas sun. She woke up about twenty minutes later, disturbed by the sound of someone snipping shrubbery close by. For a moment she lay there listening and then, realizing she was hot and thirsty, sat up and opened her eyes.

She almost gasped when she saw him. Trimming the shrubs, and not even seeing her, was one of the most beautiful men she'd ever laid eyes on. No older than twenty, clad in nothing but cutoffs, he had an Adonis-type beauty that left her breathless. She stared at him not believing the perfection of what she saw. Charlotte was flooded with conflicting emotions. It had been so long since she'd felt what she was now feeling that she thought she'd lost those feelings forever. She didn't know what to do or what to think. Her throat and mouth grew parched. Then she dabbed her forehead with a towel and remembered how thirsty she was. Her maid had never come.

She was about to get up when he looked at her. She was startled. He stopped clipping the shrubs and studied her. Then a slight smile appeared. He didn't say anything. He didn't have to. She gazed at his eyes and knew immediately what a fool she was being. Charlotte felt naked and vulnerable, as if he were probing her mind, picking up every thought, every insecurity. She turned away and began fumbling with the magazine, the sun lotion, and towel, but then glanced back and saw that he was still looking at her. She swallowed hard and finally decided to say something.

"Excuse me . . ."

With an impish grin he said, "Yes, ma'am?"

"Uh, I was just wondering if you'd be so kind as to get me a . . . a large glass of iced tea from the main house. Lucinda, the maid, was supposed to come down and bring me something, but she never did."

He put down his clippers. "Sure."

As he walked up to the main house, Charlotte said to herself, he's perfect. Absolutely perfect. I've never seen such a body . . . and eyes. Those blue eyes are enough to—then she remembered *who* she was. And *where* she was.

She was still trying to remain collected when he returned a few minutes later.

"Lucinda apologized. Nobody told her," he said.

Charlotte smiled. "The agents must have forgotten to tell her."

He reached down and was about to hand her the glass when Charlotte took off her sunglasses and looked at him. Their eyes locked. Charlotte felt very hot and weak, almost overcome by the power emanating from his eyes.

"Where . . . where did you come from?"

He stopped, still holding her glass.

"Pardon?"

"Where did you come from? I . . . I've never seen you here before."

He smiled, almost laughed.

"You're never around."

Charlotte felt uncomfortable. He was teasing her.

"I mean, this is our ranch and I've never met you before. When did you start?"

"Last month. Your foreman hired me to come in every other weekend and trim the hedges, fertilize the grounds around the main house and guesthouse, and stuff like that. I stay in the guesthouse when I'm here. Then I go to other ranches in the area and do the same thing. It's good money for the summer."

"You're in school then?"

He nodded.

"My tea."

He reached out to hand it to her, then suddenly pulled it back.

"And you? Where did you come from?"

Charlotte stared at him, not believing how he was teasing her.

"From Austin." She shook her head. "I mean from Dallas. We live in Dallas."

She swallowed, not knowing what else to do.

He was gazing at her with a smile that could kill. For a moment she thought she would die. Thank God, his back was to the house.

"And your husband?" he asked.

"He, uh, he's in Dallas." She fought for the right words and grew frustrated. She didn't know what was happening to her. This was ridiculous. She was old enough to be his mother. In fact, her own *son* was older than he was.

"My tea," she finally said with some conviction. "Do you mind?"

He handed it to her, but his hand didn't leave the glass. Instead he moved closer and pulled the glass and her hand up close to his firm stomach. She looked up at his sunbaked chest, and then at him, as if she were looking into the eyes of Adonis himself.

He moved his other hand close to the one she had on the glass and slowly, gently, ran his fingertips over it. Again and again he stroked her hand, as lightly and delicately as a butterfly's wings and, although Charlotte wanted to move, wipe her forehead, or pull the glass away, she was paralyzed. This had never happened to her, not in twenty-five years of marriage, or even earlier. She had seen beautiful men before, men who literally took her breath away, but they'd always been at a distance, and she'd almost always been with Cliff. Now she was alone. Alone and looking deep into sensuality itself.

"You . . . " Speaking became difficult. "You've got to let me have my tea sometime, you know."

He squatted down in front of her so they were at eye level, then let his hand fall away. She took the glass.

"It's yours," he said softly.

"The tea?" she asked weakly.

He stood up. His crotch was barely three inches from her face and she could see the outline of his penis just beneath the cutoff jeans. He stretched, almost pushing himself against her, and then went back to his clipping.

Charlotte drained her glass and gathered up her things. As she passed him, she stopped and said, "Do you know who I am?"

He turned and looked at her.

That smile.

"That's why I want you."

In her bedroom she poured herself a very strong scotch and lay down.

That evening Charlotte ate with two of her agents, talked to Cliff in Dallas, and then said her goodnights.

In her bedroom she poured a drink and turned on the CBS "Sunday Night Movie." She tried to concentrate on what was going on but couldn't; the incident by the pool had been consuming her since the afternoon. She had tried to write it off, but found it impossible. The more she thought about it, the more confused she grew. She couldn't believe what had happened to her. Her nerves had gone haywire. When he looked at her, she thought his eyes would literally lift her up in the air. She had never seen eyes like that. Penetrating yet teasing, almost mischievous; when they looked at her, they totally disarmed her, leaving her as helpless as a puppy.

"It's ridiculous," she said to herself, pouring her third scotch in a row. "Absolutely ridiculous . . . I . . . I've never been caught like that . . . and I'm married. To the . . . to one of the most wonderful men in the world."

By her fifth drink Charlotte was getting to that familiar point, where her inhibitions were lowered just enough so that she was honest with herself, but not so honest that she would openly hurt anyone. And hurting someone was what she was worried about now. If Cliff even knew or even suspected some of the thoughts that had been running through her mind, it would shatter him. But she couldn't help it. The thoughts wouldn't stop.

She drank slowly while the late evening news was on, occasionally holding her glass up in front of her so that the television images become distorted when she looked through it. Thoughts came haphazardly now, a curious blend of reality and nonreality so that it was hard to distinguish between the two.

Even ... even if he did know her thoughts, what's the big deal? All ... he ... he's interested in is this ... this damn campaign. Me?

She sighed.

No! I can't do this! Not to Cliff or myself! I just can't! But ... but ...

Charlotte drained her glass and gazed toward the sliding glass doors, the chintz draperies now covering them. Beyond the patio was the guesthouse. He was staying there. He had told her that.

But there'll be one of the agents out there ... on the patio ...

No, I just can't ... not ... not unless ...

She stared at the curtains, imagining the patio and Secret Service agent behind it.

Unless I wait for him ... for him to take a break ... go to the bathroom or something.

Yes.

Charlotte waited. She turned out all her bedroom lights and pulled the curtains back. Sure enough, she could see one of the agents in the moonlight, standing on the darkened patio. His back to her; he was looking off toward the pool and guesthouse. Her eyes went instinctively to the guesthouse. She knew the guesthouse so well she could even tell which light it was she saw: the one next to the bed. She moved away from the door and lay down on her bed to get a full view of the patio. She could not fall asleep. Occasionally her eyelids drooped, but she forced them open again, afraid she'd fall asleep. The longer she lay there, the more she debated about what she wanted to do, but then, just as she was beginning to sort things out logically, the agent walked away.

Charlotte sat up. Now what am I going to do? She went to the patio door and gently slid it back. A soft, cool breeze blew in. The Hill Country nights were quite cool, even in summer. She stepped out and looked around. The agent was no where in sight.

Oh, no ... what am I doing out ... out here? This is so wrong. I ... I ...

She heard something. A rustle in the wind perhaps, but maybe not. She glanced quickly back at her bedroom, then at the guesthouse. The light looked so inviting, almost like a beacon calling her in the night, and the longer she looked at it, the more hypnotizing its power became.

She heard another noise and knew then it was leave or stay. Quickly she shut the sliding glass door and hurried down the trail.

* * *

She entered the guesthouse without knocking, opening the door softly and stepping in. He was propped up in bed with a sheet up to his waist, bare-chested, reading a book. He looked up at her and smiled. Determined not to appear drunk, Charlotte went over and stood at the foot of the antique brass bed, steadying herself. He still didn't say anything, but she knew what he was thinking. Just as she knew what she was thinking.

"You said you wanted me. So here I am."

He put down the book and gently pulled away the sheet. Her heart pounded as she gazed at his body, nude and flawless.

He got up and came up to her, taking her face in his hands and kissing her softly. Charlotte started to shake her head, moved as if to run out of the guesthouse, but he kissed her again, this time brushing his lips quietly across her cheek, then down her neck. She knew she couldn't. She was his.

Slowly, effortlessly, he unbuttoned her blouse and slipped it off her. As it fell to the floor, he unhooked her bra and pulled it off. It, too, fell. Lightly he touched her breasts. Her nipples grew hardened. He ran his fingertips over them, then bending down, kissed each one, licked them. His hands moved slowly over her breasts, stroking, feeling, squeezing, and his lips ran down between them, his tongue leaving a sensuous trail of moisture. Charlotte moaned as she ran her hands slowly through his hair and his tongue moved down ... down ...

Her breath quickened and inside her the warmth grew. As he probed and licked, she felt as if her entire body were being consumed by fire. He wrapped his arms around her. Their tongues met and ran over each other's mouths.

Together they fell on the bed and his hand found the top of her jeans. With his teeth he unsnapped the top button. Slowly he slid them off her, then her panties ...

Charlotte woke some hours later with the puzzled realization that she wasn't in her bed. Then she realized where she was and, horrified, raised herself up. He was sleeping quietly, his body silhouetted against the moonlight. She let out a sigh of relief. At least he hadn't left her. She looked at the room in the darkness, making out various shapes such as the small stone fireplace, the sofa and chairs, a table. Then she shut her eyes, reliving all that had happened. She took a deep breath and opened them, looking at him with more pain than she had ever known in her life. She was so confused. She wept.

Oh, Lord, what have I done? What have I done?

How could I have ever . . . let it happen? Oh, God, help me, I'm dying inside!

The more she thought about what had happened, the more panicky she grew. Finally her weeping woke him up.

He reached out and softly brushed his hand over her cheek, wiping away her tears.

"Don't be upset," he said quietly.

Charlotte looked at him. Her lips quivered and her throat tightened. She felt as if she couldn't breathe. "Oh, God . . . I've really messed up!" she murmured.

"No, you haven't."

She turned away, "You don't understand. You'll never understand what I'm going through right now . . . it's . . . I hate myself."

He leaned over and pulled her into his arms so that her back was against his chest. He held her tightly, lovingly.

"Don't. You're a beautiful woman. I understand that."

"But I'm married! And I love my husband."

"That's good. You should."

She turned toward him and started crying again. "But I shouldn't be here. This should never have happened . . . because I do love him. It's just that . . . it's so hard at times."

She pulled the sheet up over her, covering her breasts.

"Being his wife?"

"I don't know . . . I guess."

"Trying to live up to his expectations?"

She nodded. "Look, I'm a good person. I am. And I'm a Christian. I believe Jesus Christ is my Savior and I pray that I'll have eternal salvation through him, but . . . I'm not perfect."

"They say only Jesus was."

"I know," she sighed, "but it's just that I . . . I'm under such pressure. Appalling pressure." She pulled the sheet closer to her and said, "You can't know what it's like. Nobody does. Especially my husband."

He didn't say anything. She feared she'd given away too much of herself already, she still sensed he wanted her to stay. He pulled her back against him and they lay holding each other and listening to the sounds of the world around them.

Finally Charlotte sat up. "Do you have a watch?"

He nodded and rolled over, picking it up from the night table. "It's almost six."

"Oh, I can't believe this." She swung out of the bed and searched around the foot of the bed for her clothes. She dressed quickly.

Now he was sitting up, back against the headboard, hands behind his head.

"I . . . hope this remains between us."

"It will," he said.

She smiled, "Good-bye. And please, don't trim the shrubs today." He laughed.

Charlotte shut the door quietly and hurried back up to the main house. She saw the agent stationed by the patio door looking at her as she approached. Behind her the guesthouse was surrounded by huge, overgrown oak trees that offered enough camouflage in the morning's darkness to disguise the exact direction she was coming from.

"Mrs. Hawkins?" the agent asked, astonished.

"Wonderful time for a morning stroll, isn't it, Frank?"

"But—we didn't know you were out. You really need to tell us these things so we—"

Charlotte smiled as she briskly passed him. "Oh, Frank, you worry too much!"

And with that she slid back the glass door and went inside. She closed the curtains and collapsed on her bed, still amazed at what she'd just done.

Later in the afternoon, after she had caught up on her sleep, she stood in her bathroom staring at the two bottles of Chivas still left under the sink.

"They're breaking me," she said aloud, the tears beginning to flow again. "They're really breaking me."

She felt as if she were losing her mind. She leaned against the bathroom counter and braced herself. Then she slowly lowered herself to the floor, wiped away the tears and studied the bottles. Anger swept over her. Anger and regret and guilt and sorrow.

"No!" she said through clenched teeth. "No . . . no . . . no. They almost destroyed my marriage twenty-five years ago, they're not going to do it again!"

With all of her strength Charlotte pulled herself up from the floor and grabbed the bottles. Opening them, she quickly poured the scotch down the sink. And within an hour she was on her way home.

43

CHICAGO

The delegates began streaming into Chicago as early as two weeks in advance of the convention. They came from all over the nation, including the country's newest state, Puerto Rico. They came with campaign buttons, bumper stickers, inflatable toy elephants, plastic trumpets, Bibles, crosses, crucifixes, polyester outfits in red, white, and blue, hot plates, thermoses full of coffee or whiskey, lots of money, and plenty of enthusiasm. During the day they poured out of their hotels to shop and eat, often running into other delegations at the Adler Planetarium, the Lincoln Park Zoo, the racetracks, museums, restaurants, and, of course, the hotels' bars. They were biding their time until the night when they would cast their votes for the man they'd been elected to support.

The next week more delegates breezed in and with them came alternates, delegation leaders, a sprinkling of celebrities, old politicians, officials from the Republican party, hordes of television newspeople, journalists, novelists, columnists, protesters, groupies, hangers-on, peddlers, con men, thieves, whores, and more religious leaders than you could count. Billy was there, as were Jerry and Oral and Pat and Ted and Billy Jim and Jim and Tammy, all eager to show their support for the man who was going to bring God back into government.

It was a circus fitting for a city known as the convention capital of the world. Professional, business, and political interests had been holding conventions here since the 1800s. Republican Abraham Lincoln was nominated here in 1860—but only after his supporters encircled the convention hall, known then as the Wigwam Building, and refused to allow anyone to leave until his vote was cast for Lincoln. Teddy Roosevelt, Adlai Stevenson, Hubert Humphrey, and Otis Meade were nominated here as well. Humphrey's nomination was one of the most turbulent in history. His name was placed before the delegates inside Chicago Stadium, while antiwar demonstrations and riots raged in nearby Grant Park and Lincoln Park and in the Civic Center. Meade's was the most boring. Every convention was different, and this one promised to be no exception. Although the gays and feminists and proabortionists had sworn to demonstrate against Cliff Hawkins's nomination, nobody expected anything on the scale of what happened during Humphrey's. In fact, the really exceptional thing about this convention was not what was different, but who was different. Not only was Hawkins a man of politics, but also a man of God. A curious juxtaposition if there ever was one.

The manager of the Conrad Hilton had told Cliff Hawkins's staff that the candidate's suite on the twenty-sixth floor was the finest any Hilton hotel could offer. The Imperial Suite was elegantly appointed, with antique furniture, exquisite paintings, Waterford lamps, fine linens, and other furnishings usually found only in the pages of *Antiques* magazine. If offered a breathtaking view of Chicago. At twelve hundred dollars a day the staff realized it was a bargain, though none of them had time to appreciate it.

All day and well into the night secretaries scurried through the suite loaded down with papers and reports, while aides came and went with polling data and delegate changes. Phones rang endlessly, coffee pots percolated, and teletype machines chattered away. But perhaps the most constant sound came from the hall, where two of the best political speech writers in the business sat at identical desks pounding out separate versions of Hawkins's acceptance speech.

The candidate spent the majority of his time interviewing and reviewing the backgrounds of those still under consideration for his running mate. Hawkins had expected to have his mind made up before the convention, but by the end of the first day, as a prominent aging Republican senator gave the opening address to over two thousand delegates on the convention floor and millions of television viewers across America, he was still pondering over the three men on his final list. No one more than Cliff Hawkins was aware of the potential advantages or damage a running mate could bring the campaign. It was one of the few elements in the campaign, perhaps the only one, that he had complete control of. Party leaders, fellow religious leaders and evangelists, a former president, and his own advisers and staff members had offered endless suggestions and opinions, but nothing settled it. The responsibility was tremendous, and the fact that he was almost deadlocked in his decision didn't help.

Then, as his list of alternatives dwindled, the name of Tom Kelly grew more prominent. It stayed that way through four cuts. Although the personal chemistry between them wasn't the best, his aides and several party advisers argued with Hawkins to keep his name on the list. Kelly was the junior senator from Pennsylvania, who had quickly made a name for himself during his first term. He was the recipient of numerous awards and citations from various civic and political watchdog groups and was probably the most charismatic and charming senator on the Hill. He was tall, handsome enough to be a model, and young-looking, though he was in his forties, and he had made a good showing in the primaries during his own short-lived run for the presidency four years before. Had Kelly's campaign not been plagued by a shortage of cash and internal fighting, some politicians predicted he would have made it to the convention. Some said he was the Republican incarnation of Jack Kennedy; like Kennedy, Kelly was Catholic. Kelly's Catholicism hit a particularly touchy nerve in Hawkins—though he admitted it only to his closest advisers—but it would be a strong counterbalance against charges that Hawkins was going to load his administration with nothing but Baptists. Hawkins needed the Catholic vote almost as much as he needed the Jewish and black vote, and Kelly's religion, along with his youthfulness and energy, began to look more and more attractive.

It was three in the morning and Cliff still had not decided. The Imperial Suite was silent now. Everyone had gone to bed an hour ago, but Hawkins had stayed up to think. When he realized that he was too tired to make a decision, he decided to turn in.

He showered, toweled himself, and stepped back into the bedroom, flipping off the light behind him. Charlotte lay asleep, a dim night table lamp casting a soft light on her face. The sheets covering her rose and fell with her breathing, like gentle ripples on a calm sea. He paused and studied her. Slowly his eyes traced the outline of her body and then came to rest on her face. The campaign had been having its effects upon them both and it bothered him. He was especially worried about her. Had been for almost two months. The reports the Secret Service were sending him had been much more encouraging lately, particularly during the past few weeks, but he could tell she was still on edge, still having trouble dealing with the media and the pressure. He had asked her staff to lighten her work load, but, much to his surprise, Charlotte refused, saying she wanted to stay busy, wanted to continue her pace, even though anyone observing her could tell it was wearing on her nerves. Her hands trembled more now, she was more easily irritated, and she often had a short fuse with her staff. He sighed, not really knowing what to do, but knowing he loved her now more than he ever had. She was such a beautiful woman, both physically and spiritually, he thought, and he was blessed to have her.

Crawling into bed now, putting his arms around her, he closed his eyes and held her close, content with the realization that whatever problems there were, the Lord would take care of them.

Perhaps he was right.

One floor below Hawkins's suite Randy Perrin was hunched over his telephone talking to one of his convention floor managers while an aide scribbled notes.

"Well, we knew he was going to pull something like this . . . right . . . right. It's simply a matter of saving face? Bull. He's just trying to push it into an open convention, but it's not gonna work. Baby, we got the numbers. That's all that matters."

Perrin laughed out loud.

"So what, he can try, but wait until it gets down to the vote. . . . Sure, I'm sure."

He nodded his head to the phone. "Yeah, I can understand why they'd be upset. After all, that's why they're our delegates. Because they knew he would push that kind of platform through . . . right . . . right. Well, you tell them there's no chance. Got it? No chance."

Perrin hung up and looked at his aide, still scribbling.

"What are you doing? You didn't have to write that down."

"Memoirs."

Perrin rolled his eyes. "As if we don't have enough nuts—"

"What was that bit about the platform?"

Perrin shook his head, "Oh, you know, we got the platform vote tomorrow night, right? So Broder's being a jerk, saying he isn't going to release his delegates to us until we make some compromises on the platform."

"He doesn't have the numbers."

"He thinks he does, but like I told him, so what? We *know* we've got 'em. So, if it takes a rules fight or something like this to prove it before the actual roll-call vote, then fine, we'll just embarrass the twerp in front of forty million people."

"And some of our delegations were upset?"

"Yeah, that's what he was calling about. They wanted to be sure Reverend Hawkins wasn't going to give an inch to Broder. Of course, I said he wouldn't."

"And he won't."

"Won't need to."

The next morning the entire Imperial Suite was bathed in sunlight. After breakfasting with several top party leaders and telling them he still hadn't made a decision concerning his running mate, Hawkins sat down on one of the living room sofas to go over yet another draft of his acceptance speech. In less than thirty-six hours from now delegations from around the nation would be casting their votes to nominate him, and the night after that—Thursday night— he would be standing before them and millions of television viewers accepting it. Even as he sat working on his acceptance speech, he found it hard not to think about what was going to happen. After all these months! Thoughts of the momentous night drifted into his head as his writers showed him his speech line by line. Finally he forced himself to concentrate, and began to work on it seriously, adding a line here, deleting one there.

Two hours later he flipped the last page over and looked up. He was beaming. The speech was finished.

An hour later Hawkins was holding what he promised would be his last series of meetings with the men being considered for the vice presidential slot. Staff eyebrows were raised when Tom Kelly arrived. They all knew Hawkins didn't particularly like Kelly, but they also knew that, compared to the others, he offered the political edge that Hawkins needed. Nevertheless, Cliff Hawkins was no ordinary candidate, and just what he did and did not need politically was up for debate. After all, he'd already overcome a vast number of typical obstacles, so whatever the rules in the past, it certainly didn't mean they were applicable now. Especially with regard to religious matters. His staff knew it was Kelly's religion that Hawkins cringed at, but how much he was going to let that influence him, they didn't know. Hawkins was already on record saying he would rather have a nonbeliever who shared his moral and political concerns than a "recommitted Christian" who was diametrically opposed to him.

Kelly and Hawkins talked for well over ninety minutes, and before Hawkins got up to show him to the door, he said, "You realize if we lose this race, you could be out in the street without a thing. That's speaking figuratively, of course, but you know what I mean."

"Yes, sir, I do."

"There are a lot of people out there who are going to oppose us. By the same token, as you've seen by those delegates on the floor, there are a lot of people who're supporting us. It's going to be a decisive race for this nation. I really believe that. Even more decisive than '88 was, and it's going to be tough. If we lose, there are a lot of people you're never going to be close to again. Simply because of your association on this ticket."

"I realize that."

"And it doesn't bother you?"

"Reverend, I've always felt you've been one of America's greatest patriots. I haven't always agreed with you and still don't. But you do fight for a great number of things that are very dear to me. And you've pushed for some legislation that I've felt was long overdue, and did a damn good job of helping to get it through. I admire that. There's no way I would ever regret being associated with anyone who's working as hard as you are for the betterment of this nation. And I'll tell anyone who asks me that."

Hawkins cleared his throat. It was the only time Kelly had ever given him any serious praise and he liked that. The others had been so effusive it was almost nauseating.

"Well," he said, slowly getting up, "I still haven't decided, but I'll let you know soon."

Kelly left not knowing any more than anyone else.

* * *

At the convention center that evening the platform came up for consideration and approval and, just as Perrin has been warned, Larry Broder, speaking from the podium for his platform proposals, gave a highly charged speech pleading for the inclusion of several planks that were in direct opposition to the Hawkins planks. He could not in good conscience release his delegates until those planks were included. "Because," Larry Broder shouted to the crowd on the floor, "these are issues that I have fought for year in and year out since I became a public servant, and not to stand up and fight for them goes against every fiber in my body!"

At this the delegates cheered and stomped and waved signs for Broder and gave the television camera the display they were looking for. But Randy Perrin, having known in advance that this was going to happen, already had his staff and floor managers and delegate chairmen working quickly to put the platform up for a vote. And the Hawkins delegates, also forewarned, readied themselves for a loud voice vote, while Broder's supporters went on cheering and clapping and stomping and sign waving.

The convention chairman called up the planks, asked for a voice vote, and, hearing the Hawkins delegates shout their answers over the Broder demonstration, gaveled the original platform into the record. It was done so quickly that one of Broder's aides rushed up to him, just as he was getting into his limousine to go back to his hotel, and told him it was over.

"Christ," he snapped, "It doesn't surprise me."

As the limousine doors shut, he knew it was finished. The platform fight was a good test of whether his own people had been successful in wooing enough of the Hawkins delegates over to his side to make a difference. As he'd just seen, they were firm in their support for the evangelist. It was true—Hawkins did have the numbers. More than enough to be nominated.

Broder, depressed and tired as his motorcade pulled up in front of his hotel, was greeted by a sea of cameramen and reporters. He wished that he didn't have to face them.

"It's over," he said. "We've given it our best, but I know political power when I see it. The Reverend's got it. It's over."

Later that evening he released his delegates to Hawkins and then phoned him to wish him the best.

* * *

The next afternoon, Wednesday, Cliff Hawkins's suite was chaotic. Telephones were ringing, flowers and telegrams poured in, celebrities and television evangelists and party officials stopped by, and everything was coming together for that evening when the Republican party would place his name before the delegates. After Cliff and Charlotte ate a quiet dinner, a dozen guests and journalists began arriving to watch the convention proceedings. The suite looked as if it was decorated for Mardi Gras, with balloons floating up from chairbacks, streamers running from chandelier to chandelier, confetti strewn about, and "Hawkins in '92" posters covering the walls.

The guests chatted and wandered to an elegantly draped table spread with trays of smoked salmon, cheese, raw vegetables, breads, petits fours, and a bowl of mock champagne, all hovered over by uniformed caterers.

One evangelist stood stuffing his mouth with salmon while trying to explain to a *Newsweek* correspondent that it was not true he and his wife had bought their Mercedes with donations from his evangelistic organization. Tammy, whose husband Jim had his own born-again talk show, talked about her bouffant hairdo and newest chiffon dress with an unimpressed congressman's wife.

In another corner of the suite Charlotte was playing host to several women, all of whom agreed that life on the campaign trail wasn't as glamorous as everyone thought, and trying to smile sweetly as several photographers snapped her picture and cameramen filmed her. Inside she was thinking, if one more flashbulb goes off, I'll scream.

Over by the fifty-inch television screen Hawkins, standing with Gordon Wade, Randy Perrin, the party's only living former president, several congressmen and senators, a movie star, and some reporters, reflected on his primary races, trying to explain the difficulty he'd had in choosing a running mate.

"Then you've made a decision?" a reporter asked.

Hawkins laughed. "No, not yet. But, believe me, you'll know when I do."

By nine thirty the convention's activities began picking up speed. Cliff Hawkins's name was placed in nomination by the governor of Arkansas, an ardent supporter, after he finished a rousing speech calling for Republicans and Americans everywhere to support the fight to restore God, morality, decency in our government and nation.

The atmosphere in Hawkins's suite was electric. Everything, going smoothly, was overwhelmingly received by the delegates. Then the roll call vote began. The first two states, Alabama and Alaska, went without a hitch, their chairman announcing unanimous support for the nomination. This seemed to set a precedent and, as state after state voted and each state chairman turned away from his microphone and another one stood up, it drew Hawkins closer and closer to clinching the nomination.

In the suite everyone started talking at once.

"Two more states! Two more states and we're over!"

"Oklahoma and Ohio'll do it!"

"And wait till they see the Ohio vote!"

On the screen the Oklahoma delegate chairman stood before his microphone and listened for the roll call.

"Oklahoma!" announced the convention chairman.

The Oklahoma chairman announced, "Mr. Chairman! The great state of Oklahoma is proud to cast all sixty-two delegate votes for the next president of the United States, Clifford Hawkins!"

A roar of applause and cheers swept over the convention floor and up through Hawkins's suite. Cliff nudged Charlotte closer to him and squeezed her arm. Inside his mind he was already racing ahead of the next delegation's vote. In front of him Randy Perrin puffed nervously on a cigarette, while Gordon Wade stared at the screen, mesmerized.

"Ohio!" boomed the convention chairman.

Everyone in the suite edged closer to the screen.

The Ohio delegation's chairman stood behind his microphone and a rumble of excitement swept over the floor. Photographers and television Minicams crowded around him. The chairman gave the cameras a broad smile, then, a little shaken by all the attention, removed his enormous elephant campaign hat and wiped his brow.

Nobody in the suite moved.

"Mr. Chairman! The great state of Ohio takes pride in nominating Clifford Hawkins with 130 delegate votes!"

The suite erupted in cheers.

Hawkins turned and grabbed Charlotte and hugged her, then both of them burst out laughing and everyone around them laughed too.

Somewhere on the convention floor "Happy Days Are Here

Again" started up and everyone was out of their seats. Horns blew, flags and signs waved, and on television screens across America the words HAWKINS NOMINATED! flashed across the bottom. Then came a panoramic shot of the floor as thousands of balloons and streamers showered the delegations.

In the suite everyone was talking and congratulating Hawkins at once.

They had done it!

"Senator Kelly's suite. . . . Yes, he is, who's calling please?"

The aide turned to Kelly and mouthed the words, *It's Hawkins.*

"Yes, Reverend, just a second." He handed the phone to Kelly.

"Hello. . . . Fine, thank you. And congratulations, you've earned the nomination."

Kelly listened for a moment and then said, "Yes, sir, I'd be honored. Yes, sir, I can support the platform completely. Fine, thank you, sir."

Kelly hung up and looked at his family and guests. "Well, let's get ready, gang."

"Where are we going?" his wife asked with a laugh.

"The convention. This senator's on the ticket!"

The limousines and Secret Service advance cars rolled down the rampway into the underground garage with red lights flashing and headlights ablaze. Newsmen, photographers, and cameramen jogged alongside the motorcade, all clamoring to get a shot of the presidential nominee and his running mate.

When the motorcade came to a halt, Hawkins's limousine door was opened and, as he stepped out, a new wave of camera flashes went off. Microphones were thrust into his face and questions came at him from every direction. Then Senator Tom Kelly emerged from behind him and together they stood facing the cameras, waiting for their wives and the senator's children to get out of the next limousine.

"Reverend! Reverend!" the reporters called out.

"How does it feel to finally get the nomination?"

"When did you decide on your running mate?"

"When did you call him?"

"Senator, how does it feel to be on the ticket?"

"Do you both support the platform planks?"

"Reverend, does the senator's religion bother you?"

"Will you be campaigning right after the convention?"

"Or wait until Labor Day?"

Charlotte and the senator's wife and children joined them and, as the Secret Service formed a tight circle around the group, they moved through the crush of journalists, party officials, security agents, and police to go into the convention center.

Inside there was another stream of quick, unnerving camera flashes bursting before their eyes. They smiled and talked and waved while the photo session went on, realizing that somewhere beyond the dozens of television lights and guards and photographers were over four thousand Republican delegates, alternates, and guests. And beyond them over forty million people throughout the nation watching on television.

After Hawkins was introduced, the roars of thousands upon thousands of people overwhelmed the center, and flags and placards and soaring balloons filled the air. He moved swiftly onto the center's platform and, as he went up to the podium, he saw before him the cheering faces of the hordes below. They yelled and waved and tooted their horns in an ovation that lasted almost twenty minutes. They had finally accepted him. The night was his.

Then he gestured for quiet and began to speak.

" 'You are the light of the world. A city on a hill cannot be hidden. . . . No one lights a lamp and hides it in a jar or puts it under a bed. Instead, he puts it on a stand, so that those who come in can see the light. . . . Let your light shine before men, that they may see your good deeds. . . .' "

44

WASHINGTON/The White House

Rain fell throughout the District. On Capitol Hill. Around the Tidal Basin. Over by the Watergate complex and the Kennedy Center. And at the White House.

As a jagged knife of lightning streaked over the West Wing offices and a clap of thunder followed, Howard Hickman stopped reading the memo before him just long enough to look out at the rain. Water streamed down the windowpanes. He could see his reflection and thought how perfectly the weather reflected his mood.

If the memo lying before him was correct, the president was slipping badly in two key areas: the East and the South. Meade was behind by seventeen points in the East and twenty-seven in the South. There were indications that he was also losing ground in the West and Midwest. To make matters worse, the president had decided to go ahead with a trip to India, planned since last winter. Hickman argued with him for almost a half hour, telling him he should hold to his "Rose Garden strategy" and not leave Washington. But Meade was tired of being stuck in the White House, parading out to the Rose Garden for the press to watch him giving congressional medals, posing with poster children, shaking hands with hundred-year-old war veterans—octogenarians made him especially nervous after the black man died on him in Pennsylvania—or showing off the First Dog's newest litter. It was all nonsense. Hickman said it made him look "presidential." Meade countered by saying the trip to India would do more for his image as a president and world leader than any ceremonies performed at home. They were going to New Delhi for the first annual World Economic Conference, a summit between the Western and Eastern nations to see how the West could help the East in its economic and industrialization problems.

Trying to get his mind off India, Hickman turned his attention back to the memo and stared at the figures. Seventeen points in the East, twenty-seven in the South. What are we going to do?

Then, knowing he didn't want to answer himself, he got up, closed his office, and went home in the rain.

The next morning Hickman had other things on his mind. He was late for the Indian conference briefing as he took the elevator up to the second floor of the West Wing offices. Tony LaCross, the president's chief negotiator for the Mexican pipeline agreement, was running late for a meeting of his own.

"Tony, anything on the negotiations? Is Portillo coming around?"

LaCross shook his head. "Nothing. They're watching our polls as closely as we are. Hawkins is leading right now and they don't like it. Portillo thinks he would never honor the agreements if he got in. He's so conservative."

"Damn," said Hickman under his breath. "Thank God, they haven't seen this week's polls."

"Worse?"

"To say the least."

"Maybe this conference will pull him up."

"I doubt it, but you can't tell him that. He's going regardless."

Hickman looked toward the Oval Office. "Look, I'm already late. Keep me posted on this thing. I want to know any progress you make, okay? We've got to get them back to the bargaining table. Once they're there, it shouldn't take long to wrap the agreement up, should it?"

Before LaCross could answer, Hickman was gone. LaCross went to his own meeting, and later that morning phoned Mexico once again.

The president was seated in his big leather chair behind his desk.

"Howard, good of you to be here on time."

"Sorry."

Meade turned back to his chief of protocol. "Where were we?"

"Initial remarks."

"Oh, yeah. After the Indian prime minister makes them, I give a short toast, right?"

"No, sir. After his toast at the end of the dinner."

Meade sighed. "Right. You'd think I'd remember all this crap by now. Now what about the language? Customs? All that?"

"Mr. Vijaya will be here this afternoon to brief you on their customs, idiosyncrasies, and whatnot."

"Language?"

"English primarily."

"What are we taking as a gift?"

"A painting from the Michener Collection and a prize head of Angus cattle from Florida."

Meade raised his eyebrows. "A steer? They don't eat beef!"

"No, they're sacred. That's why the gift will be appreciated."

"The creature isn't going to be on our plane, is he?"

"Believe me, Mr. President, the steer won't be on Air Force One."

After Meade showed his chief of protocol and the economic advisers who'd been at the meeting to the door, he turned to Hickman. "You still think this is a lot of bullshit? Our going to India and all?"

"Yes, sir, I do," Hickman said taking a chair in front of the president's desk.

Meade went back to his desk and sat down. "But you think it will work?"

"That depends on how our media comes across."

"Is Jody Allen working with the press?"

"He's in a meeting right now."

"What's he telling them?"

"He's trying to work on the sympathy end, hoping to get the best coverage he can for us. He's telling them that Hawkins polls are up, as everyone knows, and you realize that you could probably gain more politically by staying here and campaigning before our convention. But, as president, you have to make personal sacrifices in the name of leadership and this trip is one of them."

"Good," said Meade, satisfied with the way his press secretary was setting the tone for his departure. "Now do you have the latest polls?"

"Do you really want them?"

Meade nodded. "I've already got a good idea as to what they say. I'm assuming they're bad."

"They are."

"How bad?"

"You're seventeen points behind in the East and twenty-seven behind in the South."

Meade took off his reading glasses and tossed them on his desk. "What in the fuck are we doing wrong, Howard? This is ridiculous."

"I know, but don't think about it now. McClellan's coming over with a full report right after that guy from the Indian embassy leaves."

"I don't want to see it."

"To tell you the truth, McClellan doesn't think it's as bad as it appears. At least not now. Public opinion typically goes toward the candidate who receives the most coverage, and Hawkins just finished a convention watched by over forty million people for four days."

"That's exactly why I want to go to India. Hell, I'd go anywhere if I thought it'd help, even Acapulco!"

"Speaking of Mexico, I saw LaCross this morning just before I came in and the word's not good."

"The talks?"

"They're still hanging over us, Mr. President. Completely stagnant."

Meade leaned his frame on the edge of the desk, propping up both elbows. "He hasn't gotten anywhere with Portillo, then?"

"No, sir."

"Damn it. Portillo's not putting a helluva lot of faith in us. That really pisses me off. Whether I get reelected or not, I'm still the president now and he knows damn good and well no president in his right mind would renege on a deal that's already been made."

"Also there's Gianni."

"I know," grumbled Meade, "and *that* pisses me off too. I've never liked dealing with him anyway, but all the fucking money we owe him is wrapped up in the signing of this agreement. If he thinks we're going to lose, too, then he's going to want to collect while I'm still in office. Losers are always harder to collect from than winners."

"I know, Mr. President."

"Well, if you know and LaCross knows, then push this fucking thing *through!*"

Hickman assured the president he would and left.

Afterward, sitting behind his desk and eating lunch off a tray brought in by one of the White House stewards, Meade tried to focus his thoughts on the conference in New Delhi, but found himself continually wandering to other subjects, especially the latest polls. He couldn't believe he was so far behind. Did the country really want a return to Republicanism? If the Republicans had had a stronger candidate running against him in '88, would he have been elected over Meade? Perhaps not. One columnist the other day had written that the American people, seeing that almost everything had failed to revive the economy, reduce inflation and unemployment, and deal with the growing Soviet imperialism in Europe, were now turning to God through Cliff Hawkins in the belief that, if anything could put the country back on its feet, it would have to be through divine intervention. And what better man would the Lord work through than Cliff Hawkins?

Meade had seen the column in his news summaries. It ruined his breakfast. Thinking about it now, he was still disgusted by it. Even the very insinuation that Hawkins's candidacy might possibly be divinely endorsed was ludicrous. Worse was the columnist's conclusion—that nobody would know for sure until after the election in November. Although Meade was raised an Episcopalian, attended church semiregularly, and believed that the Lord was there whether or not he prayed regularly, he would be considered a lukewarm Christian by Hawkins's standards. But to *imply* that the presidential election could come down to the religious commitments of each candidate was enough to make anyone sick. Meade especially did not relish the idea that, if he lost, his defeat might be thought of as a divine ouster.

He picked at his lunch awhile longer and then pushed his tray away and buzzed for the steward. Just like snapping your fingers. The hell with it. He was still in control. Still capable of getting the things he wanted, doing what he wanted. The electorate talked to him through the polls, but they did not own him. Nobody did. Not them. Not Katherine. Nobody. There were a lot of things he wanted, and he was going to get them. Now and in the future. But particularly now.

He picked up his intercom and asked his secretary to have the head of the Secret Service White House detail come to his office. Within a few minutes Charlie O'Rourke was standing before the president in the Oval Office.

"Charlie, this won't take a minute."

The president tore a piece of paper off his notepad and handed it across the desk.

"Is Mrs. Meade still going to the Kennedy Center tonight?"

"Yes, sir, she is."

"Good. What time's she expected back?"

"I don't have her itinerary with me right now, Mr. President, but I believe it's around eleven thirty or so, because of a reception afterward."

Meade nodded, then motioned toward the note. "There's a name on there. She's in the East Wing offices. This is her name. I want to see her tonight from nine to eleven. Harrison's already screened her."

O'Rourke shook his head in exasperation. "Mr. President, do you really want to do this? You know the problems we had with Miss Vásquez. Not to mention the First Lady. I wish you'd reconsider what you're—"

"I don't have to reconsider a damn thing," snapped Meade. "Remember that. If you don't want to carry this out, then I'll find someone who will."

O'Rourke nodded slowly and asked, "Is that all?"

"That's it."

"Yes, sir."

After O'Rourke left, Meade's afternoon went quickly. Mr. Vijaya from the Indian embassy came over and gave him some pointers, as a refresher on some Indian customs, to consider before flying into New Delhi and a complete rundown on the joint activities he and the Indian prime minister would be participating in. Later McClellan came over. Like Hickman, he didn't think Meade's slippage in the polls was as bad as it looked. But, unlike Hickman, McClellan *did* think Meade's chance of gaining in the polls were greater by going to India than by staying at home. The rest of the president's afternoon was filled with more duties based on the Rose Garden strategy: receiving an ambassador, greeting a man who'd recently saved a deaf and dumb girl from drowning in the Potomac, and meeting with two of Hollywood's hottest stars who were filming parts of their next movie in Washington. He dined early with Katherine and their daughter, who'd been in the mansion since the weekend, and together he and Kat said good-bye to her in the Diplomatic Reception Room before she headed back to Wellesley. Then Katherine went upstairs to get ready for the evening at the Kennedy Center, where a new play was opening, and Meade retreated to his bedroom to read the briefs the State Department had sent over on India.

The president, propped up in bed with only a robe and his reading glasses on, read for almost an hour. By nine o'clock he finally took his glasses off, removed his pipe, and shut the last folder of briefs.

He glanced at the clock and took a deep breath. The intercom by his bed rang.

"Yes? . . . Oh, okay. Fine, send her up."

In a moment there was a soft knock at his door. The president crossed over and opened it. Meade looked at her, taking her in at once.

"Hello, Barbara."

"Mr. President."

"Come in."

She stepped in. And moments later Meade was caressing and undressing her . . .

Katherine stepped out of the elevator on the second floor of the private quarters and glanced at her watch: 11:10 P.M. She was a little early, but the reception following the play hadn't lasted as long as she'd expected. She was glad. There was still a mountain of correspondence on her desk that she hadn't answered as well as a few other things to do before going to bed.

She said goodnight to the military aide in the elevator and, as the doors closed, started in toward the West Sitting Hall and her bedroom. For an instant she thought she heard what sounded like a cry. She stopped, glanced at the center hall behind her, and waited a few seconds, then shrugged and turned back. Then she heard it again. It was a cry. She looked toward the West Sitting Hall, then behind her again, trying to decipher where the noise was coming from. Across from her was the door leading into Otis's bedroom. She crossed the center hall and cocked an ear against his door. The sounds were more distinct now, and the voice definitely a woman's.

Katherine leaned heavily against the door and listened as someone cried, "Oh God! Oh God! Don't ... stop! Don't stop!" Then, realizing what was happening, she covered her mouth and fled to her bedroom.

Tears were streaming down her face.

45

EN ROUTE TO INDIA

As Air Force One gained altitude, Katherine leaned back in her seat and stared out the window, watching the world rush by. The president's plane had left Andrews Air Force Base ten minutes ago and they were already over the Atlantic. Thirty minutes ago Katherine had been standing in her bedroom trying to decide whether or not she was going. A few days ago she had thought the trip might do them some good. It would get Otis away from the White House and the campaign and give him a chance to really be president again, to flex his authority and talent and experience among the other world leaders and rebuild his strength. She had also thought it would give them a little time to themselves. They both needed that.

But last night everything had collapsed. The cries and moans had raped her ears of any illusions she'd had left about him. He was the same as he'd always been. Nothing she had said or threatened or done had changed him. She knew that now. It had cost her a night's sleep and more heartache than she thought she was capable of feeling. The wounds hurt like hell. And there were moments like now, when the tears needed so desperately to come. What she had heard wasn't totally unexpected, just shockingly real. She had seen it coming for months, even years, she guessed. Last winter, during the pri-

maries this spring, during Acapulco and afterward, when he came
back from Camp David—oh, how she remembered that—and many
nights since then. So the tears of last night were slowly giving way to
anger and resentment, leaving her parched of feelings and with a
burning desire to save herself by getting the hell out. To do that,
Katherine realized now, things *had* to be said. But she needed
strength to do what she had to do.

She glanced down at her hands. They weren't trembling now.
Half an hour ago they had been. After they had stepped out of their
limousine at Andrews, Otis had briefly—and gently—held her hand
as they walked toward the plane. She had pulled it away and, when
he touched it again, she stared at him. Her lips quivered and she
didn't know what to say. When he smiled at her in front of all those
cameras and told the press they were looking forward to the trip, she
wanted to scream and kick him in the balls. In only a few seconds he
had accomplished that. Her emotions weren't under control then.
Now they were. As they soared high above the Atlantic, the chatter
of journalists and flight attendants and the Secret Service filling the
plane, Katherine got up from her seat and walked the short distance
to Otis's office. There was no other time but now. She knocked on
the door and stepped in.

"We need to talk, Otis."

Meade lifted his head up from a stack of papers and looked at her.
Three of his aides had left when Katherine walked in.

"About what?"

"A lot of things."

She took a chair.

"Right now?"

"Yes."

Meade took off his glasses. "Okay. What's on your mind?"

"Us."

Meade massaged the bridge of his nose.

"Us? Do we have to? Right now?" He looked exasperated and
started trying to get out of it when she said, "I'm not in the mood for
it either, but we are going to talk."

Meade shook his head. "For godsakes, Kat, let's not get in an argument on this trip. Please. I've got a million things on my mind,
fifteen briefs to try and remember, and a hell of a lot of polishing to
do on our resolution. So, please, can we avoid anything personal
and heavy?"

Katherine glared at him. "Nothing personal? What kind of relationship do you think this is? A marriage-by-the-hour? This is the only time we're going to have and I've got a few things to tell you, goddamit."

Meade sighed. "Why do we have to go through this every few weeks? This is getting old."

Katherine slammed her hand down on the desk. "Of course, it's getting old, but I've put more time into this marriage than you've ever thought about. And what have I got? Nothing. Absolutely nothing. Up to this point my life has been nothing but negatives. Negatives, do you hear me? I'm tired of it. I've tried every way I know to put our relationship back on the right track, but the efforts have all been one way. You haven't thought about it, given it any of your time, or done anything else except whatever's right for you. Why do I always have to come to you to talk? Why?"

He sat silently, looking at her.

"I'll tell you why," she said. "It's because you don't give a damn. Not about anything or anybody. You've always been like that and you always will be and I see it now more clearly than I ever have before. Well, things are happening around you, Otis, things that are going to affect you whether you like it or not, so you might as well get to know them."

Meade sat upright in his chair, pulling it closer to his desk. "What are you talking about?"

"I'm talking about us—about you. The fact that even though you agreed to work on improving our situation, you haven't. Instead you've done exactly the opposite. Well, I'm tired of the charade. Of your coming to my bed as if it were some sort of *duty,* of your placating me in that condescending tone of yours whenever I ask you questions. Tired of letting you believe you've got me fooled, that I haven't got any idea as to what's going on. I know more than you ever hoped to hell I would. So," she said taking a long breath, "I'm through and I want you to know it. Through fighting for you and crying for you."

"What do you mean?" he asked slowly.

"I mean I'm finished trying to make this thing work, holding on to hope when there isn't any. I've suffered too much. I stayed with it, tried to show you I loved you, tried to help, but it hasn't done any good. So it's time for alternatives."

Meade leaned back in his chair. "Kat, it's just the election. The pressure and all. I know it is . . ."

"Don't placate me, Otis."

"Well, what is it you want?"

"Out."

"Meaning?"

"Separation."

He shuddered.

"Or divorce."

Katherine stood outside his office door as the chatter from the fore and aft sections of the jet mixed with the hum of the engines. She tried to fight back the tears, but couldn't. She closed her eyes and winced. It had taken all the strength she could muster to propose divorce and now that strength was fading fast. Otis held the cards in his hands now, the next move was up to him. She had done all she could.

Hours later, when most of the plane was quiet and the passengers were trying to sleep, Howard Hickman slipped into his boss's office, where he found the president slumped in his specially contoured chair. He was writing in his diary, a practice he'd begun on the advice of his predecessor, who said it would be a great help in getting a multimillion dollar contract for his memoirs. As he wrote, Hickman noted the president's face was puffy and his eyes were unusually shadowed. Even the lines in his face seemed more visible than they had been earlier in the day.

"Mr. President?"

Slowly, as if drugged, Meade looked up.

"Mr. President, I hate to bother you, but we just got word from New Delhi that some changes have been made for our press. Seems the Indian government's sealed off the hotel next to ours, where the press was scheduled to stay, because of a foul-up with where the Russians and Germans were supposed to stay. So our group's going to be stuck in some fleabag dump halfway across the city and they're giving that hotel to the Russians and Germans."

Meade did not respond.

"Mr. President, did you hear me?"

Meade nodded.

"Well, you know what that means don't you? Our press corps is going to be bitching more than ever and there isn't a damn thing we can do about it. I've tried calling our embassy to find another hotel, but they can't get anything. A bad hotel means bad press relations, which means bad press. Which is just what we don't need."

* * *

Meade didn't respond.

Hickman leaned forward. "Mr. President, are you all right?"

Meade looked up and Hickman would never forget what he said.

"I told myself yesterday that nobody owns me . . . and you know, it's true. But I just realized I don't own anyone either. I didn't make the fucking game. But damned if she isn't making me play by the rules."

His words were so out of context that Hickman didn't wait around for an elaboration or explanation. Instead he made an excuse to leave. When he shut the door, the president was still looking at the space in front of him, as if Hickman were still standing there.

46

INDIA/New Delhi

The American press had taken up quarters in the fleabag hotel Hickman had warned the president about and, just as he had feared, the press complained the entire time.

The First Lady and the wives of the other heads of state toured New Delhi and the surrounding area, while their husbands were gathered about the World Economic Conference round table.

Otis Meade suffered through the three days of the conference with as much enthusiasm for it as a crippled bloodhound, though he tried very hard not to show it, especially when the press was around. Nevertheless, other people noticed. By the end of the second day members of other delegations were whispering to each other about the president's spirits and wondered what was wrong. Some speculated that it was the campaign back in the States, the prospect of losing to Hawkins. Others thought the president probably just wasn't used to the dry, dusty weather of India. A few sensed that his mood had something to do with his personal life since he and the First Lady seemed unusually detached, even for a formal visit abroad when so many demands are made on each other's time. Of course, they were right.

Meade had said nothing to anyone about his discussion with

Katherine, but the effects it wrought were unmistakable. Something had happened to him inside. Pain and anguish were visible on his face and discernible in his tone of voice. He had been given an ultimatum. It showed on the remainder of his flight to India and the following three days. It showed even now.

The Indian prime minister finished his remarks to those gathered in the packed ballroom and then sat down. As protocol required, Meade stood up and, greeted by spontaneous applause, went behind the podium. Seated before him, just in front of the main banquet table, were Howard Hickman, several men from State, Hickman's assistant—Jerry Ecklecamp—and several members of the Indian foreign ministry. Hickman's eyes watched as Meade unfolded a small white piece of paper that he'd taken from his breast pocket, and hoped the president didn't come across on television looking as tired as he did here. He leaned over to Ecklecamp and whispered, "He looks bad. Did you take him that bottle of Wild Turkey?"

"Uh huh. He just nodded and told me to put it on his dresser. I saw it this morning and he still hasn't touched it."

"He'd better do something to get himself in shape."

"You think he's flipping?" asked Ecklecamp.

Hickman glared at him and hissed, "I think it'd be wise to watch what you say and listen to the fucking toasts."

Ecklecamp shriveled and the man from State stared at them.

"Mr. Prime Minister, my honorable friends and guests, I bid you both welcome and thanks from the United States and all Americans. We have had the opportunity within these past three days . . ."

Hickman glanced over at the press section, saw two of their press corp members yawning and another one playing with his microphone cord.

"The president isn't impressing our media," Hickman said to himself.

". . . seek an unprecedented accord between the world's most powerful nations in an effort to bring about peaceful economic solidarity. When the World Economic Conference accords are made public tomorrow, I do not doubt that the world will begin to be a better place because of the work we've done here. But, before then, I wish to say that this conference would not have been possible without the tireless help of our good friend and ally, a true leader among the third world and a most gracious host, the nation and peoples of India!"

The lapels of Meade's dinner jacket shimmered in the spotlights as he raised a champagne glass and gestured toward the Indian prime minister. A round of applause welled up in the ballroom. The prime minister nodded his thanks and acknowledged the warm response of the audience. The applause continued and the ballroom rose to its feet clapping.

Suddenly Hickman felt a light tap on his shoulder. He turned around and faced a member of the United States Marines.

"Excuse me, sir," the marine said in his ear, trying to be heard over the ovation, "but you have a phone call from the White House."

Hickman's face registered surprise. "Who is it? What do they want?"

"They didn't identify themselves, sir."

Hickman's face turned in puzzlement.

"Did you tell them where I was?"

"Yes, sir, but they wanted to talk to you anyway."

"All right, let's go."

The marine led Hickman through a maze of tables as the dignitaries from various countries began sitting down again. Behind him he heard the Soviet president being introduced and, as he left the ballroom, heard him say, *"Stasivo,"* greeting the audience.

Outside the ballroom Hickman walked through the ornate hall, where uniformed guards stood among luscious palms and beautiful tapestries.

"There's a phone in the minister's office around the end of the hall. We've secured it just in case."

Hickman glanced at his watch. "Nine o'clock. How long ago did it come?"

"Just a few minutes ago."

Hickman nodded and they passed a small group of Secret Service men mingling with some British agents. "Tell me, what's the time difference back there? Twelve hours?"

"Yes, sir."

"Umm, that makes it nine in the morning then."

They went into another office, a small room obviously used by the minister's secretaries, and through to a much larger, more elaborate office used by the prime minister himself. Two other marines were guarding the phone. They left the room when Hickman picked up the receiver.

"Hello?"

Over a static-filled line came the voice of Tony LaCross.
"Howard?"
"Yeah, what is it? Why the call?"
"First off, it looks like the president's getting some things done over there. Coverage here is good. Is it true?"
"What?"
"That the participating nations agreed on the accords?"
"Yeah, big deal. You and I both know they won't mean anything for at least a year, but the principles sound good."
"Still, the coverage is good. It's keeping him in the headlines here and on all the networks. He could come away with some real gains."
Hickman said, "That's encouraging because he's been going through these meetings like a robot. I don't know if anyone else noticed it or not, but he's definitely not himself."
"The reports say he's been rather low-key."
"That's not the word for it."
"Anyway, I thought you and the president would like to know that some things have been happening here as well."
Hickman prepared himself for the worse. "Like what?"
"We've been dealing with Mexico almost nonstop for the past week and it looks like the negotiations could start up again."
"When?"
"Anytime. We're waiting on word from Portillo now. Maybe this India conference will encourage him. Regardless, I'll let you know as soon as we do. Will you tell the president?"
"Are you sure they're going to open up again?"
"I'm almost sure. I'd bet on it."
"Well, let's tell him when we know positively. I mean, Christ, I don't want to put this on him and then have them fall through. He's already got enough on his mind."
"Howard—"
"I mean it. We'll tell him when it's definite. Just call me when you know."
With that, Hickman hung up.

Later that evening the hotel suite in which the president was staying was dark, and in one of the bedrooms Meade lay in bed wide awake, reflecting on the past three days' events, the conference, the dinners, the receptions, the tours. The conference, for all he could tell, had been a moderate success, yet he had an underlying feeling that he had succeeded at nothing during his entire stay here. He knew he had carried himself off as best he could, knew that he'd said the right things while bantering with some of the other Western leaders, as he usually did at these things, knew that he'd made the right points. But it had all been perfunctory and no one was more aware of this than he. The reasons, of course, went back to their flight and the ultimatum Katherine had given him. He supposed it shouldn't have come as such a shock to him. It was her timing that surprised him—and her finality. He didn't know she had it in her; perhaps up until now she hadn't. However she had mustered up the strength to do what she did, he knew that he was the one responsible for it. He had been pushing her into it all these years, testing her subconsciously to see how much she would take, flaunting his ambivalence toward her almost under her nose.

Yet he didn't know why he had.

He used to think he loved her, but that was years ago. Even then, thinking about it now, he knew he never really had. He married her because politically he had to. It was that simple. The fact that his marriage to her had helped his career was undeniable. To this day, much to his irritation, people still said it was Katherine who had put him in the governor's mansion and the White House.

It was true that their relationship had always been more or less one-sided. He knew that she loved him deeply, had given him a beautiful daughter, and had always played the role of the political wife, even when she didn't want to. He respected her for all of it. Appreciated it. But lying there, thinking about her and about their marriage and her background, he knew something was very wrong. He did not *like* Katherine. For all she had done, all she had sacrificed, none of it made as much of an impression on him as the fact that he did not like her. He had never acknowledged it until now, but it was true. Although the reasons were not wholly clear to him in his own mind, resentment was certanly the biggest. Resentment toward her background, her wealth, her social standing. The fact that she had had everything in her life that he had always wanted—but never could have had without her. She had been the key. It was her money and power and status that forced him to rely on her for the past twenty-some years to get everything he had now. Envy still burned within him after all these years, envy he couldn't shake. He had been forced into doing what his father had done—his weak, pitiful, washed-up father—and rely on his wife instead of his own abilities. And the worst part was that he needed her now more than he'd ever needed her in his life. Once again he was in a position where she was the key, where she was capable of either keeping him on top or tearing him down. It infuriated him. And now he had made a mistake. He'd pushed her too far, squeezed whatever love she had for him beyond its limits, and Katherine, realizing it, now wanted out.

But, he couldn't—wouldn't—let her. She still loved him, of that he was sure, and he could use that love to his advantage, if only for a little while. He had to try, if for only one last time, to keep her with him.

In the morning the stillness of the dawn hung over the bedroom like the calm before a storm. There were still hours before Meade had to get up for the breakfast he was giving in honor of the Indian prime minister, then there were the economic accords themselves to sign, and later the flight back to the States. So his mind began to drift, thoughts filtering through and mixing with emotions, especially bitterness, and always . . . always . . . Katherine was at the center. When the sun began to creep through the sheer curtains, Meade finally pulled off the sheets and sat upright in bed. The elegant rug beneath his feet was a warm welcome as he walked across the room to a door on the opposite side.

Yes, he had to try.

Katherine heard the gentle creak of the door and knew it was Otis. She lifted her head from the pillows and stared at him through sleepy eyes. He had nothing but his pajama bottoms on and for an instant she thought about how good his body looked even now. Their eyes met and before she knew it he shut the door, unsnapped his waistband, and came toward her.

Katherine smiled and, seeing her smile, Meade told himself that he was doing the right thing, what needed to be done. She was vulnerable for love, and he was going to exploit that. That was all it would take.

Katherine, reaching out her arms and pulling him into bed, said silently, That's right . . . come to me. Yes, that's it. Kiss me. Make love to me. Tell me you love me, that you didn't mean it, and there's been some mistake, that we can still work things out. . . . Yes, run your tongue up and down my neck like that . . . hear me moan, tell yourself you're turning me on, you're giving me all I ever wanted . . .

tell yourself whatever you want, you bastard, but I'm finished. Finished, do you hear? . . . That's right, squeeze me there . . . keep whispering to me . . . and just remember that it's not going to change things. I'm staying on through the election so nobody can accuse me of abandoning ship, but after that, you're on your own. I'm going.

Yes . . . that's the place . . . rub me there . . . kiss me again . . . do all the things you did to *them*.

Bastard!

47

EN ROUTE TO WASHINGTON

Below there was nothing but the vast green waters stretching beneath Air Force One as far as he could see. For Howard Hickman, a man who rarely thought of what he saw in the context of its beauty, it was stunning. He pressed his face close to the oval window and gazed at the mirrors of light bouncing off the water below.

India had worked for them after all. Meade and the other world leaders had signed the World Economic Conference accords that morning, and the press, who had seemed unimpressed by the conference until then, made a great fuss over the significance of the pact. If there was ever such a thing as a media snow job, this was it. Meade's press secretary, Jody Allen, who had noticed the press's lackadaisical attitude before they even left Washington, had been working almost nonstop during the trip to turn their perceptions of the conference around. His job had been even more difficult because Meade seemed so detached from the proceedings. But this morning it had been different. Meade had recovered from his malaise and had regained his usual self-confidence, telling everyone who would listen that the economic accords were the most significant set of agreements accomplished during his administration. Again Americans everywhere could be proud of their contribution toward making the world a more stable and economically healthy place in which to live. Allen and Hickman lobbied the press to concentrate on Meade's abilities and talents in getting other Western nations to agree to the accords. Now, having read several reports Allen had secured before they were filed, Hickman knew the journalists were doing just that. He smiled to himself. Yes, the conference had been a gamble, but it looked as if it would pay off. And back home the only direction Meade's polls could go was up.

He was about to recline his seat for a nap when Jerry Ecklecamp poked his head out of the door of the rear cabin office and said, "You've got a phone call, Howard. It's Tony LaCross."

Hickman's mind snapped to attention, remembering his long-distance call yesterday.

He unbuckled his seat belt, got up, and stepped into the office. He took the phone and, turning to Ecklecamp, said, "Step out and find something to do, Jerry."

Ecklecamp, looking hurt, turned and left, closing the door behind him.

"Tony?"

"Congratulations, Howard, it looks like the old man pulled it off. They interrupted all the network shows here to bring live coverage of the signing."

"Is our press still good?"

"The only really negative thing I've seen is Atwood's column."

Hickman grunted. Atwood was the columnist who caught the president lying about taking a disturbing phone call in his limousine right before running into Cliff Hawkins at the Waldorf-Astoria. Hickman loathed him. "What did he say?"

"Something to the effect that the trip was nothing more than an official excuse to get out of the kitchen because the president couldn't stand the heat."

"That sonofabitch."

"Forget about him. I've got some news you'll love."

"The pipeline?"

"You got it. Portillo's been keeping an eye on Meade's performance at the India conference and it looks like he bought it. He's betting on the president's still being in office after November."

"Meaning the—"

"Meaning the negotiations have started up again."

Hickman clutched the phone. "Good! Good! When?"

"We got the call about an hour ago. We resume the talks the first of next week."

"He's going to love this," Hickman said. "It's icing on the cake."

INTERLUDE

BRITISH WEST INDIES

North of Haiti and east of Cuba, about halfway between Miami and Puerto Rico, there is a stretch of eight islands and forty cays known as the Turks and Caicos archipelago. It is a place where the rich come to escape the rigors of life at the top, a place where there is no income tax, sales tax, inheritance tax, gift tax, real estate tax. A place still unspoiled by commercialism and tourists, with unbelievably white sands, spectacularly clean beaches, crystal-clear water, and some of the best bonefishing in the world. It is also a place of privacy with entry to the islands gained by either private plane or boat. And it was because of all these benefits that Francesco Gianni built a home there.

The gentle waves ran up the sugary white sand beach of Provo Island, then retreated as quickly as they had come. Francesco Gianni sat comfortably in a chair on his back deck, his body sheltered from the sun by a multicolored canopy. Sipping his piña colada, he looked out at the ocean, watching in amusement as some dolphins played in the distance. This had been paradise to him for so long now that he wondered if he could ever leave. This was his own private retreat, an escape from the law and the climates so harsh on his bronchitis; but he knew he would have to leave eventually because there were too many business interests awaiting his attention in the States. The thought saddened him.

The radio beside him had been playing soft music out of Miami and he turned it up when the news came on.

The accords were signed yesterday morning and it seems assured the United States achieved its goals at the conference. Insiders in Washington are speculating that this could very well be the beginning of an upswing for the president. Although none of the economic policies proposed will go into effect until next year at the earliest, White House officials say the accords are of major significance in that they have brought together a consolidated statement of policy with other Western allied nations in dealing with economic development in India and other Eastern nations. This is something they say the president has been seeking for some time. . . . In other news Palestinian terrorists attacked a . . .

Gianni listened until the report was over with, then turned off the radio. Behind him he heard the patio door slide open, but didn't bother to turn around. He knew who it was.

"Sir, you have a telephone call from the United States."

Gianni coughed and wheezed and turned around. He asked his houseboy who was calling.

"The White House, sir."

Gianni knew the boy could read the surprise on his face. He got up. As he walked inside, one of his bodyguards handed him the telephone.

He grabbed it, pausing to cough first. "Yeah?"

"This is Hickman. I just wanted you to know the negotiations have started up again. Mexico is coming along fine."

Hearing these words, Gianni's eyes brightened. He even laughed. "Sonofabitch! It's about time you people got your asses movin' on this thing. How long's it gonna take to get the agreements settled?"

"We don't know. A month, maybe two, maybe not until after the election."

"After the election? What the hell—"

"Look, we're pushing it as fast as we can. We're doing our best to expedite the proceedings, but we've got to handle the whole situation with kid gloves. You know that."

"Yeah, well, look. It better not be after the fuckin' election. That's all I gotta say. You keep me posted on this thing, you hear me?"

Hickman curtly replied that he would and rang off.

Gianni handed the phone back to his bodyguard, then turned to his houseboy and said, "Get me another piña colada."

The houseboy disappeared toward the kitchen and Gianni stepped back outside. Standing on his deck, he looked out at the magnificent Caribbean, thinking about what Hickman had said. The time factor irritated him, but he had to admit it was damn good the talks were even going again. And this thing . . . this conference in India had gone well too. Who knows? Maybe the president could still pull himself together.

Maybe . . .

Two weeks later Otis Meade won the Democratic party's presidential nomination.

BOOK
FOUR

THE
ELECTION

48

CAMPAIGN TRAIL

It was amazing how quickly time had passed. The lazy weeks of August, which were filled with sluggish heat-stricken days interrupted only briefly by the lackluster Democratic convention, turned quickly into the energetic fleeing weeks of September.

As was traditional, both Hawkins and the president kicked off their campaigns on Labor Day, but the fireworks of what was building up to be one of the most unusual presidential races in history had erupted weeks before.

Hawkins had been hitting the campaign trail almost nonstop since his nomination, trying to draw attention away from the fact that, as the press reported, his advisers were having more trouble bringing their fall campaign strategies into a cohesive plan than they'd had with the primaries. Part of the problem was how to attack the president. Hawkins was in a particularly vulnerable position because he had been nominated for his Christian beliefs and principles, and to do anything extremely negative—such as going venomously after the president as he wanted to do—would strip away that image and a lot of his support, giving credence to his opponent's charges that he was a demagogue. During his televised crusades, he had been able to attack the president because, as a religious leader, Hawkins was seen as a politically concerned candidate. During the primaries, he was such a celebrity, and his candidacy such a novelty, that the public didn't pay particularly close attention to how he said things, but to what he said. And what he said about Meade was what his supporters already knew.

Now, however, the situation was much more sensitive. Hawkins was not in a field with three other Republican contenders, but the Republican party's sole representative for the presidency. Thus the public was much more scrutinizing. His celebrity aura was wearing off, and the fact that the public would have to decide between him and the president in November was difficult enough. So his staff advised him to stay away from attacking the president directly, which would help maintain his Christian image, and concentrate on the moral, economic, and social issues that the president was especially vulnerable on, thus attacking him by association. But even that caused Hawkins problems. Instead of directing negative attention to the president's beliefs, he quickly found the attention being drawn toward himself.

At a question-and-answer session in Dayton, Ohio, following a rally, the evangelist was asked if it was really so important to have a recommitted Christian in the White House.

"Yes, it is, because unless you have a truly dedicated Christian in the White House, devoted to turning this nation away from its present course, you'll see things not only continue to deteriorate but also reach a point of no-return. The Bible explicitly states: 'Misfortune pursues the sinner, but prosperity is the reward of the righteous.' So the ultimate choice is whether you're going to vote for a nation under God or a nation under man."

Hawkins's press entourage snapped to attention when they heard this. Did Cliff Hawkins just say that, if he were elected, the nation would be under *God?* If Meade were reelected, it would be under man? They looked at each other and dashed to the nearest phones to call in the story.

Before the rally was even over, Hawkins's road advisers realized the bomb he had just set off. His remarks were the lead stories for television stations and newspapers across the nation.

In Washington the president said facetiously, "I might as well throw in the towel. I didn't realize I was running against the Lord himself."

* * *

A week later Hawkins found himself in deeper trouble in San Francisco. He was being interviewed by a beautiful but tough young woman journalist when she asked him to expand upon his opposition to homosexuality. Hawkins was used to the question and said he based his opposition to it on the Bible.

He told her the Old Testament was explicitly clear on the issue when it said, "Do not lie with a man as one lies with a woman; that is detestable."

The journalist, "That passage continues by saying that both shall be put to death. Do you believe that, Reverend?"

"Not in the sense that the Lord will strike them dead or anything. He is a loving God, after all, which is why Jesus came down from heaven and died for us on the cross. But I do believe they will be denied God's kingdom, which is worse than being put to death. It is death itself."

"And you back this up biblically too, don't you?"

"Yes, of course. In 1 Corinthians, chapter 6, verses 9 and 10, it says that neither the 'sexually immoral . . . nor male prostitutes nor homosexual offenders . . . will inherit the kingdom of God.' That's pretty clear, isn't it?"

The young woman nodded her head slowly, then asked Hawkins the one question that would probably lose him the entire San Francisco vote.

"Reverend," she said, "what do you think *causes* homosexuality?"

Hawkins studied her for a minute and answered, "Jennifer, I really believe it comes from the men of this nation who falter as leaders."

She tensed.

"What we have had in this nation is a situation that *feeds* the ingredients of homosexuality into our children, then, when they grow up, they're gay."

"Meaning?" she asked, astonished.

"Meaning that it's men who have left their homes, who have left their sons without a masculine image to follow, which has eventually led them to homosexuality. The son doesn't have his father's image to follow, so he begins to pick up on his mother's. And before you know it, what have we got? A nation of grown up Sammy Homemakers instead of Suzy Homemakers."

Jennifer Collins stared at Hawkins, not believing what he'd just said.

Neither could the thousands of San Franciscans watching the interview live. The television station's switchboard lit up with irate viewers demanding to talk to Hawkins, screaming for Collins to get him off the air; one even threatened to blow up the station.

The remark created a controversy that raged on throughout the next week. Gay activists as well as psychiatrists, psychologists, sociologists, ministers, educators, and politicians called it everything from ludicrous to misguided. Their outrage plagued Hawkins from California to Michigan to New York and back again, and only after repeated explanations and clarifications of his statement did the gaffe even begin to be overlooked.

The Meade campaign took full advantage of the situation. Volunteers began passing out literature at Hawkins's campaign stops, quoting similarly ill-thought-through statements that he'd made in the past—from his opposition to the women's movement ("The Bible says, 'Wives, submit to your husbands as to the Lord.' ") to his thoughts on rock music ("If a true Christian reads the lyrics, he'll easily see the demonic influences behind this music."). It wasn't as if the public hadn't heard his opinions before, because they had, and millions of Christian voters had agreed with him—which was why he had the numbers of supporters he did. But there were still millions of voters who hadn't heard these statements before, even during the primaries, because of the brouhaha over Hawkins's candidacy itself.

Leaders of the Meade campaign, delighted that the evangelist was finally facing some serious heat, beefed up their grass roots organization—already strong thanks to the Democratic party's considerable help—and quickly recruited more volunteers to hand out literature, handle phone banks, canvass neighborhoods, and do all they could for the reelection.

The Republican party, already nervously aware that their candidate would be either the hottest commodity or the worst liability they'd had in years, responded by pumping bucketfuls of additional money into Hawkins's campaign. They had already raised enough money to outspend the Democrats three to one.

As the battle raged on, it quickly became apparent that the greatest expenditures of money by both sides went to buy media time. In 1992 the typical American was now watching almost seven and a half hours of television a day, with access to four major networks and an average of 128 cable–satellite stations across the nation. Although the candidates and their vice presidential running mates were making personal appearances on the campaign trail, the real differences of emphasis between the two candidates were the result of television advertising by the parties themselves.

In some market areas, those in which the president was somewhat weak, the Democratic television spots would emphasize what the next four years would be like under Cliff Hawkins. How vulnerable our liberties would be under someone as rigid and dogmatic in his beliefs as Hawkins was. How simplistic his views on the world were. How his lack of experience in government would be disastrous for the nation and earn him little respect from world leaders. In other areas the spots would emphasize Meade's leadership abilities, his experience, and the fact that as president, he had had to make some tough decisions even though they weren't politically popular. Meade himself had seen one of these spots the other day in the Oval Office and was quite impressed.

On the screen the president was shown behind his desk filmed through the outside windows of the Oval Office. It was nighttime and the curtains were still parted. The office was well lit. The camera moved in closer and the image behind the bulletproof glass came into sharper focus. The president was shown leaning over his massive desk, tie undone, shirt sleeves rolled up, going over a stack of papers. He took a pen in hand and made notes. It was all very presidential. The only sounds heard were those of crickets and other sounds of nature. The camera moved closer. His image grew more defined. Then it took the television viewer through the glass pane into the Oval Office itself. The viewer is clearly expected to feel awed. This was an angle the camera had never given them during those televised speeches. They were sneaking up on the president. Observing him. Seeing him work. His face—stern, serious, presidential. It told them he was so concerned with his work that he was unaware of the camera's presence. Then, as the lens moved in closer and a camera from a different angle zoomed in for a close-up, the viewers saw an enlarged image of the president's eyes, his skin, his expression. This was obviously a man of all work and no play. Then the camera pulled back a little. Meade laid down his pen, massaged the bridge of his nose. Everyone watching knew that whatever he was doing wasn't easy. And the voice-over made this perfectly clear:

> After we leave work at the end of the day, there is still one man who stays at his job. He stays because the job is never finished. The world around us is constantly changing, and it is his

job to protect us, lead us, and work for us, even if it means staying at the office late into the night. Who is this man and what does he do?

He's President Otis Meade. His job is running our nation and it's a job that is never finished. We elected him four years ago to do this job, and he has worked for our nation tirelessly . . . late into many many nights.

You don't find dedication like that in everyone. Let's reelect the president.

The positive approach was good, but it quickly became apparent in both the polls and the public's reaction that the negative spots on Hawkins were more effective.

In one of those spots a series of pictures of Hawkins was shown—Hawkins shaking hands, Hawkins giving a speech, Hawkins laughing and waving to a crowd, Hawkins behind the pulpit—with an ominous voice-over intoning:

Cliff Hawkins is against women having equal rights.
He is against children having protection under the law.
—against the right of women to govern their bodies.
—against single parent homes.
—against secular groups that disagree with him.
—against religious freedom.
—against the separation of church and state.
Two hundred years ago the founders of our nation left their motherland to have the very freedom and rights Cliff Hawkins is against. If he doesn't want Americans to have these—then where would he like us to go now?

Although everything the spot claimed that Hawkins was against wasn't entirely true—he had already answered the questions on church and state and religious freedom dozens of times—it still was effective and instilled the fear in the electorate that through his powers as president, if Hawkins were elected, Americans would lose a great many of the freedoms they now enjoyed.

In another spot, this one attacking Hawkins's lack of government experience, a mechanic was shown with his head under the hood of a car. As the camera moved in, he rose and with a wrench in his hand said in a neighborly fashion, "Hey, there's been a lot of talk about who we're gonna choose for president. Some people say experience doesn't matter. Others say it does. Well, I been around for a long time and I know when you need someone to work on your car, you call me, not a plumber. And when you need someone to work on our government, you call a leader, not a preacher." The mechanic smiled. "So for me the choice is clear. Go with experience. Go with a leader. Vote for the president—again."

The Hawkins campaign came up with some very effective spots of their own and, armed with almost three times the money of the Democrats, could run them in more markets, at better times, and for longer periods than their opponents could.

One particularly devastating spot resurrected the disastrous raid Meade ordered on the Acapulco Princess Hotel.

Watching the advertising spot, viewers at first saw nothing but blackness, followed by a graying that was transformed slowly into evening lights. There was dancing, twirling, and a shot of smiling foreigners. Americans. There was joy and relaxation among the Americans, here in this faraway place. Then suddenly the faces on the screen froze. There was no movement. They were held in a trance. Then machine-gun fire was heard, first at a distance, then, unexpectedly, very loud and very near. Ear shattering. Screams were heard. Cries of anguish. Pain and suffering. There was no pause in the firing, no mercy in the agonized cries.

Cut to President Meade, working his way through a mass of people, smiling, waving, obviously enjoying himself. The screen went black, and the Acapulco Princess was seen from afar, erupting in a wave of explosions. There were flames, flames of death. Cut back to Meade, still smiling and waving, and at that moment the cameras froze. An ominous voice-over asked: "How can this man smile? How can we give him another chance? Like people, the chances have died. The time is now to elect someone new—Clifford Hawkins." Another series showed shots of unemployed, poverty-stricken and starving people in various ghettos around the country and then the question: "If the system is working so well under our current president, then why are these people out of work, trapped in poverty, and hungry? The president says one thing, we see another. Isn't it time we told him that we know better? Let's vote for a change. Let's vote for a man who will put compassion and understanding back into government. Let's vote for Clifford Hawkins."

All of these campaigns began to make an impression on the electorate and, as both sides watched their polling data, a pattern began to emerge: the president was slowly going up in the polls and Hawkins was coming down. Hawkins had held a comfortable edge over the president since his nomination in July, so he still had a way to go before actually falling behind Meade. But his campaign had gotten off to an embarrassing start and involved so many gaffes that Meade's polls had been rising since he returned from his trip to India. The race was clearly getting tighter, and no one acknowledged this more emphatically than the candidates themselves.

Hawkins stayed on the campaign trail, but, to avoid more political fumbles, his staff made him virtually inaccessible to outsiders. Interviews were rarely granted and, when they were, all questions were prescreened. He was advised to stick as closely to his text as possible at rallies, and was hustled from limousine to platform and back again at almost every stop.

Meade was advised by his strategists to limit his campaigning as his polls continued to rise. He was told to stay around the White House and look "presidential." Afer all, the trappings of the White House with all its pageantry and officialdom allowed Meade to control his end of the campaign by appearing calm in the face of opposition, not "chasing after" Hawkins or his lead. He accepted his advisers' logic, and knew, too, that he had a small army of surrogates out there plugging for him, including the vice president and his wife.

His wife. Since their return from India, he'd paid special attention to her, making love to her as often as he could. For all Meade could tell, it was working. Although Katherine had always made it clear she loathed campaigning, she knew that Meade's staff wanted him to stay around the White house and that he needed as much field support as he could get. That meant getting the First Lady out on the campaign trail. At first Meade didn't think Katherine would go for it, but she readily agreed. That had been over two months ago. For the past month she'd been traveling six days a week for him, hitting the key states he needed to win.

But if Otis Meade thought he knew his wife, he was wrong.

CALIFORNIA/Campaigning

The limousines and Secret Service halted traffic for three blocks. Outside San Francisco's fashionable Stanford Court Hotel on Nob Hill, well over a hundred reporters pushed and shoved with the mob of spectators and police crowding around the hotel's entrance. People poured over the sidewalks and into the street and hung out of the windows of surrounding buildings.

Katherine Meade had noticed the crowds from her suite. The agents had advised her to use the rear service entrance, but she refused. After all, if she campaigned for her husband, she was going to do it right—by meeting the people, no matter how exhausting it was.

She took an elevator downstairs. While she chatted in the lobby with the Stanford Court's manager and posed for pictures, some of her Secret Service detail went outside and began forcing the crowds back. Agents took up positions along the roped exitway or weaved their way through the crowds, their eyes peeled for anything that looked remotely suspicious. Katherine's limousine, Secret Service backup cars, and police cruisers and motorcycles revved up and flipped on their lights. A rush of excitement swept over the crowd. Cameras were raised, heads craned, and people stood on tiptoe, eyeing the hotel's entrance.

The doors swung back and more agents sprinted down the steps and suddenly she was there. The First Lady, gracefully moving past the doors, waving and smiling, as the hotel's manager led her out, her movements precise and elegant.

She made her way quickly down the steps and the crowd surged forward. They were pushing to touch her, feel her, be near her. The agents encircled her, but the crowd grew more pressing. The limousine was only a few steps away, but it seemed like a mile. Hands. Pens. Pads. Voices. Mouths, oohing and aahing, were saying a hundred different things at once. And cries of "Mrs. Meade! Mrs. Meade!" over and over.

Then a firm arm lifted her and thrust her into the limousine.

She was safe. The doors slammed shut. Locks were activated and she was secure in her cocoon. They began to move. Sirens were ahead of her, voices—her staff traveling with her—were safely around her. On the outside people pressed their faces and hands against the car's windows, smiling, waving, mouthing things to her she could neither hear nor understand. They were everywhere.

It was the fourth week for her on the campaign trail. September was almost over and all that was left were October and the first week in November. Then the voting. God, if she could only make it until then. In the past four weeks she had made over 112 stops in 36 different cities and towns. She was averaging at least six speeches or talks or interviews a day. There were times—now almost every day—when she wasn't sure where she was or whom she was addressing. Four times in the past two weeks she had misnamed a place. Two universities, one city, and one entire state. Not bad, but not good either. The man from the Washington office was with her now, along with two of her secretaries. She hadn't acknowledged any of them since she'd gotten into the car, perhaps because she hadn't had a chance to recover from the melee outside the hotel, but that didn't stop them.

"You're doin' just fine, Mrs. Meade, just fine," the man from the Washington office said. "It's always more impressive when the crowds are like that. Always."

"Now, as soon as we leave here," her senior secretary was telling her, "we're going over to Sacramento, where you'll address the University of California at Davis. Then you'll be jetting down to Newport Beach for some yacht race, then motorcade into L.A., where you're scheduled to be the guest of honor at the Heart Association Ball at the Beverly Wilshire. After that . . ."

Katherine began shaking her head wearily as she stretched her feet.

"Midge, please! Can we take this two at a time? I'm really bushed. And the crowd back there—"

Her other secretary spoke up. "Of course, Mrs. Meade. We understand. Look, how about signing some letters? That'll—"

"No!"

They stared at her.

Katherine sighed.

"Look, this morning I just told over thirty-five hundred Legionaires to reelect my husband, met with three labor groups, some reporters from the Hearst paper, inhaled my lunch back at the Stanford Court, and, now, if I don't shut my eyes and relax until we reach wherever we're going—"

"The VA Hospital," reminded Midge.

"Fine—if I don't shut my eyes for a minute, I won't be dedicating that new wing, I'll be dying there."

With that, Katherine closed her eyes and laid her head against the seat. She could feel the limousine's movements, the vibrations beneath her, but they didn't bother her. What bothered her, as it always did when the pressures were closing in on her, was why she was doing this at all. She could have stayed out of the campaign and let Otis and the committee and the party work their asses off. But she was damned if, after the campaign was over and she finally did leave him, anyone was going to accuse her of not having lived up to her obligations. Oh, no, she was going to continue just as she had, playing the pretty First Lady and the still-loving wife. Then, once the dust had settled and the next president was inaugurated, she was going back to South Bend without him. The hardest part was times like this, when she didn't know if she could stand it until the election.

God, she never thought she would feel the way she did about Otis now. But in the past six weeks it was as if someone had suddenly pulled up a curtain and shown her what she'd been trying to avoid seeing for years. Every time she thought about it her determination to get out of their marriage grew stronger. She had spent years considering other people, but now she didn't give a damn. For the first time in years Katherine was thinking only of herself. And feeling damned good about it.

"Mrs. Meade," her senior secretary said, "we're coming up on the hospital."

Katherine opened her eyes, straightened up, and smiled. "Good, I'm ready."

In Florida another woman was trying to find strength of her own.

FLORIDA/Miami

Charlotte Hawkins glanced out at the audience of developers and realtors, then looked down at the notes on the rostrum before her. She continued speaking. This was the largest predominantly Jewish audience she'd ever spoken before. The reception they'd given her was polite at best. A second ago she'd seen several rows of stoic faces of people whose support they needed. The staff in Dallas sent her to help establish enough trust between the Jewish voters and her husband to put Cliff over the top in a state that was otherwise up for grabs. For fifteen minutes she talked to them, getting her points across. When she was finished and stepped back, the audience leapt suddenly to its feet with a roar of applause.

Hours later in her hotel suite, as the surf rolled in on the beach below, Charlotte watched segments of her speech on the local news.

She thought about how ironic the entire situation was. She had opposed the very idea of Cliff's running for president before the draft movement had even been formed. She had continued to oppose it after he plunged into the primaries.

She had been through so much because of this race that her ideas had changed. To think that she was actually surviving in it—and without scotch—was incredible. Hadn't she gone out and played the perfect, obedient candidate's wife? The campaign could have easily destroyed her.

Charlotte was not about to let that happen, just as she had decided not to let scotch destroy her marriage. She believed that more strongly now. It wasn't easy to keep politics from driving a wedge between them, and Charlotte was aware of how the campaign was changing Cliff. But her love for him was unwavering. She could see why it was changing him and, seeing this, she was more aware of the changes taking place within her.

But there were times ... times when dealing with these changes wasn't easy. She was a woman who loved her husband deeply, but she was lonely and thus vulnerable to many cravings that her husband would hate—that she should hate, but couldn't. It made it hard, because what she craved most, both physically and emotionally, was what would bring her down the fastest. When she was on the road in places like Miami and in hotel rooms like this, with only Secret Service agents and staff memebers for company, it was especially difficult to remember this. But, now, seeing herself on television, seeing the influence she was having on the voters, seeing the good she could do, Charlotte had a sense of peace—strength enough to persevere.

But every day she faced the struggle all over again.

49

WASHINGTON/The White House

From the start the fall campaign was tougher than the primaries. The White House's continued barrage of attacks, as well as those from other opponents such as labor unions, gays, and feminists, made the race particularly difficult for Hawkins. Now the tables turned and it was not the president's administration, but the evangelist, who was suddenly in an unwanted and embarrassing spotlight.

It was the first week of October and the president was holding to his advisers' strategy of staying close to the White House, letting dozens of his Administration's representatives—from Cabinet members to the First Lady—stay in the political trenches of America to sustain the momentum in Meade's polls. From what Reed McClellan and his staff could tell, their strategies were working. Hawkins's lead over the president in nationwide preference polls had fallen to a mere four points, and the president's deficits in the South and East had dropped to nine and seven, respectively. McClellan thought that, if the pattern continued, Meade could go into the last weeks of the campaign with enough electoral college votes to win.

Then everything went haywire.

One of Meade's cabinet members, Secretary of Interior Morris

Finner, had flown into Texas to help solidify the president's base there. Even though Hawkins was from Dallas, Texas was still up for grabs. Finner flew in to win over as many Texans as he could. If anyone could accomplish this other than the president or the First Lady, it was Finner. With his impressive oratorical skills, charismatic looks, and quick humor, Finner could make even the worst enemies into friends.

But it was Finner's humor that turned the trip into a disaster.

He was heading back to Washington from Houston after speaking on behalf of the president to the National Petroleum Club. Like everyone else who'd been out on the campaign trail, he was tired. He really didn't feel like doing any work during the flight, so he loosened up with a few drinks and found himself chatting with some reporters in his cabin office. They talked about the campaign, about some legislation Finner was going to have to testify about on Capitol Hill, about the weather, and anything else that came to mind. Someone told Finner a joke and, feeling he had to top it, Finner told them one. A couple more were tossed around and then, after another drink or two, Finner told one he shouldn't have.

"Hey, did you guys know they had two blacks on 'That's Impossible!' the other night?"

The reporters, feeling a little lubed themselves, snickered and said, no, they didn't.

"Yeah, one of 'em had a job and the other one knew who his father was."

"How about three French words every black knows?" Pause. "Coupe de Ville."

The reporters and the secretary howled, but two days later the jokes were leaked and made the national news.

Reactions to the secretary's jokes were volcanic, to say the least. Civil rights leaders, ministers, congressmen, senators, columnists, and dozens of prominent Meade supporters all cried out in shock. Meade's staff made a frenzied effort to keep the explosion of reactions from further damaging the president. It didn't work. As the week wore on there were calls for Finner's resignation. Meade, knowing full well that much of his support on Election Day was going to come from Democrats who prided themselves in belonging to the party known for its support of civil rights and the working class, issued a statement expressing deep regret over his secretary's remark. He followed this with two more statements even more strongly worded. To make matters worse, a former assistant to Finner told newsmen that the interior secretary frequently cracked racist jokes when he was working for him and then repeated several of them. Another wave of outrage erupted.

By the second week in October Finner resigned, but the controversy stayed in the news. According to the polls taken from the previous week, it was costing the president dearly. If Cliff Hawkins's remarks about homosexuals had lost him San Francisco and a chunk of the rest of the California vote, Finner's remarks lost the president a major portion of the liberal vote. They had never been comfortable with Meade anyway, and now they had an excuse not to vote at all. Meade slipped behind Hawkins in the national surveys by almost seven points, putting him dangerously close to where he'd stood before the fall campaign began.

Meade was furious.

"I'm not going to be fucked around like this!" he roared.

His top six advisers had been summoned to the Oval Office minutes after Meade received the latest polls. They were now seated around his desk. The president was pacing behind it.

"This is the biggest campaign of my life and I'll be damned if I'm going to let Finner or anybody else cost me this election. You people either tell me what we're going to do to turn these fucking polls around or I'm going to get people who will!"

"Mr. President," Joseph Krantz said, "you know we're doing everything we can. We're trying to overcome a temendous image problem that's developed. They're not only getting us on Finner's remarks, but on your administration's hiring of blacks and chicanos and your minority appointments to judicial posts."

"We were supposed to be *handling* all that crap!" snapped Meade. "Why didn't anyone *tell* me we weren't hiring or appointing enough minorities?"

"Mr. President," Howard Hickman said slowly, "I sent you several memos you never responded to. There were other issues to deal with."

"We knew it was going to cause us problems, but Finner really sparked it," said Reed McClellan.

"Well, you people had better damn well start telling me how we're going to put out the sparks or we're all going to be up shit creek."

"Mr. President," said Paul Rampling, "we're utilizing every available resource we have, but the Hawkins people are killing us on this. They're riding this the way we rode them on the gay thing."

"And outspending us three to one," added Krantz.

Meade stopped pacing and put his hands on the back of his chair and leaned forward. "I don't give a damn what they're spending, it's what they're saying and how they're saying it that's going to cost us the votes. If we need more money, we'll get more money!"

Meade's aides glanced at each other. What he'd just said was ridiculous. The campaign was heavily in debt, and they had already borrowed so much that the banks weren't extending further credit, even for the president.

"Mr. President, there isn't any more money to be had. All we've got is what's being reserved for the final week and that's absolutely off limits. If we spend that, Hawkins will have a media blitz during the last few days and tear down everything we've built up," said Joseph Krantz.

It was not what Meade wanted to hear.

"What do you mean there isn't any more money? There's *got* to be. We've got friends in New York, we can *get* the money—"

His aides shook their heads.

Hickman said, "Our sources have dried up on us. We've got to come up with something else. Something that won't cost us which we can use against Hawkins."

"Like what?" barked Meade.

For a few minutes nobody said anything. Meade took his chair and nervously chewed on the end of his pipe.

Finally Joseph Krantz said, "How about a debate?"

OHIO/Columbus

Randy Perrin walked through the suite that had become their command post during the swing through Ohio, passed several Secret Service agents sitting down to a late dinner and a small group of aides typing and talking on the phone, and stepped into Hawkins's bedroom. Hawkins was supposed to be putting some final touches on a foreign policy position paper that the party experts had drafted for him, but that was not what he was doing. Instead he was fast asleep, fully dressed, his face buried in a pillow. He had been going on stored-up energy for weeks now, not getting the sleep or food he needed, and it was beginning to take its toll. Perrin stared at his boss for a moment and sighed. For all the pomp and glamour of a presidential campaign, the motorcades, television cameras and reporters, luncheons, rallies, and thousands of people you meet in the process, it was one hell of a way to elect a president. It boiled down to a man like this, fast asleep in some hotel in a city far away from his wife and his family, hoarse from talking too much, underweight from eating too little, exhausted as no man should ever be, pursuing a dream and hoping, just hoping, he would win.

"Cliff?"

Hawkins stirred.

"Cliff, come on, wake up?"

Hawkins raised up, squinted his eyes. "Yeah, Randy, what is it? . . . foreign policy paper? . . . I'm . . . I'm not through with it yet."

"Cliff, it's not that. We've got to talk to you, Gordon and I."

Hawkins put his feet on the floor and stretched out his arms, yawning.

"Something come up?"

"Yeah, we got a phone call a little while ago from Meade's media director, Joseph Krantz."

"And?"

"And I think we've got the president right where we want him."

"Why?"

"They want to debate."

Hawkins, Perrin, Wade, and four other staff members discussed the idea for well over an hour. But the question looming over everyone's mind was whether he actually *needed* to debate the president. On that they were evenly divided. Gordon Wade told Hawkins he didn't think it would do them any good and could cost them the election if he did. If Hawkins made one serious gaffe, the way Ford did in '76 on the question of Eastern Europe, or came across the way Carter had against Reagan in '80, they might as well hang it up.

Wade said, "The press builds them up and tells the public the debates will be the deciding factor in the race. Sure enough, that's what they become. Right now you're ahead. There's no need to open yourself up purposely for attack. Not if we can hold on and let Meade ride these racial slurs by himself."

Perrin was shaking his head. "Cliff, you've got to see the advantages too. There're a lot of undecideds out there. At least 10 percent of our support is soft. If you put that against the president's figures, we're really not that far ahead at all. In fact, we'll probably be neck and neck. Unless . . . you turn the debate in your favor."

Winny Foster spoke up. "Randy's got a point. This thing would be a great chance for you to appeal to the undecideds. You can show that you're not what Meade and his flunkies are making you out to be. After all, you *look* presidential when you're on TV. Everyone admits that. And you've got a lot more experience before the cameras than Meade does. You'd be in control."

"But," interrupted Wade, "he'd be next to the president of the United States. I don't care what you say, that's still an awfully hard act to compete against. It's a matter of presence. Also Meade's going to be in a better position to come across as president, pulling lines like, 'As your president, I know that what my opponent is saying just isn't true,' et cetera, et cetera. It's experience and he can use it against us."

"But we can use his *record* against him," Perrin said.

They talked it over for another hour, but it was not until two days later, when Hawkins was campaigning in Pittsburgh, that he told them to go ahead and tell Krantz he would debate. Once the decision was made, a group from his Dallas offices flew to Washington to start working out the details with Meade's people and the League of Women Voters, which would sponsor it.

Meanwhile, the media war continued. In the latest series of spot ads run on the television screens both sides used religious crosses to take swipes at one another. The Hawkins campaign ran a spot in the southern and northeastern states showing a huge cross burning at the top of a hill with white-hooded men marching around it. A voice said, "Thirty years ago crosses like this burned throughout the South. Crosses symbolizing racism. But our attitudes changed . . ." Then the cross tumbled over in flames and the voice said, "Or did they?" By reversing the motion of the film, the cross then rose back up and continued to burn. "For some people racism is an attitude that still burns strong, but it is an attitude that we southerners will not tolerate on Election Day. This time we're going to vote for a real change. A change in the hearts and minds of Americans everywhere. This time we're going to vote for Clifford Hawkins." The spot was altered slightly for the northeast, particularly the references to southerners, but it caused enough of a stir to prompt retaliation.

Meade's campaign spot showed the flag on the roof of the White House being taken down and a huge cross erected in its place. Then a voice asked, "When our flag is replaced with a cross, will we still be a nation under God, or a nation under a man who thinks he's God? This Election Day let's not find out. Vote to reelect the president."

50

WASHINGTON

After extensive pressure by the White House to direct the national media's attention back to Hawkins and away from the controversy surrounding the racial slurs, public opinion toward Meade stopped falling. Two weeks before the election it leveled off. The president's advisers told him he was either going to have to storm the South and Northeast to bring up his polls or write off the election. He was still going to need more points than the debate could win him, and the only way to get that, they argued, was to take his case to the people. So, while the president's campaign people worked on the details of the debate with Hawkins's staff and the League of Women Voters, Meade blew into one city after another, riding through countless motorcades and giving an endless string of speeches, in a determined attempt to save his presidency.

In Washington Howard Hickman had just finished reading a dispatch from the American embassy in London detailing the latest British opinion polls on the race and, though it wouldn't do them any good in terms of votes, he was thankful the British were still on Meade's side. London's bookies were giving Meade 5-to-4 odds over Hawkins.

His phone buzzed.

"Howard?"

"Yeah?"

"This is LaCross. Can you come up to the negotiating room?"

"Why? Don't tell me you've run into a snag you can't handle. Christ, I thought you'd almost gotten that thing wrapped up."

"I had."

LaCross had been working on the pipeline agreements with Mexico almost nonstop since the negotiations resumed almost three months ago while Meade was in India. Then a week ago he had told the president and Hickman that the talks were coming to their conclusion. Both men, seeing the bomb they could drop on Hawkins and the public by announcing the pipeline before Election Day, had told him to wrap it up—and fast. LaCross had.

"So what's the problem?"

"There isn't a problem, it's just that the Mexican delegation would like to see you."

"Me? Can't you handle it?"

"We've ordered champagne."

Hickman immediately knew what that meant.

"Tony—you mean you've *finished?*"

"Finished? Howard, these agreements are ready for the president and Portillo to *sign!*"

Hickman swallowed hard. "God, this is great! We *need* this! The president's going to love it." Then suddenly Hickman paused, and asked, "What about the seventeenth? Did you get it taken out?"

"Earlier this week. It was the last major snag, but we finally convinced them that the success or failure of a project of this magnitude was not worth being held up by one little law. Besides," he said ruefully, "Portillo's going to get more money out of this than he knows what to do with. What else could he do but agree? Now come on up!"

"Give me a chance to phone the president."

"Mr. President?"

"Howard? How's it going?"

"A lot better than you'll ever guess, Mr. President."

Meade perked up. With the campaign being in the shape it was, he was anxious for any good news he could get. "Good, what is it? Don't tell me Hawkins has put his foot in his mouth again. Or maybe he's been shot?"

"Unfortunately the answer is no to both questions. But, after you hear this, it doesn't matter what Hawkins does. We're still going to have his trump."

"This sounds good. What is it?"

"LaCross has wrapped it up with the Mexicans."

Meade actually laughed. "You're kidding! He pulled it through?"

"He called me just a few minutes ago. Everything's ready to sign. They're sending Portillo a copy of the agreements by special courier tonight. As soon as you both read them and give your okays, we've got the pipeline."

Meade didn't say anything for a moment. He was trying to grasp what Hickman had just said. He had known it was coming soon, very soon, but he didn't think LaCross would be able to seal it before Election Day. And now . . . now they had it.

"Howard, when can we sign them? We've got to get this out just as soon as the ink dries. It's going to change everything. Everything."

"Portillo should be able to come in within the next forty-eight hours. How's that?"

"Excellent. How long am I going to need to study this thing?"

"Well, you don't have to actually read it, but LaCross does have to give you an extensive briefing so you know exactly what we're getting. I hate to say this, but the sooner you get back the better."

"Christ, and we're scheduled for three cities today and four tomorrow. Screw it, I'll fly back after Atlanta."

"What are you going to tell the press?"

The president thought about it for a moment. Would he be able to come up with something the media would buy?

"That's the problem," said Meade. "If I tell them I'm going to go back and an announcement will be made within the next week, they're going to jump on it with their usual skepticism and build it up as the president resorting to dramatics again."

"That's exactly what I thought," Hickman sighed. "Well, you can always take a chance and not tell them anything."

"They'll make hay of that too. Damn. I don't want to be rushed on signing this thing without knowing exactly what LaCross has gotten us, but we've got to get this done as fast as possible to get the most mileage out of it. If I come back early without an explanation, cutting off two critical cities in my tour, they're going to make a lot of noise. Christ, I can just see the stories now: 'President's Campaign in Deeper Trouble—Forced to Fly Home.' "

"That's true, but everyone's going to know the truth as soon as you announce it anyway. They'll forget about those stories."

"You're right. Okay, I'll be back tonight."

ABOARD AIR FORCE ONE

After the president rang off, he summoned Jerry Ecklecamp, who was traveling with him. Since Ecklecamp had been privy to the negotiations from the start, Meade told him the latest news and his decision to head back to Washington.

"I want you to tell the press before we leave Atlanta that there's been a change in plans. At my direction we're canceling the rest of our tour for today and tomorrow, and going back to D.C. Got it?"

Ecklecamp nodded. "Yes, sir. But . . . what, what should I give as an explanation."

Meade flashed him an irritated look. "Don't explain a damn thing. Just tell them you don't know why."

"Yes, sir."

"Now, if you'll excuse me, I have some things to do."

Four hours later, after Meade had flown into Atlanta and had been given a chilly reception by the city's black mayor and an even chillier reception at the NAACP annual meeting at the Civic Center, he made a quick stop at the state capitol building and the governor's mansion. Then he went back to Dobbins Air Force Base, where his plane was leaving within the next ten or fifteen minutes.

As journalists and Secret Service milled about in the aisles, drinking Cokes and exchanging small talk, Jerry Ecklecamp huddled with Meade's press secretary, Jody Allen, and the head of the Secret Service detail. He told them of the change in plans.

Then he made the announcement.

There was considerable grumbling and a wave of questions, but Ecklecamp fended them off by pleading ignorance. Most of the journalists began speculating among themselves about the sudden change of plans, but there was one who had more reason than the others to want to know.

Scott Houghlin sat in Air Force One absorbed in a number of thoughts. In six months time he had come a long way from that day he leaned over his fucking editor's desk wanting to know why in hell he was going to spike his story on Cliff Hawkins and the questionable contributions he'd received from Francesco Gianni. Instead of getting the story in print—he'd left the office in such a rage he forgot his file and he was sure his editor shredded it—he stormed out of the office, went home, packed, and headed straight for Washington. Although he had been careful never to exploit his friendship with his wife's uncle, the syndicated columnist Joseph Atwood, Houghlin was out of a job. Needing the contacts that Atwood could offer, he told the columnist what had happened. Atwood didn't believe Hawkins knew about the contribution, but he was impressed by the trouble Houghlin had gone to and the contacts he'd used to get the information. Atwood said, "Why don't you come to work for me?"

So for the past six months Houghlin had done a lot of the columnist's legwork, becoming more and more fascinated by Washington politics and the unusual turns it often took. Turns such as Atwood catching the flu at the last minute and Houghlin getting his first crack at covering the president. Turns such as the sudden—and unexplained—announcement that Jerry Ecklecamp had just made on Air Force One. Turns such as the unusual phone call he'd received several days ago, just as he was leaving his office.

The call had come from Maryland, and the woman on the other end had asked for Atwood. Houghlin explained that Atwood wasn't in. She said she would talk to anyone if she was sure the information she was going to give would get to Atwood. Houghlin had become quite accustomed to taking such calls in the months he'd worked for Atwood, since people were always phoning in with "top secret information" about conspiracies and Russian agents in the White House and evidence that American companies were deliberately poisoning the nation's food. He settled back with pen and pad to listen to another crackpot. But the more the woman talked, the more eagerly Houghlin listened.

Her name was Maria Vásquez. She was currently working at an exclusive drug-treatment center in Maryland, after having successfully completed therapy there. Earlier she had worked for the White House. Unofficially she had been the president's mistress. She gave him names to verify, dates to check, Secret Service agents to talk to, and one helluva story about being the president's mistress. She had debated long and hard about whether she should tell her story, but, seeing Meade's face on the television screen everyday, seeing the way he was conducting his campaign against Cliff Hawkins, and, most of all, knowing him as she did, Maria decided she didn't have a choice. The public deserved to know what sort of man they might be reelecting.

Houghlin was fascinated but cautious. It was very tricky stuff. Her story might be partially true, but it could also have been fabricated to bring Meade adverse publicity before Election Day. So Houghlin thanked her and started his groundwork the next day. Then Atwood got the flu. Not wanting to pass up a chance to cover Meade himself, he gave Atwood the information he had on her and took off on Meade's campaign tour.

As they were heading back to Washington, Houghlin couldn't help wonder whether Meade's sudden change in plans had anything to do with Maria Vásquez. Why else would he cancel the rest of his southern itinerary? Especially since he was running behind Hawkins? Surely it wasn't anything overseas. Even the Middle East had been unusually calm lately. Besides, they would have heard any late-breaking news over the plane's communications setup or caught them on the wire reports.

No, Houghlin decided, this was something else. Something personal. Something Meade didn't want let out. But what? The more he thought about it, the more Scott Houghlin was determined to see one man as soon as they landed, one lowly, vulnerable man who was at this very moment sitting six feet away from him—Jerry Ecklecamp.

51

OHIO

In Ohio Cliff Hawkins's campaign was in its final round. If Meade had relished the evangelist's stumbles during the first few weeks of the fall campaign, Hawkins was enjoying having the advantage now. During the past two weeks Hawkins had made substantial inroads among Meade's constituencies. Still being careful not to attack the president directly, Hawkins was using Meade's own record as the best case for not reelecting him as president. He also reminded the voters that at no time during the past four years had America received any real moral or spiritual guidance from its leaders.

"And the less guidance we have," he told one audience, "the more we're going to founder!"

As Charlotte had done in Miami and was now doing in New Jersey and as Tom Kelly was doing in the West, Hawkins was trying his best to touch base with blacks, Jews, blue-collar workers, the middle class, and the poor. He did it in settings that guaranteed him good media: a synagogue, a housing project, a ghetto, a mortgage office, and a union hall.

At the same time he stayed close to the theme that had prompted his draft movement for the presidency in the first place, America's

Five Greatest Sins. It was true that the Meade campaign ads were having an effect on voters' opinions about a man running for president who was extremely dedicated to his religion, but Hawkins also knew that if he could successfully combine the philosophy of government *with* God as opposed to one *without* God in a context that told people that this was nothing new, that it was what our forefathers had intended from the start, he just might *win*.

At a rally in Lexington he said, "This is a nation created by men who believed that God Almighty had a place not only in our lives, but in our government as well. While they were very careful, and rightly so, to protect the personal religious preferences of every individual from an official state religion, they never intended to leave godliness out of government. We see this on our coins, which have the words 'In God We Trust,' and on our currency we see, besides these words, the inscription 'Annuit Coeptis,' which in Latin means 'He has favored our undertakings.' We see this even in the houses of Congress itself, where we find the words 'In God We Trust' on the walls of both the House and the Senate . . ."

And in Columbus: "Patrick Henry, one of this nation's greatest patriots, is supposed to have said, 'I would only wish that I could leave my family my faith in Jesus Christ; for without that nothing else is worthwhile.' Well, I wish I could leave all of you standing here today my faith. Because only by believing in him and in ourselves can this great nation survive. Once we do believe, then we can start on the process of turning this nation back to the principles and government upon which our Republic was established."

But Hawkins was not relying entirely on his campaign stumps or media time to win him the election. On the contrary, every night, regardless of what city or state he was in, he sat down with policy experts and was drilled on everything—from grain crops to Latin America—for the debate, an event just five days away.

But the debate was not going to decide anything, though nobody knew it at the time. Instead the man who became president was going to be decided by a series of circumstances beyond either candidate's control.

52

WASHINGTON/The White House

Twenty-four hours after Meade returned to Washington, he and Mexican President José Portillo met secretly in the Oval Office.

Meade sat behind his beautifully carved desk glancing over the formal agreements. Portillo stood next to him, watching. Meade turned the pages of the agreements skimming each clause and its provisions. On page 24 he came across the reworded seventeenth clause for the first time. He read it carefully, realizing it involved many obligations and potential complications; it was the one clause that could effectively deal with, and resolve, his financial obligations. He nodded his head in a sort of private agreement with himself.

Its stipulations met his approval. An American firm, chosen by the U.S. government, would construct the pipeline, provided that 51 percent of its employees came from the Mexican work force. Mexico would receive 55 percent of all profits from the sale of Mexican oil coming out of the pipeline as well as 30 percent of the profits the American construction firm would receive for building the pipeline. Although the percentages were steep, Meade felt that if the United States wanted more oil, the American people would have to pay the price.

Meade looked up, smiled at Portillo and the few aides gathered about, then signed. First his copy, then Portillo's.

Portillo, who had already skimmed the Spanish version, flipped the pages perfunctorily and signed his name. He was well aware that his country was going to need the profits from the pipeline sooner than he'd expected.

Meade, standing up and shaking the Mexican president's hand, believed that, by the constitutional and congressional powers invested in him, his executive agreement with Portillo was valid. Meade was thinking that not the Congress or the public or Cliff Hawkins had any idea of the magnitude of such an agreement. But they would realize it soon enough and, when they did, Meade would become a hero and a reelected president. A president with a pipeline for all America—and a place for himself in the history books.

53

VIRGINIA/Alexandria

Scott Houghlin stood in front of the apartment door trying to gather his thoughts before knocking. He had wanted to get over here before now, but Joseph Atwood, still down with the flu, had him double-checking a lot of facts about Maria Vásquez. Facts that were quickly turning into one of the most explosive columns Atwood had written since Meade had taken office. While Houghlin had been away, Atwood, using the "cleared" phone in his home to discuss the affair with several moles within the White House, had been able to work on the information Houghlin had given him. By talking to the moles as well as drawing on other information he had been privy to over the years from his intelligence sources, Atwood was able not only to confirm Maria's story but also to come up with a string of other affairs, some even lengthier than the one with Maria, that the president had been involved in since taking office. Affairs that, at least, in one instance, could have seriously jeopardized national security.

This was going to make one helluva column, Houghlin thought. But what fascinated him even more was the feeling that something bigger was building in the background, something that might swamp even the column Atwood was writing now. Why? Because over the past several days they still had not been able to find a reason for Meade's sudden return to Washington.

Until today.

Today one of Atwood's sources at Andrews Air Force Base called to ask if he was aware that an official plane of the Mexican government had flown in unannounced. No, he wasn't aware of it, nor was he aware of any scheduled visit from a Mexican official. Atwood called Houghlin. He had him check at the White House's northwest gate, to see whether Blair House, the official visitor's residence across from the White House, had been sealed off and whether there had been an increase in the Secret Service detail at the White House? Was there a call for more limousines by the Service?

Houghlin discovered a number of things. For instance, the plane currently in the hangar at Andrews was the Mexican president's personal Boeing 707. Blair House had been sealed off by the Secret Service. And entries at the northwest gate of the White House revealed that an unusual number of officials recently had been coming and going at the Mexican embassy. Finally several Secret Service automobiles were missing from the motor pool, including one of their best bulletproof limousines.

This was why Houghlin was now standing outside Jerry Ecklecamp's apartment door. Houghlin's research had confirmed what he already suspected: something big was up. The question was what? Did it have anything to do with Meade's sudden return to Washington? Houghlin thought so, but one man could tell him for sure. He might not want to. But that was okay, too, because during the past six months that he'd been working for Atwood, Houghlin had also uncovered a fact about Jerry Ecklecamp that the aide had kept hidden for many many years. It could destroy him. Houghlin himself would never do that, but he wasn't above threatening to.

He knocked on the door. After several more knocks Ecklecamp finally answered.

His face showed his surprise.

"Houghlin, what are you doing here?"

"Well, I wasn't just passing through the neighborhood. I need some information, Jerry."

Ecklecamp cringed. He had never trusted reporters. He especially didn't trust this one.

"No, I'm sorry. Get it from the White House information office."

Houghlin stepped forward and Ecklecamp winced. "Jerry, that isn't the type of information I need. I don't need a lot, but I need it straight."

"Really, I have things to do and—" He started to shut the door.

Houghlin put his foot between it and the frame.

"Jerry, I said I need it." And with that Houghlin stepped in.

Three and a half hours later Houghlin was sitting with Joseph Atwood in the columnist's sprawling living room listening to the tape of his recent interview with Ecklecamp. When it was over Houghlin snapped off the recorder and said, "Now you know why I was in such a hurry to get over here."

Atwood was obviously impressed. "I never would have believed it. It's absolutely remarkable. I'll give the president credit. One of the most valuable resources this nation could use and he got it for us. It also explains why he's called a press conference for tomorrow afternoon."

"But the sad thing is the whole agreement is corrupt. From the seventeenth clause down to those criminal profit percentages."

"And giving Gianni's construction firm the contract. Nobody would have said anything until it was too late, and by then Meade would be reelected, sitting behind his desk telling the American people he didn't know anything about who was behind the firm that got the contract. I can just see him smiling the way he does, shrugging his shoulders and saying, 'But does it really matter? After all, we're going to be a nation with a pipeline the whole world will envy. There are more important things we should be concerning ourselves with.' "

Houghlin sighed, "Exactly."

"And Meade comes out smelling clean. He's reelected, he's got the pipeline, and he's paid off Gianni."

"Well, what are we going to do?"

Atwood laughed. "You know damn well what we're going to do, what we *have* to do—burst his bubble. Meade thinks he's got the whole thing wrapped up. The election. The pipeline. All of it. But if the presses don't break down tonight, he's going to have his hands so full explaining why he jeopardized national security simply to get a piece of ass that he won't have time to announce the pipeline."

"And if he does?"

"If he does, then we're going to hit him with the second column: 'The Pipeline Scandal.' "

Houghlin sank into the depths of the couch, amazed at how one column was going to affect the whole outcome of America's history.

"You know, there probably won't even be a debate after this. I mean, it's only three days away and Hawkins would slaughter Meade from the very start. The president'd be the perfect illustration of all the charges of immorality and ungodliness in government Hawkins has been hitting him with."

"Well, it's better not to have a debate than not have an election."

"You mean an election of truth."

"Right."

"But, Joe, are you willing to take responsibility for helping to elect Cliff Hawkins?"

"I'm not going to have to take responsibility. The American people are."

54

The next morning, the day Meade planned to drop his political bombshell and announce the pipeline agreement at a nationally televised press conference, he was hit with Joseph Atwood's bombshell before he even got out of bed.

"Mr. President?" the voice over the phone asked.

"Jody? What is it? It's six o'clock."

"I'm sorry to wake you up, but I'm afraid I've got some bad news. I need to see you right away."

Meade sat up, putting his feet on the floor. He ran his hand through his hair.

"Tell me."

"Maria Vásquez."

"Maria? What's happened?"

"Nothing's happened to her, but I need to talk to you."

"All right, just give me a minute to get awake."

"Well, it'll be about fifteen minutes before I can get there anyway. I'm still at my apartment."

"Okay."

When Jody Allen entered the president's bedroom, Meade had already showered and shaved and a servant was pouring him a cup of coffee from a silver service. The president watched as the servant dropped two lumps of sugar in his cup and added a little cream.

Allen set his briefcase on the president's bed and popped it open. He handed Meade a copy of that morning's *Washington Post,* its pages already folded back to Atwood's column. "We've got big trouble. I mean big. You and Maria Vásquez are starring in Joseph Atwood's column this morning."

Meade almost spilled his coffee. "What?"

"That's right. The story of your affair with her is making its way across the nation in over 260 newspapers today."

"There's got to be some mista—"

"It's all there in black and white."

Meade set down his coffee and nervously looked around for his reading glasses. Finding them, he held them up and skimmed the column.

"Oh, Christ . . . oh, Christ . . ."

When he had finished, he went back and reread it carefully. Massaging his forehead, he said, "National security? . . . But she was cleared. She . . . oh, shit, it doesn't matter. It's just that . . . oh, *shit.*"

By seven Meade was behind his desk in the Oval Office, conferring with Howard Hickman, Jody Allen, Joseph Krantz, Reed McClellan, Paul Rampling, and Tony LaCross. They discussed the column for almost a half hour. They had no idea how they were going to handle it.

"Well," Allen said, "I've got a press briefing in an hour and I'll tell you right now this is one briefing I don't want to give."

"Then don't!" snapped Meade. "We don't owe them a fucking thing! *Not one!*"

Hickman tried to calm the president down. "You're right, but Jody can't cancel it. He's never canceled before and it would only confirm the gravity of the situation. We've got to come up with a better way to handle it."

They couldn't. Meade argued for denying the allegations in the column, saying it was a malicious and vicious personal attack. His advisers told him to forget about that approach. Atwood's integrity rating was almost twice as high as Meade's in the polls, and his reputation had been built on the accuracy of his reporting. They had witnessed that for themselves when the president tried to bluff his way out of not shaking Hawkins's hand in New York and Atwood tripped them up. It was Atwood's version that was believed, not the president's.

"Then what in God's name are we going to do? What am I going to tell them this afternoon? They're not going to give a flying fuck about the pipeline. They probably wouldn't believe me anyway. Jesus Christ, that sonofabitch has really done it. He's completely ruined everything. *Everything!*"

"You could always plead no comment," Joseph Krantz said.

"I can't say no comment! They wouldn't stand for it. We're not just talking about who I've slept with, but allegations that I may have breached national security, of all things! You think they'd take no comment on that? Christ, that would look worse than standing up there and lying to them!"

"Then what are you going to say?"

"What can I say? I've just got to face those bastards!"

By the time Jody Allen held his regular morning press briefing at eight thirty, Atwood's revelations had soared through Washington and out across the nation. All the networks were using it as their lead on their morning news shows, and Allen's usually calm briefing was turned upside down the moment it started. For the first five minutes the noise level was so high Allen couldn't hear himself speak. Finally he had to shout at the journalists to get some order. When things quieted down, he started to answer questions one by one. But the furor erupted all over again, creating such a storm that Allen eventually gave up and shouted, "Save them for the president's news conference!"

The president's appointments were canceled for the rest of the day. The press kept a vigil at the White House, filing updates throughout the morning and waiting for Meade's afternoon news conference. The president spent most of his time in the Oval Office trying to keep a lid on things.

One of the main concerns he'd had since the story broke was what Katherine's reaction would be. He had tried to reach her in Tennessee, where she was campaigning before her return to Washington at noon, but he'd missed her. Now he was going to have to face her cold. Damn sonofabitch Atwood, Meade thought to himself. Things had been going so well and *he* had to throw everything up in the air—Meade's pipeline announcement, his marriage, and quite possibly the whole fucking election.

Meade stood at one of the full-length windows in the Oval Office, looking out into the Rose Garden, and wondered just what he was going to say to Katherine. What he *could* say. It had hurt her enough when she found out about Maria and the others in the first place. It was only after she'd threatened to divorce him that he knew how precarious his relationship with her was, how delicately she needed to be treated.

One of the things he thought had kept her by him was her relief in knowing that the public wasn't aware of their marital problems. Now that was blown. He didn't know if he could keep her.

He turned away from the window and silently cursed Atwood again.

When Katherine's limousine and Secret Service escorts pulled up to the entrance of the Diplomatic Reception Room, Meade was pacing back and forth in his bedroom. He had decided to remain in the private quarters to spare her any embarrassment, but he asked Howard Hickman to be on hand to greet her and discreetly ask if she wouldn't mind seeing the president at her earliest convenience.

As she walked into his bedroom a few minutes later, he braced himself for a torrent of verbal abuse. When he looked at her and started to speak, he noticed she had the most unusual expression on her face. He could have sworn it was one of joy. That was unsettling enough, but, when she came over to him without saying a word and put her arms around him and hugged him, he thought he would die. This wasn't at all what he had expected. It certainly wouldn't have been the way she would have reacted three, four, even five months ago. He got control of himself and hugged her back, whispering, "I'm so sorry," over and over in her ear. After a moment she wouldn't listen to him anymore and gently put her index finger to his lips. Then she reached up and kissed him more passionately than he remembered her doing in ages. At a loss for words, not knowing what to say or how she expected him to react, Meade's instincts told him what to do. He responded warmly, kissing her neck, her cheeks, caressing her breasts, and hugging her as he had never hugged her before.

When she started to undress, he stopped her and undressed her himself. All the while neither of them spoke, but continued touching, kissing, hugging their way into his bed. When he finally made love to her, it was with a passion and intensity and desire for her that he hadn't felt since that first night in the guesthouse on her estate.

When they finally came, it was explosive yet tender. They cried out in ecstasy.

Afterward, as Meade lay on his back breathing deeply, Katherine got quietly out of bed and dressed herself. Then she looked at him.

"Where's your wallet?"

Meade raised up. "My wallet? On the dresser. Why?"

Without answering him Katherine went over to the dresser, picked it up, and pulled out a hundred dollar bill.

Now she glared at him. "That's the last trick you'll ever turn with me, you sonofabitch, and it just cost you a hundred dollars."

Then she walked out.

55

Meade held his press conference in the Rose Garden. He opened with a statement saying he had originally called it to make a major energy announcement but, because of the current developments, would postpone that until tomorrow. He opened himself up for questions and it was grueling.

He stood in the cool afternoon sun, the wind blowing his hair, as the questions were fired at him one by one like bullets from a gun. He tried his best to answer them. But his best wasn't much. His voice wasn't as strong as usual, and his hand movements, normally under control, reflected the intense pressure he was under.

For over forty minutes the questions came, and then the conference ended abruptly when a reporter from the *Times* asked, "What's been the First Lady's reaction to all this?"

That was when Meade lost it. He glared at the reporter and snapped, "It's none of your damned business."

Then he stormed off and the journalists were left with their mouths open.

Howard Hickman watched the press conference in his West Wing office. He flipped it off when he couldn't stand it anymore, missing the president's abrupt ending. They were losing. Losing in every aspect of the campaign, and Hickman was pissed.

The administration was sitting on one of the most significant agreements to come along in years, and Meade couldn't even announce it because it would have been too damn incredible for the public—and the press—to handle. Besides, the whole fucking thing would have been overshadowed by Atwood's column. Hickman knew that for a fact they were too damn interested in the president's extramarital escapades. It was like something out of the *National Enquirer*. The fact that it came from one of the most respected journalists in the nation infuriated him more than anything else. Atwood was destroying them and he knew it. He was costing them what had taken millions of dollars and thousands of miles of campaigning to build up.

Meade had to announce the pipeline agreements tomorrow. So what if some of the people called it a desperate ploy, Meade had the signed agreements to back himself up. Then . . . then maybe they could start to undo the damage this thing had done.

But an hour later everything was falling apart—though Hickman wasn't told until it was too late.

Hickman had been working at his desk, trying to get rid of some of the papers piled up around him, when he looked at his watch and thought, fuck it. It was time for a drink. Just somewhere nearby. So he went to his closet, grabbed his blazer, and told his secretary he'd be gone for a while. If anyone called, she was to make the usual excuses.

He was about to go into the hallway that led to the other West Wing offices when he heard a phone ring. It wasn't his regular line. Someone was calling him on his private phone.

Damn, he would have to answer it. No one would be calling him on that line unless it was of the utmost urgency. More problems. Boy, what next?

He went back into his office and slammed the door.

"Yeah?" he said grabbing the phone.

"You and I have got to talk as soon as possible," the voice, which Hickman recognized immediately, said almost in a whisper.

Hickman raised his head and looked out at the dreary gray Executive Office Building across the way. He stared at one of the windows. He was there. Hickman knew it.

"What about?"

"I can't talk about it on the phone, but it's *extremely important* to you and your whole operation down there. Understand?"

"When?"

"Ten, fifteen minutes."

"All right," he sighed. "Meet me in the bar at the Hay-Adams in ten minutes."

"Okay. I don't like public places but I guess it'll have to do."

Hickman walked the short distance to the Hay-Adams consumed by thoughts of what this meeting was all about. He'd met the man behind that voice only twice before and hadn't regretted either meeting. In both instances he had supplied them with information that had helped the White House, especially the president.

Hickman took an obscure table in the back of the bar, far away from the ordinary roaming eye. A waiter, obviously impressed by Hickman's standing at the White House, took his order. He checked his watch. Ten minutes. Five minutes later he checked it again and wondered what had happened. Something wasn't right. He could feel it, sense it. Then Hickman saw him, weaving his way through the tables and patrons, consciously searching for his man. Hickman coughed loudly. The contact turned and made his way over to the table.

"You're late," Hickman said.

The man took a seat and said, "Fuck it, but I couldn't find the damn earphones that went with this." He placed a small tape recorder on the table.

"What is it?"

"You'll hear it, but first I want a drink."

Hickman snapped his fingers and the ever-attentive waiter immediately came over, this time appraising his guest. Obviously not someone from the White House. Look at that tacky suit. Nobody important.

"What'll it be?"

"J and B on the rocks."

The waiter nodded and left.

"Now," Hickman began under his breath, "what's this all about?"

The man brushed back his thinning hair and glanced around.

"You've got to keep this under your lid, understand? Just keep calm, especially in here."

"All right, all right."

The contact took a deep breath. "You remember when you asked

us to investigate the leaks that were coming out of the White House
during the coal strike talks?"

"Yeah, it was the people with the United Mine Workers after all."

"Right, but you remember your orders before that? Tap whoever
you have to—"

"Yeah, yeah, of course."

"And do you remember your orders after the talks were over?
Keep the taps going?"

"And you have. And you've given us two reports and we're grate-
ful."

Well, here's another one."

Hickman leaned forward. "Who? What?" His anxiety showed.

The man leaned down and pulled a small folder out of his briefcase. He opened it and said, "Your aide, Gerald Ecklecamp. Listening devices were placed in his apartment, office, car, and his phones.
They've been there since last December."

"Is *he* the one who gave Atwood the information on the president's affairs?"

The man pulled out a microcassette and popped it in the recorder.
He handed Hickman a small lightweight set of earphones.

"Listen to it yourself. If he gave him the information on her, we
don't have it down. But he has been talking to Atwood's assistant
about something *else.*"

"What?" Hickman's eyes zeroed in on the recorder. He punched it
on, and put the earphones on.

"No, I'm sorry. Get it from the White House information office."

"Jerry, that isn't the type of information I need. I don't need
a lot, but I need it straight."

"Really, I have things to do and—"

Hickman pressed the fast-forward button and after a few seconds
flipped it back to regular play.

"Just wait until the press conference, okay? The agreements are
already signed. Everything's wrapped up. I really—"

"But why weren't we told he was negotiating with Mexico? It
would have given him a much better position in the campaign.
This is something other presidents have dreamed about."

"I don't know, he has his reasons."

"Bullshit! You're not leveling with me. Meade's too smart to let this be kept from the public when he knows how much he could gain from it. What's the reason for keeping it secret?"

"I told you, I—"

"You haven't told me anything. You're lying and you know it."

"I am not."

"You are."

"I'm not. The president didn't want word to . . . never mind. I've already told you too much as it is."

"Didn't want word to get out about what? Com'on Ecklecamp, *level* with me for godsakes."

"Investigations. He didn't want investigations. We . . . we've been working on these things for a number of reasons. Not just to get oil. Meade—the President—has a very . . ."

"What?"

"A very large debt that he owes a member of the mob. His name is Francesco . . ."

Hickman listened. With each revolution of the tape he slowly became madder. It was Ecklecamp who was destroying everything. *He* was going to bring down an entire administration. The fury Hawkins felt was uncontrollable. On and on the tape went, revealing more and more.

Hickman's hands began to shake. He balled them into fists, trying to contain himself, and the veins bulged to the point where he thought they'd burst. He was drawing on every ounce of strength he had not to scream out at the madness of it all.

Finally he ripped the headphones off and slammed them down on the table.

"That no-good motherfucking sonofabitch!"

Heads turned.

"Keep it down!"

"What do you mean? Do you realize what he's done? That stupid motherfucker—I can't believe it! Giving that fucking reporter everything we had. We're going to hang him by his balls for this!"

"Will you *please* get a hold of yourself? This is why I *didn't* want to come here."

"I can't believe he'd do this to us. Not after today. Not after everything that's already happened—"

"I'm sorry I didn't get this to you sooner, but we didn't check the tapes until this afternoon."

Hickman's mind suddenly focused on another thought. "Wait—when was that tape made?"

"The conversation took place last night."

Hickman groaned. "Oh, shit. That means Atwood's going to hit us with *another fucking column!*"

Hickman stood. He looked like a man ready to cry.

"The president—I've got to tell the president."

"Look, get ahold of yourself. This—"

Hickman had slapped a ten dollar bill on the table and headed toward the door before the man could finish his sentence.

Inside the West Wing executive offices Jody Allen was just coming out of his office when Hickman went rushing by. The press secretary followed suit.

"Howard!"

"What? I've got to see the president!"

"I've got to see you! I just got a call from someone at the *Post.*"

Hickman stopped. He froze. "The *Post?* What'd they want?"

"Atwood's running another column tomorrow and—" Allen stopped when he saw the shock on Hickman's face. Before he could say anything, Hickman was off toward his office, yelling at his secretary to find the president, goddamit! Allen listened in horror. Something dreadful was happening. The White House was going berserk.

56

INDIANA/Campaigning

Cliff Hawkins had just finished another of his practice rounds for the debate two days away when the local news came on. They were in Indiana now, Otis Meade's home state, and Hawkins thought it was ironic that on the very day he was stumping the state for support Joseph Atwood publishes a column that surely would make even the most ardent Meade supporters reconsider their vote.

The press had been after Hawkins all day to make a statement, but he had opted to remain silent, fearing it would look like a cheap shot. After all, this had to be one of the most embarrassing situations the nation had faced in a long time. They didn't need anyone reminding them of it. But there was another reason he kept quiet. He had a feeling that he wasn't going to need to say anything, that what was happening, and would continue happening, was coming forth through the divine guidance of God Almighty. There was nothing he or anyone else could say or do that would change what was supposed to happen.

And perhaps he was right.

WASHINGTON/The White House

The final blows were coming. The campaign was crumbling around them like the very pillars supporting the White House. It was only a matter of time—of waiting for the next column—before it was all over.

Hickman knew this, he felt it with such a passion that made the vengeance he was going to get seem entirely justifiable.

He tapped a pencil on his windowsill and waited. It was almost seven in the evening.

Tap. Tap. Tap.

Outside Hickman's office Jerry Ecklecamp stood, hesitating for a moment before he entered. He was edgy. Especially now, after what had happened today and after last night with Scott Houghlin. Houghlin had promised him anonymity, but how good was that? He wondered about it as he stood there waiting to go in. Hickman had told him over the phone that he needed to see him, but it was the way he said it that didn't sit right. His boss's words were slow, deliberate, as if he were trying to control himself. When Hickman spoke, it sounded as though he was seething through his teeth. Well, he couldn't wait out here forever.

Ecklecamp finally opened the door . . .

Hickman turned from the window. He wanted to get this over with as quickly as possible. Ecklecamp stepped in and began removing his coat.

Hickman said, "Don't bother—you're fired."

His aide stared momentarily, then said, "What?"

"I said you're fired. It's not that hard to understand. You've got ten minutes to clear out your desk, then the guards come."

Tap. Tap. Tap.

Ecklecamp began shaking his head, wondering if it wasn't all some horrible joke. "Howard, you're not serious are you? I mean, this is a joke, right?"

The pencil snapped.

"A joke? You know I don't joke, you sonofabitch! Get out of here before—"

"But *why?* I don't believe this! I haven't done anything—"

Hickman suddenly rushed forward. He seized him by the collar, the bulk of their bodies slamming against the door. He shook him, his eyes filling with fury. "*You* haven't done anything? You fucking wimp! You know damn well what you've done and don't tell me you don't!"

"But he coerced me! He—"

"*He* didn't do a fucking thing! You did! You sold us out. Now it's going to be in *another* Atwood column tomorrow! The agreements! Gianni! Everything! You thought we'd never find out it was you."

He slammed him against the door again.

"Thought your secret would be safe, huh? Well, see how long that lasted?"

Ecklecamp's knees buckled under him and Hickman shoved him back up against the door.

"Howard, please! Someone's lied to you! They must have! You've got it all wrong! I swear, I never meant to tell him a thing! Not a thing!"

Hickman released him, but went on raging. "You sonofabitch! You shouldn't have said anything at all! Not a fucking word! Now—now the whole damned world's going to know. And they're going to know *all* of it! You've ruined us! Ruined the greatest administration this country's ever known! And ... and you're going to put Cliff Hawkins in the Oval Office! Hawkins! Do you hear me?"

Ecklecamp nodded, terrified as he stared into his boss's eyes. They were red and furious. His breathing was hard. Ecklecamp had never seen him so outraged.

"How," he began weakly, "how did you find out?"

"We know everything, everything about you."

"What do you mean?"

"You imbecile. Do you think I'm stupid enough not to keep tabs on my staff? Give me a little credit. I know everything about everyone, including you."

"But—how?"

Hickman crossed over to a file cabinet and, opening it, pulled out a tape recorder. He slapped it down on his desk.

"This is how, fuckface. Everything's here. Complete and unedited."

Ecklecamp recoiled as Hickman flipped it on. Immediately he heard his own voice and that of Houghlin's. Both were as clear as if they were now talking in Hickman's office. He listened and, with each passing second, each phrase or question caught on tape, he grew weaker. He felt nauseated and slumped down in a chair behind him.

"Howard, it was never supposed to happen like that."

"It never is, is it?"

Ecklecamp couldn't take it anymore. Weakly he rose and placed his hand over the tape recorder and turned it off, tears streaming down his face.

"Howard, *please*—" he begged. "You've got to understand. I never wanted this to happen. He put words in my mouth. He . . . he tried to get me to say things I—"

"Liar! You fucking liar! We've got it all! I heard it all! He didn't put anything in your mouth! You said what you wanted! And now it's going to be in every fucking newspaper in the country! Four days away from Election Day!"

"I'll say anything. I'll deny all of it. I'll go on television and tell them Houghlin's lying, that—"

"No!" Hickman hissed. "You won't do anything! You're finished." He turned to his file cabinet and pulled out an envelope. "And this . . . this is a parting gift to you. A thank you for what you've done. I think it's something Houghlin might like to see. Maybe some newspapers too. Maybe the same ones that are going to get Atwood's column. After all, it's your *complete* story."

Ecklecamp stared at him in puzzlement.

Hickman pulled photos out of the envelope. Dozens of pictures of Ecklecamp having sex with young boys. Very young boys.

Ecklecamp let out a cry of anguish and buried his face in his hands. He sobbed uncontrollably.

Hickman leaned over his desk. He was smiling. He lifted Ecklecamp's head up and, feeling a great sense of satisfaction, said, "Had enough, pervert? Now get out of my office and go find yourself a little kid to stick."

57

WASHINGTON/Georgetown

Rain showered the Washington streets and made for a cold stormy night over the Capitol, a prelude to the winter months ahead.

Inside the small Georgetown bar Ecklecamp sat in a booth all to himself drinking his sixth double bourbon. It was more than he'd ever had in one sitting, especially alone. An hour earlier he had phoned Scott Houghlin at home, begging him to get Atwood to pull the column. Houghlin was sorry. They were reporters and had to report the truth. Besides, even if they wanted to pull it, it was already too late. The first morning editions would be on the streets by 4:00 A.M. Ecklecamp hung up, feeling more remorse than he had ever felt in his life. Everything was over. Gone. It was all gone. The campaign, the agreements, the administration. The votes on Tuesday would only confirm what he already knew was going to happen. Meade was going to lose. They had already lost. And at the White House the president was sitting down to a late-night meeting with his top advisers, thinking the same thing. He had listened to the tape himself an hour before.

Ecklecamp sat in his booth until the cocktail waitress informed him she'd like to close out his bill. She wanted to go home. He was the only customer left. He made his drunken way outside and into the street.

Before long he was stumbling aimlessly toward the Potomac as the wind and rain beat at him. Coming to the Memorial Parkway Bridge leading into Virginia, he stopped, turned around, and was about to head back to get his car when he leered toward Virginia. No, forget about the damn car. He didn't need it anyway. He would walk home.

In the middle of the bridge, at about the dividing line separating the District from Virginia, Ecklecamp stopped, and, feeling as though the world had enough destructive forces in it without him, he stepped up on the concrete shoulder. He stared into the black rainy depths of the Potomac, stole one last look at the shimmering Washington Monument, and took his final step.

The waters were cold and turbulent. Death came quickly.

WASHINGTON/The White House

At precisely the moment Ecklecamp stepped off, Meade was saying in a low voice to those few close aides who'd been summoned to his study, "It's over. We might as well face it and cancel the debate."

"But, Mr. President," Joseph Krantz said, "if you back out now, it's only going to compound everything else."

Meade took off his glasses and said, "But, if I stay in, I'm going to be opening myself up to more than I want to deal with right now." He shifted in his chair and said wearily, "Look, what's been done has been done. We've all heard the tape. We know exactly what Atwood's going to hit us with tomorrow. There's no way we can survive it. Not with our polls being where they are now. Even without those polls. Right, Reed?"

McClellan looked up from a list of figures. "I'm afraid so, Mr. President."

Meade slumped back in his seat and crossed his leg. "You see?"

Krantz still wasn't convinced and neither was Paul Rampling.

Krantz began to speak, "Well, I still think—"

"Gentlemen," sighed Meade, "it's over with. We've lost. That's all there is to it. Hawkins is in."

"Heaven help us," one of them said.

"No," the president said, "I think that's the last place our help would come from."

* * *

The next day, as the president was again facing the press with the latest Atwood column, the Washington police were pulling Jerry Ecklecamp's body out of the Potomac.

Back at his mansion in Dallas Cliff Hawkins had remained secluded throughout the day, watching the stories come out of Washington. Finally he retreated to his study to pray not only for himself and the nation, but for the president and the soul of Jerry Ecklecamp as well.

When he came out, he found Charlotte sitting by the study door. He could see that she had been crying. He knew from looking at her that her tears were not ones of joy.

"Oh, Cliff," she said, putting her head on his shoulder, "I feel so bad about the way things have turned out. It all seems so tragic. And yet . . . yet I . . . oh, I don't know what to think."

"Don't worry about it," he said softly.

She looked up at him and thought, I can't help it. Because of you, I can't help it.

EPILOGUE

His hand was placed on the Bible while Charlotte held it.

It was an old Bible, one that had been in the family for years. Its edges were tattered, and it was limp and weathered. Cliff knew no matter how old the book was, it would endure the short ceremony that had just begun, the ceremony that two years ago had seemed completely out of reach.

"I do solemnly affirm that I will faithfully . . ."

Charlotte stood between him and the chief justice, listening as the words resonated in her ears. Beneath the Bible her hands trembled.

". . . execute the office of the president of the United States."

She thought about everything that had happened this past year . . . about all the doubts and fears and anxieties . . . about all the people she had met . . . all that she had done. Looking at Cliff now, hearing him take the oath of the most powerful office in the nation, she knew that it had been worth it and that her love for him was greater than anything that might ever come between them. Thinking about that, she felt the tears stream down her face.

After the oath was finished, the chief justice congratulated Hawkins, saying, "May God be with you, Mr. President."

There was applause around him. A spark at first, which spread across the platform and then multiplied. A few supporters clapping became hundreds which expanded to the thousands crowding the Capitol grounds and then hundreds of thousands. People cheered. Across the District of Columbia that bright and glorious January day there seemed to spread a feeling of optimism even among those who had been adamantly opposed to him. A feeling that perhaps, just perhaps, it wasn't going to be so bad after all.

The applause and cheers continued, and he turned to shake hands all around him. Protocol dictated that he shake hands with the former president first. When he reached out and took Otis Meade's hand, Cliff Hawkins smiled and said, "Mr. President, this is a new beginning. I'd like to bury the hatchet."

And the former president, looking somewhat surprised, said softly, "I don't think that's a problem."

But his eyes said something entirely different.